THE BLUE BOOK

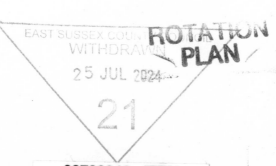

THE BLUE BOOK

A.L. Kennedy

WINDSOR
PARAGON

First published 2011
by
Jonathan Cape
This Large Print edition published 2012
by AudioGO Ltd
by arrangement with
The Random House Group Ltd

Hardcover   ISBN: 978 1 445 85998 9
Softcover   ISBN: 978 1 445 85999 6

British Library Cataloguing in Publication Data available

Printed and bound in Great Britain by
MPG Books Group Limited

For

W. F. N.

He reaches the opposite fence, swings himself over easily, fluidly, fast. His body is made of long, hard balances and strengths which take constant practice: there are days when he stumbles, breaks things, fails. Today, though, he is neck and neck with his own growth. Tomorrow, it will probably beat him again, muffle him up in clumsiness. In the end, he will be the bobbing head-and-shoulders-above in almost any group, will feel his height as a responsibility, a potential trap. He is already beginning to know this, but the knowledge is still light and he has taken to the pleasures of being visible, selected, dominant. His hair also draws the eye—fair, currently close to white at its tips, a salt white that deepens into honey against his scalp, his skin. He is not unattractive, but will always assume he is simply passable, scraping by. This will often seem charming.

He takes the only possible track onwards—a snug route between high blackthorn hedges, like the start of a maze. He enjoys being hidden in the din of bees, the scuffles of dunnocks and wrens, of fugitive lives. His feet run in the centre of the path where the cropped turf dips as if it were being bowed, stretched down beneath his special weight. Trees reach across and shadow him. With the green below and the green above, he could be in a tunnel, could be bulleting into the secret of something, unlocking it. And the tunnel leads down, tilts headlong down, until it balks at the cliff's edge and flexes into a sudden turn, then tacks back and forth across the face of a sharp descent, plunging on in a kind of crouch, huddling as far as it can from the threat of winds and the bright sea's watching.

The tunnel is no longer constant from here on: the boy sometimes breaks out across tawny exposures of stone, lopes beside tumbled drops and distances and the wide blare of sealight. Sometimes the branches clasp in over him again with a thick press of humid air, cobwebs, bramble tears—they touch him like music, stroke and cling and prick. Inside he is mostly filled with music, seems to himself that he shudders and glows with it, with so many beautiful details: names and lyrics, sleeve notes, playlists, artwork, mystically important anecdotes. On his best days, he is racked with music to the point of helpless smiling.

Only once, the boy pauses in the crook of a naked turn, is shaken by his own breath, folds over to touch his knees and stares at the howling, unsteadying blue of water. He feels its breath rise and brush him, sees the white gnaw and fumble of it against rocks and the seam where it fits under the sky. The blue stares back, bullets clear through him and out the other side. The boy feels it does not care about him, is only a terrible, hungry dazzle.

And then his intentions take him again, harry and press, and the grass underfoot steepens, sheers away deep into a final slither, an excuse to be out of control before he reaches the brink: the metal post, the first of the fixed ropes. He almost grins.

Descending is difficult—he has learned it is much easier to climb. Here, he can't see where his toes kick in and bounce, has to control his body as it swings, one line dropping to another, from post to post, threading the twists of the route and winding him lower. He bears his own weight safe, hands clever round the fat, stiff strands. He likes the effort, sweat, wishes it were more, for torn hands and bleeding, for the test of a fall.

Below him is the Pot: a tiny cove pocketed in

behind a high, containing wall and floored with a fawny-grey chaos of rocks. The boy makes his last spring, looses the rope and lets his feet land with a grinding clack amongst the wreckage and cold echoes. There is a sense here of something temporarily absent, a power that will return and overwhelm. The boy feels his shins tickle with its thrill and wishes he could properly savour the fear, believe it and be transported by its possibilities. He stepping-stones across the foreheads of the flatter boulders, aiming for an archway to his left.

At one time, he supposes, the Pot must have been really like a pot, a round little space sealed up from the tide, but the fabric of the island is never reliable. The whole place has worried itself into passages, landslips, caves, stacks. And long ago the miners worked at it: he imagines them, imported strangers with candlelit talents, grimly burrowing down between *magnetite, haematite, sphalerite, bornite*— the boy keeps the rhymes hot under his tongue like a spell. He likes to whisper the musical complications of *argentiferous pyrite* and *hornblende gneiss*. He belongs to the island, because he can name its bones. But it is unforgivably delicate: even the granite headlands seem shattered by some terrible, ancient impact. They are more shocked heaps of weight than permanent features.

And the Pot's feet-thick defences have been breached: a dark, lithe passageway leads along a fault line and will let in the high water. It lets the boy go out. He scrambles to one side of a huge, dropped boulder, fits between stones smoothed into contours that might be the flanks of some strange living thing. Above him is the nice threat of other faulting, sudden falls—ahead is sunwarmth on

5

surfaces, the rasp of limpets and a small shore which is his: in its heart, it is his and should be his and was meant to be forever his. This was the only certainty he wanted. There will only be one other he ever will.

Back in the cottage his mother will still be packing. Although she is very familiar with moving, she will take hours to fill and then unfill her bags, to rearrange and start again. The boy has told her he will deal with his own things. He always does.

This afternoon, he lies down on his back amongst the lowest rocks, settles and shifts until they can properly dig in and bite him. There are buttresses and thrones here ready for him, granite platforms that lift him so he can observe, but today he won't use them. He shuts his eyes and lets the roar of daylight bleed through and the reek of the sea is already tight around him, nearly wicked—it has the hotmetal, weird, stark taste of himself doing bad, himself at the start of sex, of his whole, red lifetime's allowance of sex. It's the scent, to be truthful, of being beyond the start and lost in a newness of want, of blurred demands and lapping, tidal fears.

But today is about something else—not being scared, not being a body, not about coping with any of that.

The boy swallows and he pauses and he parts his lips and then he is angry. He is furious.

At last.

At last, he is beside himself. He is raging.

And he's also determined that he won't be sad, or cut, or split, or harmed in some way that is bewildering and lodged in his stomach and his lungs and in his face—but mainly in his stomach, in this emptied place where he had a stomach. Those feelings would

6

be bad, so instead he is fully and hopelessly raging. He claws his fingers into the pebbles and gritty damp and he is never going to cry, never going to be the boy who has to leave here and not come back, lose this and then have to remember it, never going to be the boy who was stupid and let this in and loved it, who made plans.

Instead, he will be the boy who climbs down the ropes into his secret, into his perfect place and makes sure, before everything changes, that he is changed first. He has decided that he will be somebody else. He is going to lie here until he gets faster than death, until he is nothing but velocity. He is going to summon his future so powerfully that it will weather the cliffs in moments, boil their crystals, shock their strata until they break. The day when he steps from the harbour to the boat, the day when he walks to another new school, the day when he gathers his mother's clothes and folds them, tidies her away and finds he is only thinking of whether he'll make a sandwich when he's done—those times will have passed him, hardly touched him, and he will be grown smoothly older, will be fine. Before he stands up again, brushes off the sand from his adult self, he will have gathered powers, dignities and skills— he will be a man and complete.

This is his wish. He believes it so hard that his arms shake and he feels sick and, if the world were fair, his efforts ought to be rewarded.

The boy's breath speeds, is shallow, injured and animal. He frowns. Sandflies bounce and cloud, closed anemones shine like blood clots in shadowed fissures, the whole shoreline seethes mildly with thoughtless life. He puzzles on, leans against nature, needs it to give.

7

An hour passes, more.

The boy keeps on. He is a determined person.

But in the end he is tired and thirsty and not altered and the evening is coming and with it the tide and, because he does not want to drown, the boy eases himself back through to the Pot and stands for a while where the late sun is prying amongst the rubble and he braces his feet and then yells his name. He screams it. He intends the word to catch and stain somewhere, to hide itself away for later, like a spell. Then he grabs hold of the rope and begins to pull his body up.

He knew his intentions would fail him, but they were all he had.

He was right about this, though—it is much easier to climb.

Later, more than thirty years later, a man and a woman wait to board a boat—a liner, to be more accurate. They stand in a nicely murmuring and generally well-dressed queue while suffering a sense of gentle disappointment. They had expected and, only half jokingly, discussed the quayside bustle in which they would want to be immersed before embarkation: stevedores hefting cabin trunks through the clean tang of seaside air, other couples walking up brisk wooden gangplanks in handmade shoes and waving.

The woman has hair like her father's: a thick black with illogical spasms of curl. She would rather this were not the case. She has also inherited what is pretty much her mother's figure, so at school she was mildly dumpy and, having spent her twenties and thirties getting away with being more curved than actually fat, she imagines that her forties and a slowing metabolism will force her into increasingly vague knitwear and mail order slacks with elasticated waistbands. She does not anticipate that she'll enjoy this, although in some ways she'd have to admit that she's had a good run. Her full name is Elizabeth Caroline Barber and she is thinking—*I could just fancy a bit of waving. I have no idea who we'd be waving to, though. Or to whom we would be waving. There's something about queuing for a liner that makes you want to get your grammar right . . . No one ashore we **could** wave to. Except the stevedores—and I wouldn't be sure about waving to them—all greasy caps and Mickey-Finned drinks with Humphrey Bogart, your stevedores.*

I think.

But not really a job that exists any more, is it? Or it does exist, but not in Britain, because we don't have docks, not really. Shore porters—do we still have them? Do we still have real jobs here at all? Ones you need to train for, that have titles, special hats? Jesus, the postman had a uniform when I was a kid—now he looks like the man who mugged the man in the uniform and stole his sack. Not that he has a sack any more either.

The jolly postmen's Christmas race with loaded sacks—they used to show a bit of that on telly every year—the light-hearted end to the news. Or did I make that up? I'm fairly sure it used to happen. A manifestation of postal pride—vaguely servile and sweaty, but pride, nonetheless . . .

Is this the way I'll be now? I'll climb aboard, get more and more nostalgic, then judgemental, then

9

terrified of change and eventually I'm going to be right wing? Just happily fixated on the noose and the birch, detention centres for foreign miscreants, sterilisations for the poor and/or thick?

It's because I'm annoyed.

Being annoyed is almost indistinguishable from being right wing.

*Correction: being annoyed **in a queue** is almost indistinguishable from being right wing. That kind of unpleasantly bottled fury and tedium isn't going to break out in celebrations of your brotherhood with one and all and the commonality of human experience— not when one and all are in your way and your own experience is uniquely pissed off with every other human on earth.*

If State Socialism had been more sensible, it wouldn't have generated all those queues—that's what cut its throat in the long run—everyone a bloody fascist before they got their four-ounce loaf of bread. I would imagine.

*Naturally, I'm thinking of State Socialism because that will make me even less comfortable when I'm already, as I might say, exquisitely aware that only contemplating—from a distance—the outside of this luxury bloody liner has made me feel slightly filthy, a bit **wrong**.*

Behind us, the country is being cut up and auctioned off for meat and we couldn't care, apparently—we're just sailing away.

Guilty, that's what this makes me. I'm starting to feel sticky with it.

Probably not starting—could have been building for a while.

Has been building.

I want to wash. Lie down and wash and then lie

10

down again. And then wash.

And, of course, I am undemocratically irritated by the utter lack of luxury at this stage in the proceedings— cheap carpet, prefab walls, grey-sounding announcements relating to technical/nautical difficulties and delays—which may or may not be alarming: I understand none of them—and a rank of vaguely shoddy check-in desks, behind which women in uniforms do almost nothing very slowly.

*Why are we **here**? We're not **cruise people**. We're **not quoits and gin slings and rubbers of bridge people**. Or **being driven past monuments at speed with optional commentary people**, we are not **tonight will be the 1974 theme disco in the Galaxy Room people**. We will not be getting tattoos while in altered states, or buying Moroccan boys, or toppling wealthy aunts over the side, and we will not be—hopefully—dying in an unfortunate but historic mid-Atlantic calamity.*

Why are we here?

Why am I here?

Why am I here with Derek?

Why is Derek here with me?

Why are we standing in a non-moving queue which, at best, threatens to funnel us into a holding area equipped with unadventurous vending machines and a lady who seems to be selling tea and shockingly rudimentary sandwiches. She may also have biscuits, I can't tell from here.

At least there are toilets.

Currently out of reach, but it's good to know they've been provided.

Over there.

Where we can't use them.

Not that I couldn't nip away and ease discomfort should I need to, although Derek might not like that—

11

my leaving him.

He's in a mood.

Hasn't said so, doesn't need to, doesn't speak during moods. Self-explanatory, his bad temper, by dint of its heaving great silence.

Nevertheless, without using the medium of language he is still making it plain that he doesn't want to be surrounded by the staggeringly ancient as they whine about their pills and their luggage and their feet, or—should they, by some miracle, have actually been processed—as they shuffle between the tea lady and the toilets while mouthing sandwiches and apparently coming close to coughing their last.

We are, by miles, the youngest couple here. We are also the tallest. Well, Derek is the tallest. Just about. No doubt, should he—like our queue-dwelling neighbours—live to be 180, his own vertebrae will have collapsed into powder and aches and he will be smaller, or else hooped over like that guy there who is practically, for goodness' sake, peering back at life through his own knees. Which must be novel. Then again, at his age, would he want to keep on having to look ahead?

In front of Elizabeth, Derek hunches and shrugs his shoulders inside his jacket, then rubs one hand into and through his hair.

Dirty blond.

And she remembers this morning and lying on her side, newly awake, still softly fitting back into herself and being bewildered by a thought, by the idea of holding—she had this perfectly clear sensation of holding her arms around warm, breathing ribs, a lean chest—her hands meeting over his breathing—a dream of her resting in tight to the curve of his spine. But she wasn't holding anyone.

Hypnopompic hallucination. It's not uncommon.

12

Might be linked to stress.

I have stress.

My stresses are considerable.

A long spine, clearly enunciated, and then the dream had closed and made her miss him.

Silly.

More than silly—quite a lot more than that.

More than silly being currently the absolute best I can muster.

Derek had been out of bed and clattering about in the hotel shower, trotting to the sink, tooth brushing, spitting, throat-clearing, shaving, forgetting and then not forgetting to comb his hair. He had been readying himself while Beth was quietly left with a hot illusion, finding it deep, convincing.

Later, she'd held his hand in the taxi as they headed for the docks. She'd felt his knuckles, she'd suffered that tiny bump of nervousness as the pale side of the ship approached them, a higher and higher slab—like a building, like something too large to float.

Although it will. I have every confidence that it will. Massive boat for a massive ocean, that's not a problem.

And it's not as if we've had to pay for this—not exactly. This is a—what would you call it?—windfall. A possibly fortunate happenstance.

Then again—no such thing as a free cruise. Which isn't a popular saying, but could be—it might be appropriate . . .

Not that we're on a cruise, not honestly what we could say is a cruise. This will be **transport**—*Southampton to New York—like catching a bus.*

Well, not so much like a bus.

More like being taught to appreciate the romance of taking tea at four and cabin stewards and sunsets off

13

the stern before an early night.

Sunsets off the bow. Heading west—it would be the bow. Where you'd be exposed, wind-lashed, freezing. Not romantic.

Just the early night then.

Like willingly falling unconscious in a vast disaster movie with a cast of the virtually dead.

Christ, I don't know why I'm doing this.

I just do not.

'Boring, isn't it? Or else, perhaps not so much boring as *unsettling*. I mean, *I'm* unsettled . . . Can't speak for anyone else. Sorry . . .' This is the man who has ended up standing behind her in the line.

Behind him is the brittle lady with aggressive jewellery—the one Elizabeth has decided to think of as a quietly alcoholic widow, the one who genuinely does seem to be accompanied by what might once have been called A Companion.

Bet she'll turn out to be less quietly alcoholic.

Elizabeth is starting to gather hypotheses about many of her relatively-soon-to-be fellow passengers.

She has no theories about the man. He does not seem to be anything in particular. He has one hand in his trouser pocket and whatever bags he is travelling with must have been handed over for loading, because he is carrying nothing beyond a dark brown overcoat. It is a noticeably good coat, although he does not seem to care about it, keeps it haphazardly folded across one arm.

It'll crease.

And he'll be sorry if they lose his luggage.

No. No, he won't.

His suit, although vaguely ill-kempt, fits him suspiciously well.

Made for him.

14

He would buy other luggage, if they lost his. There's nothing he couldn't replace.

That's what I'd guess.

Even though she knows this is unfair, she believes there is something despicable about a person who can't appreciate his own belongings, who doesn't need his clothes.

Should this happen to be the case. Judging the book by its cover—which one never should.

'I do apologise. Perhaps you didn't want to talk.'

'What?' She doesn't want to seem rude. Saying *what* to a stranger would be rude, in almost anyone's opinion. Ignoring someone when they speak to you and thinking about them instead is rude, too. 'Um . . .' Doing it again would be ruder. 'I'm sorry.' Whether you know them or not.

'Ah. So we're both sorry.' He rummages violently in the pockets of his coat and then stops. He inclines his head and apparently gives his entire attention to the notch in her collarbone. He addresses it earnestly. 'I . . . by myself, you see. Long voyage ahead . . . not incredibly long and there's the cinema, shows, entertainers . . . probably far too much going on to deal with, in actuality, *uncomfortable numbers* of possibilities—but familiar faces . . .' He breaks off to gaze beyond her, as if he is searching for something troublesome and fast moving. He is pale in a way that suggests fragility, illness. He sighs, 'There are occasionally times—*will be*, I beg your pardon, occasionally times when one would like to chat—when *I* would. Apart from *this* time, of course, which is *excruciating*—but hardly a time at all, more a type of solid, liquid maybe, that *has to be got through*. Probably, though, you don't *want* to chat and so everything I've said is . . . *irrelevant*.' The

15

man blinks, considers. 'Or else . . . chatting might not be involving, *distracting* enough.' He shakes his head briefly and steps towards her, his left foot splaying very gently, not inelegant, but outwith his control. He walks as if his shoes are too stiff, or too heavy, or not his.

Or as if he's afraid. I would say he's afraid. He walks like a man on glass, on ice.

He falters to a halt. 'Are you good at maths?'

'I beg your pardon?'

'Maths.' He smiles past her, aims the expression quite carefully at her partner's doggedly mute back. 'Arithmetic? Numbers? One and one equalling two. As an alternative to eleven. Or three. In the binary system, three—but not in the decimal, not in the one we'd be used to using. So many ways of saying so many things. Two would be what we were dealing with here and now.'

'I know one and one is two, yes.' She tries to smile calmly, because this might be the correct response.

When he looks at her directly there is something about the deep of the man's eyes which makes her reach and find Derek's hand, tug him round by it to stand beside her. Elizabeth is not absolutely surprised when this doesn't make her feel more at ease. She seems only to be demonstrating a public weakness, a lapse in taste.

The stranger continues, apparently concentrating on forcing himself inside his words, increasing their density, and yet staying as motionless as he can be while still managing to speak, 'Then what would be the number you would pick—just a game—can we play a game?—one number between one and ten— what would you pick?—you might want to think for your number carefully, search, maybe discount

16

inappropriate options—or else you could choose the first one, your very first choice, the one that seemed right, that immediate choice. Or you could change your mind. Because everyone's free to do that. Of course.'

He could be an entertainer.

Either very successful, or very not.

'No. Really. Indulge me. Genuinely think of a number between one and ten. You can't be wrong. Just give me a number.'

He waits politely.

A paid entertainer.

He continues to wait, but with no suggestion that he doubts she will eventually oblige him.

'Seven.'

'Really? Seven. You're sure?'

Stage clothes and pretending. An act.

When she says it again, 'Seven,' she sounds sharp and has the sense that she has become a small focus for others' interest. She wishes the man would go away.

Instead, he very carefully smiles at her. 'And another?' He shows her exactly the face of an understanding friend, a man to whom she could say anything in any way and be entirely understood, a gentle man and a gentleman, a rare thing. He shows her precisely and tenderly calibrated fellow feeling. For the space of two words it roars and flares and is unpreventable. It comforts. It is built to do nothing but. Then he puts it away. 'Another? If you wouldn't mind.'

'Two.'

'And another?'

She can feel Derek's arm leaning against hers, but he says nothing to help her. She is the one that

17

speaks. 'Five. No, eight. Eight.'

'You're good at this. Now reverse them—those numbers. Do you need a piece of paper to work this out? I think I have a piece of paper . . .' He contemplates his coat and its pockets again severely.

'Seven five eight in reverse is eight five seven. I can remember that much.' Which didn't seem petulant and ungrateful before she'd said it, heard it, but it clearly was—undoubtedly she is being a bad sport. No, she is being put in the wrong—when none of this is anything she asked for.

The man blinks, takes himself close to the edge of a grin, conspiratorial, charming. 'But you chose seven *two* eight . . .' He pauses to clear his throat. 'If seven *five* eight would be better . . .' The amusement flickers in again.

'It would.'

'Beautiful.' Although for an instant he frowns, considers, then, 'So now you can subtract them from each other—seven five eight from eight five seven. What would that make ?'

'That would be . . . Nine . . . That would be ninety-nine.'

'As opposed to sixty-six, if we picked another point of view . . . And if you add those numbers together— nine and another nine—that would be . . .'

'Eighteen.'

'And then subtract the one from the eight. Because we can't leave it be. Poor eighteen.'

'Seven.'

'Seven. Which is the number you first thought of, isn't it . . . ? Oddly. Seven. And I'll show . . . I'll show you seven. In a manner of speaking. I have it here.' This time he is more assured as he manhandles his coat and fetches out a thumbed book from one of its pockets—she can't see the cover. 'Would you say you were determined, a determined person? If you don't mind my asking . . .' The man angles his head towards Derek and grins, rapidly boyish and then smoothed again. 'Is the lady determined? I have no idea, but she does seem that way—admirable, if I can say so—which is why I asked—I wouldn't ask if I thought it wasn't probable—determination, that shows in the face—like . . . *mercy*, for example— *kindness*—betrayal, grief . . .'

He can't shut up. He's stuck in this, talking it through to the end. Patter. Spitting out the patter, no matter what. A man who memorises nonsense and then inflicts it.

'You're her husband? Boyfriend? None of my business—but *lovely* idea, to go on a cruise together. Nothing better, I would say.'

And the stranger nods back at Elizabeth, refocuses, winks, while he speaks and speaks, voice quiet but unavoidable. He hands her the book and tells her, 'Determination can change who you are. Changing who you are can alter almost anything. Do you believe that?' And no space for her to answer, because rattling, bolting in after it comes, 'I can prove it. In a way. In a trivial, though perhaps diverting, way. If you take the book and you think of your number, you think of *seven*, strongly enough— if you feel *seven* in your chest, in your pulse, if inside your head you scream it—if you internally *yell*—and that seven becomes so *true* that its *essence*, its *strength*, is irresistible—and when you do that and keep doing that, then you can open up the book and turn it to page seven and you will see . . .'

Obedient, she opens the book where she's told to and sees nothing unusual.

19

'And you keep on screaming and you turn over that page . . .'

Which she does and finds that neatly, predictably, there is no page eight. There are only two pages, one after the other, both numbered seven—as if seven were somehow contagious, had soaked through the paper.

'And page eighteen, as we might imagine . . .'

Delivers itself as another page seven.

'The numbers.' She passes him back his trick. 'Clever. Thank you.'

'Don't mention it.' And he puts on his coat, which seems unnecessary—the waiting area is bleak, but not cold.

'It must be odd to read—a book like that.'

'Maybe.' He repockets the book which is maybe odd to read, shakes his sleeves, his lapels, until whatever order he sought to impose has been established. 'Books aren't about numbers, though, are they? They're stories—words. They're people's stories. The numbers wouldn't be the part you'd notice, I'd have said. Even if you ought to . . .'

The man forces out his hand abruptly and surprises Derek into shaking it.

And, perfectly normally, Elizabeth is next for the chill, smooth pressure of his grip, the tamp of his thumb in the heart of her palm. There is something overly naked about the man's skin, as if it is a terrible, white secret. She tries to disengage a moment before he allows her to which makes her feel rude again, intolerant. She tells him, 'Some people would notice.' Which is intended to sound placatory, but is mainly patronising and also mumbled.

'Many wouldn't. Many, in fact, *would not*.' This as he turns from her, as he is leaving with that faintly dragged and staggered walk, that atmosphere of discomfort, the uneasy head.

All at sea.

Elizabeth intends to keep an eye on him, watch where he goes, but then the queue fusses around her in a kind of irritated ripple and manages to propel itself forward by at least a yard. The excitement of this means she loses the man completely.

'God save me from amateur magicians.' At least the incident has broken Derek's sulk. 'I think we're getting somewhere finally, though . . .'

And he's right. As mysteriously as they were trapped by inaction, they are now bustled through and can fully partake in the joys of flip-up plastic seating and sturdy tea, no biscuits. Elisabeth feels she might want to buy a bag of chocolate nuts from the machine, but then reconsiders her intention, does nothing.

Docile blocks of humanity are summoned from their benevolent detention and disappear through doorways which smell of oily mechanisms, fuel and— unmistakably—salt water.

Almost on our way.

And this thought squeezes her with panic, raises a true, sick welt of fear that means, when the appropriate passenger grouping is called, Elizabeth almost stumbles from her seat. She has small difficulties with her hands as she picks up her bag. Over to her left she can hear voices.

'And if we subtract two hundred and thirty six from six hundred and thirty two . . . ? We get?

'Um . . . three hundred and ninety-six . . . ?'

'And three plus nine plus six?'

'That's . . . seventeen.'

'That's . . . ?'

21

'Oh, eighteen. Yes. Eighteen.'

'And we can't leave poor eighteen alone, though, can we? Poor eighteen. One from eight?'

'Is seven.'

The second time around it's less impressive: the working starts to show and maybe she's sorry for the man and his puzzle which no longer does.

*   *   *

And maybe you're sorry for him also, have compassion for his inadvertent and public failing. Perhaps you would find it uncomfortable if your book mentioned the way Beth continues to watch the man until he shakes his head, glances away from his work and—before Beth can stop this—meets her eyes again. He tries to construct a type of smile, but his face is soft suddenly, perhaps ashamed, and he turns away and seems to sink slightly. He drops his book, has to stoop and fumble for it—nervous fingers.

This is unfortunate for him and you can imagine how he feels.

You're aware of how easy it is to make these minor errors.

There are times when you've personally known things to misfire—the sentence that fell badly, the dull gift, slapdash comment, hobbled punchline, tight-fisted tip—trying to be too stupid, trying to be too clever, too silly, too carefree, too caring, too free. You can think back to those long and hollow pauses when you realised that you'd misjudged a mood, weren't paying attention, had taken the wrong risk.

You don't worry about these occasions, or not that much. There are a few past humiliations which, yes—if you ponder them, truly enter in—can still raise a significant sting and that queasy and sticky ridiculousness of you being inappropriately yourself. But there's nothing destructive about your reflections and you can laugh at them with ease. You can enjoy allowing others to laugh, too. You don't stand on your dignity, you aren't stuffy or prickly unless you've been given good cause and this means you can be relaxing company. Those who know you would say this, if they were asked.

And those you know, the people you care about—mistakes with them can be more serious. Going wrong can hurt so much when you're only beginning to care, when you're delicate and don't know your situation and something extraordinary could be ruined before you reach it. But it's probably worse when you love, fully love, what you've got and yet could still crash in and spoil it. You want to avoid that—anyone would.

You cope, though. In some areas, you excel. For this and many other reasons there's a good deal about you that others could admire. You're a survivor, although people might not notice this and you don't make a fuss.

You're a good person at heart.

You're sure of this and your book's sure of it, too.

There are things good people shouldn't do. Most of these are well established, codified as precepts, but you can be certain that—with laws or without them, overseen or unobserved—your own nature would prevent you from straying too far into harm.

You wouldn't consciously injure, wouldn't murder, wouldn't steal.

Although stealing can sometimes be difficult to define: more than your fair share of mints in a restaurant, hotel soaps, ashtrays in bars—some objects can seem ownerless, lost, attractive. This doesn't mean that you would take crockery from the restaurant, or light fittings from the hotel, or fire extinguishers from the bar—any more than you would walk out with the mirror from a changing room, or a coat set down for an unguarded moment on a chair, or drive away with someone else's car.

You wouldn't study a person who, in a strict and pedantic sense, belonged to someone not yourself—you wouldn't slip into wanting them, imagining, overtures. Just as you wouldn't defraud an insurance company, or falsely claim a benefit, or avoid paying any portion of your taxes.

Not to an unacceptable degree.

You only have these ideas, just very occasionally these quite natural ideas. When, for instance, the person ahead of you in the bank queue is carrying bags of money, just obviously a great weight of unmarked cash, or when security guards stroll past you with simple, tidy boxes of who can say how much—you do very slightly have this impulse to find out how heavy solid wealth could be, to make yourself better informed on that small point—

24

to grab, to snatch and run.

This doesn't imply that your integrity is tarnished. You have thought a thought, no more than that.

And maybe you have picked up coins, banknotes in the street, or from the floor of a shop, a cab, a bus, in the car park at the back of a rowdy pub—so many people have paused there—rendered careless, eccentric, helpless by their pleasures—and have burrowed into pockets and bags for their keys, have ended by dropping, losing everything as they search. This wasn't money which was yours and yet you kept it. Like a stranger's little gift.

But there was no fault involved, not on your part.

And you would never damage an animal or a child. Unless, of course, it was to spare them greater hurts. And perhaps animals are frightened, sacrificed in the production of your food, even though you do everything reasonable to avoid this. You assuredly have good will, but also distractions—it is sometimes hard to apply yourself for others' sakes and to stay comprehensively informed. Child labour, for instance, can ooze into places you might not suspect and undoubtedly ruins lives, but you may unknowingly support it, buy its fruits. Nevertheless, if you heard of a young individual who was growing without the benefit of an adequate education, who was forced to work, who lost a finger in machinery, or an eye perhaps, then you would act. You would make complaints.

You have defended those weaker than yourself. You were pleased to discover you couldn't do otherwise.

You have a great capacity for kindness.

That's why you give to charities—you can't donate to everyone, wouldn't be foolish about it, but you

25

still try your best. And there have been times when you have enjoyed doing something for nothing and payment would have been unwelcome, if not insulting.

You like the way it feels when you can help.

It's clean.

It makes you feel useful and clean.

And you can rest assured that you're more honest than most people.

Which means you'd prefer to be careful about your employment and it could only seem strange to you, quite terrible, if you slipped into earning your living by doing wrong.

You wouldn't choose to be associated with an unethical company, or criminal behaviour, deception.

So you wouldn't do this.

You wouldn't stand in a moderately spacious civic theatre (with poor acoustics) and address 750 people (the place is full to capacity this evening) having assured them that you have knowledge of their dead. You wouldn't present yourself as being controllably possessed, rattled by the voices from buried throats, gone flesh. You wouldn't peer off beyond yourself into what observers might believe to be a stirring but vaguely melancholy space in which you'll seek out messages of love.

You wouldn't do this.

But your book has to show you the man who would.

This man: tall, pale, golden-headed, and an ache in him that's plain when he raises his hands—long fingers, delicate, uneasy—and when he paces, rocks. He offers his audience—mainly female—a pain that's as bright as his hair, as his skin under the lights. He is alone for them and burning in the bleak space of the stage and any reasonable spectator might want to help him, to touch him, to believe.

And none of this happens by accident. He is not an accidental man. He is prepared. He is never, if he can avoid it, outside in the day—night walks at home and sunscreen with the homburg when he's on the road. No red meat, not ever—rarely meat in any form—a diet he constrains to thin essentials, minimums, as poor in iron as can be survivable. The anaemia refines him, tunes him, lets him flare.

Because appearances matter. Everyone judges the cover before the book.

The man wears a good suit, elegant, his tastes beginning to turn more and more expensive. A quiet tie which he may loosen but not remove. And the jacket stays on, no matter what. Dark, hard leather shoes with a good shine, an uncompromising impact at each step. Dark socks. Plain cufflinks. Shirts of a definite colour, not distracting, not flamboyant and not white—he needs a firm contrast to his skin, a way of quietly showing he's almost translucent, all fragile veins and watered milk. A sense of austerity in his haircut and a hint of service, also the suggestion of precious thinking, perhaps, of heat in the stubble gleaming at his neck.

And his thinking, if not precious, is certainly precise.

Deception is only unforgivable if it is incomplete. Leave any access for doubt, for exposure, bad revelations, and then you're much more than failing— you're committing a type of delayed assault. Be utter and undetected and then no forgiveness will ever be required.

The man's job is to be the perfect liar, because that's what his audience needs. Blood, words, skin, face, eyes, breath, bone—he must lie in his entirety.

27

The enquirers deserve nothing less. So that when he names out relatives and pets, describes familiar jewellery and clothes, episodes of romance, pleasant outings, birthday parties, misfortunes, habits, griefs, coincidences, arguments, birth signs, jokes, uncommon journeys, illnesses, cars and motorbikes, hospitals, buses, armed intrusions, injuries, scrambled efforts at evasion, running and narrow paths, terminal bewilderments—most particularly when he speaks of the terminal things, of deaths—they will be true. He will give them, most particularly, true deaths.

His job to be the window that lets them see through, the door that will open so they can walk back to the times and the places he'll resurrect. And when he tells his enquirers worlds, they will seem true worlds. They will be truer and better than the world they have.

Tonight 750 strangers have watched him convincingly let other souls slip into his blue-white self and then speak through him. Over and over, he's brought loves closer, invited them, called them in. This has been his little gift to everyone.

And he's the best. No one is like him.

Not sure that anyone would want to be.

And almost done and tired and tired and tired, he's shaken his head as if freeing himself and let his shoulders drop, he's sighed and rubbed his cheeks and felt his audience lean their will against him, the broad, warm press of how they still want more, could easily stay here—row on row—and drink him all away. But this is it, show's over: a nod and a handful of sentences, an appropriately small and quiet bow and he'll walk to the bland little dressing room and wash his face and sit, lean back and sit.

'You didn't let me speak to Billy. When you were

here before you let me speak to him.'

Woman right at the front—quite naturally right at the front and in the centre—directly at his feet, in fact, only the height of the stage between them. 'Why didn't he want to speak to me?' She has left her seat, is tensed almost on tiptoe.

Pink sweater—polo neck to deal with slightly ageing skin, overly glamorous jewellery, trying too hard—and she is yelling. The man assumes that she is mentally unable not to yell. The man has met this kind of thing before.

'Didn't he want to?'

The theatre stiffening, clinging round him while he remembers his previous visit—it was in the spring—and having made this woman happy about her dead son. This time, for three hours—plus interval—she has been carefully avoided. Too anxious, too bereft.

Female, 35–45, single and childless: difficult, they lack the usual entry points, are all needs and lacks and fretting and last-minute hopes, they suffer cruel and salty lunges of impossibility. So you offer them dreams.

Female, 35–45, divorced after her child was taken: easy. Give her back the boy.

But just because it's easy that doesn't mean I should.

The room waiting for a proper remedy, the man's authoritative resolution.

If I help her now she'll come to every session when I'm in town, she'll start to follow me about.

The man can taste her: something sour from her like illness and panicky—the flavour of instability there and obsession. He always understands things partly with his mouth, is currently swallowing bitter metal and earth, something moist and stagnant

29

mixed up with dark earth. Having paid attention, he would know her in great detail if they were ever to meet again.

'No.' And a beat while the rest of the audience almost relaxes, prepares for more trust. He pulls in a breath and lets his hand twitch. 'Last time I was here Billy said his goodbye. He said he loved you.'

She cries at this—happygreedy tears—hands curled and lifting near her lips.

'He told you what he couldn't, what he didn't have the chance to say. That satisfied him and put him at rest.'

Nobody is with her, she came by herself, is pursuing this by herself—arms falling to flutter at her sides: if someone was here for her to hold, they would catch the signal and step in, she would be embracing and embraced. Grief seeping around her, rises in clouds, travelling.

'He told you.'

She nods, little girl nod, all compliance and listening.

The man straightens his spine, widens his attention to take in the room. 'We do have to finish.' He watches this make her tremble. Of course, it would. 'But if he gives me more for you I will tell you afterwards.' He's firm when he looks at her, pauses until her eyes lift, and is firmer still until she sits and the man can roll on into the final phrases, can coil up his performance and tidy it away.

He's slightly too fast as he walks for the wings.

And he won't tell her anything afterwards.

He won't see her.

He'll use the office exit and be in his car and gone before she gets outside. No stage door rendezvous in the rain.

The man feels this is for the best.

He wants to be a good person. He wants to find the right ways to do wrong.

There are fireworks.

Naturally.

There would have to be fireworks.

Elizabeth stands on her cabin's balcony.

She has a *balcony*.

For that matter, she's *in a cabin*—and she watches mildly impressive fizzes of rising colour, detonations, splayed fire. Without a crowd to appreciate it, the effort seems slightly peculiar, if not sad. Derek is paying no attention—he's inside unpacking, *stowing* their belongings—or actually, now that she looks, he's sitting on the end of their bed and holding a life jacket, peering at it, as if it is failing to reassure.

Elizabeth knows how he feels.

Passenger Emergency Drill—scare the bloody life out of you, that would. Maundering herds of visibly breakable pensioners and couples with ideological reasons for never consenting to walk—being self-propelled letting their side down in some way—and yet they're out and tottering about in what amounts to a communal suicide pact—every stairwell just an accident in progress, just a slow-motion invitation to crushing injuries and fractured hips—and nobody getting anywhere, it's simply this huge release of the bewildered.

And myself amongst them—no use pretending—myself more than confused and liking it that my head's run to a blur, because then I don't have to deal with

31

it, don't have to cope with any part of my fucking brain. I need only be trapped and watch strangers coagulate while the words plunge by.

Distracted.

Exactly what I'm after.

Exactly what I am. Pretty much.

Except for this bit—which is too close to being aware and will need to be stopped.

So.

There I was with Derek and there Derek was with me and both of us having mistaken the unspoken rules of the occasion and not dressed up for a cocktail party with optional death later. Derek, in fact, might have ambled in from weeding, or light DIY, perhaps something electrical and I'm there in my current moderately smart slacks but slovenly jumper, weak blouse peering apologetically out at the collar and garish shoes—plus, the sea air had made my hair frizz. Red shoes and amateur clown hair, accompanied by a passing handyman—we were getting looks—cornered in this area of wall-to-wall piss-elegance and tweed while no doubt other scruffy souls were easing along unremarked.

*And these guys in their Elegant Casual Dress Code get-ups, they wanted to barge—clearly they wanted to ram their wives softly ahead of them like delightfully scented and tolerant little snowploughs, but they couldn't—or rather they weren't sure if they should— they were genuinely conflicted about shoving a way through, because they're the type who are meant to win at everything and be survivors, but the ship **wasn't** actually going down—was still at anchor, in fact—and nothing was at stake and everyone's status was as yet ill-defined and there was always the risk of causing significant—and later disastrous—offence and* *meanwhile they'd hoped to appear as sporting, likeable, gallant, which tends to preclude punching out old ladies—life's so difficult . . .*

And all of us, bumbling along together and hugging our orange buoyancy aids as if they were wallets, or kittens, or children and locked in this big, thick, dreamy inability to save ourselves.

Even when we finally dribbled into our Assembly Station—the stylishly appointed theatre: wartime good cheer from the stage and advice from ex-Navy passengers about donning jerseys before immersion and two pairs of socks: you would want to drown comfortably, not be cold—even then, it took half an hour for everyone involved to actually place their life jackets over their heads.

We would die.

We would horribly die and be lost because of our sheer inadequacy.

We would deserve it and good riddance to us. We are clearly of no use.

And there was me trying to remember if it was the forearms or the buttocks of fellow unfortunates that open-boat-drifting and starving mariners are meant to eat.

Although we'd never get as far as that; bobbing and bloating, we'd be, and no one left to fish us out and snack.

Oh, Christ.

It doesn't bear thinking about.

So I won't.

Would rather not.

Forearms and buttocks of women—I think that's what's recommended.

And sadly I have both—all four.

Imagine.

33

No idea what I'd do to live, to be alive and stay that way.

Below her, over the handrail, are the layered edges of other balconies and fat rows of plastic pods which she supposes would expand in some startling way and turn into what would be, given the passengers' manifold incapacities, relatively pointless lifeboats, should the need arise. Here and there she can also see the calm metal side of the ship. Out of her sight it must drop into the water, clean down and vanish, angle in through the cold and the dark until it meets the rest of itself, folds and seals monumentally into the hard depth of a keel. Around them the yellowish spill of their lights spreads across gently progressing water: a careless halo pouring out into the night, showing the white gleam where they cut the water's skin.

For a while, she'd had the wavering impression that somewhere a band was playing brass instruments with a degree of vehemence—this was when the quayside was still safely tied beside them and a stirring march and uniforms could have been thought an appropriate farewell gesture. She couldn't be that sure of what she'd heard, because of the explosions ongoing overheard. And there was a breeze rising—enough to tousle sounds and make them unreliable. The music's stopped now, anyway—they've left it behind. Although she supposes that the pianist who played as they strolled aboard may be playing still, or could perhaps have been replaced by some combination of other musicians and instruments, maybe a harp. She feels sure that a harp will appear at some point. And on broad, soft-carpeted decks fruit machines are winking beside the type of green baize tables that promise exciting loss and there are bars and lounges, the theatre, the programme of stimulating lectures and lessons and entertainments and then there are the restaurants and the tiny, pricey shops and the spa and there is, of course, the library—currently closed, but on two storeys with a communicating spiral staircase, which must count for something—and, in short, there is an overwhelming sense that she has entered an environment prepared for people who are quite terribly afraid of being left to their own devices.

But Elizabeth likes her own devices.

Sometimes.

'She's got money then, Margery.' Derek emerges and leans beside her at the rail, slips his arm around her waist and nestles—she can feel the hard shape of his hip. Probably because she is slightly chilled—she's not wearing her coat—his temperature is surprising, warmth caught in his pullover. He kisses the top of her head and it makes her shiver. 'Hello.'

'Margery? No . . . Not particularly . . .'

'She pays for a pair of these . . . That's a four-figure cabin in there. That's two grand. Twice two grand.' Derek likes to say that kind of thing—to mention money obliquely, disrespectfully, as if he understands it and can't be impressed.

Not that he doesn't have money himself. A man of substance, Derek. And all his own work, doesn't take it for granted.

'It wasn't a special effort, was it? She hasn't got cancer or something—wants to leave everything to you.'

'She's my friend, Derek. I was worried enough about her when she had to cancel. I don't need you . . . adding that jolly idea.'

'Sorry. Only kidding. Sorry. Really.' He peers at

35

her until she can let him see he is forgiven. 'I am.'

'Her husband—second husband—he had money. And then he died. He was older . . . And . . . she doesn't have that many friends. And she, ah . . . likes me.'

'Oh, I see . . . Me, too.' Derek squeezes her waist in a way that suggests they'll have sex later under their mustard coverlet, in their fawn with additional mustard and really quite—it has to be said—1970s accommodation which is not moving, not absolutely— not pitching or rolling, they're still only creeping along the Solent, after all—but, nevertheless, the walls, the floor, their surroundings, are unashamedly *lively* with engine throb, and beyond that is the faintest, faintest give, a sway, like an anxiety—or rather, a tease, a promise to be surprising in days to come.

January in the Atlantic—we have to be out of our minds.

Derek kisses her again, moist heat against her neck. 'Bet I like you more than she does . . .'

She wonders how cold she feels to him, how strange. 'You both like me in different ways . . .' Her hair flutters, unhappily disturbed—it stings slightly when it hits her cheek. 'Since the husband, she does have money, I suppose. Not *her* money, though. Well, it is hers, since he . . . So . . . yes. She's well-off.'

'Shame she couldn't come in the end—I'd like to have met her. Someone you went to school with—bet she's got stories . . .'

'Not that kind of stories, no.'

'Stories about lovers . . .' He puts the words in close to her ear and they flicker, nudge.

'I didn't have a lover at school. I didn't even have

36

boyfriends.'

'Yeah, I've never believed that *late starter* stuff. I think you're just being modest.'

'I have lots to be modest about.' This odd desire he has occasionally to rework her as a sexually rapacious teenager—all pouting and gymslips. Sometimes it's sweet and sometimes it's just annoying and borderline weird. 'My dad wanted me to be academic. So I was.'

'Always did what your dad said . . .'

'Always.'

Not absolutely always, but that's nothing to discuss at this juncture.

Derek begins to steer her indoors and she allows it to be comforting that she gives him control, steps inside and is waylaid by the awful decor, the seafaring neatness, smallness, the practical lack of clutter to pre-empt rough seas and breakages. The effect is claustrophobic, but also endearing.

Derek sits on the tiny sofa, his legs aimed mostly at the bed and thus avoiding the minute table, his whole frame slightly compressed, designed according to a different scale. 'Not fair, though . . .'

'What isn't?'

'That she pays for you to come along—for us both—and then she ends up being stuck at home herself. Do you think she got a refund?'

'I didn't ask . . . Couldn't be helped, though—when it's your heart, you have to . . . well—take it to heart. Sorry.'

Hate doubled meanings—once you start them, they don't bloody stop—inferences, references, cross-references—then everyone turns into the sad bloke at the party who thinks it's his job to chuck in puns, focus the room's loathing.

37

'And is she OK now, Beth?'

And, right enough, a punster does draw out the hate. Eventually even the nicest people would succumb to their darker longings and just fillet him, cut him up— still punning—and throw him into the tajine, on to the barbecue, into freezer bags for later—depending on the brand of party.

I don't hate them because they're not funny, I hate them because they mean nothing you say can stay innocent.

'Beth?'

'Yes. Yes, she called and said the tests were, you know . . . reassuring. It's just the long sea voyage thing and the insurance thing—in case they have to winch you off by helicopter, improvise on you with jump leads, that kind of stuff. They like you to be healthy.'

Elizabeth removes her shoes, lies on the bed. She looks over at Derek as he reaches for the paper and starts to read. He is folded neatly in the available space—the limbs and joints and angles of a long and wiry man, that particular shape. And in her mind she lets herself think

Love.

Such a terrible word—always demands you should be its accomplice, should comply—can't even say it without that sense of licking, tasting, parting your lips to be open, to welcome whatever it is that slips in beneath your breath, and then you find yourself closing to keep it, mouth it, learn its needs—this invisible medicine, this invisible disease.

It takes a hold.

Not like sex. Sex is a slip of a word, a slither—and it can be so simple, uncomplicated as it sounds.

Not that it wasn't a cause for concern at the

*start—because I **did** reach it later, I **was** a slow learner and usually, initially unsure—but then hasn't everyone been unsure? I don't think it's remotely unique to suffer those young, young endless doubts—If he's kissing me, actually kissing me—which is nice—absolutely nice— even so, am I quite sure of why?*

Does he like me? Find me attractive? Because I'd be hoping that both of those things is what we'll be about.

Or is he kissing me the way he kisses everyone, is he just the friendly type? Or curious? Or bored? Or has he stumbled and coincidentally fallen against my mouth?

Which is preposterous, naturally, but need not be mistaken. My insecurity may only signal that I am both ugly and right.

Right about being wrong—romantically mistaken.

Am I, for example, being kissed because there is something delicious on my face—my lips—possibly gravy, perhaps jam—it could be jam . . . Is he just hungry? Is this just to do with jam? I want to believe this is mainly about me, but I could be deluded.

I can't feel my irresistibility is likely.

Then again, what I can feel is blinding, incandescent, and offers no names for itself and is eating, is swallowing, all of my names for me—and the more I keep doing what we're doing—because he's still doing it, too: we're doing it together, in fact—except he's doing it in the opposite direction—and this works, really works—and I wouldn't have thought that a body, anybody's body, could be that, well, entertaining—the more we do this, whatever it is, the less I know about it, the less I know about everything, and the less I am able to care about not knowing.

I am perfectly happy and also evaporating.

Who'd have thought?

But eventually you're wholly free of thinking and can begin to uncover who you are with him, touch against touch.

And you make beauties together.

You and whoever he happens to be.

It does seem wrong to say so, but who he is can seem slightly irrelevant.

Not in a bad way—although it does sound bad—the specific identity of the gentleman does not, to be honest, matter that much.

*This isn't your fault. It's nearly **their** fault: the number of—eventually a not excessive but still significant number of—gentlemen's fault, because they have been, as it were, not that outstanding or differentiated and, therefore, in order to have any fun, any modest pleasure, you have become **very** differentiated. Your heart, your mind, your body, they have become discrete. You have separated into fragments that no longer communicate and which get curious and bored and stumble, and your condition is patently not ideal, but equally you're never disappointed.*

You do sometimes have a sense of waiting by which you are almost overwhelmed, but this shows you are not pathological or numb. And you bear none of the gentlemen ill will. You would smile at them in the street, be quietly fond: you would commiserate should they receive unpleasant news. This isn't love, though— this is not love, this is not in any way that word.

This is safe.

You are safe.

You are lucky and not confined—not really—it's rather that you enjoy prudent limitations, almost always have.

You are not unaware of love's damages, that chaos,

and realise you have been spared, are sparing yourself. You get to pursue what are not relationships, more a series of hobbies, indoor games for rainy evenings and afternoons.

So, on several legitimate levels, you are content.

Only then, for instance—just for instance—you may stand beside a man, a not unfamiliar man, and—sharp and hard and for no reason—every shade of him will strike in through you: his angles and his musics and the subtleties of his scents: and you cannot touch him, but want to—cannot respond, but want to—cannot move, but want to. He has, in the course of doing nothing, suspended you in want and want and want. And through you come reeling these dreadful truths: that you respect him and fully intend to be proud of him hereafter and to see him both happy and well— and you'll need him kept warm in the winter and cool when it's hot and will let no ugly breeze come near him and no wanker be permitted to annoy him and you wish for him to be comfortable, at the very least comfortable, for ever. And these are desires that ache in you deeper than sweating, or bending, or sucking, or any of the thin and predictable memories or the fantasies that might defend you from the present, too present, reality of him.

*The tiny idea of naming him **darling** is almost unsurvivably arousing.*

Which is beyond preposterous.

You are turning innocent and selfless to such a degree that if your absence would please him, you'd disappear.

You would have to go.

But you can't go.

You couldn't go.

You couldn't leave while his voice is purring in your skull, purring and curling and thinking your thoughts and you look at your hands and feel his fingers, as if you have become each other's gloves—and the sound of his breath and when he swallows could set you falling, could take you to a place where you might weep, where you are far out of your mind, but still at home in it, at liberty inside yourself as you have never been.

Many people take to this, are delighted to be found and lost, possessing and possessed.

You are not one of those people.

*You **were** not one of those people.*

But your selves have bled together now, blurred and joined. He has made of you a unified need, a piece of desperation, by being here and existing—effortless.

And his manner of existing means you will not be having sex with him.

*Which is to say, you **will** have sex with him, but you also will not.*

You will be complicated.

You will touch—will begin with touch—will slip and slither and hold and rock and cling. You will fuck—but you wouldn't, you truly wouldn't, if it wasn't entirely impossible to say what you need to in any other way.

*It won't be **sex**, it will be **speaking**.*

*And—God help you—it will also be admiration, tenderness, concern—this excruciating list of necessities which are all chained to **making love**.*

*You will **make love**.*

*You are **in love**.*

You weren't when he was leaning in the doorway.

Then he stepped over here and you were.

You are.

It isn't fair.

It isn't fucking fair.

Because you know what it will mean.

*You will lie down with him and be naked—not en route to the usual somethings and, for the sake of practicality, undressed—no, you will be irrevocably naked, stripped—you will be all skin and jolts and talking and—for fucksake—**honesty** will break out and that's when you will come unhinged, because you aren't going to leave him while he sleeps, sneak off and never come back, and you won't act as if you expect him to smother you in the night, or that you'll wake up in a quarry later with a head injury and no shoes. And you're not going to keep it brutal and light in the morning, say **you'll call**. You're going to rest unconscious in the almost unbearable mercy of his arms and want the trust of that and like it—you're going to stretch and turn into the day for more of the same and for enquiries and delicate smiles and whispers in case he's not awake, except he **is** awake—why else would you be talking to him?—he's awake and listening and whispering as well and you both keep on whispering so you can still dream each other and be not yet in the world.*

And then you'll have breakfast when it's time for lunch.

*And suddenly, unforeseeably, how much you will have to do: memorising mutual preferences, habits, frustrations, ticks—and you'll discuss—you will **have** to discuss—God knows—futures and kittens, or dogs, or stealing a baby from outside a shop—you probably won't have the time to make one of your own—and, if not that, then certainly there will be carpets and curtains to consider and accommodation, gardens, flats, renting, mortgages, life insurance, drawing up your wills—and what if he dies before you?—then you'll be upset—and planning how many you'll have at the wedding breakfast—although you might want* *something quick, a quiet affair with the cabby who drove you in as a handy witness—I mean, why not?—it could happen—it genuinely, horrifyingly might—when, Jesus Christ, you don't want to get married, not **you— marriage**, that's an institution—since when did you want to spend life in an institution?—this whole thing is unpicking you, reworking you into someone else— which means he will, in actuality, be marrying someone else and how could you possibly cope with that?—the jealousy alone would kill you—and the invading burdens, responsibilities, the claustrophobia, the shock, they are in the room with you like sump oil, they are rising to your chest—and this isn't how it should be, how you should be, because you love him, he is the closest you will get, the dearest, and surely this should not have to guarantee that being with him terrifies you more than dying—more than if you might die before him and end up making him upset.*

He mustn't be the man you'll never have, purely because he seems to be so meant, has perfections, ends your waiting, because he opens you up to your spine and doesn't hurt.

So, although you might beg to, you don't run.

You stay and can stand with the back of your hand near enough to the back of his for you to feel him, read him, the magnificent argument of his blood, and you tremble and do nothing and this is fine.

Except.

Then your lungs fill with having to dress so you'll please someone else and vice versa—and this doesn't choke you, but is unfamiliar, is odd—and then there's going to the pictures together, which you're bound to try eventually, it is something you see all the time and completely normal, yet somehow a threat—and there's wanting to buy a sofa, because that's what lovers

44

*do—and you are lovers—you **do**, there is no saving you from it, **love**—and undoubtedly you'll end up going with him to buy the sofa and looking in lots of places and not being able to see the perfect one—when only perfection can represent your love—or, indeed, be the decor and furnishings of your love—and eventually it's not improbable that you'll get tired—you don't want to imagine this, wouldn't wish it to be the case—but if you are both exhausted and perhaps your blood sugar is low then it's almost inevitable that you'll fight— perhaps not badly but then maybe worse, and this free-floating resentment and discontent will follow after—and maybe in the final furniture shop there's also a table lamp that you don't like—you despise it and you can't help your opinions, they are yours and your personal expression is protected under international law—but your lover **does** like the lamp, that is **his** opinion of it—he adores it, insists that it's superb, and this reignites your disagreement, kicks it into bitterness and rage and additionally looses the welling of commitment and undertakings and regulations and sameness and exposure, hideous risk, and the awful heap of this is insurmountable and sweeps hard down at you and before you can scream or prevent this, you've picked up the lamp—the tragic, frustrating, adorable, loathsome lamp—and you've hit him, you've knocked him right on his wonderful head and he's bleeding—he's crying and you're hitting him again— you're causing him pain and making him afraid and it's a nightmare, you would rather shoot yourself— although, of course, you don't have a gun, you're dangerous enough without one—and, Christ knows, you haven't a clue how this came about, but you are still hitting him, your darling, because this way you won't have the new wait for the failure of everything*

45

sweet in your life, its most beautiful thing, you have instead brought it neatly to a close.

You have killed him.

Because he was far too extraordinary.

You have murdered the one man you've ever tried to love.

And it takes a long breath to picture this, to see it, mourn it, understand.

And for this and many other reasons, you should save him from yourself.

*You shouldn't take his hand and shouldn't kiss him. Your mouths shouldn't make and echo and make the shape of **love**.*

But you do take his hand and you do kiss him.

Of course.

'Oh, you can't do that, though . . .'

Elizabeth opens her eyes and discovers that she is lying on her back.

All nonsense.

I'm full of nonsense.

The ceiling is neatly above her, inoffensive cream and calm.

And where would I be without nonsense.

Here.

She is frowning, puzzled by this feeling of having run in from somewhere without warning, of losing her breath. 'I can't . . . ?'

'You can't go to sleep. Not yet.' Derek sits on the bed beside her. The mattress only dips a little—it is made of stern and seafaring stuff. 'We have to stroll about and see the premises. Then we should have dinner. If you want.' He lifts her hand, kisses her knuckles. This is nice, but also gives her the slow and far impression of punching him in the mouth. 'I'm quite hungry. You hungry? We've missed our

46

sitting for the wassername—for the captain's table dining palaver—but there's a buffet somewhere. I'd prefer the buffet . . .'

'Ahm . . . I'll be hungry once we've strolled.' She looks at her watch. 'Christ, it's half past nine. Did I sleep? I didn't think I'd slept, but I must have. Anyway . . . Yes. Let me have a shower and then we'll go and check what's what.'

Before she can sit up, he nuzzles his face to her neck. 'This'll be good, won't it?'

He's a lovely man, can be very sweet-natured and he wants to enjoy an enjoyable thing, a watery jaunt in good company. That's not unreasonable of him.

'Yes. It'll be good.'

On what Beth thinks of as the Mingling Level she finds herself walking through trails of aftershaves and perfumes she hasn't encountered in years.

And why not? Choose one you like and stick with it. Eau Sauvage. My dad wore that. I'll bet you someone's wearing Hai Karate, too. And there'll be Old Spice and Brut and 4711 and Charlie and Aqua Manda and Tramp and straight Lavender and Lily of the Valley, because you know exactly where you are with them. Yes, you do.

I do not know exactly where I am.

Perhaps I should start wearing lavender.

No, where I am is on a boat.

That's exact.

In an ocean, a wilderness, a chaos—but I am also undoubtedly here and on this boat.

Somebody who, for want of a better term, may be

47

called The Ship's Photographer—not a position Beth would have considered essential—has commandeered a less-frequented corner near the lifts and has unfurled a quite extensive backdrop, reproducing the setting sun at sea. Couples are having their photographs taken in front of it—the actual setting sun having disappeared much earlier in more al fresco and unpredictable surroundings.

The photographer gently poses his subjects in a small range of sentimental configurations: the gentleman rests his arm round the lady's shoulders, the lady leans in and lays her hand on the gentleman's chest, the gentleman enfolds the lady from behind, while both peer off beyond themselves into what observers might believe to be a stirring but vaguely melancholy space.

Derek doesn't understand her interest in the proceedings. 'We shouldn't stay.' He's getting bored. Loathes hanging about, our Derek.

'They don't mind. They want to be looked at, in fact.'

'But not by us—by their relatives, or whoever—later.'

'Why don't you nip off, get hold of a list for what's on in the cinema. I'll stand here and stare at them till you come back and then we'll eat.'

He shakes his head and she can tell that he is wondering briefly if their journey will be marred by her strange preoccupations. For a moment he hovers, as if his disapproval, correctly applied, will be able to change her mind. She rubs his arm and gives him a smile until he returns it.

'I just . . . they're endearing, you know? It's endearing.'

'You don't want *us* to do that?'

'*Christ* no. Are you insane?' She rubs his arm again. 'Go and check out the films. I'll be here.'

It isn't true—she doesn't believe the photography's endearing—so many couples unable to touch without also apparently clinging in desperation, the hands slipped over husbands' hearts as if to make sure they're still beating, the oddly unconfident flaunting of savagely younger wives. The singles—grimacing, over-brave, over-dressed. It seems possible to hear them inwardly reciting—*This could be me on the night when I meet my husband / an incredible girl / an utterly boring bastard who renovates properties in Kent . . .*

There's only one pair among them who don't depress Elizabeth, to whom she has warmed: older guy, mildly elegant, and a wife who matches and he stands half in his partner's shadow, presents her, because she's still lovely and ought to be first, and he holds her, light as light, to show admiration while letting her be—her being, plainly, very much what he likes—and she rests easy against him and is happy and her face full of the sense that in a moment she will turn and look at him and they'll grin, share the secret of who they are, one with the other.

'So how are you this evening?'

Fuck.

It's the man from the queue—stepping in from her left and halting as sharply as if a wall had sprung up to fox him.

No wall, though—nothing in his way.

Elizabeth knew she would see him again.

He's the sort to be unshakeable.

She wonders how he managed to approach without her noticing.

Although his feet are apparently fixed, he twitches,

shifts, inclines his body, positions himself to obscure the photographer, the backdrop and the subjects: their nervousness, their excuses, their attempts to dilute reality's disappointments.

So he'd rather I looked at him, then—is posing himself instead. As what? Lonely and stealthy. Not a combination I'd recommend.

And we're on this fucking boat for seven days . . .

'Are you well?' He's changed into jeans and a shirt, but his shoes are still formal—shiny black oxfords—and he seems, if anything, less relaxed—there are flickers and starts of tension in his arms and the rise of his chest.

Looks like an off-duty policeman. Or a soldier—an officer trying to be in mufti—the scruffy isn't scruffy, it's still a discipline, a plan.

He glances at his feet, his shins, then shakes his head. 'I'm Arthur Lockwood, call me Arthur, and *yes*, I don't dress down well—I'm much better with up, but *still*, at least I don't have . . .' He slows his sentence to the pause where she might help him finish . . .

And Elizabeth would rather *not* help, but it turns out that she does in any case: . . . 'creases ironed into your jeans.' Her intentions were too fixed on not cooperating.

Thinking summons doing, brings it on—you know that—and what you most forbid yourself is bound to linger, is bound tight. It'll hang about like a bleak and uncomfortable man.

'Yes, I'd be the type, wouldn't I? The way your husband would be the type to wriggle and pull himself into his jerseys as if he's five and needs his mum to get him through it. *Endearing*, one would imagine.' Arthur Lockwood, call him Arthur, smiles at her with unalloyed sincerity and it is difficult to feel insulted or disturbed by someone who does this effectively and warmly and with care.

'He's not my husband.'

'Really? I'd have thought he was. Did you personally know, by the way, that three hundred and sixty-one people have been photographed so far. Not your husband?'

'No. Three hundred and sixty-one. I'd have thought that was too much, too many. He's not.'

'I could be wrong. Often am. Well, not often.' He shrugs, shivers like a man with a pain in his neck and flutters his attention beyond her, possibly into a stirring and melancholy space. 'But when I *am* wrong . . . I do then go *fantastically astray*. If he's not currently your husband then he has, *of course*, lured you off to sea and into all of *this* with the intention of proposing. What I would do. If I were him. Which I am not.'

Elizabeth knew this, knows this:—that Lockwood is not Derek and that Derek has been building towards something—tetchier than usual, more needy and delicate—she hadn't wanted to notice it, name it—*marriage*—but that is almost certainly the destination her partner has hauled on board with them. There is going to be a time when he will ask and she will have to answer. No doubt champagne is stored somewhere for just such occasions. 'I don't think that's true.'

'He didn't lure you?' Lockwood snaps a wide, clear glance right in at her. He winks. 'Ah well then . . . *you* lured *him*.' And he bowls his interest away against the wall over her shoulder. 'How extremely—I'm not quite sure of the word . . . *informative*. Oh, and yes . . .' Lockwood swivels on his heel and Elizabeth follows him round until she catches sight of Derek, who's approaching with a slip of paper in his hand. He holds it aloft—this causing Lockwood to dip forward and near and murmur to her, 'Like Chamberlain after Berlin . . .' before he strides a pace away and hard into a handshake with Derek which slightly crushes— although it does not render useless—what turns out to be a handwritten list of tonight's film screenings.

'Hello. Arthur Lockwood, call me Arthur—were you going up to the buffet, because I don't mean this to sound in any way uncomplimentary, but you do both seem to be avoiding the evening's dress code for dining and me, too, of course, to the best of my ability, and so we might go along together, if you didn't *mind*.' He contemplates both of them and Elizabeth briefly believes that if she interrupts him, if she can shut him up, then her fists will unclench and whatever wrong thing is on the way will turn aside and seek out other people, but she hasn't any sense left in her mouth, nothing to tell him, to bundle up against him, and so he digs out at her again, at Derek—these small, harsh movements of his skull, his forearms, each keeping time with the drive of his words, 'I travel a great deal by boat—freighters, liners—hate to fly—late-onset phobia—very common in middle life—and I can recommend the buffet *experience*—it's *the one consistent, one reliable element*—they're good with *meat*—have a lot of *meat*-eaters on board and they cater for them— excellent *meat*—do you like *meat*? Profess vegetarianism and you'll be the lowest of the low, they will be *stern* and brusque and give you boiled potatoes only and a talking-to . . .'

Elizabeth hears Derek admit that, yes, he isn't

averse to meat, and this establishes enough of a connection to mean it's too late for them now.

Far too late.

Beyond saving.

We'll have to go with him.

And they proceed, the three of them together, as if they are friends.They work their way over the softly untrustworthy floor and then up the softly untrustworthy stairs, while Elizabeth tells herself—*far too, far too, far too late and we should do anything but this*—and notices she pats at Lockwood's elbow, perhaps because she hopes to make him safer.

Mild shirt and beneath the cloth is bone—the unprotected hardness of bone—he is down to his bone—little bone, big bone, little—bared and taut and listening—there it is, listening—requiring.

And a jolt in the muscle.

Another.

It's waking up.

She raises her hand from him. Folds her arms across her waist as they continue to climb.

It's waking up—it said so.

I noticed it and it knows.

*   *   *

'The one thing I do love—meat.' Lockwood unloads his tray on to their table and has, indeed, collected a disturbing weight of meat—correctly pink and tender beef—which obscures a more restrained selection of vegetables.

Outside the restaurant's windows are blank water and blank air, this vast cave of night determined to confront them with their own reflections. Elizabeth watches a yellowed version of her body trying to eat lasagne, faltering cutlery, childish mouthfuls. The yellowed Lockwood shovels beef into himself intently, nods and encourages Derek into elaborate descriptions of his business, of how he first met Elizabeth, of other journeys they have undertaken, of his parents and schooling, hobbies. Derek nudges at his food, but barely alarms it. Lockwood consumes. Lockwood swallows in a way that seems near to pain, to choking.

In the end, Derek stops talking, exhausted. He blinks. He is pale, quickly paler than when he sat down, than the minute before this one. 'Excuse me.' He runs his fingers along the back of Elizabeth's wrist, gets up and walks away—tight steps, the ship adding a minor stagger on uneven beats. The sea is making itself felt.

Lockwood watches Derek go, then lowers his knife and fork, crosses them on his plate.

Elizabeth angles herself to face the window—she can feel him, though—Lockwood—his living and sitting and watching and thinking all prickle on her skin.

There are small rattles of crockery that nag. The ship is beginning to flex, play.

Oh, God.

Whatever that means.

Whatever does God mean?

Elizabeth is dropping fast into a headache and also tired, tired, tired and so hollowed, so indefensible, undefended, when she needs to be something else. When she needs to be she isn't sure of what.

'Merciless.' Lockwood waits until she turns to him and then repeats, '*Merciless.*' He is studying the window and may be commenting on the ocean, which is certainly swelling visibly, tangibly.

54

'I'm sorry?'

'No. No, you're not.' He pushes away his plate and takes a sip from his water glass, rubs his face with his free hand, 'Will you, Elizabeth . . . Elizabeth, will you fuck him tonight. Will you fuck him and will you say *yes*—will he hear your voice saying *yes*—and will he be inside you, hearing your voice—*yes*—and imagining—*yes*—that perhaps, that perhaps you'll agree to be his wife—*yes*—and his prick in you, moving in you—*yes*—when you tell him will that make him come . . .' He turns his palms down and then up and then down and studies them and seems bemused by his extremely clean, well-tended fingers, his buffed nails.

Elizabeth half stands to get away, but he simply wags his head—quietly, deeply furious—a rage so confined and so injured that it scares her: these quick shadows and signs that it makes in his eyes, the tensions in his face—and she cannot help but sit again. It is clear that even he doesn't quite know what he'll do—that the further she goes from him, the louder he's likely to ask, 'Do you use protection, or does he come right into you, can you feel it push and run uninterrupted—his semen, seminal fluid, cum, spunk—and his little—what would they be: grunts, pants, hisses? Damp words? Is that how it is with him? Pushing and damp?' As it is, with Elizabeth so near him, he grinds out his sentences, flat and soft, to somewhere beside her, some shape in the air that he can bear to look at, fix. He's unable to bear her.

Unable, perhaps, to bear anything.

He coughs, clears his throat, coughs again. And this time it's Elizabeth who wags her head and she isn't sure of why.

Wrong move—like trying to make fun of him—trying to mirror him.

Mirror and you show him you'll follow his lead, give him sympathy and dominance, you prove you're alike. People like people they're like. People remember their fathers, mothers, the peering down of family faces, smile answering smile, leading smile—seeing their own muscles apparently move someone else, a proof of mind-in-mind, of love.

Which is completely fucking obvious and he's not stupid.

Fit his shape and you might understand him, though . . .

Lockwood notices her efforts and only smiles—this young, gentle look which meets her and isn't answered, which pierces and leaves. After this he seems to relent, there's a sort of sinking in his spine, a withdrawal of engagement. His head falls and he murmurs to the tabletop, 'No, don't answer. Don't. Personal question. All personal questions and inappropriate from a stranger. My comments have been an unsuitable intrusion and I should apologise but will, of course, not.'

He pauses and the floor bucks, shivers, rests.

Then Lockwood fades himself close to whispering, each word sounding on the same low note before breaking into breath, raw breath. 'You touched my arm.'

Elizabeth can't swallow. Inside she is filling with silence. It tastes like milk—yes, it's milky and thick in her mouth.

So concentrate on that.

'You touched my arm.'

Milk and stillness.

Not that it isn't hard to hold.

Stillness.

It's the worst thing to keep, but I do want it—a rest from the gabbling, the nonsense, keeping up the pace and always being tired from not sleeping because of the noise—my noise—because of the rubbish just spooling away in here beneath the hair, the skin, the bones, just mazing around and around in the brain.

Distraction.

A distraction that doesn't distract me enough—an inadequate misdirection from the forthcoming panic, which might as well panic me now because I know it's on the way.

Then again, I no longer need the gabble. No more diversions required, because right here is the perfect fear for me and I can step out of hiding.

Should be a relief.

'You touched my arm.'

No more guesses, worries: the real thing.

And at that same moment, both of them—Elizabeth and Lockwood—become aware of Derek. He's weaving back from the toilets, greyish and heavy-limbed, skin shining with water or sweat. He is obviously ill. Both of them—Elizabeth and Lockwood—follow his progress and, if he were inclined to give them his attention, he might perhaps be puzzled by their very similar expressions of true concern.

Another and a better worry: altruistic, practical. He's poorly, seasick. He's plainly a priority.

And a reason to leave.

Thank fuck.

Elizabeth gets up from the table, 'I'll have to . . . He needs . . .' and she motions to Derek that they will go—head for the cabin and peace, take care of his ills.

Give him the tablets to settle him—he should have taken them before—and then he can lie down.
See how things are in the morning.
Not a fucking clue about the morning.

Lockwood snaps into the actions and the tones of a man who is saying goodbye to an acquaintance. He meets her eye and then quickly states, 'You touched my arm.' Before Derek is near enough to hear. Then Lockwood shakes her hand, releases, nods to Derek, nods to her.

As she goes, Elizabeth does not nod and does not tell anyone—*Yes. Yes, I did touch your arm. For 361 reasons, I touched you.*

Derek wants to lie. Nothing but that. He says so.
Like a kid.

He is curled in their bed, arms folded around his own shoulders although—if he wanted—Elizabeth would hold him. Derek doesn't want. He is miserable. They didn't make it to the cabin without him throwing up again. And he has thrown up since. Horizontal, he isn't sick, but says that he feels as if someone is squeezing his skull. Because he can't tolerate seeing, she has darkened the room and so she sits in a generalised gloom on the miniature sofa beside their broadish and expensive window, through which is clearly visible a pattern of stars and cloud, rain spatters, the idea of a moon, hints of its greater light. And the shipglow—there's always that—if she went outside she could see how they burn as they go. But she has to stay in with Derek. She draws the curtains.

Derek breathes as if doing so annoys him.

The room is too hot, smells sweaty and sour—oddly like the back of a late-night taxi—and the floor is pressing up beneath them and then flinching away. They have entered a storm, or perhaps simply the ocean's accustomed state: no more pretending, a week of this.

Derek is a dim curve, there's a deeper shade of shadow where he is slanted across the bed—on his side, knees tucked—the shape is vague, more a suggestion, but he's familiar all the same.

I should think so, by now—we've been together for nearly a year.

More like thirteen months. And they didn't move in with each other until quite late. She went to him.

Slightly surprising.

His place was nicer than mine—bigger.

Surprising nonetheless.

Beth still has some furniture in storage, odds and ends—that's mostly to do with lack of space, not to provide her with resources should she ever wish to bolt. Derek lives in a thirties bungalow with strangely extensive gardens, even a stream transecting it and adorned with a Japanese-flavoured bridge. The interior is markedly less generous, because of the clutter. Derek inherited a plethora of ugly pieces from his mum and dad—vast sideboards, grandfather clock like a coffin—and he hasn't been able to throw them away so far—sentimental.

Sentimental man. Soft areas. He's still cautious in case I damage one.

And I'm not absolutely unguarded myself.

And this is not a disadvantage—it means I can be clear-headed and take care of everyone. It means that I know Derek shouldn't see Lockwood again—we'll dodge him. He's the sneaking type, but we'll manage so there'll be no more enquiries—nothing about what Derek and I may or may not do, or how.

It's nobody's business who I fuck.

Or that I do fuck.

And I do fuck—we do—we do fuck.

Lockwood's voice still there in the verb, his taste—so she uses it to spite him, tries to.

Derek's like a kid when we fuck—when we do fuck— and once he's over, once we're there, he's all pleased, like a boy—happy the way he would be if he'd learned a trick and showed it and you'd been honestly amazed.

Cute.

Not that he knows any tricks.

But still cute.

Sort of.

Cute could describe it.

In the distances of the ship, components she cannot name are chafing and whining. There is, intermittently, the reverberating slam of big water against the bows and—although she can't currently say so—this sense of struggle is enjoyable and what she'd hoped for. She wanted the din and fight of a genuine journey, of something large being achieved.

Derek, in contrast, is much quieter than he has been and she guesses he's fallen asleep.

Good. So I can stop failing to comfort him.

Her efforts have been mainly useless and uninspired. She has cleaned up the bathroom, set a cool cloth on his forehead—which he liked—refilled his water glass.

Which he did not like—the water bounced back up and out of him as soon as he drank it.

Horrible how sad he's got about this—a bit of his holiday spoiled by a misfortune and him not feeling

60

*the way that he'd want. He's disappointed—as if he's
five and needs his mum to get him through it.*

Horrible and—again—cute.

*So he's abject and I find it appealing. Does that
mean I'm peculiar?*

*I don't think so. We tend to those we love and more
so when they're troubled.*

Not that I'm being his mother. Not that.

*Too many wardrobes and antimacassars and
ottomans involved with that.*

Ottomans or ottomen?

Undoubtedly there are stewards and sundry other
members of staff who are practised in the ways of
mal de mer and its relief and she should probably
call them—but Derek really wouldn't want strangers
pestering in at him.

*Tomorrow morning—we'll check on his progress
then and decide the best course.*

And meanwhile—because he's well out of it—she
won't have to keep on throwing him perky sentences
of invalid-encouraging stuff.

It doesn't matter.

It's all right.

There's no need to worry.

You'll be fine. It'll all be fine. You'll be all right.

She didn't necessarily believe these things were
true, but they seemed constructive, padded out
uneasy pauses and have been—naturally—a
distraction.

*Can't beat me for that. Past master. Past mistress, I
suppose, except that sounds louche.*

And distracting Derek has prevented her from
being forced to hear what she's saying and saying
inside—the slither and pelt of that.

Noise is all I'm full of and no one should have to

61

tolerate noise. It's harmful to health and safety.

She folds her arms, adjusts, clutches her shoulders. There's a shiver in her breath and she can't stop it, has no way to halt the fretting as her time sheers by.

Let me yammer away for long enough and I'll maybe just drown myself out.

Which doesn't make any kind of sense—my only emergency plan and it makes no sense.

She's been talking crap again, inside and out—but it doesn't matter. It's all right. There's no need to worry. She'll be fine. It'll all be fine. She'll be all right.

Some people whistle, or doodle—Beth chatters. It doesn't mean that she's silly, or callous, or weak.

You understand about this. You're an understanding person.

And, like Elizabeth, you've attempted to lighten a mood when no positive information was to hand—so you've made something up, built it out of optimism and eagerness to please and if you thought of it as mainly music rather than meaning, you've been able to absolve yourself for passing on information that's actually false. And if the information is good—has good intentions—then it might even end up making itself true. Any word can work a spell if you know how to use it.

Plus, honesty does have its savage side—you're well aware, quite frankly, that it wouldn't always be your first or even last option. The fabrications of kindness, of courtesy, of optimism: they're very necessary—and, by accident, or in a pressured circumstance, there may have been occasions when you haven't been utterly accurate in what you've said.

This can feel ugly and uncomfortable to you, alien—because you have integrity, and dishonesty doesn't suit you, how could it? But nobody is fastidious all the time, unremittingly brave: you can be scared off to this or that edge of the truth—like anyone. And if, for example, you did in actuality do some unfortunate thing and it was completely unlike you—the word, the thought, the act, the total mistake—if it was so far from who you are that describing it, admitting it, would be misleading— then a deception might be called for, a silence might be justified.

And what if you're simply finding a way of practising your dreams, letting them play, sharing? What if you're pronouncing incantations, inventing happy prophecies? That surely must be pure and harmless. The friends, the relatives, the loves, the ones who know you: they can see through to your heart no matter what you tell them, so your fantasies can be something they'll enjoy—secrets that join you closer to them, enlarge their definitions of who you are—a person's choice of lies being dependably diagnostic.

Not lies, though—that's too harsh a term. When you thoroughly study yourself, you know that you're better than that, than a liar. You've only avoided being truthful, pedantic, when it would hurt somebody—somebody including yourself—and self-defence is nothing shaming.

It's an indication of your moral sensitivity that you do sometimes feel ashamed.

You have in the course of your entire life occasionally erred, drifted, been too instinctive. You admit that.

And not everyone would admit that.

Also, there were days when you said the true thing even though it would hurt. You withstood the injury. You could make yourself admired for that, but instead you don't talk about it. There are several things—when you reflect—that you don't talk about and it's significant that the very good aren't mentioned any more than the very bad. They can both unnerve you.

You tend to give others your middle ground. Which is prudent. Human beings are not intended to be comprehensive in their expression of themselves. If they were, they would be terrifying. They would always mean too much.

There would be layers revealing layers and meanings that double and on and on and where would it end?

It would end in a room.

It would end with a man standing in a doorway and walking back into a room.

It would end with this room.

He's in this room.

The man is in this room.

In another hired-for-the-evening stuffy little room—stage at the far wall, away from the door, and the rows of stackable seating set out neatly with an aisle—a shuttered hatch to one side that will roll up and open through to the tiny kitchen where someone will make the tea and coffee, serve up biscuits in the interval.

And every room will never be anything but stuffy— what the man does perhaps affecting the atmosphere's density, he can't be sure—and the biscuits will never be anything but stale—snack density *not* down to him: it's because they buy cheap biscuits—no matter who or where they are, they go in for own-brand,

64

nasty biscuits and ignore the sell-by dates, don't bother to store them in a tin, which shows a breathtaking lack of foresight. Tight-fisted town after town and in every venue the fund-raising raffle to open the evening and the prizes of unconvincing electrical goods, or personal readings at later dates, free healings, the sending of amplified prayers on the winner's behalf.

And the man is there with her—with the woman, with his love—and they are there together and smiling where no one can see it, giggling just beneath the skin. They are being the secret of who they are, one with the other, and everything of them that's important is tucked out of sight. The man and the woman are hidden in amongst these strangers and having their fun, a tight fit so that they're cosy, no matter what. They could do this forever, the pair of them—if forever could be reached—swapping and making the codes: the counting, the signals and counter-signals—like kiss against kiss.

They'll give the full show tonight, a good one—no one will ever understand how good. A night to remember all ready and dancing in them, wanting to start now, to play: they can feel it like breath on their necks.

A night made of what they have on file from last time and what the man's found out since he arrived—this in the days before Facebook, Twitter, before lives were bent over for better inspection everyfuckingwhere. The man has to work for what he knows, gather overhearings and gossip and newspaper cuttings and In Memoriams and graveyard tours and averages, statistics and guesses that are always educated—unless he and his love just busk it, improvise—unless they're riding the room and it's racing them somewhere and they let it. And they like the riding and racing—it's what they perfectly do and—for this evening—they'll be doing it in the Church of Eternal Love, Light and Hope.

Says so on the posters and the song sheets— Eternal Love, Light and Hope upstairs and to your left, second floor of the Municipal Hall.

Have to be upstairs if you're after Eternal Love, Light and Hope, stands to reason.

He takes it they didn't go for the Hope, Eternal Light and Love option—H.E.L.L. not being quite the initials they'd prefer.

Shouldn't knock it, though—either you tour the churches or else it's the pub function suites—clattery stage and a star cloth background if you're lucky— might as well be a stripper, ventriloquist, some shaky-handed magic boy wadding silks into his thumb tip, clanging a dove pan—no dignity there.

Not much here, unless you bring it—which we do.

His crowd's in and he's had a look round—it's the usual selection of regulars, virgins, occasionals, desperates: big women in sparkly tops, short sleeves on hefty arms, purple spangles and silvers and pinks, butterflies, starbursts, little girl images of fun.

No black, you won't see black unless it's on a sceptic: the way they insist on mourning for everyone else: all pain, no consolation and fucking smug.

But no sceptics tonight—tonight is leather jackets, smokers' coughs—lockets and bracelets and necklaces with names on and even more so for the men—they get the heavy gold, thick links, substantial watches, the sovereign rings and Mason's symbols, Pioneer symbols, Union symbols, AA symbols, lettered fingers and swallows inked on the webs of thumbs and solo earrings—whole libraries of themselves set out on offer—and the loud shirts and fastidiously well brushed hair. Mainly women here, though—this a matter for women, a women's mystery—chatting women, raucous women, thoughtful women—little love heart tattoos, or coloured stars—in couples and groups and outings: family resemblances, office parties—borrowed clothes, shared clothes, pinched clothes, eBay clothes—styles of make-up—special friends—and they're giddy, nervy, anticipating—good night out— they'd like to be entertained and have no commitment, not noticeably: they're keeping it light-hearted, they imagine—but odd silences, nevertheless—curiosity, mild interest is what they'd admit to—they'd explain how they're nobody's fools, would love it to happen, a contact, they'd be overjoyed, they'd be put at rest, but nobody's bought and sold them—even the man hasn't bought and sold them—they're going to keep an open mind—this being, although they don't know it, the Great Requirement—just open the mind.

Then we'll open it wider still, until it trembles, until you couldn't stop us if you tried.

And you won't try.

And then we come in.

And we'll work in you until we've split you, fathomed who you are, until your everything is different, absolutely—which is what you want, what everyone always wants—to be naked and opened and seen and touched, but still loved—to be absolutely known and proved absolutely lovable.

Not in spite of ourselves, but because of ourselves, our whole terrible selves—that's how we all want to be loved.

We know it would change us, make us complete.

And in underneath the smiling and excitement, the man is already harmonised with his audience, the enquirers—he understands them and he does love.

And he's taken the time to examine them, to be comprehensive and find it—their truth. Because it is there: the grey in their faces, the void in every dawn, the scream in the eyes, the howl, the moment, the one and forever moment, the instant when they heard, felt, knew that the world had left them, had fallen away—these intolerable losses they carry with them, unspeakable. Anyone could see what he does, if they tried—it isn't hard to notice the humiliation of too great a pain. There's no hiding the indignity of that.

There's no bearing the indignity of that.

Which is why the man and the woman are so needed.

The man and the woman together.

Double act.

He assumed they'd work better if they masqueraded as brother and sister. A kind of a joke, this—he's not remotely like her. She's rounder—or rather, fuller—has a smaller nose—her body, hands, mouth, they are modest, but suggest capacities for pleasure, sensuality. He tends to be attenuated, has a body that might be brittle, that's near to alarming and alarmed. He has dyed his hair until it's dark as hers—if less enthusiastic—but this has left him startling, bleach-skinned, like some kind of warning— an illustration of symptoms arising from an ill-judged life, bad habits, excess.

As a pair, they don't match. But the ways they move, the ways they *are* with each other—that convinces.

They don't go on stage pretending they're husband and wife, or admitting—truthfully admitting—that they are lovers. They try to be more, to offer themselves as two people born for other worlds. They spread rumours of childhood visions, terrified neighbours, baffled parents, hypnotised cats.

This was the man's decision and he's sticking with it. Ever since they became completely partners in their types of crime, he has insisted they put a pretence around the pretence, around the pretence.

It seems a good idea. Because he's young.

Complications taste sophisticated to him—like salt and protein, acquired preferences, treats—and he thinks they're harmless. And he is packed with ideas of invulnerable success and the illusion that being definite in his planning will somehow aid his progress, impress reality. He imagines a clandestine marriage at some point and then a life of enjoyable narrow escapes, of passions that always stay feverish because they are pressured, denied.

And he's still affecting the long hair and a beard— anxious to seem a Victorian, a wannabe Golden Age psychic in an off-the-peg twentieth-century suit. As a gesture it's faintly pathetic, but he does enjoy acknowledging former practitioners, traditions, the faked niceties and restraints of another time—all frock coats and surnames until the lights go down, then seance rooms that filled with busy fingers, licensed reliefs and sticky little trinkets hauled out from places propriety couldn't mention. He feels he is wearing a private joke—one even she doesn't really get. In fact, almost no one appreciates the reference and meanwhile, it has to be said—has been said—he looks like General Custer. Custer, only not blond—not any more.

So he is, in a way, ridiculous.

And aping a man who is famous for losing.

But he loves his persona, embraces its implied fragility.

Because he's young.

And he's assuming—and the woman is agreeing—that people wouldn't trust a married team, any kind of romantic team. So the man and the woman have created their own niceties and faked restraints. They say they are family and wandering together in a happy no man's land, called to serve, to ferry messages across. And this means they do have to be absolutely sexless—not the vaguest hint of anything untoward can be permitted—the consequences of a lapse apocalyptic—excitingly so—rumours of incest would finish them. Even a brotherly squeeze of her shoulder might leak heat, a hand-clasp could show inappropriate thought—they couldn't come back from that. So discipline has to be total, merciless.

And he loves that, too.

Because he's young.

No options for either of them but to seal what they are and need into the brief conclusions of their nights. The strain of this assists them, he thinks—makes their demonstrations, their readings, thrum with opaque and yet unnerving energies. They both savour them, translate them later, race and ride with them in hotels, in B&Bs, in the flat where he sleeps and stays awake with her, because they are lovers: not related, not married, but lovers—lovers who hide to keep strong, to stay effective.

So very often, as the bedroom door closes, while it's still on the swing, they're already tasting each other, releasing. Prohibition has become a necessity,

70

infallible foreplay, the deepest tease.

Because he's young.

He lets the work stroke him, raise him, keep him raw so he can feel.

And he does feel—everyone and everything—he feels like a flayed man, a burning body, like the end of himself so that he'll be right for her and right for them, the enquirers.

For tonight.

And every night.

Tonight.

This night the man and the woman are side by side, tucked in the kitchen with the polystyrene cups and the twitchy strip lights and the curls and peaks of conversations tumbling in from outside.

And they are telling you, if you will listen—and how many people ever listen—how much pace they need, or laughter, if they can concentrate, if they'll be arsey, boisterous, sad.

You shouldn't ever meet an audience, meet anyone, for the first time—not when the second time's better. Prepare and you can be their friend already, close as blood.

And it's time.

They stride outside and into nowhere, into forever, into every fucking thing that should be and never will.

Easy.

He introduces his sister, establishes a peace, respect, ground rules: the dead will be returning—were never gone—but have no fear, they are more known and knowing, more familiar than they were—also, they are eccentric and they wish for reconciliations, they hide small objects about the house, they spend slightly inexplicable hours

71

overseeing driving tests—that's mainly a little laugh for the family in the corner—daughters, mother, aunt—they'll get advice about something: not paying too often for others' meals and drinks—and what about the drinks?—they do have a few too many, every now and then, well don't they?—and relaxing is one thing, but don't let it slide, be cautious. And don't buy unnecessary shoes. And don't buy uncomfortable shoes. Older relatives speak their minds, they're often feisty once they've passed and forthright and they appreciate practical footwear, traditional undergarments, their grandchildren, unexpected pregnancies, rainbows, penetrating and inexplicable sensations of delight—they are, in perpetuity, holding their new offspring and overwhelmed, promising bonds of affection to conquer time.

This is reliable, expected.

And the man has told his lover what he heard while he strolled about beforehand, had a non-smoker's convenient cigarette. So she's ready.

She does the work, mostly. He does the minding, guarding, watching—mostly—the actual readings tire him, leave him feeling too unusual.

He's already reported that second row, centre, girl in the criminal sweater, she's on-the-nose already asked for her grandmother: unfinished business, sore stuff, guilt, it's running off her—and the dyke couple at the back, there's clearly some unhappy person they want: a young and troubled, druggy thing, smells of suicide, dark contemplations, insecurity—tact required and gentleness.

New procedure this time—he's always tinkering with changes, improvements—now if he pats his hands together, that's when she'll start to count the silence, she'll stop and register the number when he touches his ear—he'll potter up and down the aisle for that, keep an eye out for tensions, focuses, half-motions: the special ring, medallion, the small something that matters, that has a memory. If it's named by miraculous processes then he can take a hold of it, pass it up to his love and she'll tell what it transmits.

They'd both fancied a spot of psychometry—object-bothering, he calls it—and it sits well in the current repertoire. Take the object, reveal its owner, histories, emanations, importances. When he hands it back, it's something to keep the enquirer warm and confident, it's the charm to bring them luck.

Some luck—they're either dead or here.

But they'll go home happy. They'll be absolved, accompanied, and loved. They'll be fucking loved.

We'll see to that.

*　　　*　　　*

And it's running well. So far, they've had two grandmothers back from the beyond and an uncle who's like a father and a grandfather who seemed more like a friend—two watches and a bracelet of heated significance.

And then a mother.

And she's a good one and a deep and a genuine hit. The idea of her returning, the possibility of her thinking, being, watching in the room beside her living daughter—this thickens the air around them—and the congregation truly silent, listening into their spines—and this hauls at the daughter where she sits, jerks her.

And then—here it is—it really is—here's the Six

73

Inch Jump—reality springing forward, paying attention differently, more closely, fitting tight at the man's skin.

It's wonderful.

And then the daughter cries. Of course she cries. Everything demands it. There was some terminal misunderstanding, some apparent wrong that's unforgiven and she carries it, has carried it for years. And how easily, beautifully, matters unwind and are how they were meant to be: time and truth annihilated by will, united will—and the daughter is little Irene again—she is little Irene and she has her mum—she is Irene and happy again, because here's her lovely mum: tiny memories in splinters, the photograph that should be framed now, the burned dinner, a fight at Christmas, the incident with the pet—a dog, she was a dog lover—Irene's mum in the kind years, the sweet time—and this is the nonsense and smallness that means the room can understand we will stay human—that both sides of death will be human, the still-dying and the dead, but they declare themselves eternal also. This proves it—this is living beyond doubt.

A miracle; handmade, perfectly fitted. And a Good Mother, which is to say a Bad Mother—and they're the best—something for everyone, for players and spectators.

Very easy to love this—what the man does.

Times like this, he is almost nothing but love.

Because he's young.

And then—last enquirer—five minutes left—and the man is standing in the aisle—tired, tired, tired—and this Vicki woman is up on her feet and talking about a cousin—he's distracted and Vicki's a bit of an anticlimax, she's barely upset—or oddly upset—there's something about her that may be unspoken—and Vicki's leaning infinitesimally forward and to her left and her hand is in her pocket—and her mind is elsewhere, just as the man's mind is slipping away to mouths and breaths and being finally unsecret: not long to go—but then his enquirer is thinking harder, louder, biting in and distracting his distraction—in her head, there's **right hand, right pocket, big shape, heaviness, car keys**—he's close to hearing a tiny noise of metal—the man is being saturated with this **car keys** thing, **car keys** taste, he is at the edge of seeing them they're so sharp and Vicki continues to lean and gives a tiny glance—it's aimed at a guy in front—over there and in front—a guy on his own—unlikely spot for a rendezvous, but that's what it is—undoubtedly—they are waiting for mouths and breaths, too—and Vicki's bloke is listening too much, twitchy, bluffing casual—the pair of them acting solo, but they're lying.

They live where the man lives. They are made out of fucking and hiding and planned surprises.

And the joy of this opens in the man's chest, it sparkles—and the service, the evening's session, is nearly done, Vicki's consultation dribbling to a half-hearted close: it turns out she's called Vicki Konecki, which is just odd enough to be true—and what she actually wants, loves, what shouts in her is **car keys, lying, sex**—and the man needs to touch her, suddenly and urgently needs to confirm how she is, what she's told him without speaking—he wants to know what her kind of interesting feels like—and his palm is held open towards her back—as though he might comfort her if required—and onstage his partner is winding up and Vicki the liar, this conductress of affairs, this tangible excitement, she's starting to sit down, so he chances it—her change of position excuses a small goodbye and he indulges in this little brushing pat and she'll forgive him, does forgive him—she hardly registers him, to be honest and why should she—but the man is roaring with her after one contact—**door, lying, muscle, door**—and like a red thing in his thinking, she's **pushing** and **coiling** to **kick** down the **door** and she is the **door** and **sex** is there, **sex** will be there—**keys**—and she will **follow** and he has her pulse, she has soaked him with her pulse.

Vicki leaves him shaking.

When he remounts the stage, he is still unsteady.

This doesn't prevent him producing the blessings expected and the kind summation.

And after this the sacrament, the demonstration, the evening's entertainment is concluded and he runs.

He makes his apologies—his lover puzzled—hints that he's ill, that he'll head for the guest house and maybe an all-night chemist first and he runs.

He shakes off the stragglers, sleeve tugs, unfulfillable enquiries, scrabbling requests and emerges outside, breathless and **following—car keys, lying, sex**—darkish street, inadequate lamps and there she is—**lying**—there's Vicki—**sex**—the crowds about her dissipating—the audience, the congregation, the gullible going home.

But there's no sign of her bloke.

I could be wrong.

She turns right and right and right again and then a final turn before she's inclining, stalling, last-minute ducking in for the door of a car and unlocking it. She sits inside.

76

Lying.
But she won't drive off, not yet.
She won't.
I'll bet anything that she won't.
The man has to pass on, walk by her and keep going.

He crosses to the opposite pavement, turns left and left and left and left and there's the car, still parked—no engine, no lights, but Vicki is there in the driver's seat.

She's waiting so hard it distorts the street, makes his palms tingle.

He slows up and studies the window of the solitary available shop—it is, thank God, an estate agent's and invites consideration. He brings out a piece of paper and pretends to take notes with a pen which is still in his pocket, because he's good at pretending.

Lying.
Car keys.
Sex.
There's a sound, an impact, a door snugged shut, maybe, maybe, he can't be sure.

Don't look.
He hears an engine start. But, if it's her car, she can't be driving away—and not alone—she can't be, he won't believe it.

I can't be wrong.
I won't be.
Oh, and there they go, they fucking do and I am not fucking wrong.

Her car pulls tenderly past him and he can peek: two inside—Vicki and her bloke—same bloke—he's beside her.

I was right. Exactly right.
Nailed it.

A hit.

The elation—it's on every surface like the shine from a new rain.

I unlocked her—I fucking read her—been pushing towards this so long that it's finally let me, given way and I'm through—I'm free—I'm mid-air and not fucking falling—I am in fucking lovely flight.

The man walks—faster and then faster—hungry for other people and deeply and tenderly struck by every face, each body that moves past him, by the opened catalogues they offer as they pass beneath the street lamps, as they modify and amplify their states, confess their natures: drunk, drunkhorny, oddanddepressedwildpain, absent, drunkscared, recklesshorny.

He understands.

He knows them.

And he knows he's a phenomenon.

Sad to think that he's almost unique, because everyone ought to be willing to let themselves see, find one another.

But everyone can't, won't, can't and I can.

And he adores it.

Jog-trotting across the late pavements: here he is and here is his species anatomised, luminous with information, secrets, wishes, fears—enough to enchant him, turn him giddy.

He can read anyone.

He is a burning man and reads by his own light.

* * *

Somehow it's after midnight when the man sneaks up and into his shoddy B&B—optional shower room across the landing, no TV—and wakes his love. If

78

anyone can join him in this—and somebody must, to be alone would rob out his delight—then it will be her.

It will be her.

Shaking her shoulder and gabbling while she doesn't quite listen, is not overjoyed. No codes, no cheats, no significant numbers, just ordinary talk— the straight experience—but she won't have it, is barely interested. His lover doesn't want to hear him, is out of step.

A cool weight settles against his ribs and doesn't shift.

Eventually, they have a fight and no amends after.

Not what he expected.

Can't read everybody, then.

The lack of connection tightens his skin, pains it.

For a moment he's scared she is too far away, irretrievable.

And more scared that he's lost his new talent, that it wasn't permanently his and tonight was simply an accident, or a mirage he'll never regain or even be able to describe.

The man and his lover lie on their backs, separate and unsleeping in narrow twin beds. At last they stumble up into the morning when it arrives—no tolerance for food, no chatting—more silence on a bleak drive to their flat.

But the man believes that his lover continues to have him and hold him, whether or not they seem close—he is bound through and through her and she through him—no undoing that.

He will solve this—their first real difference of opinions—and they'll carry on—the man and the woman together, side by side.

That's what he expects.

79

Because he's young.

After a while, the cabin is so oppressive—and so tedious, because Derek is so unconscious—not his fault—and Beth is so tired of sitting and staring, or creeping about, or easing out on to the balcony for a dose of salt and oceanic rage—that she decides she has to slip away. Her going won't disturb him and will therefore do no harm.

Elizabeth eases out into the passageway, delicately pulls the door to and lets it lock. She's bundled her coat out with her like a foldable shame and puts it on in the corridor where it won't disturb.

I need a walk. That's a perfectly normal impulse. I've been pent up all day, one way and another—and I have this energy, spare energy, rattling energy and it ought to be burned or it'll turn septic, run to fat, some terrible something will happen.

And air—Christ I could do with some of that.

Elizabeth has the idea that a whole storm of air might do her good. She isn't exactly rushing but—side to side and occasional stammers—she is progressing rapidly. She is moving like a woman with a goal.

Which, fuck it, I am.

Fuck, fuck and fuck it.

Just let's be practical about this and head outside.

Fuck.

Elizabeth is full of shouting, but she ignores it, takes the stairs, moves on.

It isn't so late that the communal areas are deserted, but there is a sense that somewhere a party has finished and the guests are wavering home. Little cliques are ambling and in spite of the rolls and plunges underneath them, they keep hold of loose formations as they chat, conspicuously elated they've already found themselves usable friends for their trip. They can relax, go to bed with tentative schedules for bridge, or poker, the sewing circles, gossip, a stamp collectors' get-together, the before-dinner drinks.

The opportunities for Entertainment and Experience Enrichment are severely curtailed at this hour and the closed bars and emptied seating, while not forbidding, have certainly ceased to invite. Elizabeth is relieved when she reaches an exit that leads to an external door. A warning sign states that she shouldn't be out here, that prevailing conditions may prove unsafe, then she's pushing the door and it's giving, it allows her through and on to the narrow and relatively sheltered path that circumnavigates the ship.

The Promenade Deck—that sounds likely. Maybe.

I should learn nautical terms, preoccupy myself with that.

She battles into the open and is caught by a sidelong blast that stops her and chastises.

Definitely refreshing.

A turn around the deck. That's supposed to be the bracing cure-all, isn't it . . .

Fuck.

So she heads off into the ransacking slam of it, mackintosh clattering round her legs, but no rain—just the taste of wilderness.

Fuck.

Fuck.

I'm here, though.

81

So this must be where I intend I should be.
Fuck.
Unless I'm just some kind of accident. Waiting to happen.

When she reaches the stern, the wind is muffled. And here it's impossible not to feel—only gently, gently—that every option but the last has been exhausted, that she's run out of ship, and meanwhile, the wide, pale tug of their wake both soothes and invites. A little camera has been positioned to observe, in case anybody succumbs to the attraction, plummets in to join the creamy, long perspective.

And here he is.
Waiting to happen.
Fuck.
Last option.
Fuck and fuck you and fuck you very much.
Here's Lockwood.

Call him Arthur.

He's leaning on the rail, arms braced wide and facing out, staring. He gives the impression the weather may be a product of his will.

Of course. That's how he'd want her to find him—looking authoritative.

Fuck.

An additional pitch in her stomach, because whatever does happen will be undiluted, no interruptions, no distractions, they will *meet*.

And how long before he makes a point of giving his authority away . . . ? Smart manoeuvre, that, to snag you in.

'You're late.' He's quiet, intending that she strain slightly to hear him. He shuts his eyes, lets the breeze press at his face, fair hair lifting, hands deep in the pockets of his long, brown overcoat. It flaps

82

expensively. Now that everything else is moving, he can be still.

And Arthur is always beautiful when he stops to let you see.

Which is appalling, so it's important for Elizabeth to be angry. 'I'm not late. You cued me in and then repeated it four times—and this is four hours after I left you.'

He smiles at this—*after I left you*—as if he has more delicate emotions than she does, as if every doubled meaning cuts . . .

'And could you have said the word *meat* any more loudly? I'm neither deaf nor imbecilic. Neither is Derek.' She offers him a pause within which he does nothing to help, so she has to begin again. 'Well, we're *meeting,* aren't we? This is what you asked for.'

He turns and catches her with a hot look. He's good at that kind of thing. 'I'm so sorry. I was thinking four hours after we *met*. And sorry for the dreadfully unsubtle repetition. I'm out of practice.'

So he's going to be the calm, calm gentleman. Which means I have to be the unreasonable bitch.

'You're not out of practice, Art. You're never out of practice.'

'Try not to make that sound quite so accusatory. I'm out of practice with *you.*'

'And could you make *that* sound less accusatory . . . ?'

'No, I don't think I could, actually.' But, somewhere, he *is* calm. Somewhere he is just glad to be looking at her and he's letting it show, leaking signs and tells like an innocent, like a civilian. 'It's not as if I *meet* you often and it's not as if I'm *meeting* anyone else, or have been for a while—ever really do—and it wouldn't be like this if I was, so it wouldn't be practice, Beth . . .' Of course, he isn't an innocent—when he gives out tells, he means to.

'But you can *meet* someone else if you want, Art. We're allowed other people.' Which is not the direction she should take. Their terms and conditions have never been clear-cut and shouldn't be discussed for fear of savagery and damages.

But Arthur doesn't argue, is only firm with a dash of sad. 'Yes, I know that. I can *meet* people and you can do that, too. I know that.' He wants her to face him and sympathise, to let him in, but she angles her head to the side, says nothing and deflects him, so he continues, 'You're *meeting* Derek. I've been watching that all day.'

'Not *all* day.'

'Strangely, it feels like all day.' He winces. 'I do apologise again. I'm not allowed to say that sort of thing. I withdraw it. Consider it unsaid. Blame it on the unaccustomed protein—heavy meal, rush of blood to the head.'

Elizabeth won't feel guilty—has no plans to be anything like guilty. Nothing here is her fault.

It isn't my fault this is insane, that when we meet it's always going to be insane.

And this was his idea.

Therefore insane.

*A weekend, two or three times in a year, forever and ever and ever, irremovable—that's bad enough. To keep on **meeting**, for ever and ever and with no amen, that's fucking futile—corrosive—infuckingsane—but a **cruise**? This long together on a fucking **boat**? I should just have said no. And then Derek—Derek who is normal—he wants to come along. And how to explain why not? I'm heading out with, as far as Derek knows, my school chum Margery—the Margery that I've been* *meeting for years, since long before I **met** Derek—so why shouldn't he come and join us? Hang the expense, he'll sort out the details—it'll be fun . . .*

Fuck.

*And if Art isn't **meeting** other people, that isn't my fault, either. I've never asked him to be lonely.*

The gale is humming and crying through some gap, around some obstacle—it's singing and the sound is almost wonderful and she would like to listen to it and not deal with Arthur, or anything about him.

*I did leave it late to tell Art—didn't want to mess him around—I never want to mess him around—but I do and he does me—and then Margery's falling on her sword—this isn't my decision, but she won't attend—Arthur provides her with an illness—dodgy heart—and we'll ignore **that** double meaning—fuck, is there a meaning he doesn't multiply, is anything ever just itself? And the lie about the heart—the heart lie— that meant we'd solved the problem—or not solved, but altered . . . me stuck on a boat with Derek who wants to propose instead of being otherwise stuck with Art who never will, or who might if I would let him, but I won't. I can't. I couldn't . . . Main point, main fucking point—my fucking question would fucking be . . .*

'Why the fuck tell me you weren't going to come on the cruise and then still fucking come?'

'You knew I would.'

'You said you wouldn't.'

'But you know me.' He's smiling again—putting a melancholywounded spin on it.

'Stop it.'

'Stop what? I'm not doing anything. Beyond reminding you we have *met* before. Have been

85

meeting for years. My body has been *meeting* your body for y—'

'Stop it.'

'I'm saying you know me. That's all. And anyone like me in my circumstances would be predictable. I'm not a story that's hard to tell—not for you. No surprises . . .'

He is standing closer to her. They are propping themselves against a white-painted metal wall—*bulkhead*, maybe, she isn't sure of the right word—it keeps them steady. And this desire to be steadied has drifted them in nearer to each other, tighter—that, and the hope to be warm.

And there may be nothing more to this: simple comforts required by them both and allowed to exert their influence without manipulation.

But Elizabeth has begun to feel pressured, as if she can taste him, working in. She isn't easing herself away again, it's true—although she'd partly like to—and she's aware that Arthur chose the boisterous location, the tempestuous cold—he could have predicted their effects. He'll always have her story worked out, too.

This being the kind of behaviour for which there's no excuse—like his rant about fucking—like saying he wouldn't be here and then being here—like being Arthur Lockwood—makes her—she feels, quite reasonably—angry and an angry woman is allowed to say, 'You cunt.'

'That's uncalled for.'

'And your . . . what would you say it was? Your *oration*? Your speech in the restaurant? That was called for? And lying to me?'

'I didn't lie.'

'I wouldn't have come if I'd thought you'd be here.'

86

'If you remember, our original arrangement was that I would be here and that's why you'd come—sorry, for the double meaning, we can act as if it didn't happen. Of course.'

And he is making her be—letting her be—furious, which she doesn't want. Any large emotion would be bad—it would let the others in.

'I wouldn't have dragged Derek along to be—'

'Oh, I think he's been dragged along from the start, hasn't he? Doesn't realise he's being dragged, but that's hardly putting you on the moral high ground . . .'

'Cunt.'

'Sorry, that's not very specific—are you just saying that I'm generally a cunt? I'm not allowed to . . . *intuit* what you mean, so you'll have to explain.' And he gives her that flinching, wearied look—consistently very effective—and he moves to face her, stands between her and the ocean, and he holds her forearms, pulls her forward so they both stand free of the wall, balance and sway with each other in the ocean's great, grey twists of thought. 'I didn't lie, Beth. I don't lie to you.' And he lets her see he's giving up and won't fight her any more—that she can win if she wants. There will be no argument.

He'll be beaten if she wants. 'I said that I wouldn't enjoy the trip without you, Beth. I said that I wouldn't enjoy it if you were with him. Which is true: I am not enjoying it, but why assume that I won't do something because I'll be hurt—why, of all things, assume that?'

And she would like to reach for him but can't because his hands are fastening more intently and, anyway, she shouldn't.

'I didn't absolutely say I wouldn't be aboard, Beth

87

. . . and *Christ* what do you want me to . . .' And he's blinking and it's hard to be sure, although not hard enough to be sure that he won't start crying.

No. Not crying. He wouldn't allow that, not when I'm with him and have to watch, when it's something too effective to ever be used. We wouldn't stoop to that.

So it would be the worst trick he could pull.

Or not a trick at all.

And perhaps it isn't a trick.

Because he takes care to avoid breaking completely and makes himself unsympathetic, fends her off. 'I can smell him on you. I can smell his pedestrian little cock.' He studies her expression then releases her, appears satisfied, sets the heels of his hands to his eyes and rubs.

She should get away now. She knows he would let her go, but she's already begun, 'Art. I can't deal with this. Derek's a good man. He's a reliable man. He doesn't do appalling things.' Before she can prevent herself or regret it.

Before they can both regret it.

And he tells her, *'Please.'*

He is so particularly eloquent with that word—*please.* No one should be able to ask so well, it lets them grow accustomed to more than they deserve.

'Please.'

She fails to leave and this means he can say, 'Beth, just let me . . . I was rude and I'm sorry and I apologise and I will be perpetually sorry if you want and I will apologise and apologise . . . I was . . . Let me . . .' He reaches out and then she discovers she's holding his hand. Anyone who saw them would think they were lovers—hand in hand in the privacy of night.

But I'm so cold I can't feel him.

And then Arthur frees her, unbuttons his overcoat—this takes a clumsy while, he's clearly also numbed. He turns himself away from the hardest edge of the weather and opens the long, brown cloth of his coat before he folds her in, hugs her in with the sky blue lining which is probably silk and shouldn't be near salt water. He gives her what's left of his heat.

And anything but this and anything but this and anything but this she can deal with.

Anything but him.

Like lovers.

We were lovers.

We are.

We were.

We are.

Cold cheeks, cold lips, like a dead man's, his words fumbling a little for this reason, or for other reasons. 'Beth, I didn't tell you where I live.' But his voice in her hair, quick beside her ear, and it feels like inside, it has the temperature of inside who he is, of who they have been together—it touches her like a long time ago and like their being other people, like her being someone else and with him. 'You don't know where I live, Beth.'

'What?'

'Ssssshhh. Why should you? You didn't want to. You don't want to. Sound decision—you needn't. But . . . I have the flat in London, that you . . . there was that afternoon when you nearly visited and I can see why you wouldn't—that's all right—and I also have regular hotels . . . but that's not where I live, not home, I . . .' He's shivering—a delicate instrument, Arthur, tends to show his shocks, his unfavourable circumstances. He's built to indicate

89

distress. He needs gloves. They both ought to have gloves, and his fists should at least be in his pockets, but Beth feels them knotted close at the small of her back. Her fingers are against his chest, his ribs, his breathing, the way that he's thin, broken back to his final limits, to the fights in his thinking, his intention. 'Listen, Beth. Listen. There are bluebells. In the spring. Campion, sea campion, primroses, thrift, violets, bird's-foot trefoil, wild garlic in white drifts—all kinds of flowers—but I love the bluebells— in the dusk, they glow—they return all the shine of the day and I walk out past the bank around my house—high, high bank—and that's what I see there and I can smell that blue—it has a smell—and the powdery, perfumey, sugary gorse: it's like cheap sweets and face powder and I love it, too—and under that is the scent of the island—like a big dog—a big, warm animal—woody and clever and dusty and living and salt and I love it the most—boots covered in live dust and after the first night I smell of the island, too, and I forget who I am and what I do and I tramp—yes, still avoiding the sun, I am mostly still avoiding the sun—you know I have to, because of . . . and I'd burn—blonds burn and it's forever since I was out in the summer, fully under it—because of the other things, too—but I can stop—I could stop, I . . . and sometimes I sit in the garden under the tree—but mainly I tramp out at night with a torch or by memory—there are no street lights on the island, not anywhere, so we're good at the dark—we all keep our secrets—we all know them, but we keep them, we're polite—and I go along the cliffs, judge where I'll be safe by the ocean's breathing—the same way it's breathing here—a dark that's alive in the dark—not too near the edge and not too far, that's what I aim for, I don't want to fall—same ocean as this—and I'm on paths that are warm still, that are skin heat—and it is dangerous—slightly— occasionally—depends where I go—but not so much so, because I remember, I have learned the shapes of places and how they are and what they want—and then I get home again safe and behind my bank, inside my bank—the place is set back from the deep of a path—it's been worn in, you see, feet and carts, cutting it down for so very long—and the house above—all hidden and hedged—wrens nesting in the hedge—blackthorn and brambles and honeysuckle, the tangle they like . . . Did you ever see a wren in spring? He's so tiny you could lose him in your hand and with the ticked-up tail and he'll sit and pour out music—huge music—flares his wings, bristles with it, all unfolded by the way he is, has to be—he wants to be bigger and he is—I have a wren—a pair—they live in next to me—and I have my house, walls of pink and grey granite made feet thick for the winters and with stones for the witches to sit on built into the chimneys, so you won't have them pestering you in your house—believe that you could have the witches and then you'll believe you need the stones—the fact that you don't see the witches means the stones repel them—that's how it works—matters of faith—I am aware you understand, even if you no longer want to—and I have a porch for boots and with hooks for hanging up—my boots, my coats, my hats—serious fireplace in my living room—the stone is old, is huge—fat mantelpiece, not much on it, I like it as itself—no ornaments on it and no photographs—no photographs—and rugs, two armchairs—mine and a spare, or rather mine and another, but only for balance because I don't

91

have visitors—lots of whitewash—and my desk is in the study with a sensible chair and some cabinets you'd want me to be rid of—you wouldn't like their contents—some books that you wouldn't like either—and a big kitchen you can sit in and eat breakfast on the table—eat whatever you like—which is what I do—and upstairs there's a bathroom which looks out to the ocean and another little room with just ordinary, good books for reading and then my bedroom with wardrobes and a double bed—and I don't need a double bed—and I can lie in it, if I prop myself up, and I can watch the sunset and everything there is perfect—it is fucking perfect—and remember that summer bedroom? Remember the rose scent from the garden at that hotel and the big squares of sun on the carpet and nobody saw us, because we never left the room. Remember? The first time after Beverley, remember? And my house is ready and it's nice and you should just once, just once . . . there are so many stars, thick stars—I can get drunk with staring at them . . . just once . . . You know I wouldn't . . . I don't . . . That's what I wanted to talk about, to tell you in the buffet. Not the other stuff. But I couldn't tell you, so you got the other stuff, because I couldn't, that's why . . . I wanted you to be here on the ship, so that I could tell you about my house. That's what I wanted.'

And what answer could there possibly be to this? It is unforgivable.

'It's . . . Art, please, I—'

'It's a kind place. All prepared and if it's comfortable for me and we're alike—and we *are* alike . . . It's a kind place.'

And Beth can't accept this and she can't refuse, so she tries, 'You really live there?'

'Yes!' It hurts her when he yells, seems to hurt him too, and they stand apart again and he refastens his buttons while, 'Jesus, Beth. Yes. I really live there. I don't lie about everything. I hardly lie at all. The bare minimum. And not with you.'

'Because lies don't work.'

'That's *not why.*'

'On your island—do they know who you are?'

'What?' And for a naked second he is baffled, simply a man she ought to help because he is overwrought. 'No. Not really . . .' And then he is Art again, defended, describing a way in which he lies. 'As far as they're concerned I'm some eccentric with money—a lot of that about on the island—and I have vague health trouble, pay a servant who gathers supplies, oversees repairs and gardening, is sworn to secrecy and who therefore lays down inaccurate gossip which is, in turn, not believed. But, no, they don't know who I am.'

'And they don't know what you do.'

'Fuck, Beth—nobody knows that. The only one who might is you.'

'Because when you tell me 361 people have been photographed . . . Look, we have to get out of this cold or we're going to get hypothermic.'

'If we go in then we can be seen, so we can't . . .' He's shuddering, they both are—perishing. 'Yeah, we'll have to go in. Yeah . . .' And he hunches his shoulders and returns very mildly to the halting twitching man he'd decided to be in the queue.

Elizabeth follows him round to the nearest door, shouts into the wind before he opens it, 'Three six one. I remember.'

'On the Right Hand List.'

'three six one.'

93

And then they are tumbled through to an aching quiet, a preposterous warmth. Ahead of them is the internal door and then the expanses of carpet, the efficient lighting, the possibilities of—although it is late—inquisitive observation. Elizabeth's cheeks and ears are stinging, being hurt with comfort.

Arthur looks raw and diminished. He is frowning down towards her and bending a touch forward, crossing and uncrossing his arms. '361 on the Left Hand List would be—'

'*Loss. Betrayal. Please listen.* But that's not what you meant. On the Right Hand List **three** is *Touch me*. And **six** is . . .' Swallowing and this airless drop that seems to take her as if she's seventeen and nothing has ever happened to her and she has been academic and a late starter. '**Six** is *Fuck me*.' Can't say it without saying it.

They stand between the doors and Beth wishes she could feel like crying, because that would be something to do and not a trick—not meant as a trick—just something for her to be with.

Arthur rubs his hand over his face in a long, anxious swipe. 'And **one** is *Look at me*.' He lowers his eyes and says very softly, 'And you did touch me when I asked, you touched my arm and I have a suite—I have a *Grand Suite*—and it's comfortable and warm and we could be comfortable and warm in it together and we could undress and we could be in my bed and you could fuck me, because I asked and you haven't done that yet and you can't start a number and not finish, you have to do the whole number and you could fuck me and then I would be with you and I would be naked and you could look at me.'

His head swinging away from her while he speaks,

as if he expects to be found offensive, and he doesn't look at her, is only turning for the final door, pushing it open into the dry, anxious scent of the ship.

Arthur simply walking himself away: 'You could look at me.'

Which means he isn't being simple.

He isn't being fair.

He shouldn't say things like that.

Any word can work a spell if you know how to use it.

Prepared.

The man sits in a bland hotel suite, curtains drawn for the third day running. Resting in the other room is a woman nobody can mend, but he will try to.

The man is hot with the idea of saving her and has already entirely committed himself to the first of his offerings: the undermining of his own fabric, the imposition of stresses, minor pains. For the woman—she's called Agathe—he has made himself unnatural. For Agathe there is nothing natural that's left.

He offers as much to every one of them, to each enquirer.

For quite a while now he's only worked with individual enquirers—the platform gigs didn't feel right to him, they lacked control. By himself in a roomful of strangers and their lacks, that never was what he'd intended.

This is better.

This is the last of three days.

The man gives enquirers three perfected days,

tailored to their needs.

Bespoke service.

Three days and then no more for ever, a definitive end.

Three days prepared by a man who is prepared.

Before the start of every session, he's careful to think—*I am a man who is prepared.* Then he fits his hands one into the other and imagines the smell of caramel and sunshine on his face and reflecting on water and the sound of an easy tidal swell—that kind of breathing, the breath of a calm sea. He revisits a number of comforting places and sensations.

Nothing too pleasant, but enough.

Because I need to be defended.

I need to be prepared.

For this morning he has drunk too much coffee and taken one over-the-counter decongestant. This, combined with his anaemia, will re-pace his heart, make it gallop in his chest. And he will shake.

Which is sometimes an unavoidable requirement.

Appearances matter.

He's in an excellent suit. He can afford it.

Bespoke service.

He's been wearing it for two days straight, though, letting it wrinkle—his shirt's fresh, but wrinkled too—because he's working, shut in with Agathe and the hours racking round, accumulating. And he won't be shaving until he stops.

Here am I, gone to pieces, lost and harried in my single-minded care for you.

Symbolic devotion to their cause.

Normally he's immaculate, keeps cleaner than clean. Shaves twice a day. Manicure once a week.

But if he's got a gig then he has to be more subtle— dishevelled but not distasteful—so no iron, and unscented soap, unscented antiperspirant. Unwanted scents can be confusing.

Additional antiperspirant for his hands.

Because he *is* devoted to their cause and his care *is* single-mindedly for each enquirer.

And, most of all, because they'll hold his hands. They will touch him.

They will become familiar with the small knock of his pulse, its eloquent suggestions. But always formality with them, restraint.

Jacket stays on, no matter what, and have to be careful, maintain the proper distances. Be a gentleman. Be especially a gentleman for the ladies.

The work is easier with women. Their orientation doesn't matter, it's just simpler for him and smoother with the gender he should love, should be allowed to love—all those echoes of experience, the terrible paths of tenderness that still lead into him, he can use them—they insist on his attention, focus him— and they mean he doesn't have to fake affection. It's a pre-existing inclination.

Plus, women live longer, survive—he gets more practice with them.

Ladies' man.

Which would be funny at another time and in another place.

And if I were another man.

But here I am, myself and working.

And here's Agathe.

Her last name is undoubtedly a cautious invention, but Agathe—that's honest. That rings in her when he says it and he can watch her hollow with the wish to hear it as it once was, familiar and spoken by lost mouths. She aches. When he sits beside her the man aches, too.

At first she was excessively wary with him, furious with a desire to be gone, numb, other than she is.

The man can understand this.

And safety: Agathe still wants safety beyond speaking.

But she doesn't believe in it, of course. She has no faith in sanctuaries.

She has seen what will happen to people who do.

A challenge then, Agathe.

Not that she was beyond him.

Very few people have managed to stay beyond him.

And, when he came down to it, with Agathe there was only one real barrier to cross. This made his process simple—either break her, which he would not ever do, or find her line and then respect it, spend their first two days showing it humility and restraint: don't cross it, not until invited.

Kindness.

All done with kindness.

We are all of us done with kindness.

Right now, she will be lying on her bed, but not asleep. Agathe rarely sleeps. She will have heard him showering in his bathroom and the mild din of his feet, his ungainly knock—tired—against a chair that sent it over and on to the carpet. Every noise will have meanings for her, sensible explanations, but each will be a horror, too. Each will be the inescapable, finally here to claim her. Even a cough can jolt her, or the clatter of restless pigeons, outside on the window ledges.

He had guessed this before he met her.

No.

He had been certain.

Because he began by letting her story overwhelm

him—the outrage of her experience and a sense of being stunned, robbed, splintered, hauled down towards weeping and giddiness: his, hers, his. He saved the flavours of this and its unfathomable size, its slipping into fury and an attentively waiting nothingness. In her absence, the patterns of what happened to her began to coalesce.

This is the least he would expect, because he has learned how to nourish facts, how to feed them and let them grow into usefulness. Threads, suggestions, scraps, they make him ready for First Sight.

Which was watching her walk out of the frost and into the milky fug of a coffee shop on the Rue Saint-Denis.

Always like the Montreal gigs—such a crazy town, so full of damage, anxious for release. And there was Agathe—the whole of her—the buried and unburied.

So there I was to be with her.

She was angular, clean-limbed, and there would have been something fluid and dignified in her walk, but it was stiffened now and locked. The upright head was anxious, throat taut. Cheap skirt to her ankles and comforting, protecting boots for warmth—nothing dainty, nothing female, not any more, just a defence against Quebec, the cold. A type of thin anorak, faded, not originally hers; quite likely that nothing was meaningfully hers except the scarf.

Karkade red, hibiscus red—impractical synthetic chiffon—hand touches it often—threat to the neck—a memory of threat to the neck—a knot, a fear, a choke in the throat made of words, impossible to swallow and impossible to scream.

That's OK, though.

I only deal with the impossible.

It's what I like.

Red bound around and around her neck. But not blood. To her it's not blood—more like giving, sharing, passion recalled, types of heat—it's something gentle near her lips, I can see her almost tasting it, a sort of response—and it isn't heat, it's primarily warmth, there's a difference, a more lasting penetration.

She has clever fingers—we can share that, don't need to translate it—only her touch has lost assurance—it's blinded—so think of gloves, keeping gloves on you, muffling constantly—and she's directionless.

There's no point to touching when what you want to touch is gone.

Hair cropped to a haze, no longer hides the skull—lovely curve there, but it's a mortified beauty. She has an impulse towards simplicity, scouring and punishment—not starting again, but freezing at nothing. No longer hiding because there is nowhere to hide. No hat. It's bitter outside but no hat.

No hiding.

But she did once, didn't she? Agathe tried to hide and it was bad. She was bad. Time enough for that, though . . .

Her mouth was used to smiling: taken altogether, she has a face that would once have been comfortable, opened, ready to show an intelligence and charm.

Charm is rare and shouldn't ever be extinguished.

Intelligence is rarer, but also more difficult to like and she's intelligent—she's bright, bright, bright.

Silly too, she could be silly, she could play—sexual play and just daftness. I would have enjoyed her. We might have flirted, talked.

She would have laughed a good deal and quite probably clapped her hands together softly when she did. She'll have covered her lips, shielded her grin for a moment, enjoyed having overstepped some tiny mark.

100

She hasn't been able to change her eyes—they have stayed challenging, curious. They look too much—it's almost a form of self-harm. She is learning to curb them, focus on table legs, pavements, floors, to behave like a refugee. But she has brave eyes, that's irreversible.

Brave and tired, tired, tired—she can no longer trust what they'll force her to see. They are beyond her.

But I'm not.

I'm right here—here with the over-priced cookies and the sugar-heavy syrups—symptoms of safe city living, this masochistic urge to spend too much on shit. We have been consistently persuaded to buy what will do us no good.

Agathe bought me.

She asked for me.

So she gets what she asked for, what she wants. People should.

She'd told him on the phone—very quiet but precise—that she wanted to meet him and to try him.

He hadn't sent for her, she'd asked.

And then he'd lifted his head on that initial afternoon, so that she could find him, and he'd sat calmly, fixed his whole strength into restfulness and tender breathing and hampered glances. He'd reached out and matched the beats and pauses of how Agathe is Agathe.

*It's an animal thing, a wilderness thing—flesh echoing flesh and leading, a sense of large defence—or the child and the parent and the parent and the child, the home they make between them—and it's a sex thing and a shared will thing and a human thing and a rest thing: it's **come unto me and I will give you rest**. It's a relief.*

This felt, as it always does, like hunger and freedom

101

and finding and wearing and racing and dancing and burning and having and laughing and fucking and bracing himself in the tide of who she is, the slap of it against his chest.

He began to fix her in his mind as the scent of syruped coffee and also green mornings, the aftertaste of Fanta—popular in Rwanda, Fanta—and the nag of over-happy music and motor taxi exhausts. There was Montreal in her, too—those flattened Québécois vowels and a park bench, sitting, being startled away by clutching mission drunks, being disproportionately frightened, scared of her multiple weaknesses and how they show themselves: that was yesterday. She had that at her surface, but he pressed until she dipped into years ago and Kigali and the sway of rounded hills—no anxiety, no shocks—simply pooled mist and dust that is a pinkish khaki, that washes down on to the pavements and the tarmac when it rains.

He chooses not to admit that Rwandan earth is a colour that makes him think of taint, of spillage, of humped soil that moves, seethes, becomes remarkable with covering too much slaughtered meat. He keeps her from that—seals every thought of her away from the slip of putrefaction, tangled cloth, unbreathable streets. The least he can do.

He's seen other countries, other places that remember selections and thefts, houndings, flights, pits—Guatemala, Poland, Bosnia, Spain—an older and newer and larger list of countries every year. The man is aware that different violated earths have different colours, so he shouldn't let chance mineralogy mislead him, or trouble her.

In his thoughts, she will see no blood, not where he saves her. His mind doggedly takes her to live in a flawless space in a sunlit room in an upper storey in a row of many mansions—he's going to keep her there. Every one of his enquirers is settled safe inside imagined houses, together with the details that made them real. They are stored away with dignity, accurate tenderness.

He doesn't forget them.

They are held under love.

This is important.

As important as the fact that he works for them and then never sees them again.

No exceptions.

His necessary loneliness.

The right way to do wrong.

The man hears Agathe stirring through the wall, a toilet flush, taps running for a bath. The accommodation they share is not luxurious, but it is pleasant, allows for privacy and space. It brought her near to her earlier existence when she saw it. There was the start of tears, an anger, a shame.

He has given her salts and oils for bathing. Neither of them believes they confer any New Age benefits. They're having none of that crap. They do make her feel indulged, though, womanly and pampered and, by now—two days gone—this is something she can tolerate again. Guillaume, her husband would have bought her similar treats at their beginning, on one of his attentive, unbusied days.

Difficult to get the scents just right—musk, Egyptian sandalwood, frankincense, tuberose, Givenchy Pi for Men and Amarige—very 1990s. He gives her ways in which Agathe can recall Agathe, ways in which Agathe can recall Guillaume.

Michel, her son, is more difficult, further away.

It hurts both the man and Agathe that Michel is

103

staying mainly out of reach.

The cruelty of sons with their mothers never ceases to disgust.

While she bathes, the man waits and leans his elbows on the table, shuts his eyes and shifts his head, nuzzling the conditioned air. Then he swallows and frowns and drops into a sense of her skin—this isn't a sexual process, this is knowing—this is, in a way, being known—this is water over her surface, their shared surface, over the no-longer-needed body, the attempting-to-forget-itself body, over the scar on her collar bone. Cupping liquid warm in her left hand.

Agathe's right hand is gone. So she can't be right-handed.

Shame, because she was.

Could be worse. And it's not as if she's pretending she'd have prospered as a cleaner, a nanny, a waitress, been happy in some abject, practical, double-handed job. Agathe is not practical. Journalism suited her: ideas, concepts, a discipline of the mind, of uncovering and talking, shaping, driving, late-night calls and letting her name be printed—her byline exposed where the radio broadcasts could find it in those poisonous last days. The new kind of journalists started work: the ones who coach murderers then set them loose to play— and they wanted her. They wanted everyone. They were ready at RTLM: nailed her up on air with her husband. She is unable to forget the adolescent, happy music, the fresh voices—Georges Ruggiu, Valerie Bemeriki—all those knowing and persuasive voices, authoritative threats, exhilarating threats, the fucking and fucking and fucking energy of threats— bloodthreats, fuckthreats, young men's threats.

Some days, she could see them shading the air above her like greasy smoke.

They only broadcast for a bit more than a year, so their influence was remarkable. What might be called their productivity was highly impressive. Then again, it was a highly productive genocide—efficient beyond imagination.

Kill rates have never been exceeded.

Not yet.

And the Brits did what to intervene? Helped the delays, assisted evasions. Eventually we sent some trucks. Old ones. Fifty trucks. To save a whole country. Every mechanism slowly failing. Doesn't bear thinking about.

But I do think about it. My job to bear.

I bear nothings, ghosts, thoughts.

A British (non-domiciled, non-taxpaying) citizen just doing what he can.

To help.

To help her.

After the killing's stopped.

Sort of stopped.

Agathe, clearly, was not killed. She was mutilated and raped.

Agathe survived, which is an extremely misleading word.

Agathe can type slowly, freelances with some francophone work, some English. She writes whatever she can, agrees to be an expert on the whole of Africa, to pretend that everywhere on the continent must be fundamentally alike. Agathe pretends she is from Burundi, which is almost true. She comments on Rwanda, on President Kagame, on how many potential *genocidaires* you can select and choose to kill before you yourself will become a *genocidaire*—

105

on how the poison still frets in the earth.

Agathe knows she had a son.

Not now.

Agathe knows she had a husband.

Not now.

Agathe had that one strong border around the privacy of her mourning and the guilt that she'd been slow once, had not understood her situation— she'd been a journalist and clever but she hadn't adequately predicted, hadn't pre-empted a single terror, had not saved anything.

And after that Agathe had decided that nobody else would mislead her, that she would be ready, even though she believed that she shouldn't be living, that every breath was unforgivable. She was walled up alone inside her watchfulness and sin.

So the man simply sang out her pain, made a methodical inventory for her, so that she could grow used to his being correct. He didn't even murmur against her defences—he sat outside them and stretched in the sunlight and searched through his pockets for redemption, held it coddled in his hand and warm and let her see.

If she wanted it, then she would break herself open for him and ask him in.

Eventually, everyone does.

Because we all need mercy, how could we not?

And I have the finest for her, because I make it.

Hand-crafted for one careful owner.

None better.

And he's set her fingers firm on his wrist, made her hold him so she can't help but notice when he's squeezed his pulse slower, flattened it, when he's raced his heart, trembled. Yesterday—his arm all gimmicked, ready—they went a little further. It

106

wasn't a cheap trick necessarily, only a plain thing, an apposite addition which would deepen confidence—it's not like he'd stooped to blood-writing, nothing shabby. Time was, he was going for 10/11 forces with Tarot cards, nonsense like that—deserved a spanking.

Now he stops his heart.

He did that for Agathe: gave her a death reversed. Nothing flash, just a sufficient halt, no showing off. She would have felt him slow, then stop, then start back up. And it wouldn't have seemed unlikely: he generally looks like death, bloody awful.

Fucking headache all the fucking time.

He'd squeezed the gimmick, let his blood apparently falter and stop, and then he let her search his intentions, eye-to-eye. He parted himself for her, let her peep in. And then he released the pressure on his arm, restored his pulse, stuttering, struggling, fighting to be with her. After that, three decongestants and his lack of effective blood had guaranteed him palpitations, something unfakeable—unless you know how to fake it.

And then The Gift.

He'd brought her Guillaume.

He'd summoned her husband, made Guillaume beyond convincing, let him find her smile—that early-love, most beautiful and delicate of her smiles. The man gave Agathe exactly what her husband would have if he still existed and wasn't bullshit and could have returned from the beyond. The man let Guillaume forgive and forgive and forgive.

Agathe had that one strong border.

Not now.

And today Agathe will wear the mishinana the man bought her—*karkade red*—and together they

107

will finish this before tomorrow morning.

Once she's opened her bedroom door she pauses, stands and is lovely and almost knows it. The cloth of the dress drapes conveniently—tradition leaving her perfect side revealed and concealing the damaged shoulder, the shortened limb.

The man seats her at the table, deft and attentive as a maître d', and then he lights the final candle—*hibiscus red*—turns out the lamps and sits down opposite.

He always uses three candles: the black, the white, the red. His enquirers decide on each colour's significance, a logical order. Very few of them choose to end with red.

Brave eyes and brave to the bone.

No food no drink, not for either of us—only this.

He sets both forearms flat on the tabletop, allows her to mirror him, which she does and tells her, 'Mwaramutse.'

Kinyarwanda—I've not had to use that with anyone else. A nice task, picking it up—adds an extra layer, perhaps a resource for the future—Christ knows, they've got enough widows . . . And speaking it has pleased her, really delighted her in some tiny way. I'm slightly proud of that.

'Is it still the morning?' She smells of roses. She settles, meets his gaze. She is asking for everything this time—whatever else he can do.

Which will be The Final Leaving and The Beginning.

Leaving is easy—it's starting again that's intolerable, deciding to walk out into your life, the way it promises and then fumbles.

I used to say I'd give them hope—but no one should have to deal with that.

Even so, he says, 'It's another morning. Last day.

Amakuru?'

'I'm fine, thank you.'

'We got through the night.'

'We got through the night.' Her voice is deeper, her words are slower than when she arrived, they seem younger, nearer, snug and unselfconscious as they touch her lips. 'We got through the night.'

Night is when the young men ran and played with their swooping, exhumed blades, their stockpiled determination to remove the *inyensi*, the *ibyitso*, accomplices of the rebels, the *inkotanyi*. They made roadblocks which could not be passed, constructed gauntlets that clotted with bodies, breathing heaps and parts. They laid waste. They took neighbours and teachers, broadcasters, politicians, shopkeepers, journalists, anyone, anyone, anyone who was marked, who was listed as a collaborator, cockroach, moderate, threat. And the running men, the playing men—they denied the rules of homes and cities and hospitals and churches and villages and farms, the rules of human beings facing other human beings. They raped in the way they might smoke a cigarette, or take a drink. They raped to prove their point—that they were raping nobody, doing nothing—that appetite and liberated thinking are invincible. They were an absolute, carried out their *umuganda* as if it was truly *clearing brush, cutting down the tall trees*— fast as *pulling out the bad weeds*—as if their country ought to be reworked into one vast, manicured landscape—like the grounds of a stately home, or perhaps a golf course. Machetes and bullets and fears so great that everyone must die before the morning.

Each time Agathe has closed her eyes it has been night. Six years of night inside her skull and the

109

noises that people make when they stop being people.

This morning she will watch the man's face and he will talk her back into April and living in Kimihurura—up the hill by the diplomatic compounds, in amongst the curved roads and woodlands—good for parties and gossip, good for sweet air.

But the President's plane has exploded and what couldn't be happening is; beyond any limits, it is. There was a plan. All along, the men with machetes, the broadcasters, the politicians who moved them— they had a plan—there were strategies and contingencies and diplomatic considerations and she never found the red, wet truth of them. So it found her. It found everyone.

And the man and Agathe and Guillaume—they are there together.

And running up the middle of the road is a naked woman and then she falls the way she might if she had tripped. She will have hurt herself, skinned her knees. There's an odd stain on her back, it glistens. A presidential guard ambles towards her, shoots her once more, this time in the head, moves on.

Agathe is three minutes away—a three-minute leisurely walk—caught in her dangerous, pretty house that has simple doors and unarmoured windows, a pleasant garden, decking for the evening sun, an inadequate fence.

None of what she has is any use to her, not now.

Guillaume wants Agathe to hide. He tells her in one hot whisper, 'Genda!' He sounds the way he never has: so small, so scared, tearing with love. And she won't go and he begs and the men are next door—outside and next door—*Abakuzi,*

Impuzamugambi, Interahamwe—the names of her coming death.

And when she remembers this, drops into this, Agathe shivers and the man shivers and when she cries—this bereft, immobile weeping—the man weeps, too.

And she's going, she's going there—completely there—and so stay with her and love her and stay with her and here she goes, all of the way.

And the man tells her that Guillaume is in the room with her—imagines a sense of being filled with this breath, with this scent, this years-ago air—and the man takes her husband's words into his own mouth—'Iruka!' The last word—good guess, lovely guess—beautiful job.

So follow up, keep hold.

The husband must have watched while Agathe hid somewhere . . . no thought of being tortured for her whereabouts—he's going to be murdered, not interrogated—and he wants to see the last of his wife, he wants her face there firm in his thinking when he's by himself and the horror comes.

Somewhere—look at her—it was somewhere tiny, hopeless, flimsy . . . she's shrinking into it, thinking of hugging herself like a girl—somewhere low that was like a cupboard—at the level of the soldiers' shins, boots—flinching, flinching, flinching—loud boots once they were indoors and kicking.

Because this is fucking obvious, the man tells her the intruders took money and jewellery and pawed through her clothes.

Mention bedding—I'd rip bedding—if I was a cunt like that.

Confusing, intoxicating—being the violated and the violator—the killer and the killed.

I'll sleep well tonight—bloody exhausted.

I'll sleep well or not at all . . .

Agathe frozen somewhere when he mentions the bedding.

Bedding.

The word hits.

Lovely.

So she was in a linen cupboard. Smell of bedding, fresh, intimate, owned—no way to sleep for her, ever after—no way out of dark and wakefulness—or there hasn't been—but I'll make her a way. I will.

Agathe hid in the linen cupboard and listened to the sounds of metal and her husband's bones.

Guillaume didn't shout, didn't want to upset her, stayed unexpressed—comes across as an odd man, very gentle, slightly distant—more suited for academia than journalism.

Either way, they'd have fucking killed him.

Agathe holding her breath in the cupboard—has kept holding her breath ever since—the only sounds letting her understand Guillaume's murder.

She heard the breaking of her husband's body— what she kissed, learned, fucked, loved. They killed Guillaume.

This would be the point where she went very reasonably insane.

And afterwards—*being the perpetrators again*—the man imagines and describes searching, giggling, drunk men, stoned men, breaking things, foulness in Agathe's house.

Naturally, they found her—cruel to dwell on that and it might push her too far, lock her beyond herself again, so be gentle over it—be gentle anyway— *fuck*—of course, be gentle.

Agathe was not Tutsi like her husband and her

112

rapists knew that. Because she was Hutu, they exercised perverse restraint, permitted everything except her murder. Or else it was premeditated torture—this leaving her alive, alone, making her see.

Trying to overwhelm those eyes. Make them shut.

The last thing they did was to cut off her hand.

The man thinks of her hoping she'd bleed to death.

Not allowed—none of those thoughts, not any more—no more dying, no rushing into destruction. Can't let the bastards make her kill herself, reach out and murder her with her own will.

The man makes Guillaume tell her that her self is sacred and mustn't be harmed, has to be held in beauty. The man allows a type of poetry to break out in his narrative because, husband and wife, they were people of words and found them impressive.

And the man talks about the way Agathe was sure Guillaume was with her and still alive when she fainted—that he was there—and then that terrible re-education when she awoke: metally bloodsmell and shit—lying in her own blood, husband's blood— broken glass, boot prints—things she cannot look at but has to, has to remember, has to eat up because they are all she has left. They were her everything.

Details, the probative details, that's what gets them and she is got.

Which is good because the man has to make her believe that she wasn't mistaken: that Guillaume did watch and wait. The man portrays her husband, invents him as being adamant on this point: that he was there beside her, beyond touching but there.

Something else for her to eat: a better everything.

And this is a type of perfection—a tenderness, but she doesn't stay with it, because her chronology is

113

leading to her son. First her husband was murdered and then her son.

Guillaume is lighting in her, he is convincing and she wants him—but she needs her son.

The man can taste her need—he makes it like chocolate in his head—hotsweet—and she never did really know what happened to her son. Michel, her only boy.

Down in Butare it was diggers and soldiers. No more tolerance for students, no more education required. Not much we can stand to see of that.

The man says he can feel Michel, that he is running along a track in open country. He isn't properly dressed, may have lost clothes, or been woken and driven from his bed. Michel is in a crowd. The men behind the crowd are quiet and busy—they have a long day ahead—they either shoot at the crowd or hack individuals down as they wish. Michel doesn't hear what happens to him, barely understands the start of it—out of breath, dust in his throat and then gone.

This feels unconvincing, not comprehensive enough. Agathe wants to understand completely: at least be with Michel, even if she couldn't do as a good mother should and save him.

Motherlove, motherguilt, motherblood—they all fuck you up.

And I'd like to please her—I would, but Michel, he'd be sodding awkward, he'd resist. Can't get a handle on more of his dying and I'm not going to try and that will work better—it really will work better than having him torn apart for her to watch.

Guillaume—he's the best bet—he's her way out of this. He's salvation.

And she should fucking have that, so I will fucking

arrange it, so fucking there.

The man lets her know how Guillaume watched her navigating Kigali. Her husband was why she didn't bleed to death and wasn't caught again. He is why the UN jeep paused where it did and she could reach it. He is why the checkpoints showed no interest in her—already dealt with.

Apparently.

Such love from him.

Bundled—always see the love in bundles, soft armfuls of the stuff.

Because I am a sentimental bastard.

But Agathe gets more than bundles.

She gets a real goodbye.

Guillaume needs to kiss her.

Yes, he does, my love, my darling. Come on Agathe, you can do this. We can do this.

The man suggests Agathe close her eyes and that the darkness will be recast, secured from this day forwards, peaceful. And her love so near her that she can smell his skin, his hair, the things of his that are forever now.

The man wants her to purse her lips.

Deep. A deep kiss. Thoughtkiss. Move for it. Please. Come on. For me. For him. Most natural thing in the world.

If she purses her lips for the ghost of a kiss, this will work.

Leastways, it ought to work. I dunno.

Pimping her for a corpse.

Come on, girl. For me. You can kiss him.

Sweet Agathe.

Open all the secrets of your lips.

She does like her poetry—shame I'm not in the mood myself—too excited—never tried this before.

But he does try talking her back to the excellent pain that was wanting and needing, that was love.

Kiss.

Sweet Agathe and a kiss.

The man leans forward and whispers, 'And he takes your hand, Agathe. You kiss him and, as proof, he'll touch your hand.'

The nerves get confused after amputations, they reconfigure, so—this can be possible, should be possible—a movement of her mouth, her cheek, can summon up what's gone: she'll feel her lost husband holding her lost hand.

And how fucking good would that be? That would be fucking good.

Not exact as a procedure.

Never tried it before, in fact.

But I did want to.

But unpredictable.

But fuck it. You can do this, Agathe. I know that you'll feel it, because you should feel it. You should have this.

You can.

And then he sees her, sees her smile and he is sure—he sees who she was and who she will be and that she is more and clean and more and strong and more and is in love.

Ecstasy. For you and me. Endlessly.

Fuck, yes.

She weeps without noticing. It rocks her, harrows her, and she lets it and still smiles. She burns.

Hurts to look.

Anything this wonderful, you shouldn't look.

Have to take care, though, stay alert.

What's left of her forearm rises from the table and her eyes still shut while she concentrates beyond the man—beyond the world—and grips, clings, touches with fingers that do not exist. She is holding her husband's hand, she can feel it, recognise it.

This is true.

Fucking true.

And this gives the man a joy approaching hers.

Fuck, yes.

*   *   *

It wasn't her husband, though.

Good thing the man only steered her, lightly kept her company and didn't crash in with a name.

Getting it wrong at this point would have been inexcusable.

Michel was the one she imagined returning, whose wounds undid themselves and fled, whose hair smelled of paradise when he touched her and of himself, of the total of his first cry, first look, first step, first hurt, first fight, of his known and secret life, of his mother's knowledge of his life.

Between them—she's between them—I can see it in her, in the sway of the head, the urge to lean on air, to rest her head on fantasies and let them love her.

Happy for you, Agathe.

She trusts, utterly trusts, that her man and her boy are to either side of her and she is breathing them in—greedy.

The red candle burning down.

I have explained.

I do make it very clear.

When the last candle gutters and goes out, then this is over. Permanently. The dead won't be home again, not for me, not for anyone else—so none of the other fuckers will take her, charge her, hook her up to the

117

weekly fixes of counterfeit affection and silly tricks.
  She's had me.
  Had the best.
  And I've given her everything she needed.
  Safe hands, me. A pair of safe hands.
  *I **gave** her this. No charge—that's **giving**.*
  And no one here but us to know. No one but me.
  I saved a life today.
  Well done, me.
  And no one to know.
The man's safe hands shaking so that he has to flatten them against the tabletop.
  She can sit for as long as she wants.
  We'll let it all consolidate and calm.

*   *   *

When Agathe finally opens her eyes, she looks at the man as if she has slept and been awoken and he clasps her hand gently between both of his and waits until she recognises him and this time and this place.
  Sorry. You have to be here and they have to be gone.
  The way things have to be.
  And it will rip you in places that I haven't got, but this is the end and unavoidable.
  And I won't do any more—I won't make you need me. I won't do that.
  Here you are and only you, and I am only me, but together we made what you wanted. Please take the love in that. Be satisfied.
She is flushed, early morning bewildered—for a moment he feels her appetite, that hungry confusion—so he lets her go. He begins to re-establish a useful distance.

Sodding candle's got a way to burn, but we can snuff it out.

Or she can, that might be better. Maybe . . . Not sure . . .

Can't just hang about here getting morbid, that's for sure.

And this is the point where advice is required and suggestions, ways to proceed into a future.

Advice from me on anything . . .

Laughable.

But nobody laughing.

Why would we.

Then off we go to our lonelinesses. No need to mention them, though. Obvious. Each to our own.

But she has her consolation, yes she fucking does.

From me.

What little there could be—from me.

Keep things brisk, definitive. Check she's fine, solid, no vulnerabilities left without at least some kind of covering.

Talking of which—will she want to take the dress off? Keep it?

She'll keep it.

I'm betting she'll want to walk out wearing it.

And undressing at this juncture is to be avoided, I would say.

This game that he's played: she never understood the rules and he could end with anything, could require anything of her and probably get it, steal it, con it out of her.

But I won't. Have to end it well for you, Agathe. Something special for brave Agathe.

So he stares at the wall beyond her and mentions she has the suite for another three days—this isn't true, but can be very easily arranged—and there is no arguing about this, there can't be: his delivery lets her understand that it is necessary, that it preserves her from the rigours of her new world until she is ready for them. The rest of her transition will take place here.

Then he bows his head for a moment and produces an appropriate smile. When he faces her again he makes it more than readable that somehow he has withdrawn from her at depth, that this is painful and troubling, will leave him less and her more, will leave him solitary, folded back into pale isolation.

He lets himself give in to being tired.

Because I fucking am.

He reaches out and levels his right hand above the candle flame—his last gift.

*Fuck the pain—there isn't any pain—I don't need to fake it, I can think it gone—and she'll like this, she'll **get** it, she'll remember.*

Then he crushes out the fire with his burned palm, marks himself with ash and hot wax, and he pushes back his chair, rises, stands. He bows to kiss her cheek, while she attempts to organise her fretting for him, her thanks and rehearsed goodbyes, but he's already up again and walking, leaving, no more to say, no more permitted—one last glance expressing confidence, affection, his gratitude—he makes himself bright as bright—and then he's out, he's over, free.

He'll send someone later to gather his things—meanwhile, she may want to inspect them, or she may leave them be. He'd like to think she might be curious about him, perhaps a touch fond of who it seemed he was. His belongings are all neutral, provide no clues, just a vague sort of intimacy about them: aftershave, laundry, a mildly used bed.

But she isn't like that. She won't check.

On Wednesday morning, he'll be in the foyer, tucked out of sight for when she leaves.

Just observing, making sure of the gig, the finale.

He expects her to be carrying the new holdall he bought her—important to have a fresh bag for fresh journeys, nothing patronising about it, not a present—and she'll still have that dreadful coat, but underneath it and blazing, singing, he'll want to see hibiscus red: a dress from home, a proud and impractical thing.

That would be a result.

Higher than average chance that she'll carry it off.

Make me cry, that would.

Women—they make me cry.

*   *   *

The man will stand and hide himself from the end of his work, another job done, and he will watch another stranger walk away and he will wonder how he came to be here. He will wonder how he came to be so far from love.

It's easily done.

You take your thumb and press it, nestle it, into the heart of your other hand. Where it most naturally rests, that's the sweet spot, the place where any touch will always raise a tenderness.

Consider whoever you love, ponder them, allow yourself to dwell, and a quiet ache will begin there—the longing you hold instead of their skin, that other skin. Clench your fists and it's that space you'll be defending—both hands curled around a lack, a thought, a tiny mind that you are out of and that your love is in.

And it's a light sleeper, your sweet spot, almost impossible not to wake it in spite of yourself—or because of yourself—not to set it off demanding satisfactions, to be touched—the little well that speaks, asks to be filled.

Best to train it if you can, start early and at least placate it, provide alternative interests to entertain. As a child, an oddly sensible child, you might start by setting a coin there, or a pebble, a medal, a talisman, charm, badge, ornament, folded paper, ticket, earring, seashell, marble, ring—pick any one of the small and precious, small and worthless objects that might litter a room, a jacket's pockets, a usual life.

And then you can teach the hollow of your palm to hold them, hide them, make them disappear. So the absence you feel can conjure up another, earn its keep.

If you would like.

Some children like.

Some people like.

And liking leads to doing, leads to practice—and a way of being compulsorily, usefully self-contained. Through evenings and weekends and holiday afternoons and on into the nights, you'll clench and furl and smooth your grips, you'll pace the beats and off-beats of any motion. The back of your hand will grow innocent, completely fair, its sides will be irreproachable, you'll even be able to offer up its soft, clean face while a marvel stays locked behind your knuckles—then you simply shift your treasure to the ledged base of your fingers, or the fold at your thumb's root, to fingertips, or into the snug of your palm, your gentle, educated palm. You'll start to be made up of refuges from every observation, all angles pre-empted, because this is how you will fabricate invisibility. You will study yourself in your mirror as if you're a dangerous stranger until, finally, you'll see you've managed it, you've changed, become completely secret, a deception. Your skin knows without seeming to know, your muscles and tendons work without seeming to work, your fingers flex and drop and catch and place and never show it.

You are magic.

You are definitively sure there's no such thing, but you can be it anyway.

You can believe yourself wonderful and enough and beyond helping.

If you would like.

If you would want that.

And the boy did want that.

The boy.

Our boy.

The boy was an early starter, in several ways precocious, and most of all with his hands, in his hands. When he is older he won't absolutely remember, but he is perhaps seven, nearly eight, when he first attempts their training. His dad can move cards to the top of the pack and can put the Queen of Hearts in any order with two of her cousins, will dance her about as he lays her down on the kitchen tabletop—first, third, first, second, second . . . wherever he wants. His dad explains that when someone else does this, it's a bad thing to do, because people can use it for cheating at bets and taking cash away from idiots. This is cruel because idiots need their cash more than most. And his dad also has a special card with holes in it which can be pulled along its sides—movable holes punched right through it which the boy cannot look at, except from far away, and isn't permitted to touch.

This leads the boy to conclude the holes are a gimmick built into the card and not a special cleverness of his dad's. The boy works this out.

So his dad has three tricks.

And only with cards.

The boy has already decided that people who think they can trust cards, or anything cards do, are idiots and should be left alone with their cash and not interfered with. He is waiting to be a grown-up and fool the other grown-ups who are like him, who can see things and can work them out. Personally, the boy would only be impressed if something amazing happened with his special piece of amber, or one of his model commandos, or his tiny dinosaurs—with reliable, familiar items. And so he intends to surprise the world with strictly proper stuff: the clean and plain and pure.

He has saved up and bought a book from a lovely and crowded, disreputable shop. It's a manual and contains instructions and thick-lined, authoritative drawings of hands and gestures and men with short haircuts and slyly concealing trouser cuffs—very serious, vintage men: ones like the black and white detectives in old films. But they're always ready to astonish with handkerchiefs and tumblers and American coins. They'd be fun to have round in your house. They are, he assumes, American men and not just being awkward on purpose by vanishing and producing inconvenient currency. He guesses about which British coins would be the same as the ones they're using, stares at the diagrams, imagines his fingers into their shapes. He stands and repeats the passes over his bed so that no one will hear when he fumbles, lets something drop. Eventually, he doesn't need the bed.

And the boy saves up again, this time for the mirror which he carries carefully, painfully back from the high street and into his room. It makes his mother laugh and talk about girlfriends while his dad frowns and the boy feels jangled and compressed.

The following Sunday, as they walk to the paper shop, his dad describes girls and girls' habits. The description requires three circuits of the play park with the rusty swings—right to the bottom trees and back, three times—because it is long and detailed. Although the boy has met girls at school and mainly not given them much thought, his father makes of them dangerous strangers and causes for concern. They will not grow into women like Dusty Springfield, someone the boy is very fond of and believes would be nice, even if she does wear spacewoman dresses and have frightening hair. In fact, perhaps *because* of that, he really does quite fancy her a bit. His father says the girls will have nothing in common with Dusty, won't be *gorgeous.* Or, if they are, this *will not be good news.*

Once they have made it to the shop, his dad asks the boy if he would like to spend this week's chocolate and comic money and the boy tells him that it's all right for today and *no* and *thank you—* because he has plans to buy a thumb tip and other indecently, nakedly misleading and deceiving stuff from the wonderful shop that smells of cigarettes and men and badness and which is called *J. Cooper & Son's Magic,* although there is no J.

Cooper and there aren't any sons. His dad gets him a Crunchie anyway, which isn't normal and so the boy eats it too fast on the way back home before anybody can notice and doesn't enjoy it.

When they are just inside the cool of the entrance— looking at where Mrs Barker keeps her flower tubs which the squirrels dig at *because they are bastards*— the boy's father hugs him and closes a hand around one of his ears and rubs it a bit, as if he might make it disappear, and then his dad looks at him and whispers, 'Arthur, always be careful.' And he kisses the top of the boy's head and asks him, almost too quietly to be heard, 'Will you do that?' And Arthur— the boy's name is Arthur, an old-fashioned name, it gets him grief at school—he nods, although he feels that he won't manage. His magic won't be adequate for girls.

Arthur lives in a ground floor flat beside a roundabout which has daffodils on it in spring and once a bloke on it in the summer, pretending to sunbathe for a laugh. The flat is in London—sort of—but not so that Arthur can notice. He is a train and a bus ride or two bus rides and an Underground away from anything notable or on postcards. There is no Big Ben and no ravens and no palace at the end of his street and when he goes to visit these things they do not belong to him any more than to anyone else and this means they make him annoyed, rather than proud or excited. His mother lives with him. She is unhappy. And his dad is there—his tall and blond and wiry father who is striking but will eventually be quite difficult to recall. His father is also unhappy.

But Arthur is happy—he makes sure to be.

And Arthur's hands are both delirious. They are

126

overjoyed.

And Arthur loves them.

First night aboard and Beth dreams in numbers. She has edged herself into the bed, curls on her side away from contact, takes care that her chill won't wake Derek, her salt chill.

Which it would—I would disturb him.

Because I'm frozen. I haven't a warm place.

Not really.

And he needs to rest.

And he doesn't need to feel there's something wrong with me, all over me, and he won't, because I'm the only one who'll notice that. My secret.

And Arthur's.

No. Just mine. I allow it to happen and it belongs to me.

I used to share it and now I don't.

*I used to be . . . walking in the street and nothing showing, respectable—riot inside, though, mayhem—with any memory of him, every memory of him—I couldn't predict what of Arthur would hit me or when—as if I'd walk straight into him, like rain—his hands on my shoulders and the press of him behind—or the shape of his fingers—confident, talkative fingers: snug. Trying to stroll and worrying I might fall with the sense of him, the knowledge of him. And I'd smile, because no one could tell and I would think—**Here's me and I'm covered in him and nobody knows it**.*

He clings and aims to be ingrained.

Like smoke.

Like water.

127

Like the scent of him.

Not that he doesn't take care to be unperfumed, neutral. But he's there all the same, he's there on you when he's left—delicate.

He finds your bones, soaks in.

Bastard.

And she has no hopes of sleep, expects simply to lie and recite and recite: *loving the unlovable is stupid, is self-harm—loving the reasonable is what I need and I can have that. I do have that. I can prefer that because I am not an idiot.*

Which depresses her because she won't believe it.

I am not an idiot.

Except when I am an idiot.

Bastard.

Sleep does arrive, though, unexpected—a strangely rapid kindness she pushes into, under. But then it turns shallow, of course, and relentless. The force of unease turns her on to her back and the bed nags and sickens beneath her and Arthur—

Bastard.

Creeping bastard—always pesters.

Arthur stands there in her mind. He's fidgeting and wears his overcoat and is occasionally crying, which she would rather not see. And with salt fingers, cold and blunt fingers, dead man's fingers, he reaches forward and summons numbers from the air—empty hand passing them deftly to empty hand—and then he puts each figure in her mouth.

She hasn't forgotten—couldn't forget—the lists of meanings, the translations for each one.

One.

Listen, please.

It's useful, one. It can slip into any sentence, any one you choose, and it can ask you.

128

Please listen.

It marks out the start of the story and Arthur's a man who wants all of the story, all of the time. He wouldn't like to miss a word.

And, then again, he's happier yet when it can mean **Look at me**—when we're working from the second list, the personal list: The Code for Peculiar People in Public Places.

He loves it if you look—shy and then not, absolutely not, lying out for your attention, blazing with it.

Favours dark sheets: purples, blues—he brings them with him to every hotel, asks the staff to remake the bed with them—give us something other than the standard white. He's the one paying—paying too much—paying for special attentions—so he gets to pick.

And once he brought black: black sheets, black towels, black curtains, black everything.

Like being exiled into night.

And Arthur lying on the night, showing the light of himself, the milk light.

Look at me.

For special occasions.

Buttoned tight, otherwise. Won't even roll up his sleeves. Then it's clever talk and numbers and playing games.

Look at me while I'm hiding, find me, come hunting, and then I'll know you love me, that it's true.

He knows too many games.

And he's too much work.

And he **ought** to always hide and be ashamed. And why **should** I fucking find him? He's nothing to do with me: shouldn't be anything to do with me. He's a Bank Holiday shag, he's play-acting pickups in hotel lobbies, he's a duplex suite with a fruit bowl and two

129

tellies when all we need is a bed, because we just fuck—no more to us than fucking, not now.

Every night a one-night stand.

Look at me.

But then she swallows **Five** which is peppery and has thin edges and is **Help** which is what she needs, but doesn't get. Or else it's **Come**, which is what she needs, but shouldn't get, because people can use it for cheating and taking things away from idiots.

Time was, they could both be together—Beth and Arthur in company—and they could ask this of themselves and make an answer. **Come.** They could both deliver and request. They could watch for the twitch of a smile, or the colour rising, the approach. They could enjoy understanding and being understood.

Out of my mind, but into yours, very into yours, and your wish is my command and vice versa.

Takes training.

And the insanity to think of training.

And no cheating—because we'll know . . .

Beth and Arthur.

In her dream she wants to see his face, because she believes it might be informative, but all she gets a sight of is his wrist, the flat back of his wrist.

And no more commands and no more wishes—they don't come true.

Arthur never did a true thing in his life.

A man you should not look at, except from far away, should not be permitted to touch.

Man is **Two**.

Tastes sweet—over-sweet—a memory growing, laid on her tongue, and it ought to be salt, it ought to be forgotten.

Man.

Long-shinned, long-footed—soft give of the skin at his throat: feels all alive—and the tuck of the muscle in over his hip: that curve, that line—and he's blond, but then a little darker, coppery too, where the strangers don't see him, what they don't get.

Two.

Clean, clean shaven—or the bristle of him in the dark—early morning—and kissing the insides of his thighs and breathing him in—hot—roaring—the shine of the boy—pale boy—silky boy—like saying silk—to lick.

Two.

And otherwise, and naturally, it's **Smile at me**.

It bloody would be.

And it would be easy to keep herself in this now, concentrate on the pictures of how he can be. This once, she would risk it, indulge it—half awake and with Derek beside her—but the dream of him feeds her **Eight**—pushes it in with his thumb—fat and slippy—**Accident**.

Always needed it for the punters—got to cue each other in so we can tell them how their loved ones left: the car, the motorcycle, ambushing workplace, fate—acknowledge the endlessly amputated plans. Rude of them, the dead—hurtful to rush away without ever saying, ever mentioning, ever finishing what they started. Untidy. We do hate to have it untidy. And we hate to know our dead have torn things that we can't survive without. They have stolen who we are when we are with them—our good selves, our beauty.

*And **Eight** is **No**.*

No.

*The other **Eight**.*

An almost entirely powerless word in life. You can scream it as long as you want, but matters will still work on as they must, reality will still ignore you. You're flesh in the mechanism, caught in its gears.

No.

*But when it meant **Later** and **Persuade me** and **At the moment, I'd like it if I was in charge**, then we loved it—horny word—the **no** in between us—tickling.*

Christ.

Christ, we fucked up.

He fucked up.

He is fucked up.

And she dreams herself away from Arthur, tears things about which she does not wish to think and moves away, free. Relatively free.

Bastard.

Awake. I want to be awake.

I'm not, though.

It's that thing—I'm in that thing you get when you can't move and you're not awake, you only think you're awake, but you're wrong. You're dreaming.

I think I'm wrong.

She's in a fluid version of her past. Its edges ripple and dart forward. It makes her tense.

And she's queuing to board the boat again and outraged for some unnamed reason—she's close to retching with disgust—and she picks up a little bag, heavy bag—which isn't hers, or else it is, but she can't recognise it—and then she flings it—intends to make a large and savage gesture but releases too early, her effort swinging wild and to her left and then she spins round after it and sees him—Arthur—again Arthur—and he's sitting—gently sitting—and the bag has hit him, landed in his lap, and he is instantly, immeasurably sad, which is her fault.

Hit him in the balls with my baggage—my baggage which is emotional.

Well, whatever could I possibly mean by that?
Fucksake.

And, although she is additionally outraged by her subconscious's lack of finesse, she responds to the scene and tries to make amends for Arthur's hurt—but there's no way through to touch him, only sudden crowds that intervene. She can't offer consolation. There is only this obvious, accusing damage: him sobbing with his arms hugging the bag and rocking, shuddering—and then he's scrabbling in his pockets, he's desperate, he wants to show her something but can't find it.

Seven.
Not my fault.
Seven.
It was an accident.
Eight.
Or else it was his fucking fault for being in the way, for being here in the first place.
He's looking for **seven.**
I'm not. I don't expect it.
And it's not my fault that he's in the way.
It's not my fault we're in each other's way.

His hands are clearly fighting with pockets that seal and shrink.

That's what you get with tailor-made: bespoke and wilful.

He lifts his head and blinks at her and is panicking and lost. He wakes her with a look.

Love.
Always the same on any list.
Seven.
Forget every other number, you could still manage a sitting, an evening, a seance, with just that.
Not that it needs a number. It's the constant.

No matter how well the enquirers lie, you can still see it in them—**seven**'s what they want, their heart's request. Why else would they come? They need you to *tell them the loves they felt were real, that the cruelty was love misunderstood, the absent affection was only hidden, that every love has been continued, will be endless. They want the dead bound hand and foot to them, chained in love.*

Which is expecting a lot of the deceased. One minute they're live human beings: fickle, silly, irritating, gorgeous, flawed—the next they're supposed to be perfect and content to adore us for ever. Nothing better to do with eternity than watch us, see everything we are and worship it.

When nobody ought to see everything we are, because they couldn't stand it.

Seven.

The best of the games and somewhere in every one of the games. Passing it between them like a note. Arthur and Beth. Beth and Arthur.

'Snow White and the Seven Dwarfs—scared me witless when I was a kid—something about the dwarfs' hats—and the pickaxes.'

Civilians not included.

'Canal holiday—boating on the Avon. Or the Severn. No, the Avon. No, the Severn. Perhaps both. It's big, the Severn. Fucking huge.'

Becoming somewhat notorious for babbling and non sequiturs, mispronunciations . . .

'I don't know if that seven is legal.'

Civilians not capable.

'Five Seven Eleven—my gran adored that. Any time of day, you'd go in—the bedroom would be full of it.'

Changing the name of the perfume to fit. Not Four Seven Eleven. That wouldn't suit them. So it's

134

Five
Seven
Eleven
Come
Love
Be beautiful
But people change.
They can't endlessly be what someone else requires, it wears them out.
So I am tired, tired, tired. I have 888 reasons for being tired, tired, tired.

Beth gets up, showers quietly, goes and sits in her complimentary bathrobe and watches the next day arrive in shades of slate. The irregular shatter of large weather is comforting as it jars the ship's spine and then hers.

She stares and imagines nothing, a beige blank, until she hears Derek stirring. Then she calls up room service for coffee—no breakfast, they'll neither of them want it—and she steps over to start coaxing at her partner—her registered with US Immigration and the shipping line official partner, the man she is supposed to be with, the man that she currently *is* with—starts cajoling her partner into sips of water and another pill.

Outside Beth's cabin, passengers stagger and shoulder walls as the ship bounces, shrugs. There are little impacts and the blurred melodies of hearty chat, or sympathy, or good mornings. And the staff will smile, because this is compulsory and they will polish and dust and varnish and paint unendingly, because this is also required and the seafaring way—otherwise chaos would triumph, water and hard weather would eat the ship.

Inside Beth's cabin, she is trying to be both hearty and sympathetic and has already said good morning. 'You're rallying.' Keeping the chaos at bay.

'I'm fucking not.'

'You don't look as green.'

'I've got a headache like you wouldn't believe.'

'Dehydration. Drink some more.'

'If I drink any more I'll be sick.'

They decide that being dressed might raise their spirits and so Elizabeth helps Derek to abandon his sweated-through pyjamas, encourages him into the shower and nods when he props himself back on the bed in a soft checked shirt and old cords.

He draws up his knees, glares weakly. 'What are you nodding about? Passed inspection, have I? I'm the one who had to do it all. That shower's a fucking joke—like being pissed on by an ugly bird.' He isn't usually coarse in this way—he is trying to annoy her.

And it's good that he has the energy to be annoying—although it is also annoying.

She rubs his arm. 'They say looking at the horizon—'

'Who say?'

'I don't remember. I heard it on the radio, I think.'

'You think . . .'

He is being petulant and insulting, but that's all right; she knows him and is sure he would be noble with a broken leg or a serious infection, something dignified with which he could contend. Seasickness is distasteful and pathetic and yet overwhelming, it has him rattled.

Nevertheless, she permits herself, 'If you're going

to be an arse about this, you can fucking well stay as you are. But getting outside and focusing on the horizon is meant to be good and we could have a go, couldn't we? And you could cope with the yard or so from here to the balcony and then we'll see what happens.'

'I'll get pneumonia is what'll happen.' He grins, though—makes a brave little halfway attempt—the good lad doing his best.

He's a fighter, Derek: gets in the ring and keeps swinging, even when there's nothing to hit.

A fighter, not a lover.

And why is it those are the rock and roll choices?

*Why not, **I'm an actuary, not a fighter** . . . ?*

And why don't you fucking focus on the task in hand?

She wavers across the carpet with Derek, arm-in-arming it, the pair of them in no fit state.

Lover: fighter—they picked the maiming occupations. Obvious. There's more drama in the fatal undertakings, the wastes.

And what are we? One of each? Two of both?

She almost falls and, as might have been expected, complicates the possible reasons why.

It's not the ocean. I'd be unsteady in any case.

Bastard.

Recovery time—you shouldn't need it just because you've looked at someone, listened to him, touched his arm.

I used to think I'd end up feeling ruined because of the physical thing, the exertion—nice word for it—because of the two or three days of fucking against his choice of high-class backdrops. I thought that's what it was.

The luxury screwing.

137

And Christ knows where he's staying on board—or what he originally planned. He maybe intended a hideaway here for me, while his suite has the resident unicorn, the lapis lazuli bathroom and Fabergé bed . . . Or maybe he'd have coffined us in together and no pretence: six nights and seven days, same bed.

Did Fabergé ever make beds ?

Oh, fuck this.

Beth cracks her knuckles against the frame of the balcony door, just hard enough to order her thoughts.

'Careful.' Derek produces a grin. 'We don't have to punch our way out.'

'Hm? No, no, of course . . . Silly. And here we go . . .'

Needle rain catches them once they've emerged in the open air. But mostly the air isn't open, or too unruly: they're boxed in by secluding panels to either side and sheltered by the balcony above. They are only mildly buffeted unless they actually crane out over the rail and ask for punishment. Which Elizabeth does.

Like being slapped.

Which I don't.

And I have nothing to be penitent about.

Already been punished. Meeting Arthur is always its own punishment—pleasure and pain and immediate payment for both.

He prefers things to be self-contained—even when they're my things.

I'm self-contained enough to scream—which makes it easier to leave him—and almost impossible. Every time.

***Seven** days and **six** nights.*

That would have been unsurvivable. Don't know what he was thinking—but I can guess. At his bloody

138

games again.

***Love** days.*

*And **Fuck me** nights.*

***Love** days.*

*And **Betrayal** nights.*

*Comes up a good deal with punters—**six**—betrayal being so commonplace in life. Like fucking. Hand in glove.*

And seven and six is too long no matter how you say it.

Seven and six makes thirteen and that's unlucky.

It's all unlucky.

Because it's him that's the problem, not what we do—it's being too close to him—it makes me ill.

Fucking Arthur—he's like catching flu.

Ideally, Beth should sit with Derek on the two metal chairs provided—just right for a couple—with matching metal table—and gaze out in refreshing circumstances. She's even brought a towel with them to wipe everything down, but the rain dodges back to whichever surface she dries off and, after a while, Derek tells her to stop. 'We can lean. It's good, leaning.' And he rests against the closed door, folds his arms, studies the far horizon with what do indeed appear to be beneficial results.

Elizabeth returns to the rail, sees the ocean mounding round them and faulted into ridges, lines of stress, as if the ship is caught and sliding in a bowl of black glass, hammering and hammering against such a depth and height of glass.

And she shouldn't have drunk all the coffee, methodically worked down the pot to busy herself, because the caffeine is scrambling in her now, dialling up intensities she can't afford.

Get yourself over your sleepless night with exactly

139

what will guarantee your next and also set a panic rubbing underneath your skin. I never learn.

Clearly.

'Do you want to try exploring?' Derek seems pinker and more assured. 'I might be able . . .'

Which is a good idea. Exercise will be calming.

And avoiding the rest of the ship would be eccentric, inexplicable. Why wouldn't it be entertaining to survey the decks? That should prove both informative and bracing. There could even be the risk of lunch. An attempt . . .

'Elizabeth?'

Somehow the day has slipped until it is almost late enough for lunch.

She can hear Derek shifting, pulling open the balcony door. 'I hope we don't see that guy again, though—the meat-eater. I could do without him.' Feral weather leaps in the cabin's curtains, lifts the ship's newspaper, starts up small howls as it fills their room and hunts and searches for ways further into the ship.

Beth nods, still facing the ocean, letting it hurt her.

The liner has kept itself amused without them. They have already missed classes in bridge and computing, several talks on health and beauty (naturally for the ladies) and on maritime history and engineering (even more naturally for the gents) and at least one quiz.

And the bingo.

But nowhere is quite as photogenically busy as it

should be. There is about the decks, the areas for leisure opportunities and the shops, an air of relinquished hope. Hunched passengers sit here and there in frozen contemplation of their own unreliable interiors. Healthy wives mouth news of their afflicted husbands over said husbands' mournful heads. Healthy husbands bashfully destroy plates of sandwiches in the lovingly recreated Olde Englishe Pub while their wives stare fixedly out of windows full of grey unwieldy shapes and disturbances. There is little chatter and the good cheer of the untroubled is slightly too strident. Nobody's plans are going to plan.

Elizabeth leads Derek on a mild ascent through the vessel's layers until they emerge in the gentlest location for more coffee: what appears to be a large hothouse for the propagation of geriatrics. Beyond the glass walls there are sturdy funnels, cables, antennae and receivers murmuring or bleating as they part and bewilder the wind. Overhead the sky races fiercely and underfoot the floor misbehaves as it seems set to for the duration, and yet here is only moist warmth and generous pot plants, cane chairs with footstools, cane tables, motionless figures under rugs and a bar decorated along tropical lines, forlornly suggesting late nights, cleavages, reckless cocktails and Caribbean flirting. A small man with a moustache lurks behind the bar, resigned to preparing tea, coffee and possibly cocoa, perhaps even Ovaltine. Elizabeth imagines him spending his evenings in a storeroom somewhere, stroking his boxes of novelty plastic straws and coloured paper umbrellas, counting the jars of unused maraschino cherries, wishing himself or his circumstances gone when neither can be altered.

141

'Shall I order you a banana daiquiri, just to cheer him up?'

'What?' Derek hasn't responded well to his journey and has laid himself flat and closed-eyed on a sun lounger.

'To cheer up the barman—a daiquiri . . .'

'Would kill me.'

'Bovril?' Which wasn't funny, so she shouldn't have said it. She shouldn't have said it, even if it was funny. He's upset—like the rest of the passengers: all of them being shaken until they break.

Derek has started taking each jolt personally, grim. 'It's not going to stop, is it?' He is gripping the sides of his seat.

'I don't know. I mean, I can ask. But the last announcement was . . .' The last announcement was uncompromisingly certain that the storm would continue today and then worsen tomorrow and be unabated the day after that. They both heard it—that was the point of the Ship's Announcements— everyone was meant to hear them. Although if you were suffering dry heaves at the time, you might be inattentive.

'I'll get you some warm water.'

And Elizabeth keeps her word—is honest and does just that—brings him back a cautiously half-full mug of something comforting and hydrating and sits beside him and wonders if she should give him another pill, because that might help, but it does say on the 'read before taking' leaflet that they might provoke headaches—headaches and nightmares, in fact, among other things—and the next dose allowed would be three hours from now and an overdose would probably be awful.

An overdose of nightmares.

So she goes and finds the stack of blankets and brings one to unfold across his legs, this joining him to the rest of the room, to the sense that some catastrophe has happened elsewhere, is still occurring, but here are the survivors and a peace to contain them and an idea of waiting.

Unclear if we're waiting for worse things or for better.

She strokes the flat back of Derek's wrist and he smiles, so she continues, takes sips of a coffee the barman made her—the last thing she needs, more coffee, should have had decaf—and an elderly woman with very red lipstick and overly whitened skin reads an Agatha Christie by herself and another, larger lady—nicely dressed, but with swollen ankles and feet: ugly shoes for her misshapen feet: and this means she is probably dying, is being murdered by a failing heart—scribbles at a puzzle book and there are yawns and there is dozing and there is full and deep and unembarrassed sleep—faces turned softer and younger, parted lips, the grace of unselfconsciousness.

And Beth remembers being with her parents at Blackpool, way out at the end of a pier in a glass garden like this—filled with deckchairs and with sleepers and with mediated daylight.

Black tie and ball gowns for the evening, but what is the ship when we come right down to it? Just the end of a pier in motion, cast adrift. Shows with a chorus and pretty bets you shouldn't make, and wear and tear dulling the glamour and souvenirs and someone who'll tell you your fortune, someone who'll pretend that he knows who you are, what you'll do.

Enough of that.

Eventually, she feels Derek's muscles surrender, his forearm drops and he's away with the others—dreaming.

I hope simply dreaming—not anything bad. No nightmares.

This means she is left to be hungry and—why not?—she goes to the buffet—why not?—it's on the same level, not far, and she needs to eat. She has no suspicious motivations.

I can get a roll, or something. Soup. Derek wouldn't want to watch me deal with soup. I'll give him peace.

And she wanders in between the largely deserted counters of vegetables under heat lamps, noodles, rice, meat—no one here she recognises—tiny oblongs of gelatinous desserts, meat, pastas, fruit platters, meat—no one she knows—an obscenely generous selection of untouched foods, fastidiously arranged. Meat.

I suppose in a while they'll take away the stuff no one ate for lunch and replace it all with stuff no one will eat for dinner.

A few souls gaze out at the storm, picking at cakes, sipping unruly liquids. She does not particularly try to find last night's table, but there it is, in any case—empty and apparently no more or less pleasant than its neighbours, no different.

While Elizabeth waits for a sandwich to be constructed from the freshest possible ingredients according to the line's traditions of fine dining, someone pads in to stand beside her.

Not him, though. It's not him.

'Hello.'

This knowledge swooping so hard through her that, for the first time, she does feel herself unsteadied by the ship, assaulted.

By her shoulder is the older gentleman from the photo shoot: this time dressed in a navy jacket and

144

comfortable planters and just faintly amused by how he has come to be in such a costume—blazer and slacks—and of an age when it might be deemed appropriate. He grins. 'I'm Francis.'

The good husband.

'Never Frank. Don't like it.' He is laden with packages of crackers, some of which he now pockets so that he can shake her hand. 'Hello. Yes.' He leans in, comfortable with being conspiratorial. 'It always seems like theft when you put them in your pocket— even though we have already paid . . . Even though we could eat it all and ask for more and they would have to let us . . .' And at this he gives her the full smile of someone who is decent and prefers to be kind and have fun and who can no longer be bothered hiding it. 'You know . . . if you're by yourself, we're just round there—past the very, very empty pizza stall—nobody inclines to pizza in a Force Nine gale, apparently—and my wife is round there and I will be directly—we're having cheese with many more crackers than we need and not quite enough fruit.' He begins to assume the role of dithering old man, enjoying it. 'Do you think if I gave you some grapes to carry . . . ? I really should just find a tray . . . Only if you'd like company. Only if you're alone.'

Elizabeth is alone.

'Bunny and I, we've heard everything that we could possibly say to each other by now. We long for strangers.'

Elizabeth is exhausted and badly wired with caffeine and quickly, sour and quickly, intolerably alone.

He cocks his head, pauses, and Beth knows he is seeing something in her that she would rather he

145

could not. 'We draw the line at kidnapping, of course.'

And he pauses again, blinks, softly cups her elbow with his hand.

So he'll feel the bone—little bone, big bone, little bone . . . But please don't wake me.

'Your sandwich is ready—looks very nice. You should have it with us. Is that decided? I think it should be decided.' Saying this while he looks away and is overly pleased with what should be her lunch. He concentrates on it utterly and so allows her to be unobserved, but strengthens his grip for an instant to show her she's still thought of before he lets go. 'Perhaps if you wanted to fetch the grapes . . . ?' And this allows her to be in motion and only to glimpse enough of his next smile to be sure that it's too intent. If he's actually concerned about her she shouldn't see it. Otherwise she knows she'll have to cry.

Francis gathers a tray and welcomes the grapes, checks Elizabeth's eyes once and sharply and then hands her the finished sandwich and walks her across to share his table, along with a lady who does indeed turn out to be called Bunny.

Classy silver necklace—he bought it for her: she has other things, but this will be her favourite—it is obviously meaningful and sweet—Arthur would classify it as literally sweet, he'd file it away in his mind as candyfloss, toffee, syrup: make it memorable like that—and I bet it has earrings to match it and they'll dress up tonight and she'll wear them. They'll dance. They'll both be movers—there and grown up for the sixties and taking part, so they'll know how. Elegant, though—you don't often see that, not for real. But she shouldn't wear black—it makes her look poorly.

146

Bunny is poorly.

'It's silly, we do realise.' The wife as pleasant as the husband. 'You can laugh if you want. It's all right.' Hair drawn back, but not severely, in a complicated curl.

He'll like when she lets it down. Will always have liked it. **Bunny, let your hair down. That's the way. Thank you.**

The husband as pleasant as the wife, 'Why would she want to laugh? If you were called Ermintrude, she might want to laugh. But Bunny is a perfectly reasonable form of address for a person.' And he fires a lopsided glance at Bunny, hot and fast. 'More suitable than Doreen, which—as you very well know—we never took to.' His voice delicate as the sentence ends. 'There being a number of things to which we don't take.'

'Francis . . .' Bunny scolding without scolding, pursing her lips so she doesn't laugh. 'We mustn't alarm our new friend.'

'No. No, we mustn't. And we won't.'

Neither of them doing it by numbers. They don't need them.

Elizabeth concentrates on biting, chewing, swallowing, biting again—on bread and meat and meat—while Bunny and Francis continue to be cleanly and plainly and purely just what they appear to be and also remain determined to accept her as herself.

They are kind to her.

They are honestly and uncomplicatedly kind to her.

Which is why she does, finally, weep.

And then Elizabeth ran away.

Which is a thing she doesn't do.

Not often.

I didn't scare them—worried them, but didn't scare them—crying too much. Francis, he expected it and that made Bunny expect it, too and **No, no, not all—we quite understand.**

Francis anxious to ease and excuse. 'It's this weather. Quite atrocious, I'll speak to the captain and have it changed.' So that her sobs start to shudder her more effectively than the deck and she has to go, to bolt.

Couldn't make him watch me fragment. Couldn't do that to a decent man, a normal man.

'We've done as much.' He's determined to understand.

Bunny also: 'I've done more.'

'Both of us have gone quite completely to pieces and in front of people we didn't know from Adam. Honestly.'

'So do stay.'

'Yes, please stay. It's all right.'

Not a chance of it, though. Battering out through the tables and down and down and down.

Fuckit.

Still going.

Fuckit.

I am not just getting clear of them and clear of the help they might want to suggest which can't actually be of any help and which I can't stand because I'm beyond helping, but would rather not remember that.

I am not just running, I'm looking.

I'm looking for him.

Idiot.
Idiot.
Idiot.
Always the same.

And every window that she blurs past is monochrome and raging and around her the lights are trying to be golden, but seeming sad and there is music from the floor below—ridiculously pretty music—and Elizabeth is too dishevelled, she is having too large an emotion not to be noticed, remarked upon, but this doesn't matter, because she is searching and not finding—this is her humiliation, that she is clearly scouring, chasing after something she can't get—this is her paying the proper penalty, her shame.

For sin, or for rejecting sin.
For him, or for rejecting him.
And there is no sign of him.
He hasn't left a trace.
Predictable.
He disappears.
Another game.
Or the end of the games.
I didn't go to his room with him and so he's staying there without me.
He is somewhere without me.
Predictable.
And he loves predicting.
*He puts a piece of paper in his pocket every day. He writes the day's date on it and then—**On this date I predict that Arthur P. Lockwood will die. Yours sincerely, Arthur P. Lockwood.***
He'll carry on until he's right.
Has a game for all occasions.
Even the one he'll never see.
He showed me the note once and explained it. But

149

he didn't predict that I'd slap him as soon as I read it.

Only time I ever hit him—terrible to hit him—never should. It was the shock. Arthur there and promising to die.

She jars herself through the drop of another staircase, then paces beside the dance floor—a dozen or so couples are dipping and bending inside piano music, accommodating to the ship as it kicks and slides, gives them new steps, propels them. Their bodies remember the turns and reverses and beats they learned decades ago, they fill the ghosts of how they moved and smiled at weddings, dinner dances, parties, birthdays, anniversaries.

Not at funerals—not the custom.

The women are dignified and competitive, dressed to make the most of what they no longer quite have, and they're tenacious, brisk—echoing who they were with stronger bones and different skins. They largely dance with each other, because there are not enough men.

The men die fast, die soonest, leave us. We are made to be durable and therefore abandoned.

Except Bunny. She'll die before Francis. It wasn't just the black of the pullover, she has something quietly hollowing her out and they are here for the last cruise, the grand gesture—they are making him something to hold, for afterwards.

The feel of her palm wrapped round his finger and tight and the pulse in it and the heat—like fitting himself inside her, but discreet—they'd enjoy that: could promenade anywhere and no one need understand it, or notice it but them.

It would be something to remember.

A thought to burn him later—to hurt in his own

150

palm, crucify him with her being nowhere he can reach.

Poor Francis.

Poor all of them.

However much money, however much they own or want to own, outside the cold is beating a way in, has all of their names.

I really shouldn't hate them as much as I do.

And she fights to slow herself—breathe, walk—until she sees them properly: all the silly, distracted people who are like her: who will die. They will dress up for special occasions and be pompous, or lovely, inadequate, languid, dull and they will make mistakes and be afraid and enjoy jokes and treats and surprises and maybe their children and then they will stop.

Which makes them wonderful.

Think of how rare they are and tender, of how they are extraordinary—no chance of escaping and still they do all this.

Makes you love them.

Makes you unable not to offer them a broad, indiscriminate love.

That's Arthur's trick, though—so he can love his enquirers into openness, trust. When he actively considers their frailty, it becomes irrelevant if he dislikes them, loathes them—because love is his only appropriate response. He loves them and they know it and that means they will let him burrow in.

He'd be ready for Francis. He'd take the good husband's hand and fold his own around it, press his thumb into its heart, touch where it's bleeding.

That's how he'd start.

Some people can sit in a café and drink coffee by themselves, be nakedly alone, eat teacakes, or something quite fiddly like pasta and they'll be fine.

But you might not be—not every day, not no matter what.

Sometimes you'll look at the café people, their bodies assured and all being well with them, as far as you can judge, and you'll think—*Who are you? How do you manage?* Because it appears they do manage very nicely, while it can seem, now and then, that you do not.

Walking across foyers, into unfamiliar rooms, half-empty restaurants, waiting for the first steps of a first date, being in parties with too many faces you don't know—you can find it taxing. But social anxiety is commonplace, a kind of bond, because you've worked out, of course you've worked out, that your discomfort is often caused by the equal, if not more profound, unease of others. And you've wished you could just announce—*we are scared here in this situation—whatever it is—all of us nervy and being tender-skinned precisely when we should not and although we are adults we feel we would like to run now or burst into tears—big children in stupid clothes who ought to be well-presented but aren't and can't think how they could be and this is, quite literally, painful and we should stop*—but you never have mentioned a word of this: you have only talked nonsense while voices pitched oddly and objects were dropped and the room became irritable or desperate for a drink, for several drinks, for anybody it could really talk to.

Because it can be complicated, having fun.

Not that you can't go out alone: to browse in a furniture store, for example, or anywhere else you might wish—take a stroll in the park, or see a movie without the bother of somebody else—it's possible to relish that kind of thing, as a change, as a rest.

The café situation, though—it can niggle. You have, if you're honest, sat there and wondered if maybe your hands weren't properly angled, if you didn't quite fit, if people who glanced at you wouldn't be horrified, wouldn't find you somehow appalling. You have felt that your aloneness might look entirely justified, deserved.

Which is why you need games—Games for Unpeculiar People in Public Places—and your book can provide them here, would like to help.

c) You can sip your coffee, tea, or beverage of choice—perhaps decaffeinated—and believe you are taking a short break from pressing busyness. This will always be, to some degree, the case and not a thoroughgoing lie—and, as your belief convinces you and others, check your watch with an air of gentle irritation, indulgence: you wish your life weren't so demanding, but what can you do . . . ?

This will seem much less unfortunate than sipping something on your own and, in an unforgiving world, what can be wrong with reassuring falsehoods?

But try not to give the impression that you're actually waiting for someone. They will—naturally, because you *aren't* waiting for them—be unable to arrive and this may seem sad to your observers.

Another option, then.

d)   Should you have such a thing about you, there's always your phone to bring relief. It can provide the necessary chore of weeding out your messages, or just reviewing them, reflecting on the fact that several people, people who know you, have formerly made efforts to get in touch—some of them wholly unsolicited. Thinking this, projecting this satisfaction, can be warming and easily done. Or you can text a random friend to say you're bored—you need not mention being solitary—and then you can smile quietly, as if you are in love, as if you have just done something new about your love. This will be additionally warming and will make you appear more attractive. Not that you aren't attractive and may not genuinely be in love and entirely appreciated: it's simply that your love is not here and not now. So you need a touch of proof, witnesses, reassurance. A gently enhanced presentation will mean you seem accurately yourself.

Although there is always the danger that, if your love is an absence or else a repeated mistake, the darkness of this may creep in and cloud you. Or it may happen that nobody calls you or texts you back. Not that you needn't still pretend they have.
    Being publicly ignored is, once again, sad.
    And miming that you have a small phone palmed in your hand when actually you don't, going through the motions—that would be even sadder. Don't do that.

h) Make little notes on scraps of paper—frowning, serious lips—as if an especially vital point has sprung to mind and must be recorded.

Or make the effort to carry a laptop and use it—behave as if you're doing business, an unassuming figure at the heart of invisible empires, or someone who's working on sonnets, a biography of Houdini, a *roman-à-clef* with more keys than a piano and no locks.

Which would be very, very, very sad.
So perhaps not writing.
Reading then: that's involving, that's company.

i) Study the menu, or flyers, advertisements, scan through orphaned newspapers and wonder who's held them before—let this consume your time with a merry glow.

And bringing your own paperwork need not appear defeatist: you can peruse your chosen material as if it is challenging, abstruse, work-related, essential to a course of study—or else something you can demonstrate, with plentiful nods and grins, as exceptional, a book that everyone sensible should be reading. It would be good if any covers or bindings involved could be stylish.

l) Play yourself preoccupying music—pipe it in gently through whichever headphones you prefer. Make it clear that you are enjoying yourself, that you inwardly thrum.

Don't simply stare into space as you might quite reasonably do while listening to something not unpleasant—this will make you look mentally stunted. But don't enjoy yourself too vehemently, either—not if you're over twenty-five. Avoid anything beyond mild finger-drumming and possibly foot-tapping. Mouthing lyrics, graphic physical commitments, the playing of imagined instruments—these are all to be eschewed.

Don't begin to fret in case your isolation indicates that parts of your life have gone wrong or astray.

That would be intolerably sad.

m) So you should turn the ugly pressure of being observed into observation—watch the other customers and staff and stand aloof from your species.

This will allow you to see that—let's say—couple G are in the first six months of a warm, but rather juvenile pairing—that couple E have not had sex, but are going to soon, although she is less interested than he is—that child N is a sociopath and his mother O isn't helping. She is swayed by his blue, blue eyes and his fair, fair hair and he's already using his beauty thuggishly, enjoys worship, believes every other woman he meets should offer it and that he should be perpetually able to do what he'd like.

But conversely, a not dissimilar child shouldn't be neglected. No one, for instance, should hold back her motherlove from a clever blond boy, or never fully meet her son's extraordinary eyes full of sea and want. This would harm him. It might drive a probably unpeculiar soul to fold himself away and make a package, a distasteful secret, of whoever he turns out to be. A good mother would study statistics and then avoid likely causes of injury and death: traffic accidents, choking, drowning, poisons, electrocution, falls. She would be aware. And she would be kind—she would love and be amazed by him and kind; she wouldn't want him growing to believe he's been defective from the start. She wouldn't want to make him alternately abject and untrusting in affection, both angered and paralysed by inrushes of hope—in short, ruined for any other woman he might care about.

Although none of this should matter to you. It's as irrelevant as the man A who might sit there, reading a book in the coffee shop. He might be both unashamed and undemonstrative about it, just reading—could always carry a book or a paper for dining out, could usually expect to eat and drink alone, stay neither happy nor unhappy, but wholly suspended in a resignation he isn't stupid or numb enough to call content. And possibly he used to be loved and a sliver of him still expects it, is alert, betraying him to every disappointment. Touch him with sufficient gentleness and he might kindle, smile.

And that would be very intolerably sad and sad and sad.

And none of your business. You have no connection to any of the café-dwellers you'll ever watch. Because you don't watch friends. At least, you shouldn't.

But anonymous lives, their being close, can sometimes seem a kind of safety, a comfort. If you let your mind out to touch the idea of someone and hold that—who they might be—they can soothe you. They're people you can decipher, who can warm you, but you'll never have to meet.

This does no one any harm. It's not intrusive.

Strangely, if you recall when you've been most lonely, you won't think of being alone, of guessing at unknown occupations, interiors. You'll remember

157

having made an effort, perhaps being well-dressed and yet entirely certain this does nothing but highlight your obvious lacks—and there will have been crowds and laughter not your own and the shock of your friends' and of your love's inaccessibility. Those who should have been closest have stepped away.

y) Consider your love, focus, perhaps briefly close your eyes and entertain its full effect, let it come awake, flare in you like music, so it touches your sides and tickles, turns and strains against you, like the finest music—no electronic assistance necessary—like the songs that change your heart, that walk you through public places as if you're dancing, that make you feel like dancing, as if you're running out beneath close thunder and letting it lift your hair and make you dance.

But not if your love is gone, or spoiled: you couldn't bear it near your thinking then. Don't try.
Because you can't.
Shouldn't.
Can't.
Shouldn't.
Can't.
A little bit of crucifixion in each palm.
Find yourself rubbing the skin.

Elizabeth hopes to get though her afternoon by watching a film, sampling the vessel's lively schedule of current hits.

Don't think of a man A and give him a name, a line to his back and knowledgeable hands. Or if you must, then imagine that he's cultivated solitude because of his own guilt, has made sad habits by choice, prefers them, and is in no way your responsibility.

You ought to leave him to himself.

Too many things have been his choice and have been wrong, untouchable.

It's been two days.

No Arthur.

She let him go and he has gone.

Which has left her—predictably, pathetically, as if she were seventeen, and helpless and knew no better—has left her with chafing evenings, hours that gnaw, with walking and waiting in public places and drinking too much coffee, because there is no more harm caffeine can do her: she doesn't relax, she can't get sleepy, she has moved beyond espressos and their minor damages, but might as well add them to the general, miserable, bad inward thrumming. She likes their taste. She wants to have something she likes, for it to be there and simple.

Two days—not a sign of him.

Two days—***Smile at me.***

Two.

Man.

Is he trying to tell me something, or not saying anything at all?

Was this the end of it?

Derek is with her. 'It's like a fucking prison.'

159

'It's like the opposite of a prison.'

'Why are you drinking so much coffee?' Derek smells of their cabin, of stale sheets and boring skin. 'Coffee always makes you weird.' Derek beside her in the cinema.

Beth, it's true, is nursing a cardboard cup of coffee. 'I've never not drunk coffee.' She has it mainly because its warmth calms her hands, because walking with a cup has always made her feel at ease—as if she were at home in a street, or an office building, or a multi-purpose auditorium plunging forwards and forwards with a ship. 'I've never not drunk coffee. Are you saying I've never not been weird?'

'Yes.' He would have started laughing by now if he was well, if they weren't trapped, if she was better at being a nurse, or being a girlfriend. Or both.

I nurse my coffee, but not my boyfriend. What does that say about me?

What does that say about him?

Beth wanted to be here, where the air is thinned with theatrical height and inoffensive and the weather is far away and does not whip, or punch, or moan and this is a dark place where nothing half-recognised will catch her eye and then hurt her.

Derek starts again, 'No, I don't think you're weird. I think . . .' And he sounds uncantankerous and small, as if he is trying to begin a sentence that is about how his plans have foundered and that all is not well with the week and perhaps them, perhaps there is something wrong with what they are.

We don't want to deal with that, though—not with so many days still to cross. Jesus . . . Especially if it's true.

She ought to rub his shoulder, his knee, be consoling, but she's tired of not being happy with

160

him and guilty if she leaves him and is without. She is also sick of weaving him along to his sun lounger—it is now effectively his and he gets ratty if anyone else is in residence. She would like to ditch fretting beside him in the Winter Garden with the blankets, the mugs of hot water, the mayhem through the glass.

'The film will distract you—it's a boyfilm with stuff blowing up.'

'Don't fucking patronise me.' Derek is clamped in his seat, virtually phobic about motion, tensed in the face of everything he can't avoid. 'This is the bow—we're in the bow—the bow goes up and down the most—we need to be in the middle.'

And, indeed, the lighting bars hung ready for the shows (all dancing displays currently cancelled, due to bad weather, the performers being unable to leap or frolic safely on an uneven surface) and their state-of-the-art lights are creaking, swinging, while the screen sways gently in the manner of a sail on a soft day.

'If you focus on the picture, it won't move.' And she does say this patronisingly, perhaps even intends to.

I know he's ill, I know he hasn't eaten properly in a while—and I will get him to the doctor tomorrow—he can have the injection, they've said that might work—but sod this. I am not responsible for his condition.

He should complain to the captain.

Several passengers already have, made requests to the skipper suggesting he ought to do something about the waves, take steps, get them not to bang against the hull . . .

Francis would be happy to know that his joke came true—any word can work a spell.

161

Or no word—doesn't matter who you are, the weather can still fuck you. The wealthy, though—they want what they want and they have to have their say—their word.

Or else they're simply optimistic.

Maybe they just have a sunnier outlook than normal when it comes to the human condition. Maybe the wealthy just believe we can change, or survive anything.

'Fuck off.' Derek's voice flat and nasal.

Survive anyfuckingthing.

It doesn't kill you to assume that.

Just sometimes other people.

'Fuck off.'

Maybe there's something about me that seems to be leaving, left, and maybe he wants to change and deal with that—decide in advance that he hates me, then he won't mind when we're over.

That's what I'd do.

That's what I am doing.

Beth has decided to hate elsewhere: a man who sits in cafés with the one book he always carries, reads and reads it like a meditation, a repeated song—stylish cover.

A book from me.

I used to give him presents.

And he gave them to me.

Now we give each other discontent.

Could be worse. The proper subject for consideration would be what he gives to other people—Arthur—the man A, full of keys to private locks.

In he comes with gifts you shouldn't want.

There's a wife at home amongst the furniture and ornaments and all the beautiful litter of a shared life and she keeps on asking for her husband, even though she's completely aware that he is dead. And it is nothing but human to breathe and feel inside a skin that knew him and to grieve—to think with a mind that heard him and to grieve—to still carry the needs that meant she would, over and over, touch him before she could even intend it, her love faster and deeper than her will, and to grieve. And it is normal, reasonable, for her to reach out and seize absurdities once he is gone.

It is, after all, absurd that she continues and he does not.

It is much less absurd to demand he come back: to be, in that way, optimistic.

To be absurd and optimistic is not the same as being stupid.

The wife, the widow—she isn't stupid.

She is hurt.

And she is—though it seems rude to mention—a millionairess. Properties, stocks, shares, she is both cash- and asset-rich, has several millions. Lucky her.

And if there was once a probably unpeculiar soul, a boy who folded himself away and made a package, a distasteful secret, of himself—who grew in a box of his own making—then he might later have become an adult specialist in hurt. And he also might be a connoisseur, a collector, of the wounded and prosperous, might gain an interest in their fortunes. Lucky them.

Or him.

There might, of course, be innumerable times when he doesn't even mention charges as he carries out his work. He might simply make it excellent, effective and an act of love and cherish the days when his spine feels upright, evolved, and he is clean and takes pride in the services he embodies: his restoration of lives through—admittedly—grotesque and intrusive lies, but if the lies are beneficial where's the fault?

In other contexts, though, there is this compromising truth: that he has to earn a living, pay his bills. Which gives rise to the question: why not pick out a few, a ludicrously wealthy few, and have them pay for all the useful happiness of others?

And there are many reasons why not—good, sane reasons—but they may be less convincing than the discomforts inherent in poverty and powerlessness: he wouldn't wish those on anybody—including himself.

So, having made his dark decisions, his compromises, he can choose his marks.

And, for them, he becomes a smiling and attentive parasite.

He would rather not.

But he does have to.

And maybe he goes to the wife, the widow—who is called Peri Arpagian and who misses her husband, who was called Mels Arpagian. And maybe the man fixes her inside the sort of assistance that will never set her free. And maybe she knows no better and is glad and grateful to him while he manipulates and deceives her and rations the warmth of his attentions to keep her weak, because maybe he needs her to be addicted—to him—and so he makes sure to arrange it.

And this means that in many other ways he'll be tender; he'll fly to New York—where Peri lives and he mainly does not—at her request. He will get on a plane, although he loathes them—although his too many air crash seances have left him soaked with pitiful, lengthy deaths, falling and lonely screaming amongst strangers, the tumble of belongings in vicious air. There are rooms and rooms inside him filled with the abandoned living, the guilty living who still remember sick confusions of flight numbers and the way they begged reality to offer survivable options: that their loves had altered flights, that plans had changed. They prayed for the salvation in mistakes—*she might not have boarded, he did mention he might stay an extra night*. Nevertheless, the man climbs aboard to be with Peri in hours, almost whenever she says he's needed. Almost. And there are Sundays when he'll go with her to garden parties, evenings when he'll agree to dine with her at the Metropolitan Opera Club, when he'll walk her on his arm into her parterre box and then sit through the onstage posturing and repetitions: the big women shouting, the men with unruly arms, the unlikely conjugations of their fat romances.

Although he dislikes opera heartily, he never suggests that she shouldn't endow it with vertiginous sums. There is plenty of Peri to go around.

He has glanced towards the Director of Major Gifts at this or that black tie occasion and known they were both thinking—*There is plenty of Peri to go around.*

And Peri has the man's numbers and, quite often, he can talk her through an empty night and into the grey hours of morning if she wants it. His silences and absences are very rare—the minimum necessary to spike her need—because he mainly aims to please.

Then again, it's not hard to please the addicted:

165

only starve them a very, very little and then feed them their substance of choice. *Let them score and they'll adore.* And if *he* is the substance, then what could be more beautiful than the way he'll descend through the cloud cover, place his seat in the upright position, secure his tray table, grind through the landing, the trudge to Immigration—*here for pleasure, visiting a friend—yes, I do visit her a lot—nothing romantic, no, she's old enough to be my mother—no, I'm not into that*—claim his bags and then look for his name on a sign in smeary block capitals—*A. LOCKWOOD*—a nod to the limo driver holding it, and the slide out of Newark, relax and roll straight for her building, walk in and chat politely with the doorman—who is called Richard and who likes A. Lockwood, thinks of him as a friend, and invites him to head on up. And then he'll ride the elevator—art deco, all original—while it rises fifteen floors and then opens, always slightly disconcertingly, right into Peri's home, which is an apartment in Beekman Place: French antiques, bay windows, East River views and a balcony furnished with manicured shrubs.

He visits with Mrs Arpagian regularly, has cultivated her devotion, her craving, over a period of years. He has sought out her wounds and then closed himself inside them like a bullet fragment left there to corrode. And he takes care—professional and conscientious—to note her furniture and ornaments and all the beautiful litter of her previously shared life and he continues to learn from them. He is in the habit of asking to use her bathroom and then trotting about through her flat: gliding into bedrooms, armoires, closets, medicine cabinets. He has gradually fumbled and investigated every tender place within her privacy. He has made it his business—because it is his business—to gather information.

Not that she doesn't flat-out tell him virtually everything he could require without his asking. Not exactly a challenge, Peri Arpagian.

Treated me like a sickly nephew from the outset, like a lost son: patted and doted and, in her way, spoiled. Gave me a scarf—not a Patek Philippe, or a Gauguin study, or an Alfa Romeo, not any of the marvels that she could afford—just a scarf and some cake. Personal gifts—no desire to impress, or dominate.

You know that you've got them, the rich, when they give you presents anybody could, when they try to be ordinary for you.

*First time I went over, it was snowing unstoppably and the weight of Manhattan halted under it, but I'd said I would be there, so I was. I walked—for an hour—round and round, up Sixth Avenue and along, down First and along, that hideous sting every time I turned into the breeze—a punishment for what I have to do, a little fee—**I couldn't see a cab anywhere and I've never got the hang of the subway**—the subway doesn't run near there: no one who matters would want it, so it doesn't approach—**I'm so sorry, I think I'm late, am I very late?**—arrived damp, dishevelled, perished—the cruel air off the river had murdered my ears—Richard looked askance. If it hadn't been for the tailoring—has an eye for a suit, our Richard, quite the dandy on his days off—if I hadn't pointed up the British accent, then he wouldn't have let me in—expected or not.*

But arriving in genteel need, I knew she'd love that, want to fuss: summon Imée to dry out my shoes and socks, make arrangements for slippers. A man in your house in slippers—you'll keep him for longer than you

167

ought. You'll talk to him. You'll give him stories that he really shouldn't have.

I stayed the night—spot of dinner, nothing fancy, meat, veg, figs with cheese, more conversation—confide in her and she will be confiding—and then we watched a Rock Hudson movie: likes her Home Entertainments does Peri, has the Recreation Room with the walnut, out-of-tune piano and the fancy sound system with walnut speakers and the fancier projector and the specially painted wall to enhance the image and the floor-shaking speakers you know she'd enjoy even if they weren't upstairs in a two-storey, soundproofed apartment—cranks them up for Saturday mornings with Dizzy Gillespie, Benny Goodman, Artie Shaw: shivering the windows, swinging the walls back a little, waking the floor almost to dancing, almost to that— like a type of fury, her need for noise, huge music, her hunger to be touched by it. She wouldn't care if she damaged eardrums throughout the block, left her neighbours sleepless, cracked their walls.

Not that she does, but that's her choice—her behaviour is always her choice. Millionaires don't like restrictions: laws—even natural laws—are so rare an intrusion, they'll always seem clumsy, blasphemous.

After the film I'm kitted out in a dressing gown and pyjamas—not her husband's, they're from the days when she had guests, when they had guests—and then a quiet goodnight and off to sleep in Egyptian cotton. I kissed her cheek before we parted—made the gesture crisp and English, gallant, non-threatening. She smelled of imported honeysuckle soap.

No work until the following afternoon and only a brief session then—asking her to lead me to an object— clasp my fingers round her wrist so they can listen— thinness of ageing skin: shy, fuzzy, indecisive and then

168

*this hardmetal, proudmetal, fierce intention, it lashes in. I'm walking with her, quartering the room, and she can't help but lead me, shout with her bones that we have to head for the little table and her husband's wristwatch. We almost stumble when we reach it, overly anxious to arrive, and there's a triumph in her, a glee, when I lift it up—**oh, yes, he was asking you to think of this**—and then letting it speak to me—**something that touched him every day: he knows my business better than me, he's very strong in this, strong man**—remains of Ralph Lauren cologne in the leather—she still keeps the last bottle, evaporating, fading: probably inhales a little when she can bear to, can stand the pain. No son to inherit the watch. No child to inherit anything. But now she has me and I can tell her about Mels, be somebody else who remembers him, who knows him.*

It felt as if we'd just been introduced.

But Peri was mine from the start, from the shoes.

That's all it took.

Sweet Peri—bending while her servant watched her, undoing my laces, removing each snow-ruined shoe, inviting me all the way in.

She was nothing but ready.

And necessary—a valued contributor to my own little Welfare State of the Beyond—from each, according to their capacity: to each, according to their pain.

But it's still like stealing, like watching a neighbour's windows while I wank, like slipping my fingers inside an old lady and working her until she pays, until she wants and pays me every time.

She sent me home with coffee cake and the scarf.

Coffee cake wrapped by the silent and observant Imee who disapproves of me, but who makes up a package which is both waterproof and lovely—sets it in a blue paper bag with blue cord handles, from a

169

stationer's uptown. Peri's household economises and helps to save the planet by reusing bags, which is cute—relatively cute. And then Peri brings the scarf—new, Italian cashmere—a little treat once meant for Mels Arpagian, although I don't say so yet—but I appreciate it, offer effusive thanks and then throw in a moment when it seems to strike me, have significance, and I let my eyes well, but control it. I intend her to notice, but also be controlled, so she can navigate our goodbye without breaking fully up against the thought of Mels—the man she lived with for forty-three years and who was named after Marx, Engels, Lenin and Stalin as a joke. Mels, who happily fed America its own uranium. (And who also mined copper and silver and gold—mainly those—and had some other interests; he did diversify . . .) Mels who defended the price of his shares, who wouldn't pay to seal abandoned workings, who contaminated water, who poisoned Navajo miners—and their families—who had a sunnier outlook than normal when it came to the human condition, believed we could change or survive anyfuckingthing—a true optimist who burrowed far and wide underneath Utah. Mels who enjoyed a joke.

Good sense of humour—clearly, in various ways, a nice man—started up from cabbage soup and chilblains, too many brothers and sisters, the unwanted offspring of unwanted immigrants—and he didn't completely erase what that was like. He could be charitable. His family had been touched by the Armenian genocide—could tell you stories that made you weep, him too. He was not socially inactive, was benevolent to people often—as long as they weren't sick or destitute because of something he had done.

I might have been his friend.

If it weren't for the poisoning issue and the breathtaking

170

greed.

Breathtaking. Like lung cancer—which is what killed him. Mels with the same illness as his miners and downwinders—unfuckingsurvivable—the adults and children who kept on breathing and eating and playing near the gaping tunnels, the abandoned tailing heaps. It's good to share, see the results—reminds us that we're all in the same species. His disease metastasised so quickly that he was finished in months, despite exemplary treatment.

Peri laying the cloth, soft around my neck—around delicate and important lymph glands, an unscathed throat—knotting it in front and then tucking it inside my coat.

Like my mum.

Not like my mum—like a mother.

And she gets my finest, close to my finest work: accurate details, conversations, songs, jokes—old Mels and his wisecracks—his pranks—his ironic phobia of smoking: immaculate material, irrevocably convincing. It is a dirty thing I do to her, but that doesn't mean I can slack—it provides me with more motivation to excel. And she'd have been dead long ago without me. Her health has improved since we started, her posture, her skin—she's back at the fund-raising dinners, the charity silent auctions—she likes off-Broadway, looking at edgy art: having safe adventures—Martin the smartly gay PA in a good suit at her elbow, the chauffeur parked close by and waiting. She no longer repeats herself, or forgets things, because she hasn't forgotten Mels, has neither lost him nor what she offered him, was for him, in herself. He's back and so is she.

Sophie Myers passed on my name to her. I do mostly rely on recommendations, on women who've had me who talk to women who might need me, pass me on

171

like an infection.

Always the women.

Sophie vouched for me. Sophie Myers, widow of Christopher Myers III—the much-lamented Kit—who heartily enjoyed his yachting and weekend jaunts to Venice and raping a range of wetlands and African countries.

Made him regret it after death. Sophie's big with AIDS orphans and conservation as a result—pays for drugs and schools, well-building, micro-loans for mums, mosquito prevention. And then there are the film crews she supports who document dolphin kills and shark-finning. She dabbles in seabird-rinsing whenever there's an oil spill. She gives generously to pelicans and gannets.

As generously as she gives to me.

But she'll never be quite as generous as Peri.

Because Peri gets scared. Her mother married up the second time around—Big Bad Step-daddy Warbucks— and, by all accounts, enjoyed it—her spirit drops in, from time to time and I have her say so—but Peri's never had faith that her own situation is secure. Enough capital to pamper villages, indulge a dozen lifetimes, but she lies awake anticipating threats.

And I help with that.

Because I am a bad man.

If I believed in hell, I'd be sure this would send me to it: frightening Peri then selling her protection.

Ask any one of the bastards who do this because they're sadists, psychos, inadequate, insignificant, blood-drinkers—who love it because headfucks get them horny and power makes them come—ask any of the usual practitioners and if they're honest—which they never will be—they'll tell you the serious money, the best way to earn, is with fear. Give people a heaven

172

with bells on: further education, enlightenment, everyone cool they've ever wanted to hang out with: and, yes, they'll pay for that. Return their dead, let them hear, speak, touch, kiss, let them reconsummate— dig in and make your prostitution limitless—and they'll pay for that, too. But give them the truth of a world that doesn't know them and won't care, enumerate their frailties, nudge them—gently, slightly—towards the sewer which is human nature, and of which you are a prime and predatory example, and have them peer in—then they'll beg you to defend them and believe every unseen monster you create. And they will pay you everything you ask.

And they will thank you.

'But we were informed that it had been a bear . . . Mr Williams, he called and told us a bear did it . . .'

The man knows about Peri's cabin in Montana— Mels heading there with her to act like a hunter; plus, youthful lopes across the country as a couple on matching caramel-coloured quarter horses— idyllic. They found the insects trying, though, the isolation—the place was more a topic for conversation than somewhere to stay. But its memory is laden with thoughts of health, incautious love-making on blankets by the lake, bug bites, roughing it with a deep freeze and a helicopter kept on call for them in Missoula.

The cabin means trust and relaxation, skinjoys and sunlight, log fires, lunging evenings, a past that was smooth and fit.

Inevitable, then, that the man attacks her there.

The way that a bastard would—a sadist, psycho, inadequate, insignificant, a blood-drinker.

Peri neat in the hard chair beside the man's—his knee could be touching hers but it's not—it

173

won't—and the drawing room is cool and cream and linens and silks and possibly not the perfect background for his skin—it makes the man slightly invisible, puts too heavy an emphasis on his suit—but she feels relaxed here, prefers it for sittings.

Not that she's relaxed at the moment. 'Wasn't it a bear?'

'I'm not seeing a bear. I see someone breaking in, breaking the door and—it's very pretty inside—or it *was* . . . you chose the things yourself—I like the colours, lots of reds—and you enjoyed the fireplace . . .' Because he needs a lock on her thinking, a blush, the flicker of screwing by firelight—that way he can pull her further in, fracture the mood, introduce damage, get her hands rubbing each other.

That's right.

She doesn't have to tell him anything—her worried hands are more than enough.

'But it ended up such a mess—a waste—all your pretty things—he left it—they left it a mess—two men, they hiked in.'

'Goodness.' He knows Peri's imagining how hardy and fit two such hikers would be—and surely armed against cougars and, of course, bears—how dreadful if she and Mels had been there—two men armed against people. 'Two? There were two men?'

'They broke up the rooms afterwards . . .'

'Afterwards . . . ?'

So much more penetrating, if she drops into a sentence he leaves unfinished—suffers its possibilities before he pretends to rescue her. 'They used knives to make it look like bear's claws.' Blades lacerating delicate air, personal belongings—he doesn't have to say it, she tells herself.

While he spins off into random thinking he

174

shouldn't permit.

That's a dessert, though, isn't it? A bear claw. It's a cake, or something . . . Jesus, the mind does wander . . . because it is unhappy and wants to run . . . but it can't so fuck off with that.

The man's face grim as he disciplines himself, becomes purposeful, intent—which makes her flinch, but he drives in anyway, ungentle. 'But that was afterwards . . . They spoiled your things afterwards—once they had what they'd come for.'

Which is frightening, but not as bad as, 'Once they had what they'd been sent for.'

Better.

Or worse.

Depends if you have a conscience and if you can still hear it.

But I never listen to mine, so fuck off with that.

'Somebody sent them?' Peri, like many of her kind, assumes that envy and conspiracy surround her. This flames through her like phosphorus.

So he ignores her, digresses. 'Frank. I think one of them was called Frank.'

Can't get it wrong when he doesn't exist and therefore cannot contradict me.

'Yes, he was definitely Frank. No name for the other one. They spoiled your flatware . . .'

Peri cares about crockery, having side plates and fish knives and spoons for honey and all the special tools for shellfish—doesn't feel born to it, so everything matters.

Flatware, which is plates and dishes—which are flat—but also cutlery, which isn't . . . you can suffer over here, for lack of vocabulary . . . Or double your chances of being right.

'They spoiled your flatware, but they also took

175

things—some clothes.'

'Oh, no, Arthur.' *She can call me Arthur, but I can't call her Peri—she's always Mrs Arpagian, as if I'm a servant. When I'm the master.* 'Do you think so, Arthur, I don't think so.' She's not really contradicting, more highlighting that he's infallible and she knows his news is still unfurling and will be bad when it's completely visible, surrounding her and cinching in. She starts patting Arthur's forearm with her hand. 'There was hardly anything left there—a few shirts, boots . . . Mels had a work jacket, I think . . .'

Outfitted to suit the territory.

As am I.

Made Richard especially happy this morning—twin vents, hand-felled lavender lining, flower loop, ticket pocket, functioning cuff slit, the usual: my work jacket.

'Small, personal objects will have gone missing and older clothing . . .'

Her voice quick and thinned with anxiety: 'But not worth anything. Why would they take things that are worthless . . . ?' Although she's already convinced this was not a normal theft, is something that obeys the rules of worlds only the man can navigate.

'Clothing that's been with you and carries your shape—surfaces that have absorbed a little something of your personality . . .'

*I'm not saying **aura**. I never have and I never will. I will not talk bollocks. I won't. I don't have to. This is bad efuckingnough without that.*

*And I'm not saying **essence**. I'm not saying **emanation**. Won't have them in my fucking mouth.*

Peri's mouth a whisper open, her horror silent, palpably chill.

Slender lady, born in the thirties, has a fragility and openness that makes Arthur want to hug her, see her laugh, bring her roses, listen to jazz with her until they both get sleepy, sit on the side of her bed and kiss her forehead like a proper son.

But instead I do this—I hound her.

'If such things are passed into unsympathetic hands—envious hands, jealous, malicious—then a skilled reader can find your weaknesses, can work against you with contagious magic.' Arthur pauses until she looks at him—gaze flickering between his eyes and lips—trying to decide which she should hide from most. And then he delivers the three small, fatal words—'I am sorry.' As if she's beyond all saving, including his.

I'm not sorry. I am a bastard. I am a cunt.

And then he waits.

One thousand and cunt, two thousand and cunt, three thousand and cunt . . .

While she cries in a small way—neat little girl in a big house crying—and she glances across at him as if she is being foolish and would like to be much more brave and

Four thousand and cunt, five thousand and cunt . . .

He can't relent.

Six thousand and cunt . . .

Liberty print handkerchief tucked in her sleeve, then dabbing, keeping good order, being presentable because he's watching and—there it is—the moment when this horror flows down and in and meets its more established brother—the loss of Mels.

Seven thousand and I'm not that much of a cunt.

Finding her wrist and kissing her knuckles, the salt, he strokes her arm, and takes both hands at this point, holds firm around them and—hush, hush—the comfort of this provoking a further

177

collapse but he'll squire her through it and could weep himself, could and does—it's the direction to take—and only very slowly, only after minutes, does he say anything else.

'All right? Peri?'

'Oh . . . I . . .'

And she can't tell him that she was recalling the funeral and wishing she'd known him back then—seeing how dapper he'd be in mourning, her tall protector, dipping to take care—she can't be particularly informative, but he nods and, 'I know. I know. And the thing I know most? Is that I will fix this and it will be fine. You will be defended and any ill-effects will be quite overthrown. That little cold that turned to flu—I'll bet you it wasn't a thing to do with you—you see your doctor every week, you're fit and healthy and—'

'Now, Arthur . . .' She gives him a smile that he feels in the pit of his stomach, like someone dropping cold coins there. 'I'm not young.'

'Well, *I'm* not young, Mrs Arpagian. We are neither of us young, but neither of us ought to catch a cold that turns into flu.' She pretendfrowns to say that Arthur hasn't fooled her and he pretendfrowns to show he has been caught in this the very least of his lies, which is hardly a lie at all—she is fit and healthy, she could last for years. He could have more than a decade of income left. 'Someone out there is practising against you and I will prevent them and overcome and we will triumph. They may have used foot track magic at the cabin and I've heard more and more lately of the *Pulsa D'Nora* . . .'

A gift, the Pulsa D'Nora—*some nonsense with tongues of fire that can pray you to death. One recitation and that's that—every opponent just vapours*

178

and ash—as if there'd be anyone left if it was true. As if I wouldn't use the hotel shaving mirror and cast it on my fucking self.

'The *Pulsa D'Nora*?'

Some Kabbala freak has already mentioned it to her, so he slides his grip and squeezes her arms and grins as if she is making him courageous and he explains, 'It's words, a thing built up from words—but every word has an antidote—and every word is letters and each letter has a value and a value is a number and I'm very good with numbers, always have been.' And he sits up straight, releases her, acts the manly man: competent, commanding. 'So then. There are ingredients to gather—some of them rather rare—although I have many—and ceremonies that I will perform. One has to wait for the old moon, one more for the new.'

Have to get a planet in there somewhere. And girls do like the moon.

'For the rest, it will take me a week to fast and watch—I must sit with a rabbi and a priest and another . . .'

Can't be too specific, makes things humdrum.

'And then for three days I will confuse and then destroy their intentions, I will cleanse your street, home, interests, your health, your peace of mind, your present and all visible avenues of your future.'

Although further paths will be revealed and need attention, further challenges will arise, which I will conjure, address and defeat—not complicated, defeating my own fictions. A form of therapy, you might say. I make the dreams and Peri swallows them—each of my ladies does—and Mr Walcott, my solitary gentleman—they eat my dreams: my endlessly vanquished and resurrected, my ingenious dreams.

179

'And then we'll have our ritual here—for us—and I'll position protection at thresholds—'

Which Imee will remove. Loves to dust and polish, remove feathers, powders, lines of silk. Naughty girl.

Not that she shouldn't—they serve no purpose.

'Windows and doors, the balcony rails and so forth. You'll be cosy.'

'Do you need the money now?'

'I don't need the money now. I don't need the money now at all. I don't want to talk about the money.'

And that's true.

'When this is dealt with and you're happy— extremely happy—and well—and sleeping well . . .'

I have to suggest that she isn't, so that she won't. That's also fucking true.

'Then I'll write it all down in an invoice and you can pay me.'

Oh, and that's as fucking true as I can get.

Or just about.

But I didn't invent it. I am nowhere near the worst.

It's just the Dream Game—strong as a dark spell could be, if dark spells existed. The Dream Game created Mels Arpagian's fortune—uranium for the cold war, the rare and precious substance to rout the phantom hosts of enemies, the overestimated peril, the reasons for spending money on ideas of death, on murder. In other times and other contexts, it has other flavours—it's still the same game. Build a stone step into your chimney, it'll make the witches rest outside and leave your house alone: no witches, then the step must be working, must be needed—it can't be that there aren't any witches, that you don't need the step. **Buy this juice or your kids will be blighted—use this cream or your skin will be haunted—give up this right** *or your country will founder—bail out this company, bail out this bank, or you'll live in a wasteland—change your life according to this plan or you'll never be happy, you'll never have sex, never properly fuck, never please or even tolerate your cock or cunt again.*

It's all shit magic, nothing more.

Our current crop of Dream Games want sacrifice and pain and heroes and terrors to burn the world and the energy of righteous torments implacably exacted, and sufficient funds to stoke our problems, not remove them—to keep the craving and the sense of arcane threats, of powers facing powers and miraculous escapes. They want hate. They work for money and hate.

It disgusts me.

As much as I disgust me.

Perhaps more.

At least I work for money and love.

And my dead are already dead and I didn't make them and I wish for no more, have enough, and all of us walking and turning and dancing to our graves in any case, no need to rush. We'll get there.

I won't work for hate.

But still . . .

He is no longer anyone close to what he'd like and occasionally he can picture this restaurant—Italian place—and he wasn't there alone, was with a woman, a cause for love, uncalculated faith. Long time ago. And the waiter—perhaps for comedy effect—had idiosyncratic English and said, with an air of concern, 'If you is me,' and went on to advise on the choices of wines—which were limited. And A. Lockwood looked at the woman's face—the pair of them amused but not quite laughing, enjoying that edge—and he tasted in his mouth—sweet,

181

sweet, sweet—*If you is me*—and the phrase seemed significant and not a mistake. It seemed that the woman could be him and that he could be her, that they were interchangeably themselves and this was glorious.

If you is me.

Then all is well and I will manage very nicely.

I will not, in the spring that follows this autumn, lie on a hotel bed still wearing my stage clothes, tainted with sweat, my evening done with—leukaemia kid, feisty grandma, car crash kid, feisty grandad, boring aunt, eccentric grandma, unresolved mother brought to her full stop, tears for two inadequate dads, thanks to the husband who cleaned up his father-in-law, dressed him and dealt with him decently in his last days. Decency should be rewarded.

And so good that such a thing is so common, is such an easy guess.

So good that we are so connected, human beings, all of a piece.

So I ought not to end up lying cold on a hotel bed.

I shouldn't be alone.

I shouldn't be without her.

That ought not to happen.

Except it will.

No words to stop it.

And I'll lie on the bed and be alone and be alive, but not exactly.

And I'll be aware that I have set myself down precisely as I was before I left to give the punters what they'd want. I will be troubled by the circularity of this. I will check my watch and it will be approaching midnight and no one I can call and no one who will call me and I will start writing—words that are letters that have values that are numbers, that will be no use to me.

But I'll write to her anyway—an angry, inadequate, pleading thing—and I will wish for magic, that she will touch where I touch the paper, I will tell her my wish, my little wish that I know will fail and not bring an answer.

And after I have written and felt sick, I will seal up my failure in a hotel envelope and I'll need to be inside with it and sent to meet her—to let her lift me, hold me—but instead I will tear up my effort, throw it away. Might as well speak to the dead.

Might as well be truthful and say I'm the dead speaking—writing.

I can say anything—she won't hear.

Then I will stare at the mirror and what it shows of a sepiaed spilling light and wallpaper that's turned alien, that seems older than it should. I will think I could be peering back into the 1950s—no, the 1940s, somewhere nicotine-stained and harsh and accustomed to loss. It's not that I'm delusional, I am simply struck by how appropriate the feel of the forties could be—that they will assist me in the work—and I have to work, have only the work and will be the work and will love the work and the work will not leave me or find me inadequate, insignificant. I will be busy with drinking my own blood and I will have nothing because nothing lasts and I will last—I will be busy to death—I will be busy with death—I will be busy.

And tonight I will shave—no more beard, or moustache—short back and sides in the morning from somewhere traditional and cheap and begin improvising clothes that will fix me in a sympathetic decade—a time before I met her, before I was born, a time for the dead.

I will be him: the man who could stand at the mirror, step into it and disappear.

Elizabeth Caroline Barber is thinking—*this is my birthday and so I should have what I like, that should be what happens, not this, which is what my dad likes, which is what my dad **always** likes—and my mum lets him always get away with it: they are not grown up.*

Elizabeth is ten which is double figures, which means she *is* grown up. Having double figures makes you grown up and only great efforts and acts of will can overturn your natural state into something that's messy and less.

Both her parents—but especially her dad—make constant efforts and acts of will.

Today, in all this unrequested crowd—her dad's too many guests—her dad is the one with the shiniest, curliest hair—black, black, black—and the long arms—also darkfurry and curly—and the mildly hitched up shoulders, as if he was hung on a peg by the back of his jacket and left to hang for a long while and has never quite got used to being freed—as if he expects it to happen again.

Her dad is the man in a black suit.

One of the men in a black suit.

The living room is currently stifled with black-suited men: they grin and lean and bump against each other, they wave and gesture, scratch their ears, pat their pockets, cough, they are all over the furniture like a murmuring infestation. Amongst them are rainbow-coloured shirts, or wild ties, big cufflinks, startling waistcoats, garish and elongated shoes—*like every time they step, they're squeezing out something ahead of them from their feet, can't help*

184

*it, here it comes—like they're walking on big shouts, embarrassing wails, or on being stupid—yes, like they're walking two planks made of being stupid, stepping out along stupid and it's holding them up—*and they have striped socks, or checked socks, or idiot socks, or no socks, or too-short trousers, or turned-up trousers, or on-purposely odd-shaped trousers and their handkerchiefs are mad with colours, luminous, and their hats, should they possess hats, have been borrowed from cartoon characters, or old films.

In short, if someone now takes a photograph—and her father may at any moment, he loves snapshots—then Elizabeth will look as if she's caught inside a tasteless funeral, a bizarre wake: perhaps one to commemorate a clown. It will seem to have been a quite happy occasion—as if the deceased was not well loved. She will, in fact, appear to have been the only person there who was upset.

Because it's her birthday.

But not her birthday—that's been stolen, as usual.

But here Beth is, dressed for celebration in her neat red tartan dress with the scratchy white lace at the front and wearing her new TickytickyTimex watch and standing on a small wooden box which is painted blue and with silver stars, and she is surrounded by her father's friends and not one of her own—she could have invited a few, but she didn't want to—and her hands are by her sides and she isn't to close her eyes and isn't to stare, she is simply to look about in the way anybody might at the men who loll and gesture with studied carelessness, who occasionally giggle, or sip drinks while they sing—as raggedly as ever—'For She's a Jolly Good Fellow,' over and over and over.

Beth is not a *Fellow*—a fellow is a man.

185

Beth is not *jolly good*—jolly good people do what their parents want—and she is only halfway to that. She is standing on the box, but she isn't really *joining in and enjoying yourself*—she isn't properly smiling and whenever her eyes meet her father's she can see that he wants her, needs her, to be happy and that she is spoiling his treat. This makes her sad, which he notices and so he gets sadder.

Her dad—Mr Barber—Michael Barber—*everybody calls me Cloudy, Cloudy Barber, that'll do fine*—has arranged the same treat for her every year she can remember, which is seven years. What he did when she was very small, she has no idea, but he has certainly given her this for at least seven birthdays— this silliness for her with the blacksuitmen.

Since 11.26 this morning when Elizabeth grew up, passed ten, she needn't want this any more, but still she gets it—here it all is: for her, to her, *at her*. They are singing and grinning *at her*, aiming themselves too much in one direction—which is her direction— and, while they do, they pass her money. She does not understand precisely how this passing is achieved, but knows that the coins and even folded notes—the warm postal orders—do not arrive by magic. The blacksuitmen are, like her father, magicians— *professional* magicians—but they don't have the kind of magic she reads about, the sort which is to do with wizards and talking animals and wonders. Her presents appear by the kind of magic which is her father's job and which is for children—strangers' children and their birthday parties, or sometimes grown-ups who are having weddings—it's a magic which makes him tired and sometimes annoyed when she interrupts him practising things that are secrets. Her father's magic is unmagical.

186

Although once, really once, it did amaze her—did terrify. She was sitting in the bath and little—five, or six—and she could hear her father's walking up to the door and then his shout, 'And now—let there be *no light at all*!' After which there was a brief, dense pause and then the sound of him clapping—a sound like her nice, warm, aftershavey dad clapping his hands—and after that it was, indeed, absolutely and violently dark.

And she had seen that the bathroom door was shut, she had closed it herself when she came inside and pulled the bolt across—she likes her privacy, Beth, and to never have draughts, and has drawn the bolt across for as long as she's known how to manage it without letting her fingers get nipped—and she plans, when she is older, to own many locked and bolted doors with secrets packed behind them: she will think up secrets. But this was not her secret, this was the door safe shut and her father not touching it, not opening it, and the light switch being in here with her—on her side of the door—but the light still going out—magic—the darkness coming—magic—the room dropping into magic—and it was winter, an evening in November and deep night outside and she was alone in her bath of suddenly thickened water, the threat of it against her—magic.

And she had seen it: the real magic, like in books. She had seen, honestly seen, her father's hand reaching in right through the door—like a horrible grey dream thing—this pale and unnatural hand pressed through the wood of the door and reaching the light switch and—*click*—off it went.

Except there was no *click*, just the pause and then her dad's hands together—normal, normal, normal

187

hands to hold and know and mend things—her dad's palms together and safe outside the bathroom— *clap*—and then her voice being very loud and screaming and echoes and splashes and this choke of wet lostness reaching into her and through her.

And then the light came back.

Good.

No signs of how.

Just a different magic—the kind to restore things, save them when they're lost.

Good.

And the door was still bolted and there was still no noise except her own, only then her dad's voice was there also, sounding worried and gentle beyond the bathroom and she couldn't hear his exact words, because of the din of herself, how it bounced against the tiles, and her mum audible next, joining her father with footfalls and then shouting, not letting him get away with anything, not this time.

Their fight coaxed Beth into quietness—a dreadful, large silence—before both of them called and promised and argued and reassured her up out of the bath and past the haunted light switch and close to the door frame. They spoke to her until she could believe that she was brave and pull back the bolt— her fingers shivering and the metal pinching her for spite: when one thing goes wrong, then all things go wrong—and she opened the door for them and they fell in at her and half tumbled and half lifted her into this thump of a hug.

Shaking and dripping with magic—this marvellous, terrible thing.

Her dad rushed a towel around her—always quick as snap when her mother is unhappy with him and means it, always cowed and puzzled and, somewhere, faintly pleased.

Beth was put into fresh pyjamas—something healing about fresh pyjamas, not that she was wounded, not exactly. And she was given hot chocolate and then brushed her teeth with her mum in the bathroom in case it was scary to be there and then she went to bed—her bedroom door open and not with a bolt even attached and no secrets inside it except that she sometimes listened to the old wireless under her covers, went to sleep with the mewling and whispers of static between stations, trying to make a new language out of them—and this wasn't a secret: everyone knew.

She sat up in bed feeling not frightened—more happy, racing, sleepless. She had survived and now she wanted to survive again, be proved impregnable. Beyond her in the corridor she could hear her father saying, 'I thought she'd like it . . .'

Beth did like it. Afterwards, she loved it. She wanted more.

'Idiot.' Her mother's voice angry and slightly amused, which was confusing, but also familiar and to do with who her parents were.

Because of her parents, Beth will never quite understand arguments—the first she saw being so pleasant, a form of flirting: raised voices and helpless glances, touches at arms and shoulders, lips trying not to part, to give themselves away. Her mother and father offered each other rows as a concentrated kind of affection. Their silences were the bad thing—the infrequent, but very bad thing. When they made each other sad, there were no words.

'I thought . . .' Her father shuffling his feet in the corridor, wriggling—she could tell—with small pleasures, as well as concern, 'Well, she might have

189

'. . . I thought.'

'You *didn't* think. Because you're an idiot.' Her mother pauses. 'Go in and make it all right . . .' This is a voice which Beth knows she is meant to hear and believe. 'You're the magician—you can make it all right.' And then softer, but not so soft as to disappear, 'Or you'll be dealing with it when she wakes up full of nightmares for a month.'

'It'll not be a month.'

'How do you know? Anyway—you'll be the one who copes, because I'll be asleep. You're the one who gets the lie-ins in the morning, the bloody night owl . . .'

'Because of my not-proper-job . . .'

'Because of your not-proper-job. Slacker.' Her voice with a grin underneath it.

'Always wanted to be a kept man.' His, too.

'Don't know if I *will* keep you. Might throw you back . . .' And a noise which was the noise of them kissing—her mum and dad kissing—which they did a lot, more than other mums and dads. It was moderately shaming. 'What on earth did you expect, Mike?'

'That it would be . . .'

And Beth will never know if he was going to say *fun* or *beautiful* or *horrifying* because he doesn't finish the sentence, only makes another kissnoise and walks into her room straight afterwards and sits on the edge of her bed—give, give, give in the mattress— the feel she will always love, of somebody's weight on her bed, such a kind and simple thing—and he tells her, 'I'm so sorry, wee button. Really.' And he holds her hand, eyes focused on the floor. He does mainly look away, her dad—unless it's for something important. He's paying attention, maybe too much

190

attention, so that he can't always look, except in darts and flinches. 'Really. Your mum's going to kill me later.' And then he swallows loudly and stares as if he has made another bad mistake, while also smiling. 'A bit—she'll kill me a bit. She won't really kill me dead. She is cross, though. With me. Not you.' And he peers at her. 'You all right, Beth?'

'Uh-huh.' She likes him being sorry and so is stern.

'Sure, love?'

'Uh-huh.'

And his face, by this time, is pained, fretting, and so she relents, squeezes his fingers, hugs his arm.

'Oh, good. Glad you're OK.' Relief lets him gaze away again and explain, 'I didn't mean to scare you. Not that much. Not much at all.' And there's this purr in under his voice, this bedtime story purr, that makes an ease, a peace, around them. 'And the light will serve you now, I've told it and I've sprinkled it with magic powder and –' he opens his fingers and wriggles them so that sparkles of white and green and blue fall to the coverlet and shine—'you get some too. And it's *all right*.' Beth knows the magic powder is out of a jar: she has gone with him to the special shop that sells it. The powder doesn't do anything, is just pretty. It's his voice that lets her rest. 'I didn't mean you to get a big scare.' She expects the music of him will be for ever, permanent in her life—a sound to stroke in her spine, to be home, to be there, reliable. 'Not a big bad one. Sorry.' It will be wrong beyond all understanding if this isn't true.

When Beth is an adult full of PIN numbers and passwords and information and memories and preferences and doubts, then she won't often consider how frightened she was in the bathroom, or how she saw what wasn't there to explain her terror. She conjured a ghost: her father's hand, but not her father's: the way he would be if he were different, wrongly different, reaching in from somewhere else. And she won't especially remember hoping for other shocks, further plummets into strangeness which never came—or being kissed by her father *night-night*—doesn't sound the way it does when he kisses her mother—and rolling over while his weight on the side of the mattress stayed, guarded, kept the blankets tight.

It will be years before one day she thinks, out of nowhere: *Of course: the fuse box was in the cupboard beside the bathroom. He just took out the fuse. Nothing to it. I bet he had it planned for ages, waiting until I'd be old enough so I'd be impressed, or pleased, or something—not freak out. And I disappointed. I made it a much better, much worse trick. I made it the start of an appetite.*

Standing on a silly box—standing just over the edge of ten years—she knows nothing about her adult self: the strains and lines and likings of who she will be are settling quietly like sediment where she can't see—later there will be fractures, extraordinary heats and metamorphoses, but she currently takes no interest, can predict none of them. She is simply miserable and glad that her friends aren't here. She has never let them watch the blacksuitmen and their work which moves in the room like a series of bubbles, warmths that ripple towards her and fluster. If she were to be honest about them, she would say the men irritate her because what they do is close to being still pleasant, almost appropriate, it could drag her back to being a baby, just a girl. Once she is older, she will be able to break it down into a series of benevolent deceptions: loading, ditching, passing, palming, misdirecting—an odd display of love. At present, it does seem enticing, appealing, that somehow—from hand to hand and man to man—intentions are approaching her in ways that aren't explained, but it mainly makes her feel excluded and not clever enough.

She will eventually become familiar with this sensation. When she is a jolly good and studious teenager, school dances will nag at her. Discos will be worrying—and the headmistress will insist on calling them *discotheques*, which will make them seem French and complicated and shady—and going out to clubs will be worse. Kisses—harmless old kisses—will suddenly be redescribed, for no clear reason, as *French*, and will change, become complicated and shady. Beth will find that ugly boys, boys she doesn't like—and there are very few boys she *does* like, she already has quite particular tastes—any boys at all can still light her, trouble her with what they start in rushed and brave and slapdash kisses, in how they speak to her body, wake places she won't let them see, in how they work transformations, imitation magics, have blunt but effective hands. Boys will startle her too much at first, or make her frighten herself with herself—she'll gain a reputation for inviting and then bolting, running away.

And the men in black suits help begin it: her confusion, resentment, fugitive nature. They stare at her while she stands out on her box and whoever is closest pulls gifts from her hair, or slips them—soft as whispers, as kisses, as lips—into her dress's pockets, or tucks money into the air close round her

193

father so that he can retrieve and then present it to her.

They are doing their best.

But they're interfering, too, they are making her a spectacle and she wishes they would not.

She really does like her privacy, Beth.

No, she *loves* her privacy.

She wants bolts.

She wants boxes that open and swallow everything, hide it, close, lock, and then seem innocent and portable as ever. She wants to be safe in the blue box with the silver stars, which will be prettier than her to stare at and peaceful.

And she believes it will be good if she can box her joys, control them—no more of her birthday money exciting her more than snow, or wishes, or the seaside, or fruit growing on trees—just growing, straight out of trees, or even little bushes—and more than ice cream with bits in, or big dogs—no more of these things being able to make her laugh, whoop, run to burn off the so much wonder of reality, the pleasures she expects, the escalation of delights.

In a while, her mum will come through with a cake—it will be big and have Orinoco Womble on it in colours of icing and *Happy Birthday*—and there will be more singing and her dad will fetch his camera—which is called a Polaroid Square Shooter—from the table by the door and he will take her picture and everyone will look at it while it develops—because in 1976 self-developing photographs are exciting. They will watch her conjured out of nowhere and she won't even be involved.

Beth will keep the picture with a number of others in a box under her bed—under her succession of beds. Eventually, when she looks at it she will see a blaze of cake, gone faces, a record of dead faces—her mother slightly blurry, but smiling in a mauve paisley patterned dress, skin warm with the candles' shining—her father not there, already not there, but only because he is holding the camera, tilting the image slightly to the left and down, which was a habit, is characteristic, makes her feel his fingers, still holding on to the edges of everything. And she will see an inrush of silences and a small girl who was petulant, frowning: who was wrong—joys controlled aren't joys at all, that's why they are so terrible.

'Cloudberries.'

'I'm sorry, what did you say?' Beth is sitting and frowning up at a tall, nervy man in a pebble-dashed jacket and bad shoes. He is standing beside her and is someone she has never seen before.

It's 1989 and not Beth's birthday; close, but this is just a party—one of her own making and in her own flat. At least, it's in the flat she shares with two other students, both of whom are slightly dull. She picked them for their dullness—uninvolving Sarah and boring Elaine. She wants to get her PhD—which would please her dad: she doesn't have to please her dad, but she would like to—and Sarah and Elaine will not be a distraction. She has shared accommodation before and been through the shouty boyfriends and strange compulsions and sad compulsions and haphazard mental collapses of too many strangers and acquaintances and very-much-former-friends to expose herself again. She is tired

195

of being a student: of bar jobs and waitress jobs and telesales jobs and learning the words and numbers of what seems a pointless game. It doesn't feel as she'd hoped: like owning secrets, like enlightenment. And she's older: this sad case the campus can't shake, because where else would she go? At least she'll have peace with Elaine and Sarah—if both of them exploded, burst into flames, they still would be proudly unable to draw a crowd.

'I said *cloudberries.*'

Beth is tucked at the top of the stairs, just inside the dim quiet of the landing—no lights on up here, guests being encouraged to stay below, keep tidy and not creep off for sly shags in or on other people's beds. The man must have crossed the landing behind her soundlessly and is, in a minor way, an intruder. The idea of this is disturbing. She doesn't know where he's come from and had assumed she was alone—meaning that, for a while, she has been defenceless.

He drops to sit beside her, knees high to his chin. 'Like when you were a kid, isn't it?' And he is, all at once, companionable, easy. 'Up late and peeking at your parents' noise.'

But he is not her companion and shouldn't be easy so Beth tells him, 'You can't peek at noise. You can't see it at all. In fact.' She feels he may be uninvited— he certainly isn't Sarah's or Elaine's style—long blond hair and a fussily shaped beard, a sense of intelligence about him.

Which he's probably faking.

He looks like General Custer—so he can't be that bright.

He looks like a fake.

He doesn't look like a part of her future—a long,

fluttering tear in years and years and years. She has no prediction in her pocket which reads *On the 4th day of the 3rd month in 1989 Elizabeth Caroline Barber will meet Arthur Peter Lockwood and they will be bad for each other, ever after.*

She doesn't even fancy him—not especially.

He sits as close as he can do without touching and there is something hot and interfering about the empty space he leaves against her. He is hard not to notice.

She doesn't fancy him—she *notices* him.

'I'm sorry?' Beth wondering why people say this precisely when they want the other person to be sorry and when they are themselves not sorry at all.

He repeats, 'Cloudberries.' And peers down through the banisters as if he has never watched flirting and drinking and smoking—the slightly pompous passing of spliffs, poor dancing to Sarah's disastrous music, relationships thriving, changing, being knocked out of shape. It seems these things are lovely to him, almost hypnotic. Then he peers at her, his face mainly in shadow but clearly enjoying its own curiosity. 'Cloud. Berries. You wanted to know.'

'Oh.' And she wishes that she was more sober, could deal with him effectively and get away. 'Yes.' He gives the impression of being safe, if eccentric, but it strikes her that no one should actually be able to seem *that* safe, *that* quickly—it's not normal. 'I see.' But meanwhile he is right: *Cloudberries* is the answer she was after. Downstairs in the living room Beth had been passionately describing—she can't think why—her long-ago Orinoco Womble birthday cake. This had led her to realise—with four or five glasses taken of Elaine's disturbingly bluish-green

197

and very sweet punch—that she couldn't remember what Wombles used to eat. And Beth had been a big Womble fan—read all of the books and had an Uncle Bulgaria doll and everything. At that point in the evening her knowledge of the usual Womble diet became important, even vital—she had been loudly distressed on the subject, only slightly joking when she tried to explain that who she was, who she *really was*, might be wholly bound up with being certain she could feed, should she ever have to, all of the fictional animals who had softened and blessed her youth.

But by now the information was less precious, almost irrelevant. 'Yeah... Wombles ate cloudberries.'

She hadn't been aware of the man when she was talking about cake, hadn't seen him, which indicates that he is good at sneaking, listening, that he makes it a habit. It may suggest—although she doesn't think of this—that her need, her dismay, were why he listened, what brought him, what gave him a chance to catch her mind slightly opened—like slipping his finger inside a book, keeping his place.

'Hi. I'm Arthur.'

Arthur the spy.

But you can't have a spy called Arthur, that wouldn't suit—like Hilda, or Bert, or Mavis—none of them names for a spy.

'Call me Art.' This said with the air of someone trying to set his first nickname, make it a good one.

Don't want to call you anything, thanks.

'Well, Art . . .' And Beth gathers her forces to leave. As she does so, he places his palm firmly, briefly, over the back of her left hand and smiles before letting her go, turning his head back towards the banisters and his study of her other guests.

198

She doesn't really want to go downstairs, sink into the muggy crush and fumble. Something horrible and Eurovision is playing when she would like the Kinks or Cream, or any other at least plausible musicians from a period when it was cool and influential and dignified to be a student. She was a toddler in the 1960s but she'd swear she still knew they were springing up nicely, being magnificent, and understood that her own generation would be dogged by mutual disappointments. She can remember, is keen to claim, her early-onset nostalgia: small, earnest five-year-old Beth in a range of handmade cardigans telling people, 'When I was four . . .'

Plasticine and blunt-nosed scissors and a gold star every day for being middle-aged . . .

Beth doesn't examine the back of her hand for maybe half an hour, doesn't notice *BETH* written there in purplish letters between the knuckles and the wrist—not until an engineering student pal of Sarah's points it out. 'Worried you'll forget your name, are you? Is that it? Worried you'll wake up in the park? Yeah? Is that it? I woke up in the park last summer . . .' He sniggers and spills some snakebite down the front of his rugby shirt.

Beth misses any further exciting details of the park incident, because she is working her way round to face the landing.

It must have been him—call me Art—just what I need, more bloody nonsense—amateur magic.

Art remains compressed in a bony crouch at the head of the stairs. She waits for him to raise his head.

They're always the same, the ones who like to play: once their trick's been started they have to see its end.

199

But he doesn't move, gives every appearance of being densely, absently relaxed.

So he makes her climb to him, seek him out.

'You transferred the pigment when you touched me.' Beth sits beside him and when their legs brush, he retreats just enough to avoid the contact, compacts himself further. 'Overheard my name?'

He lets her take his hands and lift them, see that he's now wearing gloves.

'What the fuck?'

Art keeps placid, quiet: tugs off his right glove, shows her his palm, the purple mirror-writing, her name in smeary block capitals. He clears his throat and says carefully, 'Isaiah 49: 15–16 . . . "Yet will I not forget thee. Behold, I have graven thee on the palms of my hands . . ."'

'Does that work with anyone?'

'Sometimes.'

'Seriously?'

'I don't know—you're the first time I've tried it.' And then he mumbles, struggles his glove back on. "Thy walls are continually before me."'

'What?'

'That bit doesn't help at all . . . the walls . . . and I think it sounds too religious.'

'Quoting the Bible? Yes, that might sound religious.'

'*Too* religious?' He's smiling, his mouth seeming soft and bewildered by itself, by what it might start saying. It's hard to tell if this is more of his act—being disarming.

'Maybe.'

And he leans for a moment against her, shoulder to shoulder, gentle and then away.

'Do you want me to ask you about the gloves?'

'No.' The smile again, aimed at his knees. 'No,

200

you'd better not.'

'Then I will. Why are you wearing gloves?'

And he takes this small, inward sip of air—fish out of water—fish liking a risk—and begins, 'Because I wear gloves almost all the time. I sleep in them.'

'Almost all the time . . .'

'Yes. I just said that.'

'In the shower? In the bath?'

'You're being silly.'

'Oh, of course—'

'I wear rubber gloves for that.'

'Oh, even more of course.'

He leans against her for another breath, face deadpan, voice earnest. 'It helps me feel. I sleep fully dressed and in the gloves, I keep covered and then when . . . It makes me feel better.'

'I should go.'

'If I take off my gloves and hold your shoulders . . .' His voice changed, revealed, somehow *at work*. 'Then you'll tell me your favourite person here—or which is your bedroom—or what you think is your household's ugliest ornament—that one isn't fair: it's the big glass seahorse sculpture thing in the living room which belongs to the blonde girl who likes it, but you want to break it: tonight you're going to break it and blame a guest—you ought to blame me—or you could tell me which is your bedroom, could lead me to it.'

'You've already said that.'

Tiny voice now, factual. 'It was an example.' And he takes off both his gloves—dark, thin leather, lined and creased and folded with use, like the skin of other hands—and he puts them in his pocket and he sets his fingers on her shoulders. And he eases the words in again, is himself—what she already,

201

mildly, thought of as his genuine self. 'You simply think and let your shoulders tell me. Think what you want me to know . . . Yes, I'm an arse and quite sad and quite sleazy, but not that . . . Thank you. Think that your name is Beth. Thank you. Think that you're not called Sarah, because then you would sniffle and mouth breathe in a deeply irritating way—bad sinuses . . . and why are you with them, both of them? They don't suit—you must want them not to suit . . . but that doesn't matter—why not think of your favourite person here, of the one who interests you the most—thank you—let yourself tell me that—thank you—let me know that. Your favourite person. Thank you, Beth. Thank you very much.'

Thanking her and thanking her—as if she is slipping money inside his clothes.

She feels that he may be smiling—that she can feel him smiling in his touch and in the pressure of his side, the rise of his breathing against her back—and then he lifts the contact, removes it.

They sit for a while in silence with the party beneath them.

Art withdraws, replaces his gloves, winds his arms round his knees.

And Beth hears herself say, 'That's a lot of effort.'

'Which you'll remember.'

'Really.'

'Oh yes—you'll always remember how we met—it'll make a nice story for the kids, the kid, the puppy, the cat . . .'

'Then again, maybe it wasn't *enough* effort.' Beth deciding to worry now that he has her address—is currently *at* her address—that he may be more peculiar than he looks. It would be hard for him to be more peculiar than he looks.

But he keeps on hugging himself, staring at people who are not her, troubling Beth only with little sentences, murmured in. 'Probably. I don't know. I'm guessing. I saw you tonight and guessed . . .' He rubs his chin against his forearms and she hears the rasp of his ridiculous beard. 'I am of the opinion that you should have efforts. I can't guarantee their results.'

Two or three hours later—afterwards she won't recall how long she waited—she will go downstairs through the party wreckage and half-dark and knock the big glass seahorse sculpture thing off the mantelpiece, smashing it irreparably. No one will hear her do it and she will blame Arthur for the loss.

'How are you this morning? Good morning?' Mila is the stewardess for Beth and Derek's cabin. Mila is weatherproof and cheery, her conversations melodiously penetrating. 'Your husband? Three days ill, four nights ill, that's no good. He is a little better?' Mila's interest in her charges is both heartfelt and exhausting.

Beth no longer tries to explain that Derek is not her husband, that he did, until quite recently, want to *become* her husband, but this is almost undoubtedly no longer the case, that he is currently barricaded somewhere surly and disappointed inside his head. Their room feels like his skull, somehow, like being locked in an uneasy skull, wearing itself smooth from the inside out—rabbity and stale. 'No. He isn't better. Not really.'

He isn't the better man—only looks like him. Bloody depressing to think of how often I've gone for the tall and the blond and then been sorry, spent all manner of awkward coffees, dinners, clammy nights, with the sense that I've misplaced something, that I'd glance away, turn back and see what I want.

Who I want.

And is that because of Arthur, or is that because of me: am I someone inclined towards wanting things like Arthur? Men like Arthur. Is he a genetic weakness, like diabetes? Or does some part of me harbour Nazi cravings for blue eyes and blond hair? And something broken.

Does he mean I'm a racist?

He does mean I can't think of him for long without distracting—he's too much, otherwise.

It's not that I wouldn't love to concentrate—Jesus, please—to be clear and single-minded, but not about him, it can't be about him—because then it turns out that I'm not a bigot, I'm alone. And I don't crave a type.

It's just that I know how to learn things and I learned a man, but I can't have him, because in person he's a toxin. I keep him in my skin and I don't forget, but I can't be with him. Even when we're together, we're not real: I'm not me, he isn't him.

And this is my finest time—what he doesn't get. Back when I had the skin, the bloom, the sort of ease, I wasn't ready: it's now we should be together, when I think I might have found the start of what we need to do, how we could be.

*It's different with men and women, I realise—I did read the manuals: **Female 45–55, Male 50s Professional, Immigrant Female 30s**: I memorised the classifications,*

204

the life paths, studied what to tell enquirers.

Gentlemen peak early and ladies are late.

But that's a very incomplete story.

Gentlemen peak early, but then they can find out who they are, how to apply themselves.

Ladies peak early and then can keep peaking. This can be a conflagration or a tragedy, a wound.

When I came in my twenties it seemed significant: today I could bang my elbow and find myself more deeply moved. I have capacities I barely understand.

And sometimes we almost really touch, but never quite.

We get theatrical instead. We waste ourselves. We don't hold each other and catch light. We never rest, enjoy the peace of ourselves. We are never properly naked. We do not ever truly fucking meet.

I miss him. And he misses me.

We are stupid enough to wreck ourselves at heart.

From which I should digress.

And there are very many varieties of digression.

In word, in thought, in deed.

My digressions involving the wrongly fair-haired and imperfectly tall—the spidery, washed-out imitation Arthurs and my being unable to like them. Clambering into stupid situations in case they might be feasible— trying to be under someone and to touch them but not that much—proving I'm alive and capable without Arthur and being with whoever else, but not that much. They don't quite exist—are just someone who isn't Arthur.

Like Derek.

Don't know what was I thinking. Then again, that's what I aim for—to not know what I'm thinking.

And so it's closing the eyes and lying—in every fucking sense lying—and holding whoever's shoulder as loosely as I can—imagining there's a lace doily, or a napkin laid between us, something insulating and polite—and closing my eyes and needing to feel the better man, but he isn't there because I settled for safer and stupider and less. Again.

It passes the time.

Christ.

Beth puts the Do Not Disturb sign on the door, because Derek has promised that if Mila comes into their cabin again while he's trying to sleep he will *glass her in the face*. He's in no condition to harm anyone and isn't a violent person, but he may make a scene, insist on indulging in complaints.

Mila leans on her trolley—her *luxury Porsche trolley*—which rattles with each surge and is laden with nice clean facecloths that no one will get and pillow mints that no one will eat and shampoo that no one will have the strength to use. 'He needs dry food. Like toast. Like biscuits—the way you have biscuits in the lifeboats. When we have lifeboat drill there is biscuits in the boat and water only and they say someone will give you two pills when you come in—I don't get sick, but I would get two pills, because in those little boats you will be sick and then everyone else will see you be sick and will be also sick—more than thirty people in a little boat, being sick, that would be such a terrible thing.' Mila is, no doubt, audible to Derek, and Beth is not remotely attempting to move her away along the corridor. 'I can fetch dry biscuits and give them to him, but not now—if the DND sign is on the door then we cannot knock even, we can do nothing.'

'I think nothing is what to do.'

'You are sure?'

'This evening, we can give him water and dry

206

biscuits. He's had the injection and I think he's sleeping.'

He isn't sleeping—he's flat on his back and venomous and staring, he's turning himself into something I can't love, can't like.

I used to be able to like him. Liking is OK.

Settling for less. Settling for decent and reliable and normal.

Which is less.

'We drill all the time, have exercise for when the ship sinks.' Mila says this happily, confidently, and it is plain that she would be equally sanguine in a lifeboat—her liner going down by the stern, its harpist perhaps still playing on the ever-more-slanting deck, and Mila quite content, asking after everybody's health, handing out biscuits and perhaps one or two of those mints. 'Look at this today, this morning—the whole way is DND and DND and DND . . . I will have to make report, say why I don't go in and clean . . .'

It's true: the passageway is thick with plaintive Do Not Disturb signs that swing from the handle of each door and indicate distress within. Elizabeth walks past them along the press and give of carpet, the perspective dipping, twisting ahead. She moves through the section that rattles like walnuts in a tin, the section that whines like a metal-on-metal puppy, the section that constantly bathes in a mild howling, and then she ascends, staggers round and round the stairwells. She wants to be outside: not on the circumnavigating deck, still haunted by a few mad walkers, brisk and smug in their waterproofs, clocking up miles—not where Arthur leaned at the stern, where the stain of him leaning will be by the handrail, a salt and judgemental shape—she's heading higher, high as she can, up until she runs out of ship.

Fucking Arthur—who is more, rather than less—too much and indecent and unreliable and abnormal and I didn't love him at the start. He did that to me—I think—he made it happen—I think—or I did—or we both did. We saw something in each other, something bad, and then chased it and it didn't run away.

Lying—again in every sense—by myself in bed after the party—after that first night. And I'd broken that sodding glass abomination and I wanted to anyway, but I know that I did it so I could tell him later—which will have to mean seeing him again. I already want to see him again, but I don't fancy him—it's definitely **noticing***, not fancying.*

Only I want to be near him again and that leaning against each other thing was nice and hand-in-hand was nice and maybe this makes me nice—my sudden fondness for small and friendly gestures.

I could be nice about him.

It's not as if I really want a wank.

A wank would be rude. And the fact that it's rude and to do with him is not in any way another layer of attraction.

Dear God, the utter rubbish you tell yourself.

When really you just want a wank.

When your mind's already out and predicting, sketching how he'll be, playing the cheap psychic, the way we do with everyone we love—building how they are when they're without us, how they'll be when they come back.

Habit of a lifetime.

And he made it worse.

Arthur there at arbitrary parties, at some and not others—nobody seemed to invite him, but he'd get in all the same—and seeming to know which pubs I went to and being about the place, then elsewhere, more tangible when disappeared.

Be available, then not: make your appearances random, a long tease—it never fails.

He would have realised that, but I never did feel he was playing me. He felt reassuring, let both of us be unwary in this gently hungry place. It was almost like friendship, as comfortable as that.

While—absolutely and of course, this would have to be the case—I'm studying MAD—Mutually Assured Destruction.

You couldn't make it up.

That was the subject for my thesis—great conversation-stopper, not bad at emptying rooms: simply tell them you're learning how to get a population of sane and ordinary people to be happy with MAD and convinced they could survive any conflagration—convinced they'd want to survive—how to make them optimistic enough to believe we can change, or survive anything.

Survive anyfuckingthing. Protect and Survive: take your doors off their frames and hide in underneath them, shove your head in a brown paper bag—as if you're a pound of apples. I spent months with all of those lies: the Public Information films, the plans that were no kind of plan. The bad spells, shoddy enchantments.

And then I'd come home and maybe Arthur would be there, or I'd go out and maybe Arthur would be there—and maybe he happened to be in my living room while a bunch of us watched the Berlin wall come down and were happy for other people and for a good change, an achieved change—and this was history and when I remembered it, I was going to remember him also—it'll make a nice story for the kids, the kid, the puppy, the cat: that while we weren't

209

exactly dating, the world turned wakeful, tender, changed its dreams.

*We kept ourselves unerotic for so long—which is almost more erotic than anything else—and maybe that's what he intended for those nights when I'd go to my bed alone, the nights after we'd chatted, leaned a bit—maybe he knew the condition that I would be in and was lying in his own bed and hypothesising, breaking a sweat. I was certainly thinking about him and I was a grown-up and at liberty and it's not unusual or peculiar to touch yourself on somebody's behalf— you know them a bit, but not like that, but not exactly **not** like that—actually, you know them just enough to make this awkward and yet lovely—if you imagine them being aware of what you're going to do—may do—could do—will do—why fool yourself: the pausing is preamble to a definite end—it's what you will do— you're going to fancy yourself enough as their replacement to make yourself come—but you feel naked, shamed, extraordinary, if you think of them knowing, of informing them: **yesterday, I wished my hands into your hands and improvised from there—** then it's almost too uncomfortable to continue.*

Almost.

But when we were together we digressed, we made distractions. He took an interest in my work: found me descriptions of mass shelters, their lists of provisions, amounts of fuel stored for running generators, the rules for admission and denial—survival not always the kinder option—some things intended to be unfuckingsurvivable—your wife dead outside, your kids dead outside—kid, puppy, cat—your life dead outside. No doors on the toilets in case you hid in them and tried to top yourself.

We listened to Patrick Allen being the last voice we'd

ever hear: all his announcements—sensible and inevitable wartime advice with this stink of a hell underneath it. That shouldn't be sexy. But it was.

Me full of mass casualties and damage and him full of I had no idea what—man in gloves, magic man, quiet man, man who works in a florist's sometimes, who can build things for you: cabinets, bookshelves, makes little boxes with sliding panels, private places— handy—secret—whose aim seems to be elsewhere and as yet unrevealed.

He didn't tell me what he really did for months. Took off his gloves and held my face and told me, kissed. And why not try it together—give the wounded their dead together—Mutually Assured Eternity —bombproofed.

And it made sense. It did. It seemed a beauty.

Although I was not exactly at my most coherent: lack of sleep—presence of love.

And next I'm stealing my dad's secrets, palming them, adapting, learning my new lessons on most nights— clean nights.

Leastways, they stayed clean until I was alone. Then less so.

But I could have just had sex with him—it's not as if we couldn't have started if I'd asked. I believe that's the case. But I waited. I didn't try for months. No obstacles then, and nothing wrong with me, not especially—I was only angry, justifiably, furious about things that were appalling. I cared about him, but also about strangers. I wanted to help. I was getting my education so I could help.

And I knew—start love with Arthur and it wouldn't be controlled. I'd get lost in it. We both would.

Ecstasy.

Nobody actually wants that.

211

So we restricted ourselves to lessons and structure and practice—hands with hands and hands in hands and thinking leaned in against thinking.

And we had the code—the simple one—our first code.

1—Please listen
2—Man
3—Loss
4—Child

Easy.

When she reaches it, the door to the upper air feels locked, there is such a weight of gale against it. Beth has to lean in, shoulder the glossy wood, manage a final shove when the pressure eases and lets her barrel into a merciless space. For a moment she can't see, can't breathe, is simply held—the shock of weather, its beautiful offence prevents thought—and then this joy comes, this immense, horrific pleasure in every gust that comes at her like a big dog, that flattens her clothes to her body in a knock, that maddens her hair, that can hammock around her in any direction, every direction, and push her, draw her, stumble her where it likes and the sky is above her and swooping to each horizon, a howl of blue: a tall, fierce ache of blue and its clouds in lines, in streamers, banners, dazzles, flares—it is all alive and makes her laugh.

Better.

Best.

In the end, you seek them out—your ecstasies. The ones that you can bear.

The deck dry underfoot and light, shining as if it's been bleached by sheer speed and the shuttering sun.

She stands and rests against it all, turns her neck

to let it be touched, closes her eyes.

5—Help
6—Betrayal
7—Love
8—Accident

The useful words, they had to be numbered to let us work them as we'd wish. Five steps, eight breaths, six seconds of silence after Art steepled his fingers together—we had endless variations. A word could repeat and repeat and repeat and give you loss underneath its own meaning, a stranger's little gift. Whatever we said, thought, did, the numbers ran through it, illuminated, were additionally generous, complicated.

In the end, I'd wonder how people spoke without them. As if we were normal and everyone else was too small. And both of us in the same beat, in this invisible motion. Can't think of the hours that we spent in his bed-sit counting—silent and marking the time until we were always synchronous.

As if we had one pulse.

But anyone can do it, if they want to be peculiar enough.

9—Pain
10—Now
11—Fear
12—Work
13—Sex

And on and on and on and you don't get **Woman** *until* **20***, up with the reassurances and compliments—* **Brave, Artistic, Honest, Forgiven***—the treats.*

We did give them treats.

We.

Us.

We were the people who understood: 1 is **Please**

*listen—and later we made it **Look At Me**—but also it was **the first thing to think of** which is **death** and **a passage of time**—in **time** we all do get our **death** and then **time passes** beyond others' **deaths**—and fuck me, the pair of us started to operate like this, we had to, hopping about from thought to thought for the punters, from word to work to number to symbol to—**time** is a **watch**—you may be getting the code for **watch**, so you'll imagine it in your hand, coddle it in the mind's fingers—or else announce its status as a messenger to your audience, if required—or picture it pointing to particular numbers, if you'd like: it can mean you'll remember them, group them together, a set of coded details you fit to an enquirer, something to keep you steady through a long sitting, or in case the punter ever comes back—for another sitting, that is: you don't expect to hear from beyond their graves—or else you can allow it to be just a **watch**, the enquirer's own **watch**—so many people have a **watch**—even if they use the clock on their mobile phone, that's like a **watch**—you can tell them about their **watch**—or their phone—or their kitchen clock—or how their years are passing—or their loved one's, lost one's **watch**—as you talk to them, you can feed them anything, change, qualify, redefine—and **watch** is also **Now, can you . . .** slip in 'Now, can you . . .'—Arthur can tease any sentence apart and make it fit—and he'll mean a **watch**—and 1 is the symbol of **a man standing in a doorway** and, 'I'm seeing **a man standing in a doorway.** Does that mean anything, can you think?'—an eloquent image to start, adaptable, the punters will interpret it to please them—and my whole head packed with this, streaming with, 'A dream of rising upwards and a door number which is important and has a 2 in it and a death, a passing that took place on or near to a special*

214

occasion, that happened close to something like a birthday or an anniversary . . .' Frowning into the middle distance—the place where observers assume all this shit is stored.

And on
And on
And on
It doesn't go away—my head's still caked inside with the arithmetic of lying.

The deck isn't empty, not completely. There's a woman in a flying raincoat standing behind the funnel, a couple attempting to walk. Everyone, Beth included, is grinning.

Weather junkies. We love it, want the shake, the being so kindly defeated by what could kill us—it doesn't know us, doesn't notice, but it feels like playing, like something big taking an interest in us, paying attention—as if we could influence nature by catching its eye. It makes us comfortably tiny and hugely important, both at once—like being kids again.

We're up here, leaning against nothing we can see and willing it into more than physics: inventing a story—a scene where we rough and tumble with an attentive and jovial reality. We're people, and people do that: we live in stories.

I have the story of my family, my mum, my dad, my health, my shameful and redeeming and unforgivable acts—the story of who I am and wanted to be and could be and never will and never tried and failed to be.

I have the story of my good, clean, honourable country where I live—not perfect, but what's perfect?— not perfect, but not the purgatory in newspaper horror stories—not perfect, but not the shallow paradise in television wealthporn stories—not perfect, but not the comforting, smothering, jealous and noble stories of the fucked-up past—not perfect, but not the threatening, beautiful, beckoning, stupid, pain- and death-free stories of the fucked-up future that anyone will tell you if they want you to do something for them: to buy, to vote, to die, to kill, to believe, to torment beyond believing—not perfect at all.

*I have the story of my present: the **here** and the **is**: me on a patch of somewhere arbitrary and the hugeness of each unprotected moment under its racing sky. A beautiful and terrifying story.*

All fucking stories: what makes us nice, what makes us talk, what lets us recognise ourselves, touch others, be touched ourselves, trust loves—the fucking stories.

And they're what works the magic: the hard-core, bone-deep, fingers in your pages and wearing your skin and fucking you magic—that magic. Inside and out.

What he gave me—the power to be in other people's stories.

Something I took to as hard as he did.

He didn't make me, lead me astray. I adored it as much as he did and as much as him.

And the raw air screams, sings, cries, rocks her in place, keeps her looking at the furrowing ocean, the ways it breaks and mends and breaks and mends itself. Stare long enough, you see things: heads, rocks, wreckage, darknesses, fins.

*First time out and doing a platform gig I wasn't scared. It was a way to be us—I could be him and he could be me—and, just before we started, Art turned as he stood up from the table and he faced me—back to the audience and shielding me, and he let us look, have that serious look—**here we are and working, nobody like us when we're working, when we're hot as fuck**—and he almost smiles, parts and might begin to*

216

lick his lips, but doesn't quite because this is about different satisfactions.

Christ, he was really something.

And so was I.

This woman—Sally—looked bored, chilly, a bad choice, but still I'd picked her and that seemed not incorrect, not entirely unwise, and I'm throwing her names and getting no hits and the minutes are winding by and the room apparently sagging and my voice getting quiet, dry and smaller and I'm vamping with stuff about her being off-colour and maybe not taking care—hardly a wild leap to say so: she was puffy, self-punishingly fat, cheap haircut, unloved skin— engagement ring, wedding ring, probably early forties but seemed older—and she's giving me no signs, has been taught by domestic circumstance, by close experience, that you shouldn't give signs—I want to tell her 'Your husband is a bastard. He is almost undoubtedly a bastard and everyone dead and here with me would like to say so' but other than that— which is impractical—I'm close to having nothing left, to giving up.

Inexperience.

Arthur behind me, but I know, I am aware, that he's unconcerned, so I lean in harder, insist—she can't have come here for no reason.

Which is when she gets angry—wonderfully, silently furious—she's close to shouting that she thinks I'm crap—I can see it—and it's because she's scared— these frightened eyes—so fucking scared. No one who isn't terrified needs anything like as much bitterness, as much rage, as that.

She's hiding inside it.

I pace—and I know that Arthur's sitting with his arms crossed—softly, gently—both hands visible, the fingers, but I can't break contact with Sally and really check—I think he's showing three fingers and four— that's his opinion and I agree—didn't tell me beforehand, so it may be a guess or a detail he forgot—except that he never forgets—three and four and that's Sally, her story—she lost a child.

I'm sure because of one glance—one tic of the head down and to the side and when she faces me again, raises her eyes, she's younger—for a flinch of time she's younger and just at the start of that fresh tenderness, mother tenderness, and already it is purposeless— stolen away—the woman that she had intended to be is disappearing.

A day when the world jumps up and tears out everything, but lets you live, makes you live, leaves you here to stay without the everything you needed.

They didn't take care in those days, the hospitals— not much better now—so you edge what you describe into some sense of difficulty about seeing, you say that she was in hospital and wanted to see someone.

And then you watch her break, a whole woman harrowed down to sobs. They didn't let her see the baby—and no grave—speed and corridors and numbness and never knowing—fuckers—she never knew—fuckers—she never knew her child, or started or finished or had any help—they abandoned her to this.

'Little clothes, talking to your mum about pink or blue . . .' Pink gets a hit, a sign of laceration, her shoulders tense—so a girl then, a dead girl. 'Your girl knows you had a name for her and she hears you say her name.' It's a risk, but the mouth is such a soft place, so used to speaking that it's an easy bet: if I set her thinking, then I'll set her speaking in herself—and she does, she starts to say it in herself—she permits

218

it—the unnameable name. 'Pa- pa . . .' I decipher her lips—doesn't have to be precise. 'I'm getting . . . It starts with a P.' And the mother speaking it out loud then, like a love, a pride, 'Pam.' She can't manage any more, has to grip the hand of someone to her right—she doesn't know them, just holds on for fear of falling, being drawn into the place that's always there and always hunting for anything good, that takes it away.

I risk the possibility of mentioning a graveyard—she went without her husband, of course, because he's a bastard, as previously established—she's somehow in a graveyard—she didn't quite mean it but there she is—not at her daughter's grave, she has no idea where her daughter is buried—may simply have been dumped in a communal pit, but that's what we'll never mention, I'll only imply that Sally's looked and couldn't find— and in the graveyard she's at one of its edges, an untidy place where they've grouped the untimely dead—a line of memorials, fading toys and playroom colours, cheap and obvious and sentimental and clawing you down by the legs, by the hollow in you where she grew, until you're in the turf and sinking and gone to that place— she's felt it, has often thought of the permanent numbness, the blank she doesn't want to think is all there'll be when she runs out over the edge of her life—she has wanted to leave and go to her nearly kid—she has wanted to leave and be nothing.

And when she swallows I do too and I am in her, I am her.

I am out of myself and in the miracle.

And if she believes that her child still sees her— knows, accepts, forgives and loves and loves and loves—then she'll be altered.

Better.

219

Maybe.

The deck here is painted ready for sunshine and games, shuffleboard, quoits.

But that isn't why I did it.

I did it because it was wonderful. I enjoyed it.

Cupboards rattle against securing ropes, filled up with summer chairs, cushions, toys to keep little ones occupied when they're not in the paddling pool.

Love to paddle, kids.

Love all sorts of things—love their mothers—and they are loved.

She tries to focus on the sky, the way the clouds seem so languid, while everything here screams.

It was a thing we were good at—that I was good at—not as good as he turned out to be, but nevertheless we were something. And we felt like nothing ever has or will.

She angles her face to the cold sun.

Arthur and me, we could get tight up inside somebody's story—we could make them invite us in.

I'd start with a name, any name—doesn't matter—certain ones imply ages, nationalities, religions, others are more neutral—play it safe, or take a risk, I could pick—the enquirers are the ones who do the work. If the name gets a hit from the hall, if people claim it, then I keep with it, move on with it—switch in through descriptions—one detail, two, three—until I've knocked down all the possibles amongst my audience to a handful of enquirers, a couple—my woman, my man, all mine—I narrow and narrow what I give them until only their love fits. They think that I've found them, become more and more precise, when all that I've done is allow them to identify themselves.

And Christ, they do want to identify themselves.

The process is sly and irresistible and cheap and it

220

will always impress, because enquirers have no understanding of probability: they don't know how very likely it is that somebody else in a relatively modest gathering will share your birth sign, or will believe in birth signs, or won't like opera, or will have a scar on their right knee, a bad back—get enough people together and someone is bound to qualify for any competent opening description—and then they'll get to be the heroine, the hero of a story, not just an also-ran. And they want as much for their departed—who maybe had a chest condition, bad legs—or someone they knew had bad legs—or forget it and slide on, keep talking—they had blond hair, wanted blond hair, had a friend with blond hair, had hair—they worked indoors, in an office, in a serious office, like a legal office, they were important, good at their job, they made a difference, didn't go on about it, not really, they worked there many years, had a send-off to mark their retirement and a gift, at a bit of a loose end after that, although still with interests, sometimes they'd say that they couldn't imagine how they'd found time to have a job.

The more is known, the more it's possible to guess, the more it's possible to know, because close in the places where we think we'll be unique, we are anything but—we have first jobs we got through a bit of a fluke, an element of luck, and something happened when we were children that was nearly fatal, that gave us a scare—gave other people, the ones who cared for us, a scare—involving water—and when we are with our loves, we can be clumsy and worried and happy and scared and sometimes racy—we can surprise ourselves— and we can get so happy and so complicated and also simplified in our pleasures that we sometimes wonder how the fuck we could ever be this lucky and we also

221

don't know why the fuck we have ever been this hurt, this marked, this damaged, so that anyone who knew about it would wonder how we move, how we can stand—only nobody does entirely know, they would have to be psychic to know, they would have to be in possession of strange gifts and able to see us in our deep, sweet, bleeding places—to go further than love.

Except no gifts are necessary: in the deep and sweet and bleeding, that's where we are the same. In the heart of us, we are together—joy, hurt, fear—if we paid attention, just held on, we would feel it beat.

Beth stays on deck until her head aches, her cheeks, until she is mortified, shivering helplessly.

And when the gig was done, I'd go back home and be without him, but next to the Arthur I'd built from his absence, I'd lie beneath the weight of that. I made him irremovable with too much thinking—didn't mean to—I was just scared—and rehearsing—and scared—and I thought the story of him would be more controllable than his skin, his mouth, his fingers—I didn't want to spoil what we seemed to be.

Thinking their name when you come—you shouldn't. You'll always want to make it true, summon your love so they can hear it—your spell.

Working towards the nearest doorway seems an absurdly elongated process and very distant. She observes herself fighting her way back inside, yanking, jolting the door until she is finally accepted, lost in a deafened, broiling stillness.

Francis sees her in the café before she can avoid him, before her hands are ready to gather a bland warm drink from the many bland-warm-drink-dispensing machines.

'Now.' He rises and marches at her briskly, Bunny waving, staying where she is. 'For goodness' sake—you haven't been outside?'

'Yes.' Beth's mouth almost incapable with cold.

'Mad woman.' But he grins. 'Was it very exciting?'

She nods, because he wants her to nod and because it is true.

He takes her arm and wheels her round, 'You will sit with Bunny and tell her all about it—exaggerate as much as you like—and I will get you a hot chocolate, because that is the only thing that will do. It will be extremely sweet already, but would you like more sugar in it?'

She shakes her head and lets him father her, mother her—there's no harm in it, the ways we can adopt each other and this time he won't make her cry, she is too cold to cry and too suddenly settled in her mind.

'Bunny, here's Beth again—obviously. You'd have to have had a funny turn not to remember.'

Bunny, tired perhaps, but shaking her head in a manner which is pointedly contented, 'Just ignore him. I always do.'

'I'm going to get her hot chocolate and also cake. She isn't eating enough. Look at her.' And he hands Beth into her seat, is briefly and tenderly grave when he looks at her. 'Is there any type of cake that you don't like?'

'Um . . . No. I . . .'

'I think she has hypothermia, should we tell someone?' Stroking his fingers against his wife's neck, intent on her, hungrytender.

Bunny inclining to the touch, 'Go away.'

Which Francis does with a kind of bow.

'He's an idiot.' As Bunny examines her husband's back, its retreating, mildly self-conscious line, its resilience. 'Now tell me about the waves and tempests—I can't get out in them myself, he won't let me. And we'll have a nice afternoon tea together, if you'd like—it is the afternoon, isn't it? Every day I change my alarm clock and my watch—except for today when I shouldn't have . . . I think. The ship's magazine said I should, but it was mistaken, apparently. Or else I am. And we do nothing but eat and sit and wander about and eat and then dress up and eat . . . most disorientating. I have a suspicion it may be Wednesday, is that right?'

'Yes. It's Wednesday.'

'Well, that is a relief.' Bunny pauses, checks on the patisserie area and then on Beth. 'I was in a slough of despond because I missed the Napkin Folding Tutorial this morning—honestly, does anyone attend half the things they suggest we might like?' She pauses again. 'Sloughs of despond are unpleasant, but we overcome them, don't we?'

'Yes, we do.'

'Strange situation—the ship, the crowds, the bobbing about, the dreadful couple from Windsor with whom we've been forced to eat dinner every night—they've only been married for fifteen years and clearly want to kill each other—amateurs . . .'

'You don't want to kill Francis.'

'Not often. Not lately. We've had our times.' Patting Beth's arm for a second as she raises her

224

hand to beckon him in.

'Stop flapping at me, woman.' Francis, arriving perilously with a laden tray—three mugs of chocolate and a variety of cakes, tiny cake forks, plates, napkins, the whole weight and balance of it slithering and clinking until it's set down at rest—or as much at rest as anything aboard seems likely to get. 'I can see you perfectly well.'

'No you can't, I've got your glasses in my bag.'

'I can see you perfectly well enough.' Smiling at Beth so she's in on the joke. 'I'd know you anywhere.'

And they sit and they have what Francis declares *an illegally early tea* and they talk about the storms— the good and bad weathers they have seen. They spend an intentionally pointless hour.

And Francis and Bunny tell Beth a story, give her an image of Bunny running in a downpour, chasing across a field and Francis there and also running, holding a newspaper over Bunny's head until it's no longer a protection, only this heavy, tearing thing, and so he throws it away and they stop hurrying, are dignified and—by the time they reach a little village—they are stately and do not mind that people laugh at them, because the rain is warm rain and they are together. Together and soaked.

And it is difficult to leave them.

Once she has, Beth doesn't return to her cabin, doesn't discover if Derek feels better, or worse, or the same. She goes to the Purser's Office and makes an enquiry—slightly bored manner, no commitment, even faint irritation—delivers it well: 'Excuse me. Mr Arthur Lockwood . . . He's in one of the Grand Suites . . . I think that's what you call them. Could you help me with that?'

She no longer knows what else to do.

'I am expected.'

And this is when your book can tell you about the man and about the woman and how they're both young and in a cold town, rainy, scent of dead industry thick in the breeze as they walked from the railway station this afternoon.

It's dark now and they're tired because all evening they've been concentrating and remembering and talking to strangers about other strangers and watching them cry. It is beautiful, but also tiring to watch strangers cry.

They lean in to each other while the rain flusters and link arms, working their way back to the hotel—station hotel, Victorian monster of a thing: big rooms and draughty and patches on the curtains that the sun has faded, patches where rain has caught the cloth and stained it, weary carpets, chipped tiles and thin towels in the bathroom, potentially fatal electric fires. The man and the woman don't mind the mixture of grandeur and shabbiness, it amuses them, is part of a world filled with pretending.

Although they don't have an umbrella, they almost amble, not speaking, past the ugly town hall and the emptied municipal flower beds, the brightness of shops. It takes them a long time to make a little journey and they even pause before they mount the hotel steps, as if they might wander further on.

But they do come inside, grin at each other as they stroll across the foyer, their clothes clinging. The man's thumb leaves a damp mark when he

226

presses the button to call down the lift and when it arrives and the doors open, they already know that his room is on the third floor and hers is on the sixth, because they are good at keeping hold of numbers. And a stranger who's wearing a grey mackintosh trots up—he has this jerky, trotting step they will both recall very clearly—gets in with them, smells of cigarettes and Brut and some kind of dark stout. They grin at him, too. They love that the stranger is here and let him stand between them, flurry and heat the absolute truth between them which is that they will both go to the woman's room and they will undress in the quiet and chilly dark and then they will climb into her bed and find themselves there and waiting with the story of who they are and want to be and could be and never will and have to try.

There are so many things you ought to know—for your safety, for your happiness—and your book would like to tell them all to you. It sees that you do love your friends, but you don't trust too easily, your intimacy needs to be won and sometimes you can seem inaccessible and this is unsurprising because you've trusted and been hurt before. Although keeping yourself too solitary can become abrasive, there have also been individuals, personalities that you've sidestepped and you had every right to, because they meant you harm. Others have simply been easy to forget. It's slightly embarrassing to acknowledge that there are people you went to school with, worked beside every day, and now you don't have their numbers or a current address. And there have been occasions when you've told your problems, even the large secrets of your self to total strangers—you've let them look clear into you, and this has been surprising, but also liberating. And after they'd heard all you could say they were nothing but compassionate, affectionate, humane. They owed you no courtesy, yet you inspired it. This is because you have a good heart, a quite excellent heart. And you're interesting; sometimes you doubt it, but you are. You know how to tell a story and when you do people listen. You can make them laugh, which is relaxing and a tonic—they appreciate it.

And you're beautiful.

Again you're by no means sure of this, but you do possess beauty and it can be something you ought to protect, if not celebrate. When you were younger you occasionally felt slightly muffled, you looked for ways to be expressed and—although you might not say this yourself—you wanted to let your beauty be expressed. You've allowed some of your plans for this to slip, though. They were over-optimistic. To be truthful, the creative side of your life has worked out unexpectedly—is still working out. You are not a disappointment to yourself, but equally you aren't quite who you intended you'd be.

And your excellent heart has been broken and since then you haven't been the same. You came back from your troubles in some ways stronger and you don't go on about it—you've had courage that no one can fully appreciate—but you were injured deeply. You can't say you weren't. You hope this has made you more patient, generous, but you're aware that you can also be bitter and

228

self-punishing.

And these days you don't walk into situations with your eyes shut, not if you can help it—you like to be forewarned and forearmed. It can amuse you to be cynical, before you catch yourself sounding ugly or someone corrects you, or questions what you've said. Then you can stop, take stock of what you do have, what is here for you. You undoubtedly have reasons to be grateful and when you are, you feel more comfortable—not in a pious way, you'd hope—only with this slight peacefulness about you, a content.

There was a period when you might have attributed the good things in your life to higher powers: luck, God, willpower, effort, the stars, fate, the benefits of this or that philosophy, or system, your mental fibre or moral discipline. Now these kinds of simple assumptions seem rather naïve and you are less sure of your place in the fabric of reality—or if reality has a fabric, a pattern.

When you were a child you found it easy to believe—were apparently primed to have faith in almost anything and anyone. This has changed, partly because by now you've been fooled too often, scammed and disappointed. You also believe less firmly because you keep learning: you're open to new information and this can adjust your points of view. Your opinions aren't set in stone. Nor are you changeable for the sake of it, or shallow—although everyone can enjoy being shallow now and then and it need do no harm. You are perhaps more flexible and, indeed, thoughtful than average.

There have been television programmes and movies that you've watched ironically, or not at all, but you're aware that others took them at face value and accepted what you couldn't. You often read the papers and then hear their headlines repeated later, undiluted by an intervening thought, stale ideas in strangers' mouths, and this can disturb you. You worry true believers are out there, like fierce toddlers needing to have their own way, hoping to turn their whole species their own way: to unleash the unbridled market, unbridled government, unbridled precepts from unforgiving gods. You suspect they want to mark you with mythical whips, prepare you in their stories, dreams, laws, so that you will bleed in this world and the next. Their posturing can seem ridiculous, but also a genuine risk.

What you might call your current beliefs are complex, mature. God and death are changeable ideas for you: threatening, mysterious, blank, laughable, beyond reach: both of them can be odd comforts and bad jokes. You would like to inhabit a universe that's intelligent and loving, but it has shown itself unwilling to be either. Still, you have consolations: animals, landscapes, natural phenomena, the song of birds, the continuity of genes and minerals—blue eyes begetting blue eyes, carbon in stars and bones—and so much, so much, so much music. These can be joys, whereas many of the rituals from your childhood no longer impress and there are days when you may feel disturbed if you consider them in any depth.

And you aren't superstitious.

Habits and talismans of this or that kind can aid your confidence, that's accepted, but you wouldn't want to rely on them instead of proper preparation, instead of relying on your personal qualities. You'll admit they can give you a boost during tense situations. You may read your horoscope in the papers, but that's only a bit of fun—journalists make them up, they're patently generic guesses, veiled compliments and less-veiled threats. Surely, if astrologers were genuinely insightful, they could have told everybody about those extra planets out there, circling the sun: Sedna, Eris, Vesta and the rest—surely they'd have mapped them long ago. Whole planets—they're not like your spare keys, or your glasses—you can't just mislay them. You don't think that's an unfair point to make.

Under pressure, you may be a touch irrational and this can mean co-workers or family members may appear to be obstructive, or else your surroundings may seem malign for a while: the streets and traffic clotting, geography squirming away from available maps. Some days apparently have a grain and you can feel yourself going against it, but your anxieties do pass and they're rarely so great that you can't control them. Perhaps you do knock on wood, throw salt over your shoulder when you spill it—that's more about keeping a culture in place, about practising something your grandparents or parents might have done. None of this means you'd be taken in by any kind of mumbo-jumbo.

Although not everything has a rational explanation—you know that. You've talked about this over the years and found most people have one story, one place in their lives where the ground gave way and let them fall to somewhere else. They have been amazed. And the stories they've told you weren't the usual, fragile rubbish: that someone came to mind and then that very person called them. (No one remembers the endless thoughts that are followed by no call.) Or else some scenario, object, animal, human being was very clear to them while

231

asleep and was then reproduced, or near enough, when they awoke. (No one remarks on the visions, intuitions, portents that don't come to anything.)

That kind of nonsense is easily explained. What shakes a human being is strong magic, the apparently real thing: someone is stopped by a flower seller in a foreign street, or an old man in a bar, an old woman, an uncanny child—whoever and wherever they happen to be, they make some announcement, statement, which proves miraculously accurate or useful at a later date. Or objects, circumstances, actions collide with an insistent significance which turns out to be of material assistance in vital decisions, or trying times. Or someone goes to see a card-reader, palm-reader, aura reader, colour reader, I Ching reader, psychic, obeah man, medium, santeria wise woman, healer, crystal gazer, cyber-witch, someone who claims to be a gipsy on a seaside pier—however it happens, an enquirer *is told something important.*

A magnificent force has touched them, sought them out, and a deep and golden fact is shown to them and it could never have been known in any ordinary way and it comes true—it is true, could never be anything but true—and it proves the pattern in reality, it unveils the threads and shows how they shine.

For anyone this would be special and would make them special and you realise they wouldn't like you to take it away.

Because it's happened to you, too—you've had your turn at being special. And you believed in it. It was made to be believed.

A man standing in a doorway.

It might have been something like that—an almost

232

infinitely adjustable and eloquent bundle of words. It might have been something you'd heard before, or words not even meant for you, but still they hooked in and stayed with your thinking and spoke to you until you sought them out, began to search for their vindication.

And when you look, you find.

*   *   *

Beth looked.
A man standing in a doorway.
She's good at looking, is doing it now, walking her way towards whatever a *Grand Suite* will turn out to be, to whatever the rest of her trip will turn out to be, to however, for fucksake, she may spend the rest of her life.

No pressure.

Only walking to Arthur's suite. I have walked before and have walked to hotel rooms and suites before and he has been inside them before. This doesn't have to be a challenge if I think of it like that—bite it into little pieces and then I can swallow it.

And focus on the irrelevant and harmless—everything he's not.

So.

It has its own name, like a pet: the Astoria Suite. Art's staying in rooms with a name. Because things for important people can't have numbers, they need to be personalised—the rest of us get the numbers.

She winds herself up the stairs.

'Ask, and it shall be given you; seek, and ye shall find; knock, and it shall be opened unto you.' When he still did the platform work, he'd chuck in bits of Bible—enough to add ballast, but not provoke.

233

Eventually, I learned them, too. I can quote fucking scripture like a fucking nun if I fucking have to.

For a while it had been his favourite—**seek and ye shall find**—he'd used it too much, in fact, almost as much as **a man standing in a doorway**—and when she left him, the image of that left with her, lodged and watched until September 1999—when she'd passed almost five years without him—and then it lit her, made her see.

She had taken her mother for a break—Bank Holiday weekend.

Can't resist a Bank Holiday weekend.

They'd got rooms in a spa hotel with nice toiletries and complimentary bathrobes and a selection of treatments and procedures guaranteed to be cleansing, or detoxifying, or relaxing, or just nice and hot tubs and a fucking swimming pool—as if this would be a sensible idea and as if they ought to be alone somewhere like that with too much time to think—alone because her father wasn't with them.

It was in Beverley—no reason to pick Beverley, but I did.

Beth's mother had walked the grounds when it wasn't raining and read when it was and, although the rest of the spa's suggestions didn't suit, she got a haircut and a new perm and had her nails done— nothing garish, just a nice manicure and a little bit of shine. She'd explained to Beth how the ladies who did it all—who encouraged her into it—had been very outgoing and pleasant, they had made her laugh and first called her Mrs Barber, but then later they called her Cath, because she asked them to, because Cath is unchangeably her name and isn't reliant on anyone else.

Cath had come down to dinner looking pretty for

nobody, hands holding each other, unwillingly self-contained. She wore her first new dress since her husband's funeral as if it were a sin.

Beth had paid what she couldn't afford to for massages—face down and tensing more when they touched her, when they tried to let out what her muscles were barricading in: the thoughts and thoughts and thoughts. She'd guessed this would happen and wasn't alarmed—she was only embarrassed when she got her money back for one session because she had started sobbing—full, jerky sobs—and that meant the masseur had noticed and stopped.

It wasn't unreasonable—guy by himself with an upset naked woman under a sheet—could be awkward.

Everything stops for tears.

As a general principle that would never work. Put the whole bloody world into gridlock, that would. It would send everyone chasing round boats to no purpose, set them adrift.

No. I do have a purpose. It is a bad purpose, I think. I'm not sure. It may be the wrong way to do right.

Beth has reached Arthur's deck, which is Deck Seven—of course, it would be seven—and the light fitments are more aspirational here than elsewhere and the air tastes cleaner, subtly conditioned to please those who've paid for it.

The scent of people faking it—Kings of Glasgow with looted pensions, Duchesses from Solihull who are blowing their redundancy money, couples who want to be twenty years ago and newly-weds—and they want to have white glove service and little sandwiches cut into shapes and their picture taken with the captain and dancing the night away and pretending that being British should mean you are running a loving empire,

keeping the less-blessed and foreign in line and teaching
them how to boil vegetables into submission and forget
themselves and salute the Butcher's Apron when it
creeps up the bloody flagpole every morning.

They don't want to be ashamed.

Or they just want to fake being film stars.

And the Germans fake being Brits and the Americans
fake being Brits and the Brits fake being Brits—fake
it harder than anyone else so they can be imperturbable
ladies and firm but fair gentlemen.

The French stay French. They have their own
problems. They have their own flag.

Everyone has their own flag. How would you know
what's yours if you can't stick a flag in it?

Me, I'm flying a white one. For surrender and
undecided—blank sheet.

It takes her an effort to move along the passageway—
going against its grain.

Did he want us to be here because we're both fakers?
Did he think I would be at home in this many lies?

And she'd knock on wood if there was any—*Does*
veneer count?—she'd throw salt back over her
shoulder in a trail if she thought it would help.

It has the scent of a good hotel, that's all—no need
for me to get hysterical.

Arthur is a collector of good hotels.

It wasn't unlikely I'd meet him in one. In, for
example, sodding Beverley.

In sodding Beverley, Beth had stalled outside her
mother's room, had missed the moment when they
ought to kiss goodnight, or hug, should do something
compassionate. Eventually Cath had thanked her
again for the lovely time she clearly wasn't having
and had given a small, stiff nod.

'You don't need to thank me. I wanted to . . . It's

236

good if we . . . And the office has been busy and . . .'

'You can't work all the time.' This only a quiet statement, not accusing—which naturally made it accuse Beth more and then widen to suggest a background of daughterly neglect, the waste of a university education in mindlessly administrative jobs, a consuming lack of positive direction that was clear to anyone—the usual themes.

Beth was unable to explain that she wanted to be busy, not fulfilled: that chasing fulfilment would be dangerous, would wake her. 'No, I think I *can* work all the time, actually. I think . . . Sorry.' Beth watched her mother's lips, the sadness briefly plain in them and then the irritation. When she spoke again Beth sounded childish, whining, 'It's what I do, Mum . . . Coping . . . Sorry . . .' She had no strength to be kind and do better. 'Sorry. I shouldn't . . . We should have breakfast late tomorrow—last day. Or in bed— you could do that.'

'I'd rather have breakfast with you.'

The need to have Beth around had never been there before; at least, not in this ravenous, sad form. It made Beth want to leave.

So she did. 'We'll do that, then. And I'll get off to bed. Tired. Sorry.' No sitting up in her mother's room and ignoring bad telly again, both reading to avoid being companions, or having a conversation. 'See you in the morning. Sleep well.' But they would have been together, nonetheless, which might have been bearable for Cath but Elizabeth couldn't deal with it, not yet. She only ever saw her mother with her father. Now she can't sit next to one and not expect the other, assume he'll fluster in with apologies about a gig that ran much longer than

237

expected, an awkward audience, a birthday girl who cried.

I should be more help to her. But I won't. As ever, not a jolly good fellow. But I can only stand what I can stand.

And she'd headed upstairs to her own room, padded along the carpet between perspectives of calming, Zen-flavoured pictures, door frames, doors.

Heard the noise of an opening door and I looked round. No reason to do so—I wasn't expecting anyone.

A man standing in a doorway.

And I can't recall being surprised to see him. I don't think I felt anything—no dip in the stomach, no swing—it was only like being suddenly in a wide, high empty space and having no breath.

Arthur was standing in his doorway, barefoot in an upmarket suit—thinner than she'd remembered, paler, wearier, clean-shaven and with a poorhouse short back and sides. He was holding a Do Not Disturb sign, about to close up for the night.

He looked at her.

I don't think he was feeling much, either. Although the sign shook in his hand. I noticed that: a jolt and then he made himself steady.

And there had been something naked in his eyes, caught in the open for an instant and then gone.

And I could have decided to think—'What are the chances of both of us staying at that hotel and at that time and of my passing precisely when he would be standing there and I could see him?' I could have imagined our meeting was so unlikely it must be a sign of some larger intention at work—our destiny.

But there are so many corridors inside so many hotels and so many people who have met—at other times and in other places—so many other people and there

238

are so many nights when so many sleepers might wish not to be disturbed that the chances of somebody somewhere encountering somebody else—even somebody they have kissed in the past—those chances are quite high. Even though the greater the number of variables, the less likely the event, it's still not that miraculous for someone, somewhere to see someone stand in a doorway—someone whose palms they have kissed, whose stomach they have kissed—someone they have kissed right to the root where he's hard and sweet and clever and where he wants.

She stops in the rising and recoiling passageway and can no longer think of going forward.

And he kissed me. We might have been kind and done better, but we didn't even speak that much—just acted as if we were following a plan and had decided to give each other what would keep us from having to think.

Of course.

But there wasn't a plan, not anywhere. Our meeting was a coincidence, not a hint, not a gift, not anything that means we have been sentenced to a life spent faking—play-acting that we're a pair of horny strangers, chasing the cum.

Deck Seven waits—all swaying perspectives and a reddish carpet for the movie star touch.

I can't recollect if I told him my father was dead.

I'd have told a real stranger—it would have been the first thing I'd have said.

And Beth waits, too. She can't go back, but she also can't move any nearer to the curve that will lead round the line of the stern. Turn the corner and she'll find Arthur's suite and he'll be expecting her, because the Purser's Office told him she was on her way, because wealthy people should not be

239

subjected to surprises. Beth can imagine she feels his concentration drilling and humming against the walls.

But he could have gone out—avoided the issue, done what I might do.

I am out and avoiding, in fact.

She decides she should stand and worry that she isn't properly dressed. This will pass the time.

And what exactly would the dress code be for this? What's the proper costume for not quite adultery, or for various grades of betrayal, or for the new start of something old? I couldn't face that. The new start of something new, then. Which I can't face either.

Should I be naked, get it over with, cut straight to the way we end up?

Or fancy underwear? We tried that. I tried that. The guy never has to, it would seem. He just brings fancy sheets.

More things to not face.

Nondescript appearance, that's what I'm aiming for, noncommittal, non-combatant—an ensemble that might suggest I'm not making assumptions.

I should have tied my hair back, sprayed it down, worn a bloody balaclava—it has a mind of its own. One of us ought to.

I'm not going to be as I should and he's going to see it. And I'm ugly enough where it doesn't show, so I would rather be presentable on the surface.

She closes her eyes and begins to step forward— being blinded helps.

The jeans because they fit, they're comfortable, a comfort, the sweater because it's cashmere and it might not look terrific—green, it's draining and it's clashing with the carpet—but it's soft and I need soft.

Low shoes because I would rather not fall.

Already a fallen woman.

While she progresses, the ship's life works on her, its motion making her heavier and then lighter in a long, slow rhythm, as if something is hunting along her bones, squeezing out the thoughts she doesn't want.

Derek might be awake, he might be rallying.

I'm not even sure what time it is.

It's ridiculous that she may be found like this by a steward and asked to explain herself, which would be shaming.

I don't want to be ashamed.

So I shouldn't be heading back to Arthur.

People who don't want to be ashamed should avoid performing shameful acts.

And the floor, walls, ceiling keep on shifting and her mind also shifting, running, shuddering, until suddenly it locks, is still—perhaps exhausted—and she thinks this is what it's like to be him, Arthur—a man so filled with everything that he twitches and flails on dry land, unfitted for anywhere stable, but shake him out into chaos and then he's a piece of peace.

If I knew how to be him well enough, I could maybe get by without him. I could fake that and be safe.

Bollocks.

I want to kiss him.

It isn't complicated.

I want that.

A man standing in a doorway.

The man ought to be Arthur, but Arthur has arranged other arrangements.

Loves his arrangements—surprises for everyone but Art.

When she rings the bell, Art's suitably impressive door is opened to her by a man in a dinner suit who wears white gloves and a shipping line name tag—*Narciso*. 'Good evening, Miss.'

Arthur is the one in the living room, sitting on a sofa with not enough space for his length of bone. He is concentrating on his bookshelves—this level of accommodation provides both bookshelves and books—and now he tells a random selection of tour guides and holiday mysteries, 'This is Narciso—my complimentary butler. And he is. Very.' Arthur winding his arm round under his knee, frowning. 'I think he'll be staying. He can serve us things. Snacks. Champagne.' Art is in jeans and a very fresh shirt the colour of his eyes and this is a plausible choice: not unattractive and it doesn't emphasise his skin—the pale shock of his skin; better to highlight the blue where he looks, the dodge and sudden focus of that. This isn't a working outfit—the idea would be that he's trying not to try—but it's formal enough to let him be relaxed. The shirt will have been made for him by somewhere double-barrelled—Payne & Hackett, Needham & Markham, Markham & Dunne—a place with bloody names.

'They've been trying to give me champagne since I boarded, but I don't like it because it's for celebrations and I don't celebrate.' While Arthur speaks, Narciso smiles like a man who is only half listening and used to eccentricities. He ushers Beth into a seat and stands behind her shoulder.

'We're close. Aren't we close, Narciso? We're as close as a temporary, rented butler and his not-really-employer could possibly be and we have no secrets. So he can stay. I think he should stay. What do you think?' He turns and blinks at her and is slightly out of breath. 'We could watch telly.'

And Beth feels as she is intended to: insulted and a little sick and she snaps back, 'Or you and Narciso could watch telly and I could leave you to it.'

Arthur calculates his way through shrugging, sniffing, demonstrations of unconcern. 'We could do that, we could . . .'

And the ocean is dark and torn through the windows and the weather lunges round the balcony which would be perfect for summer entertaining, but is useless to them currently. Beth watches the rain streak and shiver on the glass while the silence thickens and what else did she expect—that he would be straightforwardly pleased to see her and this would be easy and not very possibly the last of their last chances?

Narciso paces neatly away to the tiny kitchen, returns with a tinier dish of rice crackers—which are tinier still—and sets them down, stands at ease.

'Thank you.' Arthur letting this be a murmur and deciding to claw both hands through his hair. 'And I think that even though we are not in any way celebrating, you could bring us the champagne and then, as it turns out, we won't be needing you this evening and you can put out the sign on the door to that effect, because being disturbed is not a good thing and I have had enough of it and from here on in I will avoid it at all costs.'

Narciso tranquil, 'Yes, sir. Of course, sir.' And bringing the champagne, tucked into its ice and, 'Good afternoon,' then vanishing away.

It's almost intolerable when he goes.

Ought to wave the flag—run it up and wave it and admit defeat. But he'd never trust that and nor would I.

Arthur faces her, quiet, clear. 'Ahm, look. I don't know. Nothing of this is . . . and I don't know what would . . . for the best . . . I, I do want the best. For you. But also for me.' And he swallows. 'I'm very tired. Can I start with that? Should I start with that? I go every day to the spa place here and they try and put me right, relax me and I lie in the pool—sorry—I . . . mainly the hot tub and then I'm here and they bring me the fish with the seasonal vegetables and the fruit which is good for me because that's what I ask for and it's OK, it's a reliable meal and I can eat it every day if I have to—I need things to be reliable . . . And I am . . . That is, I don't sleep.' He is wound into himself, elbows and knees folded tight, long feet tucked away from her and there is something distantly horrified in his expression and she doesn't want this to be her fault—she doesn't want him horrified at all—and he keeps on. 'You know how I don't sleep. Nothing to do with conscience, just physiology—I actually sleep more when I'm working—sorry—but it's starting to matter, the insomnia—because eventually I need to sleep and I still don't, not exactly, and the problem is— apart from anything else—that I sometimes dream and you're there—and so I am avoiding sleeping, because I am avoiding dreaming—sorry, but I am— but you are there when I do get to sleep and I do want that. I think. Waking up is bad, because that

244

means you go, but I do think I want that—to dream. So I'm not sure why I'm trying to keep it away . . . I was kissing your neck the last time, that's all I remember . . . I can't . . . ah . . . I can't do what we've been doing. I can't. The visits every now and then.'

'I know.'

'It's not . . . I can't do it.'

'I know.'

'Well, then fucking help!' The start of this shouting, but then it snaps down low again. 'Stop fucking me about.' He rubs his knees, rocking slightly against the will of the ship. 'Just . . . I fuck you about too and I don't intend it . . . and . . . but I do.' He subsides, bends forward to study his hands before he lifts them to rub at his eyes and then cover his face. He keeps them in place to hide him. His back rises and falls unevenly.

'Arthur.' Beth's voice strange in her throat and she's wishing for codes to solve this, give him meanings. 'I . . .'

I can go and sit beside him and get him to believe in me, that's more effective than talk. I know how to feel trustworthy—just imagine that I love him and I wish him well and the rest will take care of itself, automatic. He'll understand.

A drumming scours through the ship and almost makes her stumble, but she does go to him and doesn't touch, does not disturb, only concentrates and then begins with, 'There was that place where we stayed—Fife, wasn't it? The baby castle with a sort of tower and it was genuinely old, but peculiar, weird furniture and made-up coats of arms on papier mâché shields.' And this is chatting, which won't be frightening.

245

Chat and the world chats with you, strive to address your issues and you'll be doing it alone.

I wouldn't even be doing it with me.

But Beth would prefer to be here and herself and not alone and not frightened, 'There was no staff— just that guy who owned it and pretended there were staff, but then when he's serving breakfast and he's clearly also cooked it and there are no other guests, he admits that he's all by himself, but not to worry because he hires the place out for weddings and that goes quite well—wedding in a castle.'

Arthur is still leaned over, but his hands have eased down and he's beginning to relax. He's letting her in.

But I mustn't notice, I'm just telling a story and he can listen and we'll be like friends, old friends, and I do love him and I do wish him well, so there's nothing here that could disturb him.

She isn't performing a shameful act, 'Our room was the library—great big purple room with a four-poster bed and these abandoned hardbacks, nothing newer than the 1950s, and . . . it was . . . that seemed . . . there was the lake at the back and tall, tall foxgloves—so many colours and as high as you.'

His spine straightens a fraction at this and shows how she is working in him and she keeps her rhythm, her pace, the engaging details, 'And tiny frogs, when we walked there were these tiny frogs—perfect little babies scampering away to be out of danger only we weren't going to hurt them and we . . . it all smelled of cut pine wood and I wished it was cold so we could have a fire and sit by it and instead we sat on the patio by ourselves and there was confetti left in the gravel—silver metal confetti cut out in the shape of a couple dancing, which was very tacky,

246

but I kept a piece. I've still got it. I found it with you and it made me remember dancing with you. I keep it because it makes me remember remembering.' So that he knows she wasn't blankly absent, was imagining her ways back to him all the while, all the months, was puzzling out towards him.

And he joins her, joins in, gives in. 'The confetti people, they had rather distanced upper bodies and high arms. That's what I remember. It didn't look like dancing. It looked like two people throttling each other. You could take your pick. Both intimate in their ways.' Which is him testing her, not making himself easy, but still willing.

He pauses and she lets him and likes that she heard a smile under what he said, but doesn't check him. It's too soon to check. He mustn't feel examined. The next thing he'd feel after that would be that she's playing him.

When playing him would be a shameful act.

Beth starts in with a gently different direction, something warmer. 'I didn't dance with you that time.'

'No.'

'That was . . .'

'Galway.'

He doesn't move. 'Galway.' But the purr is beginning in his throat, the low and comfortable sound.

Two men who had that—two men with that exact sound. And Arthur's the only one left.

'We were in Galway.' And he shifts and turns further from her, but leans until his back is tight to her side and rests with a small flicker of something like regret, misgiving, and then a fuller pressure. 'And it was another bloody wedding . . . Big

247

hotels—you'll get weddings—weddings, or honeymoons and all the fucking—and I mean that literally—all the *fucking equipment*: remote control ignition real-flame fires for romantic atmosphere, scented candles for overpowering atmosphere, built-for-two tubs with bubbles and funny lighting . . . *Christ.*' His ribs move when he jerks out a small, fast breath and she knows this is like a laugh—the way a sad man laughs.

But she can't have him sad—'We like them, though. The big hotels. The facilities . . .'

Arthur's body tenses slightly and no training or insight is required to help her read that he doesn't entirely want to start recalling the glide of soaped skin in hi-tech showers, the coddle of warm water and the tease of cold and the splaying and crouching and mouthing and the ludicrous, never-ending cleanliness of staying dirty—Friday night to Monday morning checkout of straining to keep themselves spiked, taut, stiffened, adequately bewildered to hide from who they are and to be fucks. Three nights of being a ride, faking that you're a stranger's little gift.

And this will hurt him, so he shouldn't think it and it's OK to change his thinking if it saves him from a hurt.

'Galway—it was nice.' But he's closing down into himself.

Catch him then, steer him.

'Yes. We liked Galway—and downstairs in the function suite there was a band and it didn't seem likely it could be that bad . . . and loud.' She sounds as casual as she can while the floor writhes under their feet.

He edges out to meet her again. 'Probably everyone

248

else in the place was down in the function suite, banqueting hall, whatever—there with the wedding. Us the odd ones out.'

'Like always.' And she tries to make this sound like a good thing.

'Like always.' And he makes this sound as if it's not.

'We're more the honeymoon.'

Which is the wrong, wrong, wrong thing to say.

Amateur.

'We're not any kind of honeymoon.' And he sits away from her, coughs. 'Sorry, I don't want to lose my temper and I don't want to be talking about this. I can't. But people on honeymoon are together and that isn't what we do and please don't insult me with that kind of . . . I realise you like to hurt me and you have your reasons and I have my own reasons to hurt me and they're better than yours—I know me better—but please don't.'

Twitch in his shoulders, as if I've hit him which I'd never do—only ever did that once which I regret—and arguing fatal now—we can't—I can't—but chatting—run back to the comfortable and easy chatting—he needs to be comfortable and easy—then we can do what we need to.

'They played covers from *The Blues Brothers* and *The Commitments* . . . I think they played "Mustang Sally" three times, four times—a lot.'

'Just a lot, Beth. Let's do without the fucking numbers, they give me a headache.'

Concentrate and concentrate and give him what's right.

And love and love and love and soft and smile.

And, 'No numbers, then. I'm sorry. We got out of bed and we had a dance. All those layers of floorboards and the carpet, so we were having the music filtered—still not great—but OK at a distance and . . . it was like when you'd only just stopped that wearing the gloves thing and all the rest, being wrapped up all the time—way back then . . . You were so . . . As if you weren't used to it—the touching . . . and your skin was . . . It felt . . .'

I've got this whole speech ready—about how there's this other man he keeps inside and he's always dancing and he shows, not all at once, but he's there: in the shoulders, or the snap to an arm or a spring in the walk, the melody in under Arthur's walk, and he's there, he's properly there, this happy man, the truly happy man and I love him and I danced with him in Galway—with almost all of him.

Too long.

Just hold his hand and give him the summarised version.

'You were blinding. Sort of blinding.'

'That doesn't seem likely.' But he lets her close the distance again, ghost a contact, an invitation, hip against hip and when she smoothes her hand across his back Arthur's spine is audible through his shirt and the bite of it, its kind of exposure, catches her—he is habitually lean, but now he's thin, harrowed—and this is in some way utterly appalling. Too much of his structure is showing through.

And there's his heat, his intention beneath her fingers—muscle, ribs, thought—it's labouring, slowing, adjusting, before, 'Sorry, Beth. Sorry . . . I . . . I like your stomach against my stomach. When we danced . . . That's a clumsy way to say it, but . . . In my stomach is where I get scared and when you . . .' But he changes his direction, retreats, 'We're all done by kindness—it's never ineffective . . .'

250

'Come to bed.'

'I don't want to come to bed, I don't want to be near a bed, I don't want—' And he hugs himself around his shoulders and drops his head on to his arms.

She does not kiss the back of his neck where it is pale and soft and burning, because this would be impractical. She leaves him be and says, 'I know. And I don't want. Not that.'

'I was going to take ice cubes from round the champagne and make your nipples hard with them— numb you up then suck you—some kind of crap like that—the usual . . . We make plans, you see—people make plans and they are the wrong plans, so they are laughable—but you shouldn't laugh because they can't . . . can't help it and they hurt. They hurt everyone.' Mumbling into his Jermyn Street shirt and then failing, stopped.

The horizon soars and shakes and Beth waits.

Takes as long as it takes—five minutes, ten minutes— until he's calmer. But he's mine now—all opened, all ready. And listen to his breath—smoother and smoother—he'll be able to hear and we'll begin.

'I worked out why you take the ships, Arthur. I understand. On the first night, I realised and it made me . . . When you lie down in your bed and the boat moves—the tiny rock—the tiny flicker in the mattress, the give—it's like when you were a kid and somebody came in and sat on the side of your bed—it's that kindness again—it's the best—it's . . . nobody's ever going to do that who doesn't . . . It would be someone at least looking after you . . .'

'Has he touched you today? Derek. Did he touch you?'

'Sssssshhh.'

251

'Has he touched you?'

'No.'

'Why the fuck not?'

'Christ, do you really . . . ? Because he doesn't want to, because I am being a bitch and inexcusably cruel to him, because he is ill, because I wouldn't be able to let him. He hasn't really touched me since dry land. The first night on board we were just very sleepy and ever since . . . Arthur, the pills I've been giving him aren't for seasickness. I break those out of the pack and palm them and take them myself—he's been eating . . . it's a homeopathic remedy for sinus infections. Does sod all. Won't harm him. But it also won't stop him being iller than anyone should have to be.'

And no one but Arthur would find that romantic—but he will—he does—there he is, my boy—looking at me like he's waking up.

But she takes care not to smile. 'You didn't make me do that—I did that, it was my choice.' This is a confession and therefore serious. 'It is not to do with you, but I might not have done it if you hadn't been here.'

'No. You would have got engaged.'

Which is the last little fence that he'll throw at her and so she ignores it, 'He might have asked me to—I couldn't have. With or without you, I wouldn't have done that . . .' The ship swooping and reeling with her when she realises she's supplied herself with the perfect cue—an accident, so it should sound genuine. 'With or without you—Arthur . . .'

If you're being honest it's all right to sound flat, jangled, amateur. So aim for that.

'Arthur, can I be with you? Please.'

'He kissed you. I saw him.' This isn't an objection,

252

it's an invitation.

And my boy gets to be my boy, my own boy.

'And so will you.' And she gets up, slides her hands under his ears and holds him.

When they walk to his bedroom they are exactly as unsteady as they should be.

My boy.

And Arthur climbs on to the goldenish coverlet like a very orderly boy, simply lies down across it, curls away on his side, faces out to the balcony and his dangerous view.

Beth sits on the side of the mattress, lets it give, give, give, then swings, moves, rests herself up against the headboard, the pillows. She slips her hand in under his skull, his cheek. She is glad of his weight.

'I go on marches, Beth.'

He'll talk now and I'll let him.

And she's glad of the shape of his voice against her fingers.

'You'd be proud of me. Maybe.'

She doesn't imagine the craft lying thick in his mind, the darknesses and strategies and lies. They have a weight and a shape and are beating in him, too.

And I have my own and today I don't save him from myself.

He rocks his head back and forth, warm and away and then warm and then away and, 'I think you would be proud. Not because of . . . I mean . . . I met these soldiers' mothers—in the way that I would meet the mothers of dead sons—I'm sorry, I know you hate it, but I have to say and . . . but I . . . What do they have apart from me? Their boys, they were teenagers and they wanted free driving lessons and

253

a fucking job and they looked smart with the haircut and the new dress uniform and people talked to them about loyalty and self-respect and discipline and they got very good at pressing in regulation creases and bulling their boots—I do know a bit about it—the research—some of it I read about and the people, relatives, other fucked-up soldiers with other dead—with dead friends—they told me some of it and it doesn't, in this context, I believe, matter what I was doing—or what the reality of that was—I still have the right to be fucking outraged, fucking beyond it, that they went off with minimal training to a country where they never should have been and were killed for predictable and fucked-up reasons, because that's what happens, always, when people pay no fucking attention to each other. Always. All neat and kissing you goodbye and photos in the post and emails and, after that, home in a box—how do you make sense of that without me—you aren't going to get apologies, or justice, or an undertaking that the recruiters won't hang round your shopping centre, your scheme, your school, and pick up more boys and use them to make more dead and . . . You know what they used to say?—in the First World War?—in that one? Believe me, I know my wars— half of my job has been learning fucking wars—they used to say there was one time when a king would have to salute a private soldier and the soldier could ignore him—which is when the private soldier is dead. I get tired of all the respect being given to the dead. I respect the living. The *living*—the ones who have to live, keep doing that—they're the ones I work for. And I march with them.' He pauses for a breath, presses his face against her hand. She holds where he's frowning. 'These women, they're different

now: they're not just bereaved, they're activists—
they're not the way women in housing schemes are
meant to be—they don't just shut up and take it.
And I'm there with them sometimes—no particular
use in that context, but I'm there, I want to be
there—when I can be, where I can be—and people
come round on the demos and give you signs,
placards—usually the faces of hurt kids, dead kids,
and you carry these dead kids with you and I walk
behind the mothers and they wear T-shirts, they wear
these T-shirts with numbers on them, their sons'
serial numbers—because their sons were numbers,
are numbers—everything they did and cared about
and trusted and all that's left is these T-shirts and
a number each—women wearing their sons. And I
march and I give them money because my job makes
me money and I *try to fucking help*. I try.'

He stops to let her contradict him, rolls on to his
back and gives her his hand, makes the grip tight.
'On the last march—because I do as many as I can,
because you get to know the . . . it's not just
research—the organisations, they tell you about
more and more and more of this shit—this death
shit—and the last march I was on was for refugees,
asylum seekers. Three of them had killed
themselves—my government, your government
dumped them in a block of flats where no one could
live—no one—no one *un*traumatised, no one *without*
ghosts—the flats, they're just an invitation to top
yourself—if you looked up: lousy balconies, rotten
wood, shit paintwork and the whole place is just
telling you, *Why don't you piss off and die?* There's
this guy there and he's just a punter, he's local, has
all these relatives—cousins, pals—and they've
jumped—they weren't refugees, they just lived

255

there—which is being another kind of refugee, isn't it . . . and the guy, he's telling me this stuff and he's not playing me, he doesn't need me—I'm just listening—and it's clear, more than clear, that anybody sane would jump. They would jump to not have to be in the normal blocks of those flats—and inside the block for the refugees . . . they're not allowed washing machines in their flats—there are four fucking washing machines in this one little utility room—that's all there is among Christ knows how many in the whole block and half the time the machines don't even work—and no door locks that the concierge can't open—and checking you out and checking you in—that's not a concierge, that's a jailer—Christ, we've got prisons with children in—refugee prisons—and what have they done? They've been the weakest of the weak, so we put them in prison—it's all . . . it's because we don't see each other, we don't even try . . . So there's this family in the high flats, they kill themselves—patch of the grass with some flowers on where they landed—covers up any indentations, I'd suppose—cheap flowers—and these people, concerned individuals, they turn up—call goes out and they're there—and me—and we march—with some of the guys, the asylum seekers from the flats, and eventually, you know, there's a quite a lot of us under way, we're off and we're filling the street and we're coming into town, from where the thrown-away people are to where the proper shops are and the good buildings that aren't trying to kill you—where the respect is—and these refugees, these human beings from nowhere, from hell, from nothing they can stand to remember, they're walking down the middle of the road and holding up traffic and being *guarded* by police—escorted and looked after *by the police*—who are behaving themselves—and the refugees, they're not allowed to earn, they can't vote, the Border Authority can do what they like with them at any time and no one seems to care, but today they have policemen helping them to be a parade—and there are total strangers there to prove that someone gives a shit—not just politicals: couples and kids and students and whoever—and it's not practical, not really, it's just giving up a bit of a Saturday morning to prove a point and not achieve, you might say, anything much—but the asylum seekers they're so bloody happy about what's going on—the almost-nothing that's going on—that some of them are *dancing,* they're *singing*—'cause it seems like they might exist, they might be real again and in the world, might be able to have a bit of it, and I am *absolutely certain* I could help them, what I do could help them and it would cost them nothing and I could have helped that family, they needn't have tied themselves together and walked off the edge of their lives. They had nothing, Beth, and nothing is the code for nothing—for fuck all—and no one should be left with that.'

And the sound of this seems to frighten him and make him want to pretend he wasn't suddenly thinking of himself and of small problems—she can see him blush, consider the largest options he can muster. 'I just . . . I'm not the worst specialist in death—I do not personally, directly *make* anyone dead, I do not earn my money by killing, or by allowing other people to die, I also do not go through my life under the impression that my everyday decisions *aren't* murdering people I'll never meet and I make an effort to be responsible in my

257

behaviour and I do expect—I insist on expecting—
that other human beings might try that, too. Thirty
years ago—I can't get this out of my head—thirty
years ago—what's 30 again? **30** was sport, wasn't it?
Something sport related . . . inappropriate . . . Thirty
years ago, the UN promised that every member
country would give 0.7 per cent—which is the
mathematical way of saying fuck all—of their Gross
National Income to stop the poor dying, so that
mothers and kids and other ordinary normal members
of our species wouldn't just cease to exist for no
good reason—wouldn't be executed by the nature
of their lives . . . in 2009—this is research I do for
me, it's for nobody but me—it's not practical, it's
because I like people and I don't want them to need
me and it's only when your dead have gone the
wrong way that you need me—and because I do the
research I know that in 2009 *five* countries were
actually giving 0.7 per cent. *Five*—out of all the UN
countries—five out of 102. Sweden, Denmark . . .
none of them amazingly big countries with huge
resources, just merciful and civilised.

'Five from 192—that's code for almost everyone
being a cunt. Or for the people who represent almost
everyone being cunts.'

'Sorry for the word—as a thing and a place, it's
. . .' He lets his breath struggle in his chest for a
moment. 'You know what I mean. We are not well
served by the allegedly great and the allegedly good
and the powerful.

'But I can say, Beth, I can tell them. Because of
my job, I can tell the people—some of the people—
who would otherwise spend their surpluses on
medieval tapestries, or jade, or German armour—
who would otherwise gather over-priced shit with

dodgy provenance, or no provenance, or fakes—the people who want their names chiselled into everything with gold inlay because it's classy—I can say to them, "Collect lives. Why not?"—I would say *save* lives— but *collecting*, that's easier for them to understand. They can keep a running total on a collection. They can turn up in tropical gear, fresh off the Lear jet and meet kids who'll remember their names for ever, no gold inlay necessary. The kids will be able to remember and have lives, because the people with more money than sense—me included, that would include me—did something to help—did more than they thought they could to help—or just stopped doing things that harmed. I can get people to collect other people being happy because apparently their dead will come back and suggest it, demand it, because the afterlife can be merciful and civilised if we would like. It can be what this life is not. And quite possibly never will be. The dead—the ones I bring back—the ones that I say I bring back—I can get them to tell anybody you'd like the truth: that there is inexhaustibly more and more damage to undo, more pain, and I'm tired and I'm tired and I'm tired, but I'm . . . I try to do things, I . . .'

And Arthur turns to find her and she lets him cling as if they are falling, as if he is falling, as if he is angry and afraid and the bed gives and gives and gives and he is her boy, her soft, sore boy being taken into silence.

Here now.

Here now and you can sleep and everything you've said can be true and everything you've done can be acceptable, forgivable, normal and we can be together.

I can believe that.

If I believe it, then it isn't fake.

259

Your book doesn't understand belief, it can only tell you what it sees: a hotel lounge with a duck egg and caramel carpet, fat chairs and the quiet of hospital waiting rooms. Beth is sitting in an armchair opposite her mother and staring at a magazine filled with snapshots of people she doesn't know having parties, and true accounts of horrible diseases and assaults and accidents—also with snapshots. Everyone pictured appears to be having enormous fun, regardless of whether they're toasting an over-dressed table or undergoing skin grafts.

Sodding Beverley, the morning after.

There is a grandfather clock in the hallway knocking out the time and further away, in the dining room, breakfast crockery is being cleared and places are being set up ready for lunch. The meals here are both unremitting and niggardly—neither woman is sure how to wear away the hours that are left between them. Beth can't have another massage. Cath can't have her hair cut again.

Up in the rooms there is cable television, there are pay-per-view movies, but Cath would think watching a film would be wasting the day. And probably it wouldn't occupy her mind enough. Particularly not today.

Today is her wedding anniversary, but she can't be married any more.

That's why they're here. This is the first time Cath would have spent the day alone—first in more than forty years.

Beth would be relieved to go upstairs and lie down,

260

but that would involve abandoning her mother and she's been doing that too much.

Beth is stupid with exhaustion and vaguely tearful. For little minutes she drifts into numbness and then she snaps alert, glances at her mother and, once again, wants to cry but doesn't. And Beth's clothes don't seem quite able to drown out the memory of Arthur and finding him. The rediscovery.

Sodding Beverley, the morning after.

Outside there is drizzle, so it would be unpleasant to stroll. There are tall Victorian trees in the grey distance across a lawn, planted to climb artistically up a hillside and Beth studies them, heartily admires them to prevent herself from feeling where she has been bitten and where she was most touched and how unwise it would have been to sleep with Arthur, to give him that trust, and how terrible it is that she didn't.

They parted in the small hours: phone numbers, brisk kisses, a slightly embarrassed rush.

Arthur was leaving early.

So he'll be gone now—would have headed off before she came down.

He would have walked across the entrance to the dining room, past the clock and out to his car and neatly away from any chance of her mother seeing him, recognising him, making half-right and half-wrong assumptions, shouting.

And he's neatly away from me, too.

A rising breeze makes the big windows rattle.

But there's another sound inside that.

There's a tapping—perhaps from twigs dropping, or debris, Beth can't be bothered deciding which, but her mother is standing. That's what makes Beth look up: the sudden movement, the lurch of odd

261

hope. Her mother is standing and walking, easing, slowly, slowly towards the window and gazing straight ahead and there it is.

Tapping.

There's a magpie—large and handsome bird, dapper black and white and that special sheen along the feathers—the dash of glamour that you always get with jays. And he's tilting his head and thoughtful and considering and tilting again and he peers in and then taps. He steps, deliberate, taps once more.

And Beth is also standing, didn't quite notice how, and her mother is inching closer to the window and the magpie nods and eyes her, steps, taps. He has a circus air: costumed and tricky and unnatural— clever bird—pickpocket bird—magician bird.

The magpie is unfearful. He taps with his beak and then rests—as if he's awaiting some response.

'He wants to come in.' Her mother's voice careful and joyful, delighted. 'He wants to come in.' Cath brings herself all the way close to the glass and touches it with her hand, her palm pressed flat where it should surely disturb their visitor; but he remains tranquilly determined, ponders it and then taps again not far from her thumb. 'Oh, Beth.' A girl's voice. Young and happy.

And if her father was going to visit them as a bird, come back and please his wife, give love to his wife, then a magpie would have been his choice and here is the magpie, their magpie, in a nice black suit with pantomime touches and jocular and peeking at them, familiar as family.

But it isn't him. It's a bird. It's a story her mother will tell and that will help her and will be special and will never be taken away.

'Oh, Beth.' And the broad flare of wings when it

262

leaps, finally takes flight, renews the loss and her mother's weeping. Tomorrow she'll say that she slept well and dreamed of her husband and the way he smiled, and of flying.

But the bird wasn't him. Beth can't believe it. The bird was just a bird.

With Arthur, she's the only one who doesn't get her consolation.

'Arthur.'

Beth wakes in the suite before him.

'Art.'

Panicking in case she has slept too long, because she has slept at all—the windows showing spills of shiplight on the dim balcony, rainwater glimmers across tables and chairs provided for fair-weather entertaining, elegant guests. Beyond that is a vertigo of black—it's full night.

'Fuck.' She's been lying awkwardly, they both have. *Clothes will look as if I've gone to bed in them— because I have.*

'Fuck.'

'Hm?' Arthur stirring, taking little sips of air and he shifts. 'You . . .'

It's painful when she tries to move. 'I'm here.' She must have fallen asleep and never shifted. One of his buttons has been pressing near her eye and it hurts when she lifts her head.

He swallows, 'You're?' Voice in his chest and moving like a deep and red and dreaming thing. 'You're . . .'

Arthur's hand briefly, muzzily patting her hair as

263

he twists his shoulders and hips and retreats until she is lying without him, unembraced. He turns on the lamp—the small glare stings her—and checks his watch. 'It's past seven.' Rubs his face, 'By which I mean, it's past seven o'clock. Not any other meaning. I don't mean anything else . . . I'm sorry, it's probably late for where you want to be . . . and I'm sorry . . .' He sits up and closes his eyes. 'I'm sorry, this is the last thing, the worst . . . this is the worst thing I could have . . .' Rubbing the back of his neck to be a comfort while he upsets himself. 'Waking up with you . . . I think when you go, that you shouldn't come back. I think that we would just . . .' His good shirt creased. 'I can't.'

'It's all right.'

It isn't all right—it's us on a ludicrous boat in a blind ocean and everywhere else, they're dying— willingly, unwillingly, violently, unnecessarily, badly, well, at the limit of their natural term or long before— the world is spinning with it, ruined, and I am guilty and we are guilty and everyone still living has to be guilty because of it, but I'm not having that tonight— not tonight—and I'm not having you try to end this now because you've panicked that it's going to end later when you're in too far.

Arthur is sitting with his fists braced against the bed, thumbs rubbing his knuckles. He keeps his eyes shut.

You're in too far already.

I know it, because you're next to me.

Beth kneels on the bed and it gives, gives, gives.

But I'm not going to argue—I'll speak to your skin.

'Arthur, I'm going to take off your shoes.' He doesn't answer and so she undoes his laces, pulls at the weight of stiff leather until it gives, gives, gives, until he lets her steal his shoe.

And again.

Gentle and warm feet and red socks, his not-at-work socks—' And I'm taking off your socks.' He makes a little noise when she does this, a younganimal noise. 'I'm putting them over here, out of our way but this is me back here and I'm going to stay back.'

She stands next to the bed.

Bare feet, long toes—and he won't prevent me, but he won't assist, but he won't prevent. So we're all right and I can be doing this and reading him because it's needed, not an intrusion, not a theft.

She has the impression he is thinking of being heavy, of being sunk into the mattress, of being a man who cannot give himself to this.

But we both know he will.

And she bends to him. 'And this is me kissing your feet, this is the feel of me kissing your feet.'

The Magdalene thing—it'll work. He's not a Catholic, but he had a funny mother, that's like being a Catholic. Mary Magdalene will reach him.

Lips on his instep, more respectful than erotic, 'I know you'd kiss my feet, but I'm doing it for you. I have decided to.'

The complicated bones, the smooth skin.

This isn't a violation.

'And this is my hand on your stomach where you get scared.' And slipping her fingers inside his shirt, between the buttons and there he is, alight.

Arthur sways his head to the left, as if he's trying to think something through, angling his thoughts. Obviously doesn't intend to open his eyes. He arches up in a small way to answer her, but then lowers himself again, withdraws.

Which means he'd still like his privacy, maybe his

265

dignity, and so she removes the touch. 'Arthur, it's where I'm scared as well. And this isn't going to be what we do—the way we've been. This is about . . .'

I think he'd be more convinced if I can't help faltering and anyway it's too late if it would have been stronger of me to roll on and make the statement, be matter-of-fact.

'Arthur, I love you. I want you to believe that.'

And who says they love anybody without wanting to get the love back—it isn't a generous emotion.

'And this is me unbuttoning your cuffs and this is my mouth. On the inside of your wrist, which I also love.'

Starting an inventory because that will give them a structure and a pace, 'And the other one. Can't have favourites.' Which should make him smile, but he doesn't—he's listening too much.

He's reading me—I can feel it, taste. I can read it. So I'd better get this right.

'And you know I have to do this.' Kissing his palm, his too hot and too clever palm. 'And I need to take off your shirt.' And fast with the buttons, smooth with the buttons—determined enough to make it seem inevitable and right.

And here he is—Arthur—all blue-white and tender breath—like he's hurt already.

'We have to.'

Now, slowly, slowly—kiss his throat—him swallowing beneath you—kiss the notch in his collar bone—nipples—kissing the hair—his ribs—poor ribs—poor boy ribs.

Shadows and hollows and silk, 'And I love this.' And Arthur the man and Arthur the boy again, too. 'I love all of this.'

Needs someone to get him through it.

266

Flail of his arms as she struggles him out of the cloth, tugs it away.

Kiss where he's scared. Me, too.

'I want to see you, Arthur, and I want you to feel me looking.'

Kiss over his heart and feel it startle.

'I love you.'

Not a lie.

Kiss his mouth so he can't say it back—so he can't fail to say it back. Either way, it would be our problem—and a joy and a beauty and a trap.

Kiss his mouth.

And I don't want to think, not any more.

Belt buckle—tricky and sleek and tricky.

Jeans.

Clumsy.

Unfasten.

Unfasten.

Unfasten.

Unfasten.

Break him, peel him free.

'I do love you.'

Silkhotsilk.

Crest of the hip—hummingbird tremor in the thigh— inside—under—kiss the fur—shift of the skin— shiftingundertheskin kissed balls—fleece and lovely—where he wants—round and blind and speaking and head and rim and head and shaft and this is everything and sorry and angry and sorry and perfect and tongue and mouth and needs and take him in and keep and lose and keep and play and the first taste of almost and almost and the softesthardestlostestnakedest thing in the world and he's dancing and taste the dancing and running against the tongue and taking him in and lips and taking him

267

*in and hands and taking him in and never leave him
be and take him in.*

Say nothing.

The idea of calling him darling.

Say nothing is best.

Arthur opens his eyes. The blue of them is terrified.
And she doesn't know what this could mean.

*Please not that I've hurt him. Please not that he
doesn't believe me. Please not that he didn't trust me,
but let me in any case.*

Please is it love?

She wants to tell him that she's sorry, but is a
coward and worried that he might ask her what she's
sorry for and so she lies beside him, edges her head
on to his chest. 'Can we stay like this? For a bit.'
Like this, he can't look at her.

'Of course.' Unforthcoming voice, small and
private.

And she thinks about Beverley and the night when
they started again and how in the grey, in the
pre-dawn, he'd got out of bed and gone off to the
bathroom and she'd dozed and then something had
fully woken her—the electric sense of somebody's
attention—and she'd sat up and found him there
watching her, standing in the doorway with the light
at his back, being this curious shadow—and he'd
said, 'You feel different.'

'I am different.'

Arthur waiting, his head seeming to shift and focus
on something beyond her.

Always does that—indirect.

He does see, though.

*The distracted man who's looking somewhere else—
that's who'll catch the trick. The ones who stare and
are intent, they're not a problem—any magician will*

take their careful observation and lie to it, because it is solid and therefore can be moved, aroused, betrayed.

Arthur looks away to catch the truth.

'You *are* different?'

'Yes.'

She seemed to feel him testing her silence, pressing against it, but then he nodded, walked to join her, his body cooled. 'I'm going to sleep now. If you don't mind.'

'No. I don't mind.'

'I have to leave early in the morning.'

'Well, I'll . . . once you're asleep I'll get out of your way . . .'

And he rolled on to his side, stilled his breath, but he didn't sleep—she knew he was listening when she left.

It is perhaps foolish, but happiness can scare you. The big kind, the real kind—it can be too much like a new country opening round you, strange and wide. You do love it, naturally—you'd be insane not to— you dance in it and it's the best music you've ever felt—but you can still wonder how you've come to be so lucky.

And beauty, you can't be near it without changing and what if you change to suit it and then it goes— then you won't be the right fit for anything else. Or it can be as if saying a lover's name will make them disappear—abracadabra—or as if they might say yours and you don't know what would happen if they did.

It can take a while for you to adjust.

But you can.

You could.

You should.

And your book would love to see you happy—the big kind, the real kind.

So your book wants to play with you.

Just a game.

For company.

For you and your book to be together in a little game.

In this game, you could—if you wanted, you don't have to—you could pick a number between one and nine.

You would usually be asked for a selection between one and ten—that's the standard for many illusions that might trick you. Statistically, you'd be most likely to choose seven in that case. Most people prefer seven—it has a nice corner, was easy to draw when you learned it and hasn't too greedy a value, but isn't too low—it's a number of moderate, comfortable self-esteem.

A magician, a trickster, would tend to pick a three. They favour threes. They favour three of clubs— almost worthless, a dark and peculiar card, shows a symbol like a paw print, the sign of an odd beast. This sets them apart from those they deceive.

But you can have any number, any at all between one and nine.

You'll probably avoid seven now.

You don't have to, but you can.

You probably will.

Or not.

What matters is that you know you do have a free choice.

So pick one number.

If you'd like.

Your book can wait.

It would be happy if you'd pick.

And once you have picked—if you have picked—it would like you to multiply your number by three.

And note the answer.

And then add three.

And note the answer.

And—why not?—you can multiply that answer by three once again—by the magician's number—that way you have three threes.

For luck.

There's no such thing, but if it could, your book would promise you good fortune—books have made similar promises before. Your book might have said you could be defended from every harm and that nothing will ever reach you but tenderness.

That ought to be possible and in a book anything at all is possible: once you're tucked up neat inside a story, you can find all kinds of things convincing.

But your book will only give you something honest—the magician's number. The number which can be *Touch me* or *Loss*. 3.

The magician's number changed your first thought to something else and then again and then again.

It altered your thinking and something which alters your thinking can alter you, alter your world.

If you choose to play.

Just a game.

Where you multiply your number by three, add three, then multiply by three and note your final result.

That's all.

Your book—because it never wants to lie to you—will tell you this.

Or you could pick one of its meanings in the codes, whichever spoke to you the most.

Or you could pick both and the good luck, too.

Why not—you deserve it.

Or our game might have been a type of manipulation when manipulation is usually wrong, although not always—not when it might make you happy, or satisfied, or keep you from being alone.

It's sometimes hard to say what's right, what's wrong.

But because your book doesn't want to trick you, it won't tell you that it knows you, can slip into how you think, has sat quiet in your life and watched you, been with you, has spent this many pages with its voice curled in your head, with its weight against your fingers and working at you. It won't say it predicted your choice long before you first met.

It won't deceive you.

Derek is sitting on the bed in his bathrobe when Beth slips into the cabin. He's entirely awake and alert.

Shit. Say something.

'Hello.'

More than that.

'You look better.'

'I know.' Derek nods as if he's handing over a school report, or some kind of challenging but completed project: here's his health, present and virtually correct, all neatly boxed and polished.

If I don't tell him now, I'm not sure when I will.

On shore.

272

But the shore's too far away.

'Really healthy, Derek . . . Well done.'

Well done?

Well done and by the way I have been with—sounds biblical—another man—Christ, this is giving me a headache—another man—made love with—trying to make love with—another man—I think I'm ill—not pleasantly ironic if on a boat full of geriatrics I'm the one who ends up having a stroke—no pun intended.

I have no idea what I'm supposed to say—how to explain that Derek is no longer my concern, not at all, that I look at him and get vertigo because he is so far away.

I could ask for it to be included in the ship's daily newsletter—GRAND SUITE USED FOR MAKING LOVE WRONGLY, WOMAN TRAVELLING IN CHEAPER STATEROOM EXPRESSES REGRET, BUT RETICENT ABOUT HER REASONS FOR DISCOMFORT.

Beth concentrates on the TV which is currently showing a map of the ship's progress, accompanied by the kind of charmless music she associates with crematoria.

I think I will hurt him and I think that is hurting me.

WOMAN UNWILLING TO SAY WHO SHE MEANS BY 'HE' FOR FEAR OF SCREAMING AND THEN BEING UNABLE TO STOP.

A jaunty orange dot in the Atlantic shows their position and it's not a wild guess to imagine that Derek is willing them fast into port.

WOMAN FOUND REPEATING INTERNALLY 'I CAN'T TELL HIM'. UNABLE TO SAY WHO SHE MEANS BY 'HIM' FOR FEAR OF FINDING OUT.

273

I am not a jolly good fellow.

Derek wants to be back with normality.

And I think I will hurt him again.

Derek hopes to be the way they were, because he misunderstands what that was. If he knew more, he would want her much less.

I no longer know what I am: but if I owned something this broken, I'd throw it away.

I should be thrown away.

Derek is no longer seasick, just homesick, but he also seems contented. 'I do feel a bit . . . you know—good. I slept for a long time.'

And how almost beautiful it is to be this scared—cold, sick, as if something is dying. I haven't felt this much in years.

Like ecstasy.

'Well if you slept you must have needed it'—*rules of civilised conduct*—and she kisses his cheek and not his mouth—*never kiss a man*—'Glad you're getting better'—*with another man's spunk*—'Very glad, love'—*still in your mouth*—'Very glad to hear it.'

She eases round the cabin to avoid both him and the bed, tries lurking on the sofa.

Not still in my mouth, that's an exaggeration. But it makes itself felt, nonetheless.

Derek's concentration follows her like a clumsy fumble, he irritates, but she doesn't respond.

Another man's semen, seminal fluid, cum, spunk. Which is the simplest part of this.

Beth arranges—*pressure flutters*—her limbs as if she—*in his balls*—as if she has never—*get him to where he can't help it*—as if she has never had limbs—*which isn't fair*—to arrange before—*tastes of home*—they are all shining and distracting. *He tastes of home.*

274

Not an unreasonable rule, the No Spunk Rule.

He tastes of home, he tastes of where I could live and I stole him away from himself and he knew it.

Not an unreasonable rule.

And Derek has to ask, 'Where were you?' because this is not unreasonable, either.

And it's not as if—'Massage'—I hadn't prepared an answer—'I went and got one'—good answer, allows me to seem rearranged for an innocent reason— 'Bloody expensive, but you know . . .' *And I do smell different, but not of cologne, no aftershave—no scent but Arthur's skin—'I was tense'—Close skin on me, hard to catch—'Still am, really. Funny' as if he'd designed himself to be undetectable, to make this easy for me.*

'Well, that's nice, then, Beth.'

Nice. Yes—that is precisely the word I was searching for—this whole week has been, beyond question, as nice as nice can be.

'Yes. *Nice.* Did me good.'

I could have said I'd been decorating hats, there was a hat decorating class: started more or less exactly when I pulled down Arthur's jeans.

The class not involving cock-licking, just hats. At least that's what I would imagine.

Fuck.

He didn't stop me.

I knew he wouldn't.

And I know I can't be me and I can't be here and I can't have—I can't have.

She turns to Derek without meaning to and he grins. 'I'm only just awake.' He's glad of her.

'Yeah, love—you look a bit . . .'—*may I suggest*—'Drowsy.'

'They've given me a scopolamine patch. See?' And

275

he shows her the little sticking plaster thing behind his ear. 'It'll last three days.' He is as bashfully pleased as he might be if he'd grown it.

'Three days. Wow. Strong stuff then, Derek.'

So he'll be in the way for the duration—transdermally delivered interference. Which means I have to tell him.

I've already said that.

I do have to.

He blinks docilely. 'And we've only got another two nights on board . . .' and brings back a gentle and genuine smile that she hasn't seen all week. 'Have you been very bored? On board.'

'No.' And if she wanted to, she could like the deception. 'Not bored.'

'I am sorry, though.' Derek manoeuvres himself across the bed, gently preoccupied because he is testing his reactions and finding them healthy and promising. His robe falls open unalluringly. He gets himself within arm's reach.

And I wish that arms wouldn't.

But he keeps himself delicate, only takes her ear between his forefinger and thumb, strokes her cheek and she has to let him, because not doing so would be unusual, and here he is, undeniably Derek— looking and acting exactly as he has at other times when he has been endearing and lovable. But today he isn't.

That's all gone.

She is embarrassed for him.

But I also want to laugh—like giggling at our funeral. What am I that I'd feel this way?

He is trying to make good. 'I'm very sorry, Beth. I've been . . . I wasn't the best company and I didn't mean it, but . . . I've never felt that lousy . . .' Which is what people do when it's too late.

276

'It's OK.' *He needs a shower. Mouthwash. To get away from me.* 'I understand.' *And I'm sorry as well, but saying so would be misleading.* 'You must be hungry. We'll go out and have something to eat.'

'Do we really have to leave the cabin . . .' and he gives her the foreplay smile, which isn't any more and never will be.

'Yes, I think we should.' Standing up and away from his hands—*no finesse: I used to think that was honest and maybe it is, but I still don't like it: he has bad hands*—a slight brush of his forearm as she goes, to prevent offence. 'Fresh air . . .' She holds her back to him, reconsiders the television, apparently fascinated by the details of wind direction, sea temperature, heading. 'Then Mila can get in and have a good clean while we're away—she's been waiting to for ages—born to clean, that woman—a natural taker of cares.'

'Bugger Mila.' And maybe this is who he really is: a mean-spirited man with a sour tone, the one she would end up dreading once they'd married and he'd stopped putting up a front.

Which is a comforting thought—that he was betraying me, pretending, and would have turned out to be somebody else.

He needn't have bothered. Somebody else was already there.

'Mila was very worried about you and is a nice woman.' Staying bright and firm. 'Get a shower and then we'll have a stroll, a bit of food. There's this lovely couple we can maybe hook up with—they've been keeping me company.'

I think I'm shaking.

But Derek slumps back into his mounded pillows, squinting up at her and failing to be charming. 'You

277

really want to go out?'

'I do want that, yes—that is exactly what I want.'

No it's not.

Derek sighs, stalks to the bathroom.

*   *   *

The buffet isn't crowded: the dinner rush has passed. Couples are lodged in angles, enjoying shadows—or some passengers are merrily in fours, teams by now, settled into patterns of which they feel protective on this their second-last night. They are delicate with nicknames and jokes, references to shared events and enjoyable complaints, their tiny history together. They are planning they honestly will keep in contact and meet again, go ashore with this extra comfort: *it's always wonderful on cruises who you'll end up talking to.*

An American woman in a tentative sweater sits down at a Geordie man's table. He is unpromising.

'It's always wonderful who you'll end up talking to.' She can say this because she recognises the Geordie from yesterday's lecture—which was about sand—and her announcement of their provenance is desperately confident, unarguable, and so he lets her join him and they shake hands and this will not be the beginning of a romance, or even an acquaintance, but they won't eat alone. They'll demonstrate they can be interesting and entertaining if they wish. They can be at least as wonderful as sand.

Beth scans the tables—recognises the so many faces who have seen her rushing, or weepy, or miserable with a coffee, or outside in the blustery light and staring—seeing the hinge where the world

278

swings—air into water, water into air.

*Big-earring couple, still pursuing their week-long
pirate theme—surprisingly tattooed Floridian woman
who misses her kids—dim, military husband and
silently damaged wife—gay guys from the West Country:
only one of them joking when he eyes up the Filipino
waiters—and Bunny.*

'We should head over there . . .' Beth so relieved
when she sees Bunny that she fears she may just
have surrendered to hopeful delusion.

Derek is trying to slow and incline towards a series
of seating options which would mean he has her to
himself, but she pretends she doesn't notice and
drives on. This makes him less subtle. 'Do we need
to be with strangers?'

'They're not strangers. They're . . . ah.' Beth waves.

*Because Bunny loves waving and ought to have
people that she can wave back to every day—Francis
and friends and visitors every single day.*

Bunny waves back.

'This is Bunny.' Beth almost trots Derek along to
present him. 'This is my . . . this is Derek.'

'Oh, you poor dear.'

Bunny taking Derek's arm and settling him beside
her while she gives Beth her instructions. 'I am going
to see how your friend's recovery is progressing and
I'll tell him all the best ship's gossip that he's missed.'
She deadpans at Derek and then chuckles, 'Don't
worry, I'll make it racy. And Beth will go and fetch
you appetising morsels. But you'll have to pace
yourself, you know.' An ill person being businesslike
about recoveries and weaknesses. 'Beth will also be
very kind and locate my missing husband and then
he can help her to carry things back.'

Bunny's in a trouser suit—purple, mandarin collar,

279

a tidy and sensual fit which Francis will like and her favourite jewellery again. 'I haven't a clue where he is—habitual with him, the wandering off. Watermelon. He's been on a mission for watermelon all day. I should never have mentioned it. By now he's probably insisting they lower a boat to fetch some.' Derek isn't responding to her, so she changes her focus to Beth. 'What will we do when this is all over?' The sense of a weight returning when she says this, so she adjusts, 'When we don't have servants . . . poor us.'

Beth kisses her—*with a dirty mouth*—gives her a peck on the ear—*with a lover's mouth and Bunny understands about love*—and reassures because this is expected and can be playful, 'You'll have Francis at your beck and call. I've never seen anyone more anxious to be becked and called, in fact.'

Bunny agrees to be distracted by the thought.

All of us masters of distraction.

Mistresses.

Sounding louche is the least of my troubles.

Then Bunny moves on to being coy, enjoys it: 'I don't believe we can describe him as staff, though. There are certain things one doesn't do in front of servants.' Her smile is coloured with Francis and how he would smile if he could hear her. 'Or with them, for that matter.'

Derek is, meanwhile, sullen and clearly doesn't want to consider geriatric sex or listen to Bunny, but Beth pats his shoulder and goes in search of Francis—*because I would like to eat my dinner with a gentleman.*

'Oh, I'm not, you know.' Francis quietly tired when she finds him, his tray laden with fruit—especially watermelon—and cheese, his pockets full of crackers

280

as usual. 'No, I'm just me. And she puts up with the me-ness of me. And that's all right. That's very fine. No one else would.' A fingertip smudge of blue beneath each eye.

He's spent the week breaking his heart to be cheery, a jolly good fellow.

'No, you'll always be a gentleman, Francis. It's how you're built.'

I don't give compliments. It's not a compliment, though, is it? He's a gent.

'You're very kind. Thank you. Should we meet on any future occasions—not at sea, I don't just mean tomorrow—it would be my pleasure to try and not be disappointing.' He peers at the plates of watermelon—neat chap in a blazer and slacks, doing well for his age, only really needs glasses for reading—*but it's not his health that scares him*—a tray full of gifts for Bunny, treats, expressions of affection.

What will he do when they're pointless?

Some people have problems they did not make.

'You're very good with each other.'

'What?' Francis close to alarmed for an instant— he doesn't want a eulogy yet and she should have known better than to start one—but then he simply rolls his eyes. 'We've had our moments. In both directions.' Then he stops, doesn't want to hear himself almost speaking his marriage away, out of existence. 'And I'm sure we will again . . . Christ, it can make you bloody miserable.' He pauses again, picks an unthreatening meaning. 'This *end of the voyage* bit, it's glum. Even though it's not as if you'll actually miss almost anyone you've met and you're going straight back home with whoever you came with—I mean, it's not an emotional time, or anything.

281

It shouldn't be.' He rests his hand on her shoulder. 'You, though—you have to come and see us. And I would recommend you do that almost as soon as we land. Unless you're busy, might be . . .' He stumbles when what he meant to be enthusiasm sounds as if matters are urgent and Beth ought to rush.

'I will come and see you. Both of you.'

Because any word can work a spell and then Bunny will have to be there, still all right.

Francis gathering his poise again, summoning up mock-serious nodding. 'Excellent. And that's contractually binding, you know—a promise made at sea, I'm sure that's something legal. Not the standard holiday fib. Let me give you our address.' And he moves deftly through his procedure for finding his card and presenting it. Beth suspects there was a time when having a business card was a big deal—it still pleases him. 'Here. Don't lose it. And then you can come and stay—we're deep in the country now and it's too far to travel and not stay—and if you stay for a night, then you might as well make it longer . . . See?' He winks at her. 'You were warned you'd be kidnapped . . .'

After this, both of them are aware they will need to joke and talk nonsense and not act as if anyone is dying or ever could: they will behave like human beings and make the very best of ignoring the long term.

Which could make me proud of us. I'm definitely proud of Francis.

So they improvise and she *forages*, as Francis puts it, with him in attendance, encouraging and advising and flirting in a way which implies mutual respect.

'This is very wonderful, Beth. Your being here.

And you've made the sun come out.' He steers her round to a window and proves his point. 'More wonderful. Gorgeous.'

Out on the deck a jogger in a knitted hat fights his way past the glass and they watch him and then survey the restaurant and its quietly pornographic butter sculptures and carved fruits and busied heat lamps. The room seems to halt before it drops with another wave, rolls and sighs, and while it does Beth looks at Francis and tells him, 'I'm not going to say goodbye. I would if I was going to, because it seems like the right time, but I'm not.' And she kisses his ear and he grins.

Then he kisses Beth's hand and when he raises his head again, the grin isn't hers any longer—it's for Bunny. 'Very wonderful. Now, we're late and there will be rumours and alarms. And I have already been severely scolded for eyeing up the butter maidens. Dairy produce—it makes the sculptor overly focused on milk and its associated physical attributes. Come on.'

'I can't think what you mean, Francis.'

'And Bunny says neither can I.' Still grinning as they progress round to the table.

When he arrives, Francis kisses his wife and she frowns at him until he pantomimes being sly and then they both giggle and she kisses him back. 'Did he give you any bother, Beth?'

'No more than usual.' Beth sets down her offerings alongside Francis's careful array. Her efforts appear random: cold chicken, grated carrots, dumpling soup, a slice of pizza, watermelon, something with fish in a pink sauce—the kind of things she'd bring a stranger, trying to guess what he'd like.

When I no longer care about what Derek likes.

283

And what would be a suitable meal to share with a soon-to-be-ex-almost-future-husband? Sexual Etiquette For All Occasions—I think that's a lecture I missed.

Derek has decided to be baleful. 'And what's the usual?' But then he seems unable to think of anything more to say, so he prods at his chicken suspiciously. He may have thought it might be impressive to refuse nourishment, but then Beth watches as four days of fasting kick in and he proceeds to eat everything she's brought him and then to insist on more. Otherwise he is mostly silent. Bunny, who has clearly been steadfast in trying to draw him out, makes a further attempt. 'We live in Dorset.' Although she's beginning to tire.

'Really.' Derek stokes in a forkful of risotto with a studied lack of grace. 'We don't.'

Absolutely inexcusable.

Bunny was enjoying a little slice of cake, something pistachio and ornate, but now she doesn't touch it and only studies her hands and is too quickly too frail and Francis is on his feet and patently disgusted, breathless with it, incredulous.

Taking his hand, Beth stands with him. 'I need some dessert. Francis, we'll search for dessert.' She leans into his shoulder. 'Could we. Please.'

Francis unwilling to move, his hands getting angry and considering bad things—Beth can feel when his forearms twitch.

Bunny takes a breath, steadies and then tilts her face up to her husband's. 'And a cup of tea, darling. I'm dry. If you wouldn't mind.' She gives him a tiny shake of her head, 'Go on.' Which allows him to exhale and hook his arm in Beth's.

As they step away Beth hears Derek add, too loud,

'And a cup for me.' And she has to work hard to keep Francis with her. He is trembling.

They make it as far as the tea urns before he dodges to stand in front of her, holds her quickly by both shoulders and then releases her, abashed. 'Look, I know he's your—'

'He's not.'

'He's . . . ?'

'Derek—he's not my anything. He was but he isn't and I haven't been able to tell him and I thought he would do, be all right . . . I thought he would be a safer, a saner . . . There's another . . . There is a man and Derek isn't him.'

'Well, thank fuck for that, love—because he's a *tosser*. Sorry, but really—what a *fucking* arse.' Francis blinking and checking her, wary. He winces out a minute smile when she doesn't seem upset. 'But . . . you know that.' Shakes his head, smiling more, glancing back at Bunny, watchful. 'Sorry. Of course you do. You're, from what I know, extremely bright and attractive and . . . I'm sorry, it's none of my business, but I do get tired of seeing fantastic women with appalling men. It's like some form of blood sacrifice, self-harm. I can't be doing with it. Not that I'm any great catch or one to talk, but . . .' And his fingers remember their previous intentions, tighten momentarily.

'I wish it was your business, Francis—you'd have made it all . . . neater, or . . . And I'm so sorry he hurt Bunny's feelings. I should never have brought him anywhere near her—or you—I was guessing I could manage him if you were around—and I am, I'm really sorry. And you can punch him if you want.'

Francis factual, 'I do want.' And keen.

'I know you want.'

'I wasn't always a gentleman—it has grown on me over time, like moss. He is, in point of fact, lucky I do not *punch 'is fuckin' 'ead in*. As it were. Ask Bunny.' Enjoying his accent, a gleam of who he could still be.

Can imagine him—sharp and handy and Bunny fancying this dangerous young man. Not too scary, just right.

'I will ask her. When we're alone. And I—'

He grips her shoulders again, this time slightly fierce. 'Look, this isn't the time and I truly do not normally take advantage of being incredibly ancient to give advice. Nobody ever wants it, for a start—of course they don't: *it's advice.* But I have kids your age . . . No, I don't . . .' He's rueful for a beat. 'I was waiting for you to contradict me there. My sons are in their twenties. Nice boys. And I wouldn't let them anywhere near you, you'd break them in half.' Another beat so that he can smile if Beth does, which she does. 'No offence—in fact, I mean it as a compliment. But—back to the previous topic—if I'd had a daughter . . . you can say this kind of thing when you're 180 . . .' But he can't phrase this kind of thing in a way that suits him. 'Oh, sod it. You and *that* doesn't work.' He cocks his head towards Derek, as if he wants him taken away. 'You and whoever else seems to be excruciating, but at least you care . . . Obviously care . . . So maybe that would work. If he's whoever made you look the way you look today.'

'What do you mean?'

'This evening something is not the way it was with you—and it's the sort of difference that's . . . This is a being 180 thing again—seen it all . . . Almost all . . . Some of it . . . That is . . . In the words of the immortal Jimi—*Have you ever been experienced? Well, I have.'*

'He likes Jimi. The other—'

'The other chap. I know. It wouldn't be *Derek*. And the liking of Mr Hendrix is in the other chap's favour, of course . . . Not that we're necessarily discussing quite the same experience as Jimi's . . . Then again, it's all intoxication isn't it? Eventually . . .' But he'd prefer to be with Bunny—she's upset and he has been brave for her and will again—will have to be much braver—and he would like to be more helpful for Beth, but Bunny is Bunny and is everything. So he's brief: 'Give it a go.' And then regrets it slightly. 'See if you're kind to each other. Try it. Maybe. It won't kill you.' And he shows her his face, his unarmed, unprepared face—'Lots of other things will. For sure.' He gives her that, then fusses at his collar, brushes his shoulders free of invisible lint, retires into being jovial for her—and then stern. 'Right . . .' The voice of a father with sons. 'The tosser. I need a word with him.'

'No, but—'

He won't actually punch him, though, will he?

Francis marching, bearing down and—despite a manifestly absorbing attack on a bowl of Thai green curry—Derek glances, falters, is dismayed and Francis tells him—carefully—'You are not going to eat any more. You are going to escort Elizabeth to the theatre. Don't act as if you've never heard of it. You're going to escort her courteously to the theatre and not take out how thoroughly disappointed you will soon feel with yourself on her or anyone else— you will not bother any of the staff.' Derek's head low and Francis maintaining his tone while his eyes look wicked and happy at Bunny and at Beth and

287

he lies, 'I've been in the service, I've seen your type.' For a breath, he is joyful with how unlikely this is and then pointed, sober. 'You will watch the show. That's what a gentleman does with a lady. *You escort her.*'

Derek flounders his gaze up. He can't work Francis out, doesn't know who would actually win in a proper fight, because Francis is beginning to look quite useful and threatening and it would be just all upside-down to be beaten by an old man. Mainly Derek's face is turning scared, but he's also trying to present himself as polite, unwilling to contradict a senior citizen, 'I don't, I—'

That was a bleat—definitely an unmanly sound.

I shouldn't be enjoying this.

I am, though.

Derek blinks. He is being humiliated.

But he hasn't a clue how much, how deeply and that's the part I'm not enjoying.

And Francis is right: the only place tenable for us will be the theatre. Where Derek can be diluted, where our position can be diluted, by an audience.

Francis is insistent—like an elegant cosh. 'You don't what? You don't know what the show is? I don't care if you don't know what the show is. Whatever it is, it will be a delight. And, on your way, you can reflect repeatedly on your good fortune and continuing health.'

Derek puzzles at the silence.

Then, 'Off you go.' And for a moment Francis puts his arm around Beth's waist—warm, light—kisses the top of her head. 'Starts at 8.30. Don't want to be late—it'll help you both to get a good night's sleep.'

And for saying this Beth could kiss him—so she

288

does and this time she can't avoid it feeling like goodbye.

Kiss him with a lover's mouth. Francis also understands about love.

And then she kisses Bunny, 'You have a top-quality husband there.'

Bunny who smells of Chanel and powder and constant moderate pain: 'He's not bad. But I can't tell him that—he's unbearable as it is and in a funny mood at present.'

They conduct their conversation as if Derek has already gone and he soon does bump away from the table, heads out, fast and ungainly, between the other diners and then loiters at the far door.

'I am not in a funny mood.'

'He always says that when he's in a funny mood.'

'And you always say that.' Francis sitting down beside his wife, attentively snug beside her and slightly pleased with his recent performance, excited, and Beth leaves them being themselves only mildly louder for her benefit and thinks that when she's gone they'll drink their tea and maybe have an early night and continue from there.

Derek escorts her so effectively to the theatre that they arrive fifteen minutes early.

Actually, he didn't escort me—pacing a foot ahead of me in a morbid sulk isn't escorting.

I should tell him—then he could go, or I could go. Put us both out of my misery. Let us get away, each to our own.

But I'm a coward.

After the show. I'll do it then.

After the wait for the show and then the show.

I promise.

We can manage the wait—quiet wait. Quiet as staring

numbly in a resentment-filled lift while Gordon from Nuneaton (with wife) and Ted from the Channel Islands—he doesn't say which island, or maybe he lives on several—I know a man who lives on a single specific Channel Island, who talks about it—so this Gordon (with wife) and Ted (without wife)—Ted's wife having an early night: he says it gives his ears a rest and we all smile at this, complicit in its minor hatefulness—all of us smile, that is, except Derek, who has troubles of his own, which I will add to and that's why I despise them and myself.

Despising is as good as anything, though—it's an adequate diversion.

So Gordon and Ted discuss their knee operations—and then, the lift finally letting us go, precede us into the auditorium while I ponder—as they have at great length—the benefits and drawbacks of keyhole, as opposed to open-cast, orthopaedic surgery and yet find myself truly more interested in whether Gordon's silent but deep-eyed wife will one day strangle him with a pair of pastel golfing slacks—he needed the plastic knee to continue his golf—or whether perhaps she'll swap murders with Mrs Ted, disguise herself as a hooker who looks like his mum—his preferences would undoubtedly lie that way—and then bugger him to death with some large unbuttered vegetable while he's strapped to his own kitchen table.

I don't mean that.

They were all right.

Probably.

Even Ted—sexually frightened and too old for his current persona, Ted. He thinks his world isn't working because fox-hunting scenes have been banned from Christmas cards by socialists and Muslims and the UN. This, when the Prince of Peace's tender birth, his *virgin mother's baptismal kiss, the harmoniously crowded manger, should obviously always be commemorated by drawings of borderline Nazis and admirers of Pinochet galloping out across farmland they no longer own to prove a point before watching dogs rip an almost-dog to pieces—or a cat, or some other equally tasty domestic pet.*

Christ, I don't want to be like this.

Or here—waiting for a magician.

Naturally.

Beth is almost relieved she has ended up having to watch 'Not to be missed, the personality and magic of Matt Mitchell'.

And I have to be grateful for him because he'll keep Derek out of the cabin and awake—until the heavy meal and the scopolamine kick in.

I hope.

Francis hoped.

When Francis ought to be saving his optimism for better things.

The house lights dim and then go out, but mean nothing melancholy by it.

If Derek's sleepy, docile, then we can be civilised.

Or, putting it more frankly, I would like him to be temporarily disabled, because this will work to my advantage when I admit what I have to and should have long ago and everything becomes my fault.

A swirl of portentous music clambers up to the balconies and then washes back.

And here's the lovely Matt.

Matt is vaguely tubby, something failed in the line of his shoulders.

It seems he hasn't brought his personality with him tonight. I wonder if he's got his magic . . .

Arthur said I was merciless.

291

Matt begins his routine, manipulates his velvet-draped props and scuffles limply round his strangely proportioned tables, as the stage creaks and heaves.

Black suit, orange waistcoat—I'll bet he's wearing, yeah, the orange socks to match . . . and the ladies and gentlemen adore him—and they adore his newspaper which he will now tear up and restore and then, I suspect, form into a tube and fill miraculously with milk.

This truly is the 1970s—'74, or '76.

And we're all at a sodding birthday party.

Dad, he'd have rocked the place. He had proper patter and style and he could do it—genuinely prestidigitate—I thought that word was so magnificent—he'd throw in an extra pickpocketing, or a levitation, or move that card to where it couldn't be, because you were sure it couldn't be, because you'd looked, you'd concentrated, you'd expected to be fooled and you'd been careful, but there it is: inside the card box you'd covered with your hand for all that time, for surely every minute—you wouldn't be confused about such a simple thing, or about when a trick is started and when it stops.

He would make you amazed.

Yes, he did the kids' stuff mostly, but when he performed for adults—only once in any evening—he'd shake them. He'd move their thinking; not far, but he'd move it. I saw.

And the milk is poured into the newspaper and—goodness—now it's gone.

How absolutely fucking amazing.

If I could make anything I wanted to appear, if I could take the broken and the ripped to pieces and make them whole and show the multitudes that here is a genuine, absolute miracle — would I waste my

292

gifts on newspaper and milk?

And here come the scissors and the bit of dodgy rope.

This is purgatory and I deserve it.

He didn't like Arthur, my dad—and I wanted him to: two men with beautiful voices, strange interests, they should have negotiated an understanding.

Very clear that they wouldn't—how could a dog like an almost-dog? And both of them thinking the other is only the almost-dog.

But I was being optimistic and introduced them.

*Mum was making an effort: first meeting and I've said Arthur's important and I've never brought a bloke here before and me and him, we're braced for dinner—the **finally we have to do this and just bite the bullet, catch it in our teeth, which is a dangerous trick and can kill you** dinner—and she'd got the house pristine and there were fresh flowers and candles and she was treating Arthur like a blacksuitman, a member of the tribe, one that she'd accidentally missed and should know better and that's as friendly as it gets. She made him eat too much dip—he hates dip, but he was also beyond his own skin with the effort of being the gentleman they'd favour: swallowing down this pinky goo and wearing a tie and a suit—blue suit—and taking her hand and kissing it. Dad leaning beside me but not speaking, a palpable shiver in the air around him indicating his need to be sitting in a Mississippi rocking chair, set out on a broiling porch with a shotgun on his knees and ready loaded.*

Which was only the usual fatherly feelings and I think we were aware of that and managing. Dad cared. He was supposed to. He was expecting—just quietly, not getting ridiculously demanding—a presentable wedding with tail coats and hats and photos and his wife in enjoyable tears and then kids and more photos.

Only none of us could make a magic to manage that.

We were sitting down to eat—Mum and Dad and me and Arthur—a cheery four. She'd laid out the posh Christmas place settings, only minus the berries and tinsel and we were not without tension, but working on it. Arthur and I were working, concentrating out into the room harder than we'd thought we could— trying to harmonise with Mum and Dad and each other and to calm things, trying to help. And, on the other hand, it did not help that Arthur was teetotal. He had decided he needed an ultra-clear head always, so no additives or fixes. The teetotal phase came after the gloves. Dad viewed teetotal as peculiar. Christ knows what he'd have said about the gloves.

And early on, the evening still stiff and early on, before we were done with the home-made beef broth, Dad asking him, 'And what do you do, Arthur?'

And Arthur told him the truth.

When he could have said anything and been believed.

Matt shows his audience rope in pieces, rope complete, rope knotted, rope pulled through the neck of a small and unharmed boy.

Tricks for a grandson—Dad was born for that.

The current magician laughing with his audience— an inward, piggy snort of laughter. He's filling his hands with sponge balls—dear God, sponge balls, not even billiard balls—a wilderness of sponge balls and he's snorting and shuffling his feet.

He is terrible.

Which is why they love him, why they will clap when he pushes that long needle through that big balloon— which, to be fair, is moderately tricky when the ship's moving this much.

So tricky that he bursts the balloon.

Well, that's fine, though—try again. The audience can wait.

And again.

There are two reasons for watching performances of any kind. They are both human and understandable reasons.

We can come out and see people, members of our own species, excel themselves, transcend expectations, burn in their work. And clearly these performers are bigger and finer and more amazing than we can be, but this is a good thing, this is wonderful, a gift—and maybe they have reached a place where we can go, are the truth of ourselves revealed. Maybe we have in us an equivalent light. They are people and we are people and when we stand up and applaud them, discover that we are standing, have been drawn up by this wonder they've provided, then we are applauding something of which we're a part—we have humility and pride both avid in us and are delighted. We let them heat us into being slightly someone else.

Or we can come out to see people, members of our own species, fail and be uncomfortable, unhappy, deluded, ridiculous, cheap. And perhaps we have been all these things, have felt ourselves be all these things, but tonight the performers suffer and we are safe and more competent and poised than we believe they could be. They are people and we are people and we abandon them. We aren't overwhelmed, uncovered, we get to stay the same and be quite sure we're adequate.

Tonight I am sitting in the second kind of audience. They are why I no longer have a television: too much of the second, not enough of the first. Important not to hate them for being as they are—because they are as merciless as I am and the truth is that they can transcend themselves and blaze, astonish, be amazed—probably have and could still—and, as repeatedly established, their hearts will be broken, perhaps more than once, and at some inevitable point they will cease to exist—they will be a tragedy—these things are certain for them. So they can deserve only tenderness.

But these are the people—and I'm not unlike these people—that I would want Arthur to headfuck—to take advantage of their rigidity and their hatreds and their fears.

And really that's almost saying they're the ones who deserve the best magic: not pulls and cards and linking rings and disappearing women, but eternity and love for ever, loves restored.

I think maybe Arthur imagined my dad would be able to see him that way. As a magician—as someone who offers wonders.

But when Arthur was working he said that his wonders were real—they couldn't be wonders unless he could say they were genuine—and there's only one rule in magic: you can't claim that it really is magic. That's the lie you can never tell.

'Don't bring him back here.' Dad gone from the table and Mum in amongst her best napkins, her nice things, and stricken, but I had to chase my father, find my dad.

He looked the way Francis did about Derek, 'I can't, I can't stop you . . .' the same fury and he's embarrassed for me as well and protective. And he wants to start a fight. 'Can't have him in the house.' But he has no one that he can bear to fight with.

*Don't remember what else he said, but **can't have him in the house**.*

Mum had made the special fish pie with extra veg,

296

and a cherry flan and optional cream and nobody ate it.

She was crying, but I was busy and Arthur was sitting in his car, not gone, but not in the house.

Can't have him in the house.

Dad holding on to my arm and we can't believe ourselves—we've been changed didn't mean to and I have to go and be with Arthur.

Can't have him in the house.

If they could have liked each other, borne each other.

The audience are clapping again. Derek huffs and shifts his legs. Matt Mitchell and his personality have skewered the balloon and yet it remains healthy.

Not even a drop of blood.

Perhaps maddened by his impossible success, Mitchell walks down amongst his spectators, pressing out minor waves of unease—they would prefer him to be neatly far away. He reaches out unsuavely and plucks a young lady out of her seat. She is manifestly fitter and thirty years younger than almost anyone in the house and walks like the kind of dancer who might take part, for example, in a New York Arrival Cavalcade of scenes from popular musicals in just such a venue as this, perhaps tomorrow night.

Matt leads his in-no-way-suspicious companion up on to the unruly stage, mugging and flapping mock applause until he is rewarded with a burst of relieved appreciation: he is back where he should be and the show is no longer a threat. A stagehand trundles out an improbable trunk that's draped with a yellow cloth.

Metamorphosis—that's going to be his finale: an effect which was already boring when his grandfather walked out of the music hall showing it because it was FUCKING BORING.

297

That's if his grandad took an interest in magic—someone in his family should have . . .

Or not—it doesn't exactly seem to foster functional relationships.

Matt whisks the cloth lumpily away—it is stiffened by a rod that runs along one of its shorter sides—and shows the trunk to his assistant who is amazed by it in the way that women in bad porn movies are amazed by their own and others' nudity: on a kind of big-eyed time delay. He then takes a velvet sack out of the trunk and waves it at her. He tells her loudly and clearly—the way he might speak to a senile relative or a puppy—that she must hold this sack open while he steps inside it and then fasten it round his neck before she shuts the trunk's lid over him and fastens that *very securely*.

Arthur gave me a vibrator once that was sold with a black velvet pouch to keep it in—just like Matt's sack—excuse the doubled meaning—drawstrings you could tie. It was smaller—but still a container for a dick—a fake dick.

That was in one of the London hotels—on the Strand. Our room had a window that looked on to white—a type of light well tiled in white—and he'd been to a sex shop before he arrived, bought stupid things, was in a funny mood: 'You could take this with you and think of me. I know that you won't take me.'

He's never fair.

And nor am I.

The assistant, as instructed, stands on the locked trunk. She holds the yellow cloth in front of her as if the audience have interrupted her while bathing. She attempts to look confused, nervous and sexy— each of these emotions proving too stern a test for her acting abilities. She raises the cloth. The rod

298

inside its top edge allows it to serve as a curtain that hangs sufficiently wide to obscure the trunk, her legs, body, head. Her arms are lifting high and she's swaying on tiptoe along with the general swagger of the ship, of everything. For a moment only the cloth is visible.

A synthetic melody is playing. It grows louder and therefore more sickening.

And everyone wants to see behind the cloth. We can't help it—we're all sure, will always be sure, that what's behind it will be wonderful. It's never quite as good when it's revealed, but next time—then it'll be amazing. Next time the secret will be beautiful.

Bodies under sheets—is that why we do it, put our dead under cover? So then maybe magic will happen and we'll pull back the cloth and look at them and they'll be looking back—restored.

The curtain is let fall and—alacazam—Matt is standing thrillingly on the trunk. More exciting still, when he unlocks that very trunk, his assistant is inside and tied up in the sack. There are whistles and cheers mingled in the applause which Matt dips forward into, bowing open-mouthed, the way that he might dunk for apples. His assistant bows, too— professional about it, forgetting who she's meant to be.

*It's the speed that impresses—how quickly they change places and the man can become the woman and the woman becomes the man—Houdini performed it with his sweetheart—**if you was me**.*

Funny couple, the Houdinis—the Weisses, to be more accurate. No kids, so they just invented one, made him a story between them.

The house lights nag in and obediently the rows of seats begin to empty.

Beth nudges Derek, who has been dozing, when she'd rather he saved unconsciousness for later.

But I don't think he will sleep later.

And I won't be there to know.

Because it stops now.

We stop.

He sniffs, wriggles his shoulders and seems as tender and clean as anyone just woken.

I think what he liked was how unavailable I am. He read it as a complex interior passion, something to be cunningly unveiled.

But pull back the cloth and he'd see—I'm all in pieces, no use.

'Let's get out of here.' He does sound a touch groggy.

And he's the real audience volunteer—a genuine innocent—so no matter what he does, the trick's against him.

They slip themselves in with the last of the crowd, the murmurs and perfumes.

In most paintings of the crucifixion they get it wrong—they show the nails fixed through his palms, when that would never work: you had to be pinned through your wrists or you wouldn't be adequately supported. But the artists understood: blood and metal at the sweet spot, that's what to show—everyone's had a taste of that.

Which isn't going to make what I do to him all right. I am aware of that.

Beth lets them be drifted and bumped towards an exit.

Francis and Bunny will be in their cabin, each one of them with their love, in their love.

'Derek?'

'Yeah.' Short, flat syllable.

300

'Do you like Jimi Hendrix?'

'What?'

'It's OK. Forget it.'

They are outside the theatre by this time, paused on the insistently high-quality carpet and Beth is simultaneously tired, tired, tired and beyond herself, starting to live in another place, somewhere thoughtless and taut, and this makes her unwary.

'You fucking cunt.'

She doesn't expect that Derek will grab her elbow and, loud in her face—not fully shouting, but drawing in wider attention—he will announce, 'You fucking, *fucking* cunt.'

'What?'

'I was *ill*!'

'You were . . . Of course you were ill, I was . . . I was feeding you pills for days.'

The badness of saying this thrumming in her fingers.

'Cunt.'

The foyer unhappy. A boxy-headed man in a dinner jacket jerking his head as if he's been slapped by the first use of *cunt* and—after the second and third—clearly torn between physical intervention and removing his wife from further exposure.

Further exposure to words for a place that she has and an activity to which it has quite possibly been subjected.

'Derek, what are you . . . ?' *But Mr Box would not have called it fucking. He peaked early and now he's lost.* 'There's . . . why are you doing this now?' *He'd never have said cunt.*

Lovely, round, firm name for it—cunt.

Mrs Box might have said it—she has hidden depths— hidden from him—bet she dances alone at parties and

301

scares the shit out of him when he sees her, bet she flirts with waiters.

And why am I reading them when I ought to be reading Derek?

Derek whose colour has risen and thickened, who has lost his dignity, thrown it away—upset much more than angry, eyes wet and large and steady on her, as if he can force her to reveal some strange capacity to strike him, or be poisonous, or a physical abnormality which will prove her wickedness. 'I was ill and you were . . . All today. *All* today. And where have you been all this week?' He wants to point at her and shriek.

He basically is pointing and shrieking. And all the discontented couples loitering to stare because we're obviously much more discontented than any of them.

'I'd wake and you wouldn't be there and you wouldn't be there and I wouldn't know why and then you'd come back and be . . . today, you were—'

'Derek, like you say'—*I am a coward, Jesus I'm a coward*—'You haven't been well. I've been around.'

'A-round?'

We're an extra show for everyone. 'I've been . . . you slept a lot. You don't know—' *They should thank us. We're pretty much as mediocre and predictable a gig as they would like.*

'I *know*!' This a full yell and the crowd fluttering back in case things get genuinely untidy. 'Were you with him?'

They'll send a steward, security—we're letting the side down, being inelegant and not dashingly dressed.

Soft sweater.

'Him? Derek, what does that mean—*him*?'

Soft sweater.

'That old bastard—he was all over you. Is it him?

302

Were you with him?'

'With *Francis*?'

'I don't give a fuck what he's called—is it him? He has a wife. You're screwing a pensioner with a wife.'

I need to be quiet and elsewhere. I need to walk away and leave him and he is giving me every reason to. 'You were rude to his wife.'

'And you're *screwing him!*'

It's not you, it's me. *Does anyone actually say that? Goodbye, it's not you. When of course it is you; if I'm leaving it would obviously be you.*

And me.

Why don't I feel anything?

'Francis has been very kind to me—'

'Yeah, I bet he has.'

This shouldn't be fun—to pace him, and pace him and here's his shoulders in the angle of mine and our feet—not agreeing—but now they do—and feeding him calmness and see if I win. Make him a game and he can't scare me, although he doesn't scare me—I'm not scared, shamed, not anything.

I'm not anything.

'Derek, this is absurd.'

Derek glares at her, but he would rather be pacified and convinced.

'You're being absurd. Francis is married, he loves his wife, he's . . . a nice guy. I don't know what you're talking about.'

And she leads and he follows and slowly, clumsily, they straggle into a lobby, past a winking clutch of lifts. She is taking him away from the scene of his crime and nearer to the scene of hers, while both of them are more or less forcefully ignored—some observers missed out on the previous scene and others are of the opinion it shouldn't have happened and therefore did not.

Can feel a tickle and giggle in some of the bystanders, though. The woman in the tan trouser suit especially— she's hot and wet with speculation and she'll talk. They'll all talk. By tomorrow morning this will be exciting the whole ship: perfectly sordid gossip.

Derek is also aware of the hungry and disapproving pressure set against what he would like to do—he wants the full-tilt drama and then probably a reconciliation. 'You cunt.'

I don't want Francis to know, though—not Bunny and not Francis.

'Derek, do you know what I did today? While you were asleep? Asleep again'—*always classy: blaming the victim*—'I went to the duty free perfume sale on Deck Three—a thrilling experience: village tombola meets The Poseidon Adventure'—*lying this much, it gets you light-headed*—'And I had lunch and I read the ship's newspaper for the day and tried learning how to recognise ship's officers according to their epaulettes'—*the story to replace reality, that I will believe so that it will be believable*—'And I had a massage and that meant I could use the pool and the sauna and sit in peace and read a magazine and—yes—they only had magazines for the elderly, talking about how sixty is the new forty and eighty is the new seventeen'—*and he is wishing every word into truth*—'And how to deal tactfully with double incontinence and how to bring cleaning materials with you when you go into hospital so the general lack of hygiene won't kill you'—*I'm being kind, something close to kind*—'This did not make me want to screw a pensioner. And I care about Bunny and I care about Francis.'

'Why don't you care about me?' Clean, small words. 'Beth?'

'Wh—?'

And she didn't expect this and hasn't stopped herself from facing him, studying, so that now his pain jumps up at her and sinks clear in.

'Why don't you care about me.' Soft—as if he is tired, tired, tired and would just like to know.

'I . . . Derek . . . I don't want to hurt you . . .'

Which is not a lie.

'Oh, Christ.' And he buckles and she puts her arm around him, as if he is once more sick and she walks him to some chairs by a little window full of nowhere, 'Oh, Christ. I . . .' The wave tops are closer to this deck, the blurs of disturbance flickering and plunging.

'I'm sorry.' *And I am.* 'I'm so sorry.' *Please be angry, instead of like this.* 'I didn't mean . . .'

Derek is sitting with his hands slumped in his lap and he starts weeping, 'Christ.' Making no effort to hide himself, nose wet, tears dripping off his chin.

As if he's five and needs his mum to get him through it.

Christ.

Little knocks of breath shaking him and then a halt and then another wave of losses tearing in him and she can't touch him any more, because that would be unfair.

When every part of this is unfair.

'Derek, you're a good person.'

Beth watching the cliché hit him, set him further adrift in this new place which is unbearable, but where he's still managing to plan and hope that if he breaks, genuinely breaks, shows it, he will be rescued and by her. And she can't let him think this. 'You are, though . . . good. And I'm not. I'm a bad

305

person and a bad person found me and you need a good person and a good person will find you . . . and this is shit . . . this is such shit. I'm ruining you . . .' And he holds her hand—wet fingers, hot fingers, chaos all over them—and he clings while she tells him, 'The last thing you need is me.'

Derek surfacing, gulping, 'But . . . I do . . . But . . . Is there someone? Is there someone? Is it him?'

Impossible to guess if saying she's leaving him for another man will be worse than saying she's going to be with no one. *All done by kindness*—'A long time ago . . .'—*Once upon a time.*—'Me and this guy, we were the same . . . I'm not explaining this well. But don't blame . . . It's not Francis. Please don't speak to him. Or talk to Bunny. Neither of them ought to be upset.'

WOMAN IN FRACAS FINDS HERSELF PATHETIC AND DISTURBING.

'I know if you were yourself, you wouldn't want to upset them.' There's an acid curl of a smile from him—disgust—and he abandons her hand and she lets him start to be alone. 'I know, I know, who on earth ought to be upset, or would want to be upset . . . I am sorry'—*And tell the good lie, at least do that*—'I wish it could have worked.'

'I was going to . . . I was going to . . .' A sort of horror in him and he can't bargain himself free of it, but even so—'I bought a ring . . .' It should be an influential confession.

'Derek, this is terrible, but—as well—you're really tired and run-down and . . . it'll seem worse . . . not that it's . . . Derek, nobody's died.'

And his focus snaps in, boils, 'I wish you fucking had.'

Which is fine. It's good to hear.

'Yes. And you're right to and . . . I'll leave you alone. I'll leave . . .' *He has my luggage and I can't go back.* 'I'll be out of your way.' *I'm worrying about my fucking luggage—I am a cunt.*

'Fuck you, Beth. *Fuck* you.'

Stand up and walk. He won't harm himself and he'll recover. Without me, he can be happy. Without me, I could be happy.

But he takes her wrist, pulls, harsh grip, kisses her knuckles—*every time, like punching him slowly in the mouth*—while her fists curl to keep their privacy and he scrabbles, clutches, and she has to tug loose and this is unwieldy and will make him hate himself as much as her.

But later he'll only hate me.

I hope. In the end he should do that and then he should forget, but not forgive because I'm unforgivable.

WOMAN FINDS HERSELF A COWARD, KNOWS SHE WILL BE AGAIN.

There's a man in a doorway. He is leaning at the brink of a bedroom in an unfamiliar flat and it's dark but he hasn't turned the lights on. He has a name, but he doesn't like it, so he's leaving it be.

Outside is Pimlico and it's a Friday evening but quiet because the rain is hammering, punishing down, keeping the weak and the prudent indoors. The man is staring at the pelted window and the mix of lights worming and shattering on it, caught in the loose water: the colours of the shop signs across the street: 24-hour mini-market, Fish and Chick Inn, newsagent, off-licence: open late.

The man is thirsty and cold, maybe hungry, but not taking an interest. What condition his condition is in does not concern him. He may have been leaning for a while, perhaps since this afternoon.

It gets dark quickly—November—uncivilised month.

A siren peaks and slews somewhere to his right—injury, emergency, crime—and then diminishes, disappears while a woman's voice yells. The same voice has been yelling, on and off, for a number of hours. The man has assumed that she is mentally unable not to yell.

Funny area, Pimlico—seems like it's on the way up: calm and cream-coloured Regency perspectives and high-design shops and Dolphin Square—naturally Dolphin Square, the nest of scrimping aristos, MPs and spies and shaggers, singles and nutters and incognitos—could almost be Chelsea, those bits—and then there's the iffy hotels and launderettes—did you ever see a cheery launderette—and sections of street like this one, it's got a grudge this one, off-kilter, an atmosphere of brokenness and bad stuff being done.

Not where you'd pick for your mum to live.

Not that his mother is living any more—she died last Wednesday and is gone now, passed on, called up yonder and out of the way.

She dwells forever in the Happy Summerland.

The man had not seen his mother since—he isn't absolutely certain—but probably 1984. Still, he is her only son—her only child—and so, naturally, he was located and called to identify her body. He wishes she'd had someone else to do it—not to save him the trouble, but to let him feel her life was populated, contained an affection she understood

308

and could accept. But this was what she'd ended up with: his absence and then too late arrival to view a small body, grey body, lesions on the skin. And her poor hair—it had been pretty when he first knew her, she was proud of it—crowning glory, brushed it each night—the tamp of the brush and the dry, long sound of each stroke, he recalls that clearly—her poor hair had thinned and coarsened and become sad.

Terrible to know her at once when she ought to have been unrecognisable. That would have broken her heart.

You're not seeing me at my best.

Medication.

Mental health issues.

And difficulties.

Her flat has the sweet, heavy stink of anxious drinking and is brown, everywhere brown, and there are cigarette leavings, saved newspapers with the crosswords completed neatly and less neatly and very wrongly and tinned salmon in the kitchen cupboards and microwave popcorn—that would have been festive—no guests, no sign of guests—but popcorn, nevertheless, and in the little freezer compartment hunched at the top of the fridge there are ready meals for two. So manifestations of hope. Or hunger.

Still a double bed.

He can't touch it.

Earlier, he packed up her clothes—no resonance in them, nothing to connect with except the sense of colour, a remnant of her style in certain items. It all went to a charity shop where there was conversation—you do have to explain when you bring in so much—about the sad demise.

He found that he couldn't say *mother*—couldn't use the term in public—was convinced it would be thought unseemly that he was so unsuitably far away from her—that her clothes smelled unpalatable—that she wouldn't like it known. So he told the assistants his aunt had died and here was everything.

Held in two bin bags and a cheap suitcase. Everything.

Once he'd folded and packed her things ready—her effects—he'd made a sandwich. Had to clean the kitchen worktop before he started and then used the hard bread that she'd left, that she'd opened with the same knife he was holding and then left.

You get a proper loaf and you cut it with a bread knife—she never liked the ready-sliced, said it tasted clammy.

Stale bread and home-made jam with a scrawly label that read *blackberry and apple* and a sticker marked 50p.

Christ knows where she got it.

And it doesn't taste like anything except of purple-red and sweetness.

Mildly spoiled butter—it was out on the counter in a dish, had been for days. Cold in the kitchen, though—so it wasn't as ruined as he'd thought.

Small mercies.

And he ate the jam sandwich standing up, making crumbs.

Almost inedible.

Then washed his hands.

Came and leaned in the doorway.

On the 12th of November 1997, my mother died.

Birthday on the 9th of June.

Never knew where to send a card.

And she might not have liked it.

310

Medication.
Mental health issues.
And difficulties.
When somebody dies, you're not always sorry, you don't always want to talk.

His voice seems scoured, cleaned back to the bones where it's only pedantic and wary, where it's made of darts and shadows. 'My turn, is it?' Arthur stands in his suite's living room watching his windows and their sparks and flickers of uneasy rain. He's arranged that one lamp is shining, angled down, which means the furnishings and special touches guaranteed to make his suite a home away from home are dimmed to irrelevance. 'Is it? Me now? Me again? *Lucky me* . . . ?'

Beth called him from the Purser's desk, but that was a while ago—she's been walking, the mind of the ship turning beneath her, and she has kept as empty-headed as she can, getting ready for this.

Ssssshhh.
To please him. Mainly to please him.
To let him be pleased.

Keeping herself a secret from herself so that she can manage, be as she must.

Nothing in me for him to read but what he wants to find.

Once she's arrived, it's clear he's been getting ready, too. He's made sure that she's the one held in a doorway this time, framed and feeling herself ugly while the nicely detailed woodwork of the door nudges her arm and then retreats.

311

He is difficult to see, slightly hunched, head tucked and he keeps beyond the lamplight even when he turns—in a dullish shirt and probably jeans, and barefoot: pale shapes, ill-defined as his moving hands, his face. 'I thought I'd leave it open for you, so you could *just walk in* . . . You needn't shut it—not if you can't be bothered. I have to assume that you'll *just walk out* at some point. It'll be convenient for you if it stays like that.'

'Arthur—'

'I know you always enjoy your symbols—so what does it mean? *Woman in a doorway*. What do you mean?'

Beth stays outside in the passage, the dark space beyond the lintel is tensed against her, thick with him, and it seems that stepping forward would be like walking into water.

'Are you going to come in? Which is to say, what do you want?'

'I . . .'

Ssssshhh.

'Please make up your mind about something, Beth.'

So she breaks the surface and then shuts it round them with a dull snap of the lock. 'I left him.' Three little noises, meanings, they blur and drop in the blinded space while her eyes adjust.

She can hear him rubbing at his hair.

'No. You went to him. I'm the one you left. As usual.'

And she can pick out that he's looking towards her and so she tells him the first truth, 'I said I'd be back.' He should have all of her truths; it will be difficult, but he should. 'I said.' Tell them properly and they won't hurt him, won't want to hurt him, will not be intended to injure anyone.

'You've been hours. It's past midnight.'

'I didn't know that . . . I didn't know.'

'You called me at *ten*.' Little threads of panic in this, which is going to mean that both of them are frightened and their fear will be dangerous—her fear more than his.

Ssssshhh.

So it isn't manipulative or deceptive if she stands and doesn't snap at him and pretends that she's not frightened, is no more than bemused. And inside she plays the trick on herself which means she imagines her pulse as languid, as a tranquil circulation of content and this will fool her and spread to him, because comfort is just as contagious as despair. He would rather be comfortable, comforted—anyone would—so she will be first. There's nothing wrong about this. It isn't the same as with Derek. It matters.

He sits, seems to press in on himself and his shape darkens. 'Are you going to say what you were doing? Or am I not worth keeping up to date—no bulletins on your movements? Or is this another punishment?' He sounds brittle and as if she should touch him, but she can't—not yet—he wouldn't like it. 'Because, I . . . maybe, maybe that would be—if that's what you want. If punishment is what you want . . . We could . . . You and I, we . . . if we're together and this is what you want to do to me, maybe . . . Maybe if I'm allowed to know what's coming then I can agree to it and you can punish me and I deserve it, so that's what we'll do. Is that what you want? If you want to punish me, then you have to be around to do that and I would be sure you were going to be around. That would be a *fact* . . .'

'Arthur—' Easing forward to him in the way she

313

might towards an animal, a fugitive thing. 'We . . . what are you . . . I couldn't do that, you couldn't—'

'Then tell me what I *can* do!' His voice with a tear in it, a boy's voice, something too lost to be borne. 'What can we do?'

As she reaches him there's a confusion, her being clumsy, catching his shoulder, his chair in the way, their arms colliding as he twists to avoid her. 'Don't start that again. Please.' But—accurate, quick—he reaches and traps both her hands in his and turns them sweet side up, kisses each at its heart with a wary mouth, an intelligent mouth, an asking mouth. He gives her the small, sharp presses of his breathing and the sense that he is thinking, puzzling through until he can risk, 'So you saw him and he made some kind of fuss and then you left him. Or you saw him and then you left him and he made some kind of fuss. I would prefer the second . . . And you're happy if I do this . . .' She stands and waits in front of him, her hands lighting, and he restates for clarity, 'My doing this is permissible and not unpleasant for you.'

The sound of touched skin. Lips. Tiny noises. Beautiful. No more to consider than this.

Sssssshhh.

All done by kindness.

Undone by kindness.

'It's not unpleasant for me, no. It's . . . very pleasant. And I'm happy, Arthur. Yes.'

Almost true. Soon could be true.

He keeps on, 'And you're happy if this feels like love? Which is important. Because it is.' Syllables tiptoeing out between the dab and cling of his mouth near her thumb, her wrist, where her fingers part. 'And you made what you did—what we did—the last time you were here, you were making that feel like love to me. And it made me happy when you did that.' He tenses at each point of contact and the small shocks of this travel in her arms. 'When you were here, Beth. When you were here today. With me. Yesterday, now, I suppose . . . When you were with me. I did believe it.' He lifts his head. 'Was I right to believe it? I am right to believe you.'

And the next truth, 'Yes.' Chill on her skin.

A twitch in his grip, 'You're sure?'

'Yes.'

Ssssshhh.

And the breath leaves him, rushes him empty, and Arthur raises her palms to his face and then lets her go, lets her smooth his hair back from his forehead, from his temples, stroke over the crown of his head, while he weathers something that jolts his spine, some internal decision, and drinks in what she knows will seem new and clean air for him, the scent of possible optimism.

He angles and turns his head and she holds it as he does—cradles the weight of what he's had to teach himself and who he's learned to be and where he lives and he leans to press his forehead against her stomach, to rest. She kneads the back of his neck, the tight wire in it, the signs of the fight to keep him steady and operational. And when he breaks off and sits forward she touches his smile, his proper smile.

'Beth? Do you want a seat?'

'No.'

'Do you want to lie down?' All the words shiny with smiling.

'Yes. Yes, I do.'

'Do you want to lie down in my bed?' And the shine thins to a mutter, creeping out, almost beside

315

itself with want—and then the closing rush, 'And you can be naked now and I'll be naked too and we can feel like love, we can do that.'

The ridiculous, naked, ridiculous things we say. Because we feel like love. Which is a terrible word and a terrible thing.

Ssssshhh.

'Yes. We should do that. Let's lie down.'

*   *   *

And they keep his bedroom blank: no lights—edges and furniture offering mild assaults and the darkness tilting and counter-tilting and they are unbuttoning, unfastening—they are apart and then together—her stomach meeting the warmth of his: warm and not afraid, but nervous—as if they are younger, as if they have never—and they fix in a simple hug so they'll know they're both there and both safe before they start again—fingers unbiddable—too numb, too electric—and stumbling out of jeans and then clear of everything.

Everything.

'Come here.' What you always end up saying before you know you have. 'Come here.'

And opening the bed for each other, peeling it back and clambering, kneeling, lying on how smooth it is, letting it sleek them together and into a slow embrace, an exploring embrace—live skins and astonishments and edges—both of them middle-aged, halfway, more than that, the downward slope and not what they were, but more than they were and they taste of each other and of amazement.

And he's holding her breasts, supporting her breasts, as he licks and mouths, tests them with his teeth.

Takes care.

And he suckles until the ache of it draws in her spine, until it's yelling.

Sssssshhh.

Have to take care. Always. Of every mortal thing.

Everything.

She uses fingertips, only fingertips, to chart his back: shoulder blades and the insistent frame, the bone, the sweet purpose in his fabric, moving, and she has met this before, these pieces of Arthur's information, but not known them. They simply became familiar—they weren't known.

The room filling with who they might turn out to be if they'll risk so much newness, nearness, faith, and what they need, might find and the movement of sheets and half-words and mumbles and strengthening breaths and how they shift and roll, lie face to face and halt on their brink, get stung by their forward momentum as it rolls back through them, complains while it eases and slows, but they don't indulge it—little rubs and reminders, but no more, not yet.

Arthur swallows, worries his cheek on the pillow, settles. 'Why wasn't it like this? Before. It was . . . even at the beginning when . . . When we were together, I thought we were so together—I wouldn't have said that anyone could have been more . . . It wasn't like this, though. And, I mean, thank you, but . . . When did you start hating what I did? Was that it ? When did you start hating me? It must have been the whole time, almost the whole time . . .'

'I didn't hate you.' *True. But not enough true. He ought to have all of the true.* 'Eventually I did. But

317

not really . . . And I didn't hate what you did. I was doing it, too . . . I loved it—the first year, maybe longer—it was . . . there was that one part of it that was always so . . . being *in* other people, *being* other people, feeling into who they are and how they are—and being with you and that close to you and . . . but . . . No, I couldn't stand what it meant—if I thought about it—I couldn't stand what it was. So I didn't think about it. I would tell myself *Sssssshhh* and I would concentrate on what I expected would happen which was that I genuinely thought eventually someone would stand up at some evening, some service, some gig, and say—"This is ludicrous, this is obviously, obviously fake, nobody sane could take this seriously or trust it, and you are a fraud—you are both frauds and you can go away now and stop."'

Beth brushes his shoulder, his arm, because he is too still, as if he is going away in himself. She needs his company or she can't continue. 'I assumed it would be stopped. From the outside. Kind of. I avoided doing anything about it myself by hoping we'd be prevented. But no one said a word. Nobody didn't believe. So many people, so hurt—they're not sane, not in the places we get into—they're not going to unmask us, kick away their sole support—that would be making them eat what's left of themselves alive. And we weren't big enough to get the sceptics turning up and throwing their weight around—they couldn't be bothered: not enough profile in it for them. No one was going to intervene and you were . . . committed. The enquirers, they had nothing else, nothing but us and we were less than nothing, we were giving them less than nothing. And then the money was getting serious. We were earning a living out of it, turning big. I couldn't deal with that.'

318

True.

She eases her knee a touch between his, because this should remind him he's beautiful—it's not to keep him from paying attention, not to obscure what she means, 'I didn't hate you, but when we were together and like this, you felt as if you were working and I was work—like when you'd take off those fucking gloves and then you'd undress . . . like you were going swimming or something—just *fast*—just business—not that you weren't excited, but . . . not about me. Even after you'd finished with wearing the gloves. It didn't seem to be about me. Not that you'd have to be about me, but . . . And not that I didn't still . . . We'd start and the whole of you would be listening, but not like this—it would be like a gig. You were—I'm not saying this is true—but I thought you were turned on by practising—by reading in so close—and I was another gig. Like I was a rehearsal.' Her arm tight over his waist and paying attention. 'I'm sorry.'

'No.' His voice fragile again, young. 'I'm sorry.'

'I'm not a good person. I didn't give it up and leave because I was trying to be a good person . . . I was lonely, Art. That's what it was.' And she pulls her arm in tighter, so she won't lose him. 'But I could have done . . . something. I wasn't sure. We got so fucked-up . . .'

'I made you lonely.'

'You didn't mean to.'

'I made you lonely.' He kisses her forehead, eyes. 'But you're not lonely at the moment?'

'No.'

'Tell me if you are. Because . . . I can't get it wrong again and you have to *tell me* if I'm heading that way and . . . I can . . . improve. If I know—can

319

attempt to, possibly not, but I'd have the chance . . . I mean what is the point of us both over-thinking if we can't get any use out of it.' And he kisses her again. 'I'm sorry. I'm very sorry.' With a kind of furious searching: face, neck, collar bone, breasts.

Beth has no answer for him until he slows and she can meet his mouth with her own and—*true*—'I'm not lonely. And I don't think I will be. I think it's all right.'

And something scrambles in her chest to be nearer than she is to him, to be fastened—arms straining with being so very hard fastened—and round his breathing.

He tells her, 'Yes. Hello. Yes. It's fine. Yes. It's fine.' Until she can be more sane, less almostpainful and Arthur clears his throat and quietly offers, 'But the work—my work—that is a problem. Currently. And permanently. We know that. I know that . . .' He draws one finger down—slow, slow, slow—finds her nipple, begins to wake it. 'I know that . . .' It's easily woken, grows fretful for him, but then he relents. 'Sorry. Mustn't distract—we have to concentrate . . . No hiding. Not the way we do. Because at the moment we should . . .' He leans the next sentences in, careful. 'It has to be only the scary type of thinking—one thing at a time and *about what we need it to be about, not running off*. Because I do that and you do that, too and . . . we won't. No distractions. Not at the moment. So I won't lie here and feel this and just . . .' He brushes the crown of her nipple. 'Except for feeling it then. Checking it's OK . . . You distract me. A lot. But this of you mustn't distract me from the rest of you . . .' A grin in this, an ease.

'Or vice versa.' Because she agrees and because

it's true.

So no more thoughts than necessary. Which is good.

One thing at a time and about what we need it to be about.

Not everything.

Everything would be too much.

Which suggests to her that she's being distracted by how she shouldn't be distracted, 'I mean, I want to talk.' But there are worse things.

Ssssshhh.

'And I want to talk, Beth. I do. And I have to behave. Not get disgraceful . . . I do love you being here, though—if I haven't said. I do.' Then she can feel him focus, still himself. 'I didn't know the work was between us when we were like this—or not like this, not as together as I imagined—but in this position and I am sorry. I've said I'm sorry . . . but I am additionally sorry for that. At least it shows I wasn't reading you. It shows I was paying no bloody attention at all. So sorry.'

'Or else I was too good at hiding.'

Ssssshhh.

'Well, we both aren't going to hide any more. And so . . . I want to ask you, if you don't mind, I do want to ask you . . . please don't—if I can ask—two things—please don't ever be—if I can use the word—*polite* that way again. Do tell me when I've screwed up. I'm repeating myself, but do tell me . . .' And a sense that he is calculating a drop now, judging if he will be harmed when he jumps and, 'Second thing—if this isn't what you want any more—if I'm no longer required—and you have to go, please say so and then go. Don't, please, do the slipping away thing and seeing whoever is next and pretending you're still with me. I'm not saying that

321

you would, but you might want to be kind—you are kind—but please don't let me think you're with me and we're together when we're not and you're also with somebody else. You've been slipping away to me all these years and it's the last thing I can comment on, or complain about . . . it kept me going . . . But if you do that to me, then . . . Sorry, no ultimatums—no ultimata, whatever the word is. Just, please, just, don't hide it when you're going—*if*—if you're going. I'm not criticising, I'm not . . . it's a skill, that kind of hiding, not a moral failing, and I'm not saying it's a failing of yours, or that it's habitual—it's my fault, in fact, if anybody's, in a way . . . it was circumstances . . . But please just don't, though . . .'

'I won't.' *True.* 'I promise.' *True.*

'You don't have to promise.'

'But I am. And I think I do have to.' And she feels in him how his body is restless with driving to be precise and to keep his emotions tidied away from hers and leave her free, unpressed. The gentleness in this bright against her. 'Arthur—' And if he can be precise, brave, and they are alike and with each other and together and they have love and are in love, are inside love, then it ought to be possible for her to tell him everything. Her everything.

Ssssshhh.

But he prevents her confession with his own and she lets him.

Because I am a coward.

True.

'You should know, Beth—what I do . . . It's insufficient, it's only a gesture, but something with me has become habitual . . . It developed. That is, I'm more insane than you might suppose . . . I

322

presume you do suppose that . . . You should. And I live incredibly well, unnecessarily well, and I'm used to it and I wouldn't want to lose that. I give some of the money away—of course I do—but I don't give it all away—easy to forget that you didn't have money, very hard not to remember that you did . . . I've seen that. The refugees, some of them . . . losing your money, it isn't like losing a relative, a love: but it's being less, having worse health, bad food, fewer freedoms—it is losing a part of yourself. A partial death. For them it's . . . it can eventually kill them . . . Me—fuck . . . I'd miss the boats, the tailors, the pretty hotels . . . that type of selfishness . . .' And he strokes his knuckles absently across her stomach, there's no intention in the touch. 'And . . . I'm not trying to make a point with this, but if I kept on with the work—and I did keep on with the work because it made me money and it makes me money and because I believe in it, some of it, some elements I can render acceptable to myself—if I kept on with it, then I understood that I couldn't have you—I would only get whatever you decided you could bear, the number of days you could cope with, or that you sneaked away from whoever was saving you from me . . . um, an occasional . . . well, I'd get an occasional fuck. Sorry, but that. I'd be an occasional fuck. And I believed, as I've said, in the work, but I also believed that the work is a terrible thing, so I decided I should pay for it and there's this . . . there's a plant called Jack in the Pulpit—I even enjoyed the name . . . This plant, it grows big, dark, glossy, tropical-looking leaves and in the autumn there are clumps of berries—orangey-red packs of berries at the end of a single stem. I see them growing when I'm upstate in New York and

323

brain-fucking people who are pleasant and very grateful to me while I'm earning my comforts and my stock tips and my little gifts—there are the Jacks in their pulpits: watching, growing, building up to the autumn. I always make a trip over then and I don't see anyone. I don't consult. I go and I'll pick the berries and I take them back to my hotel—to the Carlyle—where they look after me and are used to me and what I like and the guys on the door and in the lifts, they shake my hand and call me Mister Arthur, because that's friendly and respectful at the same time—first name, but I'm also a Mister—and I go to my suite, which has very pleasant views down on to Madison and 76th and I wash the berries, because they've been outside and you can't be too careful and then I sit on the sofa and I take one and I chew it. And it hurts me. If you chew the berries, they hurt. If you touch them, they sting your fingers. They contain oxalic acid and in your mouth they burn like fuck.'

'Art.' A bleak turn in her stomach and then angry with him, outraged. 'Arthur—'

'Ssssshhh.'

'Arthur.'

But, 'Ssssshhh.' And he shakes his head and is placid, factual. 'They burn. Certain indigenous nations would use them to poison their enemies: give them spiked meat, because it does act as a poison. Or peoples used it as a trial, an ordeal. I was told that . . . I'll chew a berry but I don't eat— you mustn't: the acid causes inflammation and the swelling in my throat could choke me, so I avoid it, because I don't want to die. I want to be in pain. That is, I don't want it, but I should have it. I punish my mouth. I say bad things, so I punish my mouth.'

324

Beth sets two fingers on his lips and cannot imagine, does not want to imagine how he has been living, how he has governed and ruined his days. 'Don't do that again.' His soft mouth, the soft of his mouth.

'It helps.' Words on her fingers, between her fingers. 'Then I wash my mouth with milk.'

'Don't do it again. Arthur? I want you to promise me that you won't do it again.'

He turns and frees himself to speak, 'That's . . . Yes . . . I can't. I can't do it again. If you don't want me to, I can't, Beth. If you don't want me to I can't do any of it again. I can't have anything in the way any more—there has to be you and . . . I'm giving it up, Beth. I'm retiring. Early retirement.'

'You wouldn't be happy. You'd miss it. If you still worked . . . I could deal with it. I could . . .' A misuse of her mouth.

'You wouldn't deal with it—you might tolerate it, but then eventually the tolerating would wear you out and you would leave me and I can't . . . I couldn't . . .'

His knuckles drift lower and she wishes them lower still, because otherwise this is hearing him tear down his life for her, hearing him offer everything, and how can she reciprocate and this morning is a beauty for them and it should be that they can have the beauty and Arthur can be here and happy and allowed it and she can be here and happy and allowed it with him and they can be uncomplicated.

Surely that isn't a criminal possibility.

Beth shifts her hips a fraction and he responds. *Beautiful.*

Beth feels his thinking glide until his thumb is tracing back and forth to the root of her thigh while

325

his fingers reach into the hair and tease, press—once, twice. But then he simply moves to hold her waist, snugs words beside her ear—there's a heat in them, but his need to explain is hotter. 'This lady called Peri—a few others like her, but especially I have Peri and I can't just cut her off and I can't tell her what I am, that I've lied for all these years. It would kill her. I'm not being dramatic, I'm almost certain that's what it would do and I can't risk it. I like her the best and I do the worst things to her and I have made her need them . . .' His thumb makes tiny arcs at the small of Beth's back, requesting, irreversibly interested. 'But I can, I can . . . I won't frighten her any more. I'll tell her that everything's fine and that she's protected permanently. But that will involve an amount of convincing. And she'll miss her husband, I would have to . . . I'll have to keep seeing her. She wouldn't understand if I just went away. It would take a while to finish, if you'd allow that.' And then his hand gives in, returns to her thigh and then runs and seeks and slips, it grazes the furrow that will mean there is no more thinking, only opened distraction, only themselves. His fingers prove her wet, let her be wet, make her wet and prove her wet and round and round. 'That's . . . that's for in a minute, though.' Before they calm, brush so faintly they are almost absent, so faintly that her mind aches and yelps with trying to feel them, have them more. Which he understands, 'Beautiful. For in a minute.' And chooses to ignore.

Beth needs to see his face, but they aren't going to turn on the light.

Sssssshhh.

So she tastes his mouth again—tender place, clever

place, hurt place—and he continues, 'Some of them—the ones I've used for money—they'll still want to talk to me and I can not take their money—make them think it's to do with purity, or something . . . that it's no longer pure if I do it for cash. I've . . . But I would have to keep . . . There would be maintenance—especially for Peri. Closing it down would take so long . . . Christ, Beth. I don't want to harm them.'

And she's moving for him, lifting as he plays in the groove of her, flickers a spark and then down, precise, and pushes in, clean in and, 'How many fingers am I holding up?' She can hear his purr—and his smile—Arthur happy because of her.

Like him happy.

Love him happy.

Feel in him the way he's dancing, close to the surface, the boy who's dancing, the man who's dancing—full of happy.

'How many fingers?'

'One.'

'And now.'

'Two.'

'And we won't do three because three is a crowd and two is absolutely perfect. Two is just exactly right. And I'm sorry, I can't talk any more except about you and this and that it's perfect. Can't tell you anything else about anything else. Can't. Should, but I can't. Hiding.'

'We can hide.'

True.

'Sorry, Beth.'

'I'm not sorry.'

True.

'Hiding my fingers first . . . I like it when you hide

327

me. Good place to hide. Best place to hide . . . But if you won't hold still, you'll end up coming. You know that. You do know that. And if I keep doing this. Then you'll come. Would you like that? Would you like to come round my fingers? I take off my shirts with those fingers, stir my tea, they get all about the place. And. Right. Up. You. That's their favourite. They love that.' Good hands, always good hands, speaking and dirty hands, fucking dirty and fucking extraordinary and in tight with the strength of his voice. 'And I'll love looking at them and thinking: Beth came round those fingers—we started all over again and we started with her coming and that's a good thing—she had a nice come, she had a lovely little come round those fingers—want you to come round my fingers, Beth—so it gets in my bones—and you've been wanting it for ages—and all today—it was such a bad day, love—not bad now, though—and you should have a come and I've been wanting it . . . I have . . . I have . . . Or maybe . . . If I take these away and just . . .' And the beautiful leaving, the withdrawal, almost enough, but not, 'Oh, I'm sorry darling, were you nearly there and I stopped . . . That's such a shame, Beth, when you were very close. You were. You were really very close to such a nice come.' While he folds and rolls with her, holds, sways, the small warm tic of amusement where he's neat against her. 'And then I don't let you . . . that's really very inconsiderate of me.' Almost unbearable against her. 'But there's always the possibility that we could do this instead.' And the rock of the bed and the rock of the room and his weight on her and he's feeling out and finding out his way, looking and shifting and the blunt nudge and here's itself and searching and playing and the

328

in and in and in, and the rock of him, 'And that's because I love you and that's because I love you and that.'

Flare in the skin where it works and knows and learns and wants and parts and she bites, doesn't know where she bites him and he shudders while she does and then speeds, is driving, arches his neck before he catches himself, soothes back, is sly at her cheek while he feeds her his fingers, lets her taste herself, 'Which is gorgeous—the way you taste.' He draws in a breath between his teeth, 'Oh, makes me want to fuck you. Makes me want to screw you so much. Makes me want this. Making love. Makes me want making love.' His pace lifting for a thought before, 'You're quiet, though, Beth. Why quiet? Leave my fingers.'

Which keep the mouth from speaking, from going wrong, from everything.

'Leave them, Beth—'cause it's turning me on too much . . . And I need to think. I think I need to think.'

*Almost unsurvivably arousing, the tiny idea of calling him **darling**.*

'Speak to me, Beth.'

If my absence would please you, I'd disappear.

I'd have to go.

But I can't go.

So she says to him, 'Darling.'

He flinches. Happy flinch. 'Good word. Like that word. Can I kiss you?'

''Course.'

And he does, licks the taste of sex under her tongue. 'You happy?'

'Yes.' Blurring into him, flexing to meet the clean length of his body, how he is opened and home, and

329

she fits her legs close round his waist, catches him and the way he's himself, is the whole of Arthur and delivered and here. And she whispers—simpler to say when it's smaller, 'You make me happy.' She whispers so they can dream each other and not be disturbed, 'And you're my darling.' They could walk off the boat in New York as a couple: true and changed and joined. They should be able to do that. 'I dream you. I dream this, I dream all kinds of . . . I dream you. I learned you, Art. I learned you and I dreamed you and when I'm away—when I was away—I kept you. I could feel you.'

And here's the leap in his spine, this delight in him—milksweet thing—that's fast and faster and deep in his lungs and the hook and the kick and the cleverness of his hips, and when he whispers, 'D'you want to come, Beth? D'you want to come with me in you, because this is me in you, this is me right in you, this is my cock and it's in you and I love you and come with me. I do love you.'

And you know his sweat, new sweat, and he knows you, he allover knows you, knows you wet and you know him dancing, know him inside naked and here and here and here and here and here and he's here and you're here and here and here and here, you're fucking here, you're fucking here, all here.

They shiver after.

Slowly the ship's din coming back and the swing of the bed and who they are and not being each other, only themselves, but also each other, this excellent bewilderment.

330

He curls in behind her and is dapper, nuzzled. He allows himself a sigh, reaches and winds his arm around her and under her breasts. 'I love you, Beth.'

The ridiculous, naked, ridiculous things we say.

'And I love you.'

And Beth is certain that he should have and see and know everything—all that's left. The whole story.

Everything.

True.

True.

True.

Put it in his wonderful head—give him what's ugly, what's me, like hitting him, like making him bleed.

Ssssshhh.

My darling.

I can't.

I can't do that.

So I shouldn't take his hand and shouldn't kiss him.

I can't have what I don't earn.

'I love you. I love you, darling. I love you, Art. I love you, Arthur Lockwood. I love you.'

Burns in the mouth, burns like fuck. Never said it so much and it burns me.

But I do take his hand and I do kiss him.

Ssssshhh.

There's a boy sitting outside his bedroom, leaning against the wall, one knee bent high and his other leg extended across to the opposite side of the passageway. He is staring at his shoes which are off-white Converse All Star Hi-tops. He bought the trainers for himself and enjoys them—the way they seem cool and also seedy and also laughable: when he wears them he gets close to being all those things on purpose and can own himself. Before, when he was really a child, people would peer down at his feet—his long, long feet—and say, 'You'll grow into them, then.' And he got tired of it. This is better—being his own joke—tall and getting taller, bigger, like a threat.

The boy is quiet, perhaps listening, hands loose on the carpet to either side of his hips as if he is consciously controlling them, not making fists. Inside his room there are the sounds of his mother breaking things.

This happens.

It is not his fault.

It is not her fault.

Every six or seven months it is now simply necessary. She has to destroy as much of what he has as she can find.

So he tries not to acquire belongings, or else makes them disappear, slides them under floorboards, buries them in taped-up boxes—but the best is not to bother with them in the first place. For some reason, she doesn't damage what he wears and carries with him. And the stones he has kept from the island she only throws about and hasn't broken, although his favourite is always in his pocket, just to be sure—the one with the brown and mauve and sepia wood grain, the beach agate. For luck.

He is waiting for her to be finished. Then she'll go and cry in the kitchen and he'll tidy up.

He takes the pebble and holds it like a wish. He lends it his heat.

He doesn't know that in thirty years' time he will be in Pimlico and it will be raining—will have poured all night—and these days he will be mainly Mr Lockwood, not so much Arthur and almost never Art—only one person will call him Art and she will not be with him.

And he will be standing in a sodden jacket at the pavement's edge, his feet in amongst all the wandered colours of the shop signs, the confusions of light, and he will be holding a jar, lending it his heat—dark blue enamel bands laid around turned brass that shines vaguely as it tilts in his hands—it looks like a prop, a suspicious container for onstage skulduggery. But Mr Lockwood will have no audience, no one to see when he unscrews the lid and empties the jar into the gutter and the fast, thick flow of water and of darkness.

It won't make Mr Lockwood happy to tip her away and then set down the urn, wait until the rain has washed his hands a little and then walk, leave her. He may have the sense there is something troublesome he needn't carry any more—but it might only be that he's rid of the urn: heavy thing and awkward, solid metal, respectful option, quite expensive.

Coddling the stone warm in the heart of his palm, the boy shouldn't know this—it would scare him. It's nothing he ought to be able to predict.

If this book had been with him, could be with him—company for him and the blue of it resting faithful against his skin—then he couldn't be allowed

333

to read it, not yet.

So naturally he would want to read it, because forbidden things are always best. Looking under the cloth, the sheet, behind the curtain, to see and find the tricks of things—he can't resist that. Human beings love to look and he is a human being.

Last time his dad came back they'd make trips to a wax museum—not a good one—a dusty, small place—the clothes on the models didn't fit, and everywhere had this sour, strange smell that almost suggested the use of remains: true body parts, hidden beneath the wigs and unconvincing surfaces.

The room for horrors was most popular, the fullest on Saturday mornings: it had a guillotine equipped with victim and operator and an Inquisitionist and there was Jack the Ripper, Sweeney Todd—all these glint-eyed figures who worked with death, could treat it with familiarity, let it in. And beyond them was a curtained doorway—greasy red velvet and a sign that said no one should pass through it unless they were over eighteen.

The boy is not over eighteen.

So his dad wouldn't let him go in—avoided that corner on each visit. But then the old man fucked off again, his goodbye very final, desperate, and accompanied by sad offers of money and advice and Arthur not happy about this—except that he spent a bit of the cash on his shoes and afterwards he went to the museum by himself and slipped in behind the velvet and was where he should not be and got educated.

He'd guessed it would be about shagging, whatever was being kept from him, and he wasn't quite mistaken. He stepped inside to face rows of bleached-out medical models: elucidations of sexual diseases, the pitfalls of pleasure: blisters, rashes, pockmarks. It was disappointing and repulsive—the worst of what human beings could be, their destroying. The worst he knew then.

'I went back, though.' Arthur Lockwood with Beth and telling her the waxworks story and there's full, grey day at the suite's windows and outside in the corridor the speakers are carrying their captain's last announcement—Manhattan tomorrow and it's been such a pleasure having them aboard.

Beth and Arthur have turned on the lights so they can see: blushed skin and busied and pulled and stroked hair—resting now—and lovers' faces—still almost the faces they had in dreaming—and plain white sheets, surrendered sheets—and Beth beside the man who is not being Mr and not being Arthur—who is being Art for her and here and over eighteen and stretched across his bed, in his bedroom, in his suite—which she supposes has become their bed and bedroom and suite and which is balanced on the ocean's skin, swaying on almost three miles of water that's relentlessly beneath them while she looks at him.

We love to look.

'I went back.'

'I know. You would.' And Beth not long awake and Art having laid himself flat, setting the back of his head just below the finish of her ribs. His weight and his thinking press at her breath.

'Of course you'd go back, Art. Can't leave well enough alone, you . . .'

'You weren't saying that earlier.' He glances along at her. 'You weren't saying anything of the kind earlier.' And he reaches his hand out to be held.

And she holds it. 'Earlier is why this bit gets to be

335

romantic. I think. Maybe. All new to me.'

'Not really my area, either.' He repositions his shoulders slightly. 'This *is* romantic. I would say. Because I would also say—am saying—that having to look is almost always like that—at least disappointing: you go past the curtain, or you lift off the cloth and there aren't any wonders—the secret's no use, or it doesn't exist, or it's terrible and you shouldn't have to see.'

'I know.'

'I know you do . . . But *your* secret—under *that* sheet—not that you currently are under that sheet, but there were rare occasions when you have not been completely naked or covered in me . . .' And he shifts his head so that his cheek is by her hip, blows softly, lends her his heat. 'What was I . . . ? I got distracted again.'

Although she has her own heat: 'No mental discipline, Art—that's your problem.'

'Yeah . . .' He pushes out a dry breath, his almost-laugh. 'That's my problem . . .' Then he turns back from her. 'My point was . . . there are occasions when you are very covered in very many ways . . . But I have worked out your secret . . .'

Ssssshhh.

In his lazy voice, early morning voice, unprotected voice, 'Which is that you're more beautiful than you'll let anybody know.' He squeezes his hand round her fingers, 'But I found you out.' Meeting her eyes directly, plainly.

Ssssshhh.

And she's the one who sits up to stare across at nowhere, a numb wall. 'No.' While she thinks that she wants to save this afternoon, loop it and stay in it and never move on to what comes next. 'The secret

336

is that you have no idea what I'm like for the rest of the time. You only ever see me when I'm with you.'

'No—'

'Yes. And often I have not been . . . but I've been all I could . . . I mean, I've been uglier elsewhere.'

'And elsewhere, ugly is all I can be.' He sits up in the nice wreck of their bed. 'Sorry. That's . . . That really isn't romantic . . . It's just that—in Pimlico I didn't *feel* anything. I feel with you. I always feel with you . . . it hasn't always been . . .' He goes for the diplomatic choice, polite as a stranger. 'There has always been feeling available even if it hasn't been positive. But there was nothing then. For my *mother.*' He says the word as if it comes from another language: a strange, demanding country. 'Nothing at all until I was—sorry to . . . but I'd gone to London for work . . .'

'You don't have to keep apologising.'

He twitches his head, but doesn't contradict. 'Anyway. This guy had got hold of my number—I'm still not sure how—and he kind of didn't want me and he also kind of did.' Art taking her hand again, keeping it. 'His name was supposed to be Drazan . . . I have no idea if that was true—didn't seem it—and he kept telling me that he had a ghost. And what exactly I'm supposed to do about a ghost, I can't imagine . . . wave a bible at it . . . This is not stuff that I do. And his ghost lived in his flat in Talbot Road—it didn't break things, it didn't move things, it didn't appear—he just knew it was there— and his girlfriend had left him because of it . . . Naturally . . . I nearly couldn't be bothered, but I was in town anyway, so . . . We meet in a pub opposite his building and he's fucking me about immediately.

337

It's a quiet and early pub—all bleach and last night's piss—and he's fucking me about in it, nearly giggling and talking shit, very nervy and clearly a wanker . . . but I also know . . . I *know* . . . he *does* have a ghost. He's telling me, but *not* telling me and he doesn't *need* to tell me, because of his face—what it's saying—because I have the same face—his ghost isn't a child, or a man, or his sister, or a lover, or a friend—it's his mother. His mum. I know what a bad son looks like.' Art's thumb fussing, thrumming over her knuckles, back and forth. 'He didn't like her and then something happened and he's not sorry, except he is—because he knows what happened, what killed her—doesn't need me to tell him, doesn't want me to tell him, because it was shameful—it was so bad that he thinks it shames him. He was a narcissistic bastard. Like me . . . He kept me there until lunchtime, till the place was full of punters— not our kind of punters, just . . . punters. Eventually I just said, "It's your mother. They shouldn't have done that to her. It was wrong, it was absolutely wrong." That's all I said.' The colour of his professional tone there, authoritative and gentle— the most effective blend—a flicker of who he can make himself be—and then it's gone and he's only Art, sheets gathered at his waist, thin shoulders, the long arms and their sensitivities, their tensions.

If you weren't sensible, didn't study him enough, then he would probably seem weak. But he never is. Things hurt him because he allows them to, because he wants that.

Doesn't mean I should help them to hurt.
Sssssshhh.

He waits, heaves in a long breath, then. 'I've had other Bosnians, Croatians, some Serbs . . . of

338

course—anywhere like that and eventually, I get them, get the grief—but I wasn't up to speed—mainly because I didn't want the job and I didn't trust him and I didn't like him, so I hadn't prepared. I intended to be unimpressive, but then he's . . . it's like this . . . this rancid taste that's . . . it's permanently there—it stains what he eats—I can see it on him—and he's so angry and so scared and so disgusted with himself and it can't be touched, or cured and . . . and it's not unfamiliar.' He closes his eyes, then gives her their blue when he opens them again. 'And I bounced him those three sentences—banal sentences—and he let go—spilled the lot. I was there until bloody dinner time. This woman he hated and hadn't seen in years, but he's found out they took her away from her house in Donji Grad—I remember, you know I remember, I have a mind that keeps the details—and she was held in the rape camp at Doboj, in the Bosanka factory. And the rest is self-explanatory. And it also lives in his flat . . . She was called Merima . . .' Art frowns at the air ahead of him, seems absent, or forsaken.

So she pulls him in and down with her until they are lying again, but he turns on to his back and faces the ceiling and, 'I was home and clear of him, clear of it by the end of the week—on the island. On the first day back I headed over La Coupee, kept on and then into the Pot—it's this tiny, closed-up bay and it's my place—it's mine. And all the way there along the cliffs the sea was unnatural—was beyond stillness, so flat you could see the grain of the water, its true nature—like an agate, all these blues, and every boat that crossed would leave this trail, this mark like a finger writing on glass. You could see all of where they'd been—they wrote it out for you to read.

'But you weren't there, Beth. And I dropped into the bay—it has these big walls—and then went out through the new gate—I call it the new gate. There used to be a single tunnel that let you leave, but a fresh one's opened since I was boy. There's been an additional collapse. It was a low, low spring tide and I ended up standing on the shore where there should have been feet of water, was way out amongst things I never should touch. I ought not to be able . . .'

There's no particular change in how he's resting, how he speaks, only this knowledge that he is, somewhere, fracturing and no longer minds. He will be undone with her and expects her to be kind.

'And the ravens are complaining at me—there's a pair that nest round there and they're up and shouting, grumbling—and the sun silvering their backs and I don't want them worried, because they're my favourite—not 'cause they're underworld birds, the Other Dimensions thing—because they're clever and like small, flying people—and they worry the way that people do and so I sit—and when they settle down and stop talking—they do almost talk—I can hear them flying. It's so quiet that I can hear the air pulling through those fingers at the tips of their wings. I'm up on my best rock and sitting and then they've settled too—they've landed and mewed a bit longer to each other, but now they're satisfied and the only noise that's left is in my head. It's this impossibly wonderful morning. And you're not there. You're not beside me and not saying how hot the stones are, or looking at the glitter in the quartz, or . . . and why should you be . . . There was no reason for you to be there.'

And she has never seen him cry, not in more than

340

twenty years—all the times stolen out of more than twenty years.

But today he does. 'And it's about you, but then it's her and . . . she was so sad . . . My mum, she was sad the whole time. And . . .'

And she kisses this other salt of him and, 'Ssssshhh.' And this makes him worse and his hands are wrong, lost, needy and he's labouring and broken back to the noises of a boy, back to the heart, and they hold each other and she can read, can feel the cold and deep and wrong shifting in his chest. It stings her where she touches him.

'I'm sorry, Art. I'm sorry.' And he shouldn't have to be this way, not for anything, should always be defended against it. 'I'm sorry.' Anyone who loves him would take care of that.

*   *   *

He's better once they've slept again and gathered themselves. And it seems to Beth that he's made a decision, some large undertaking around which he is building, a man at work.

Arthur leans just inside the bathroom. 'You don't mind, do you—if we don't do the two-in-a-bath thing . . . ? It's quite a small bath.'

'And it would be too much like how we were.' Beth not wearing Arthur's shirt for the same reasons—nakedness seeming more straightforward.

'There's that—yeah . . . There's that.' Arthur wearing the not-that-luxury robe provided with the toiletries and towels. Its sleeves are short enough on him to be comical, which he notices her noticing. 'It's one size fits all and the one size is not my size. They don't make allowance for the more elongated gentleman.' And because this could be rude he is smiling, but only a little, because they can also ignore the doubled meaning and because he is comfortable with himself.

Eventually, they dress—Beth in yesterday's clothes, which remind her of yesterday and complications— and then they eat an extensive breakfast, served by Narciso with an exemplary lack of surprise. He is purely benevolent, attentive. The suggestion that he should call at another cabin, perhaps with a steward or two to help him, and repossess the lady's belongings, rescue her baggage and bring it back is something he treats as if it were commonplace.

Beth's stomach doesn't like the idea. 'We shouldn't really ask him to do that and Derek could be . . .'

'Derek won't be anything if they go in mob-handed. It'll give him something else to resent, which will help him.' His mouth dainty round this unpleasantness. 'I'm not absolutely callous to say so. I'm being practical. It won't be fun for Narciso and I'm sorry for that.' Arthur considers some porridge and a fruit plate with brutally ornate garnish. 'You do need your things. You need clothes. Unfortunately. And if we buy a new wardrobe onboard you'll disembark looking like a colour blind dowager or a ladyboy with troubled self-esteem—those are the only options they provide. It goes without saying— although I am saying it—that I would still love you whatever you were wearing, but I feel both those options would be undignified.' He perches a celery baton behind his ear like a pencil, perhaps to make up for having little appetite.

'You're cheery.'

''Course I'm cheery. Entirely.' He grins at the fruit. 'I've got what I want.' And he closes his eyes, the

342

grin becoming private—as if Beth is his secret, as if he keeps her even from herself.

They pour each other coffee, exchange dishes, Art picking at bread, but clearly enjoying their domesticity. 'You'd think we'd been doing this for years.'

'We sort of have.'

'No we haven't.'

'No. We haven't.'

'It agrees with us, though. Pass the milk, could you?' He's playing—maybe the doting husband on holiday, the familiar man, the permanent fixture. And it does agree with him: deft with his cutlery, sitting up straight in a fresh fawn shirt, immaculate brown suit—enjoying a little formality—bare feet to say he's at the seaside.

Beth reads him the ship's newsletter for their day—the last before New York—and they agree to be unconcerned that they have not attended the Detox and Weight Loss Seminar, or the Improvers' Bridge Class, or the Singles Coffee Morning.

'Won't be needing that.' A tiny sharpness when he says it.

'We could go and be smug.'

'It's a while since I was smug . . .' Arthur pours himself more tea—they have a choice of three beverages—and looks up when he's done and is shy for her. 'I think I might like it for a bit.'

And he should stay like this: contented and happily sleepy, sleepily happy—all won, all well. Beth watches him, can't stop watching him, until he asks her, 'What?'

She dodges on, 'We're exactly too late for the Afternoon Champagne Art Auction.'

'Have you seen the art?' This because he wants to make her laugh. 'I'd rather be keelhauled . . .

Which they can do—it is a ship and they have a keel and everything.' Waiting for her to react and then dipping up from his seat, leaning to kiss her cheek. 'Not all the generic champagne in the world could make me gaze on it again. A stoned monkey with a brush up its arse could do better.' He winces minutely because this isn't quite as stylish as he'd like.

So she teases him very slightly because he will like that, 'A stoned monkey . . .'

'I'm tired . . . I'll do better next time . . . Need practice . . .' He does like it, is helplessly comfortable as he points out, 'And we'll need to get back into bed—as soon as your clothes have arrived. Can't come to the door in our dressing gowns—Narciso will think badly of us.'

'We've only just got dressed . . .'

Quietly: 'Love you dressed. Love you undressed.' And he divests himself of the celery and becomes serious. 'Plenty of time for both . . .' Predicting their future—gentle and authoritative. 'And we need a lot of sleep because . . . of the not sleeping. And tomorrow we'll be up on deck for . . . oh . . . Narciso suggests around 4.30 in the morning, maybe five. With which I concur.'

'What the hell for?'

'To see the sunrise.' He ghosts a smile, but almost hides that he is contented, because he is being pushed, teased, having to explain himself—because of these different touches of being with somebody else, nicely interfered with. 'It's an occasion, a tradition. End of the voyage . . . Stuff to look at. That big woman on the island with her arm in the air—she's good value. She's all lit up at night . . . Like you . . .' Almost swallowing this last. 'That is romantic, though isn't it? That is quite romantic. It will be. I promise. I'll be putting the effort in.'

'Art . . .' *Ssssshhh.* 'Art, I read this story.' *Sssssshhh.* 'There was this woman, young woman—youngish— and respectable, but she started to be a medium.'

'Do we have to talk about this?' Too hard a touch, he doesn't want it.

'It was—I can't remember—the 1890s or so, round about then, and she was a medium for her lover, this man who'd been . . . and she would talk in his voice and write things and . . . he would inhabit her.'

'Yes, I read about it.' He's only being brisk, not harmed, wants a return to the good of their day.

'And it was all sort of the usual—except that he wasn't dead. He just wasn't with her. He'd left. And . . . she still needed him. So she made him up.'

'It's a sad story, Beth.'

'It's romantic.'

'It's about someone going mad.'

'There were . . . There have been times . . . It's not that I didn't miss you.'

'Sssssshhh. Too sad, Beth.' But he isn't sad, he's relieved, he's complimented. 'And I can't do sad today.'

He'd thought he might not like what I would tell him.

He looks at the tablecloth, coddles his joy for a moment, keeps it inward. 'Not when we're saying goodbye to the ship and the suite and the bed. Nothing bad has happened here . . . I'm very fond of them suddenly. I'm very fond of everything . . .'

'I know.'

'I know. I know you do.'

Your book is an honest thing. It wants to be true for you, always has, and it can't hide that it's almost finished now, it wouldn't want to if it could.

Everything stops.

You've realised this.

You can remember the taste of Sunday evenings as they dwindled down to sleep and then school in the morning: that change. Or a favourite teacher left and was replaced by someone dull, or frightening. You've stumbled through the vague melancholy of childhood holidays in their last hours and the usual forked desires: wanting to eat up those places you've found and learned and cared about, those new kinds of fun, hoping to roll in them, hold them so hard they'll be for ever, incorporated, will speak in you beyond their limitations—either that or you'll sulk and wait with not enough time left to be as you were and more than enough to feel injured and robbed. You've adopted both positions, sometimes simultaneously.

Over time you slightly, slightly, slightly began to resent those glimmers, shivers, little tunnels into your affection, reaching out from temporary joys: other people's pets, toys, gardens, loaned clothes, loaned rooms and houses, the passing friends of friends, the other people's parents, the here and then gone—you were fond of them, but also blamed them for being transient and therefore hurtful.

And you dislike the knowledge that, once you have stepped away, events will heal behind you and continue. Your presence is never entirely indispensable.

Since you've got older, have been independently

in motion, there have been landscapes that were generous and striking, special hobbies, kind hotels, gala occasions, different pets, toys, gardens, clothes, rooms, houses and you have, as usual, agreed to be fond of them—but the more you love them, the more you cannot keep.

You're aware of this, too.

So you let go—which is healthy and adult—and occasionally wonderful. You have sometimes adored those fast days and small plunges into moments you wholly inhabit, because they are all that they ever will be and so there's no sense in having to ration your commitment. You can be breakneck, full tilt. You've tried pastimes and excitements, dangers, precisely because you were certain they wouldn't last—as if you were testing alternative versions of yourself.

And short-term exposure to people, that can be a remarkable mercy: having no cause to consider others' failings and no reasons to make you exercise your own—appearing just as you'd wish, taking part just as you'd wish and then being done, performance over. No loose ends, just experience, pure existence— this can have its place.

There have been days when you'd like to explain how perfectly fine it is to close a door and be outside it, to head off alone and have peace. Peace for a while, space and liberty to come back in refreshed.

The hardest of your losses at least always give you this consolation—a too-large freedom. That big, deep, unworkable love: that absence that still punishes, catches you in anniversaries, old photographs, silly stories; those chances you can't have—they throw you into open air. And perhaps you fly. You can be who you want now, maybe—but

347

with nobody there to see you try.
  Everything starts.
  You know this.

Beth and Arthur—Arthur and Beth.
  I'm not sure of our billing, or how strangers might refer to us if we were presented as a pair, the names and terms we would suggest.
  Not sure.
  They are together, certainly that, arm-in-arm and up on the ship's highest deck with the early crowds, the handrail-leaners, camera-carriers, the knots and straggles of murmuring shapes. Everyone seems a little stunned and delicate with lack of sleep and the large cold around them which is relatively still, but has a suggestion of merciless places in it nonetheless: Hudson Bay and the farther north, the solemnity of fatal wastes. The dark, though, is familiar against the ship, close to affectionate as they begin to abandon it: a clouded starless sky overhead, but the curiously intrusive signs of life beyond themselves now peering through to either side: low strings of shore lights and the shadows of Staten Island to port, Brooklyn to starboard.
  'We're in the Narrows.' Arthur being manly for her and giving unsolicited information of a technical nature. Right across the deck, husbands and lovers and partners are doing the same: instructing. And wives and lovers and partners are consenting to be instructed, enjoying the game of it.
  We should have our picture taken—it'll last.
  Beth is deep in the pullover and waterproof she'd

packed for just such an occasion. She has most of her things, more than she'd expected, courtesy of Narciso and a pair of largish stewards. She didn't ask them how Derek was or what he said and they didn't mention. Arthur kissed her once the bags had been set down and the men had gone, as if some momentous barrier had been crossed.

Art is in his long overcoat. When she remembers him, she will only have to picture him in this and so the image will stay precise. Which is a good thing and mentally economical.

It's not a very substantial coat, though, and she doesn't want him catching cold, or being uncomfortable.

Enough to make you weep.

She squeezes his arm.

'What?'

She asks him the second thing that comes to mind, 'Are you warm enough?'

'Yeah. In parts. We might have to stroll shortly or I'll seize up. Why? Or—if it isn't annoying—might I suggest that you have decided to be responsible for my temperature and well-being . . . I am, of course, happy that you should.'

She doesn't answer but hugs him while the tamed breeze ruffles them, smells of land and later today and another country.

He kisses her neck, 'Hello, Beth,' and reminds her of bed, of earlier, of yesterday and lets her feel where he hasn't shaved. 'Who's here with me.' It isn't like him not to shave, not to be polished. 'And mine.'

He subsides and they begin to move forward on boards which are hardly in motion, have faded.

I think he would like it if we took a picture. But we

349

don't have a camera.

If we see Francis, I'll ask him and he'll help.

I'd like to see Francis. He would make me believe that I know what to do.

And she slips her hand to the small of Arthur's back, steals the fall of the cloth, how it will still fall if she's not with him and the long beat of his walk and the way he is liking the touch of her, the attention.

Monologues about tonnages and draughts continue around them and Arthur halts, turns gently, rests his chin on the top of her head and sways with her, although the boat is still.

She will be able to recall this exactly, perhaps for ever. She would prefer it to be for ever.

'What's wrong, Beth?' But he doesn't sound concerned; it is only that he has the right to take an interest.

'I'd like to play a game.'

WOMAN WHO FINDS HERSELF A COWARD COMMITS HER CRIME THE ONLY WAY SHE CAN.

Absolutely inexcusable.

'I don't really want to play anything, though, Beth. I thought we'd just . . . see sights. Wouldn't that be OK?' He strokes at her shoulders, enquiring. 'If that would be all right . . .'

Her mouth unwilling, full of the cold, 'One game. Please.' A merciless place.

'Well, if you're saying please . . .' And he is almost beginning to be cautious. 'What's the game?'

'There's a list.'

Art stands apart from her. 'I don't like lists.' His feet braced on the wood. 'Not any more.' He folds his arms, but waits, angles his head to hear her properly. 'And if there's a list, then it isn't a game—it's a trick.'

'There's a list.'

And this makes him step to the side and then close again and then away—the anxious walk of a man back on ice—one shoe splaying out. His shoulders are rising, tensing, penning him in, so that he can be the hurt man she doesn't ever want him to be.

Which means she should shut the fuck up so they can be themselves again, come home to be as they were.

Except we would be broken and pretending and a lie and I can't give him another lie—not my love.

He clears his throat and then sounds like a stranger she might meet in a hotel. 'Is this something you prepared earlier—your list?' Each word harder than the last. 'Is this something you have memorised?' The sentence nailing in.

'Because we used to.' Her hands are stinging. 'It's a list of eleven words.'

He walks to the rail—the faltered, breaking walk—and leans, looking out to where there is a tiny, greenish blur that will soon be larger and the Statue of Liberty and that will make people excited and possibly inspired. He doesn't speak.

And this is the back of his hair, the line of him, how his weight rests to the left, the dare in his hips, the thoughtful, hurtful, lonely whole of him. He is the sweetest place.

And she has to explain, be very clear—without clear instructions nobody can be with you inside your trick. 'So, there's the list.' Very small words to bring on the end of them, what they are and what they could be, 'And the list—it's what I'll give you now.'

351

'Can I assume I should number the words from one to eleven?'

She thinks that she would be afraid to see his face and that she also misses him. 'Please if you could. I'm sorry.'

'Don't be. Please.'

It is impossible to take his hand, because it's too late.

'The words that I have for you are
'PALM
'BOY
'BLUE
'SWEET
'BOOK
'DROP
'BURN
'FIND
'SPEAK
'RIGHT
'BLOOD.'

So no one is touching him or looking after him and he is by himself when he says, 'I don't understand your list.'

'Please, Arthur . . . just . . .'

'I will.' He doesn't shout, but is near to it.

'Pick a number between one and ten.'

Winding quickly, quickly round from the rail and his hands high and, 'Christ, Beth . . . just . . . what do you want to . . . you can tell me . . . *Christ*. You let me . . . *Beth, you let me.*' Before he shakes his head and is soft, 'I'd pick seven. I would always pick seven. Seven.'

'So I count from BLOOD, RIGHT, SPEAK, FIND, BURN, DROP and BOOK is the seventh word and that means I give you BOOK.'

He addresses the bulkhead behind her, 'But seven wouldn't be right, not for today. I ought to pick six.' Testing the trick, extending it, because he knows that when it's over something bad will have followed it in and because this will make it tell him more and he's always the man who wants to know.

'Then I count off BLOOD, RIGHT, SPEAK, FIND, BURN, DROP and that makes six and you are left with BOOK.'

She watches anxieties hit him in flickers: skull, muscle, breath.

'Or three's the magician's number. I could take that.'

'And then I'd count PALM, BOY, BLUE.' She sounds angry, she shouldn't be angry, isn't angry. 'And the third word is BLUE. I give you BLUE.' He's the one who should be angry—she wishes he'd be furious.

'Two was for me, was for man. What I used to be.' Flat statement.

'Please, Arthur . . .'

'Two.'

'Then.' She's shaking—her hands, throat, breathing. 'Then I take away PALM and BOY and I give you BLUE.' All untrustworthy now.

He cradles his forehead with one hand, rubs his hair with the other. 'But in the beginning, I didn't lie.' And then he looks at her and seems tired, tired, tired. 'I'll always pick seven. I have no choice. Seven.'

Arthur smiles the way a human being does when they understand tricks—*there never really is a choice.*

'I know.' And Beth looks at him and keeps looking because this is a kind of holding and because she understands tricks, too and because she wants more than tricks this morning. Just this morning, just once, she wants the miracle and she has asked before and didn't get one, so she's owed.

There ought to be magic, just this once.

And in her pocket there's the prop.

There has to be a prop. Self-working.

And she reaches to find it, fingers blind with the cold. 'I have something for you. I made it.'

'Beth, please—'

And he stops when she brings out the book—it's in her hand, a kind weight in her hand, less than a pigeon, or a plimsoll, or a wholemeal loaf. 'It's yours, Art. I made it for you.'

And, 'I can't.'

Because it might hurt him like fuck.

'Beth.' But he takes it from her anyway and both of them are unsteady and the camera flashes keep firing, saving the moments as they die, and the shining statue is overblown on its island and falling behind and Beth only has one instruction still to give.

Too fast. The end always catches you too fast.

Then she has to leave him.

But I'll go where he can find me, where it would be possible to find me, where it would be possible.

And Beth tells him, 'Read the end first. Please.' Wishing the night would press the words back and into the quiet of her mouth. 'You always read the ends first.' Wishing.

'If you want me to read it then, please, I do have to know what it is, Beth. Please. Because I can't . . .'

Every moment racing down and disappearing.

'It's your book, Art. That's what it is—it's your book. Because I know you and I learned you and it's your story. It's the story that I wrote for you and it's your story and all the parts of it that matter, they're all true.'

Read the end first.

And I promise, everything that matters here is true.

This is for you.

This is for you, your blue book.

And it's here in your hands and it wants to feel like touching and like trust and it wants to tell you everything, but it's scared and in your hands and incomplete unless you're with it and can see. It wants to be able to live and see you back.

And it wants to start gently, evade just a little and remind you about blue books—that they are secrets.

Blue books keep the privacies of trades and crafts and carry years of practices made perfect and they are cheats and tricks and shameful and denied.

And no medium will ever say they have one. No medium will ever say they've stolen what they need of you and noted it, kept a record to help them lie at you.

But this blue book is true.

Built of one life.

This is your book. This is your blue book.

And your book has to tell you about a boy—that he was funny and clever and when he was born his hair was honey-coloured and warm and would have made you want to touch it and his eyes were the blue of love, blue enough to shock. And, as he grew, his hair would change, become more coppery and complicated, but his eyes were perpetually a startle, like a light caught in glass.

During his earliest hours the boy beguiled his nurses. Then he moved on to charm elsewhere, although he was an unflamboyant baby, generally ruminative, like an old man returned to little bones, starting again and lolling and lying in state—that, or else he would panic with all of himself, be expressed to the soles of his feet in his distress.

His mother learned what would rescue him: sometimes motion, sometimes holding, sometimes music and sometimes his own exhaustion would defeat him—and in this she knew that he was like his father.

His father who wasn't there—the boy coming home from the hospital to his granny and grandpa's house. His accommodation had been problematic to arrange, had involved shouting and types of breakages and disbelief. But then the boy turned up one afternoon, as fresh as milk and in his mother's arms—new to her arms—a wonder shifting in her arms—and finger-gripping and nodding and looking and looking and looking more than any human person ever had—eating each of them whole: grandmother, grandfather, mother—and almost immediately the household fell into kinds of peace and comfort and the enjoyment of strange hours and occupations. He made everything different.

And he became their fascination and they brought him their best. His gran fed him puréed versions of whatever the household was eating and sang to him and attempted knitting, became as compulsive a photographer as her husband had once been. The boy's grandfather resurrected old illusions to offer him—could hardly be kept from producing silks and sparkles unless the child was sleeping—and even then there were moves to practise for him, there

356

were novelties to invent.

The boy took disappearances, substitutions and transformations quite for granted, but was amazed by his grandad's eyebrows and by faces in general, and by a toy purple dog made of corduroy who had embroidered features, because buttons or anything like them might be dangerous, might work loose. The boy adored his dog. Later he was going to have a pup he would grow tall and run about with. By the time he was almost two, he'd expressed this opinion. He had many often vigorous opinions.

His mother seemed best at worrying: the boy fed nicely, but he was long-boned, basically skinny from the outset, so he didn't look like the other babies being checked at the surgery, or the ones trundled up and down in shops. He also wasn't turnip-headed and sluggish or ugly the way they were. He was extraordinary. And extraordinary isn't always good. It is outspoken and unusual, which may come to be a problem later on. And he was quick—maybe walking too soon and damaging his legs—but no way to stop him walking, pottering, tumbling— another worry—although he was usually unconcerned by falls unless he caught sight of her fretting—then he would yowl. And his mother wasn't sure if a grandfather and no father would be enough.

She wanted her boy to have enough. At least enough. If not everything.

But she wasn't with his father any more and it had been too difficult, so difficult, to leave and she couldn't go back. She couldn't. It would have hurt everyone.

His father having been who she'd lived with and worked with and thought with for months, years— not very long, not all that long, but years, five

357

years—and his father was extraordinary and his being extraordinary wasn't always good. His heart was clean and hot and right, but other things weren't good.

And, almost as soon as she'd left the extraordinary man, the first signs of their boy were irrefutable and more arriving, along with this sense of the child puzzling, assembling himself, coming clearer and clearer.

But it had seemed there was no fair, or kind, or always good way for the mother to say what she ought.

You have a son. We made a son together. We have excelled ourselves.

But don't see him. Don't see us. Don't hurt yourself that way.

Don't hurt us.

Don't hurt me.

Don't hurt him.

Except when she first met the boy and took him up, all alive and thinking and who he was going to be there and sharp in him already—and his father in him, too, clean and hot and right—she could have made the phone call then.

She would have.

But she was busy.

The boy made her very busy. It doesn't bear thinking about.

And he was a summer child, born on the 14th of June—14th of June 1995—and his grandpa full of plans for birthdays, although his mother did try to restrain them.

When the boy turns one, there is cake and there are balloons which he receives graciously, as his due, along with the way his granny and grandpa's hands throw shadows up on a white wall—small magics, making animals and adventures—these he studies in deep silence and then screams about when they go. And his grandpa works through an elegant effect involving a butterfly which bores the child until he can hold the butterfly and suck it. He does not have his little friends round—they aren't real friends yet, they're simply random people of his age who are stupid and unattractive and who waste everybody's time. His mother feels their first year is something to celebrate with his own people and in his own home.

He does keep often with his own people and talks to them and asks them for only red jam and how to say hospital and what dark is for and he kisses them goodnight and goodbye, but not hello. And he totters and jumps about naked in front of them between bath time and pyjamas, because there are few things finer than being naked when nobody else is allowed it, because of being old. And these are the people who love him, the people who go to sleep thinking of what he'll do next and of how he'll be slightly more of himself in the morning, more every day.

His second birthday is different: there are plans, outsiders will be coming—not magicians—other children and their parents. And it's hot, fully hot already, so there will be maybe a kind of picnic—which can happen indoors when it, naturally, rains—and there can be games and naps and, yes, some tricks, a small amount of tricks from Grandpa.

Because the boy is fond of splashing and having his skin in the air—with the jaunty hat and the sunblock: he's ambivalent about the application of sunblock, but he gets it anyway, is protected anyway—because he wants water, there will be the paddling pool—a small thing, inflatable thing. He's tried it before and been demented with how remarkable it is. It renders him speechless—and then compelled to sing.

'Addle Pool.' He demands this more often than he gets it.

'Addle Pool.' He can say *paddling pool* perfectly—his speech is well advanced and modulated and a gift. He just doesn't want to say *paddling pool*—the Addle Pool is so magnificent it should have its own name. His purple dog is Uff and then there is Addle Pool—two glorious things.

The weekend before his party is sunny. Saturday afternoon is spent in the park with his family and judder- running after pigeons and dropping ice cream and the boy has a balloon—he does appreciate balloons—and this is a posh one with silver sides that bobs beyond his head as he walks with it. He will let no one else have it—until its string escapes him and it flies, soars.

The four of them are hypnotised by its ascent and the boy not unhappy—it climbs so marvellously, he is proud of it. But all the way back in the car he asks if his balloon will be waiting for him when they get home and where has it gone and what is it doing and when will it be home and it ought to come home. The balloon is his first trouble. It is the beginning of his being sad.

On Sunday, his mum and grandpa set up the Addle Pool and fill it, because—apart from being delightful—it may compensate for the lamented balloon and prove a distraction.

The boy does, indeed, splash and run and slide in the pool until he's rendered fuzzy-headed by his undiluted pleasure and agrees—eventually—to be

360

dressed and re-sunblocked and to lollop on his blanket with his cloth books and Uff.

And his grandmother's in the kitchen and making a roast chicken dinner which she won't again.

And his mother is in the garden and talking to his grandpa and also shouting towards the kitchen but not hearing any answer and—this will only take a moment—she trots to the kitchen door and peeks in and she is distracted, she gets distracted and she's backing out to the garden again, because she's asked what she wanted to about the dinner—when it will be ready—and this doesn't matter, could never really matter, cannot be important—but then she's thinking of what might come after, of how their evening could turn out to be. So she decides she'll make arrangements for later and drifts in from the sun again, re-enters the kitchen and chats.

And it's hard to tell if even a minute passes.

And then the child's grandfather is standing in the doorway.

He is standing in the doorway and his arms are wet and the boy too—the clothes the boy has barely worn are soaking wet.

There is a confusion.

There has been a confusion.

The mother was distracted in the kitchen. The mother had said she would be a moment, would glance in and then be back, hardly gone.

The grandfather was misled. He thought he saw his daughter emerging—heading for the lawn—doing what she ought to and walking towards her son, seeing her son, calling him into the rest of the day, into the rest of their time, his time.

The grandfather had turned for the shed and left, as far as he believed, his daughter and grandson safely together. The grandfather kept his secrets in the shed and had intended to nip in and fetch some magic powder, bring a pinch of it back to the boy because it would look very fine for him in the sun.

And the boy had been on his stomach on the blanket, summer blanket, soft blanket and with his toys.

But he's quick.

And maybe, maybe, maybe the boy had believed that Uff—who is very like him—would enjoy a swim and so he took Uff to the water and dropped him in, saw him changing, sinking.

There is no way to know if this is how it happened.

It is impossible to ask the boy how everything was lost.

It will always be impossible to ask him.

The boy is called Peter.

The boy is called Peter Arthur Barber.

The boy is still warm.

The extraordinary boy.

Still warm.

They try everything.

It is unforgivable.

Peter Arthur Barber.

He shouldn't have been alone.

It will always be impossible.

And you know this.
346
346
346
losschildbetrayal
losschildbetrayal
losschildbetrayal
18
18
18
Pleaselistenaccident
Pleaselistenaccident
Pleaselistenaccident
345
345
345
losschildhelp
losschildhelp
losschildhelp
3
Touch me
3
Loss
3 times 3 is 9
9
Pain
9
Meet me
You learned this.
You taught me this.
Where we could meet.
How we could meet.

And, Arthur, this isn't a book. This is me and this is you and you were meant to see him. Once things were settled and he was confident in himself, then you would have been with him and known him.

I promise.

I thought there'd be time. There wasn't any reason to think that there wouldn't be time, but I stole him from you, because I was stupid. I stole every part of him from you and I lost him because I was stupid and now I'll lose you.

And I'm a coward, so I didn't tell you.

I didn't want to lose you.

When you said I felt different, and I said I was, that was the closest I got to saying. But we were happy then and you were beautiful—we were beautiful—seemed it—and there hadn't been anything beautiful for so long.

And I understood eighteen when you said it to me in the queue. You know I did.

And you understand me.

And this whole thing, it killed my father, left my mother without both of them and how would I tell you this and not hurt you, too.

And you were smiling today and you have his smile.

And I never didn't love you, but I avoided it, I kept distracted, because that's what I do, because I am a non-working human being.

And before this I always have kept distracted.

But I remembered you. I always remember you.

And this morning I saw you, with nothing in the way. I saw who you are and you saw me.

And now you know the rest of it.

And that I made you a book.

Because you can have this and hold it and you can look at it and see it looking back and where your hands are mine have been.

And I do love you.

And if you don't want that, I understand.

But I do love you.

And there is nothing I can help or solve and I am wrong, a wrong person, but if it would please you I can give you this which is my voice to be with you, my mouth with your mouth and soft.

And you should have the story of a man who stands very still on a ship's deck—broad wood under his feet: tiny shifts in it, gentle—and he watches an island city as it grows to meet him, bluepink in the first hour of the day. He is facing east and the new sun boils at the foot of every cross-street as he passes along the shore—it climbs the sky and is a fury of colours, a hunger, a beautiful rage between buildings that seem cleaner and better than they should be, perfect and eternal as dreams.

And this is beautiful and dreadful and the man is used to beautiful and dreadful things.

And windows gild and flare and are extinguished and the water burns, silvers, splits and then heals behind him, while quiet gulls kite above. There are no sounds except the calm of the slowing engines and the man's thinking, the words in his head.

And when the man comes to land, walks on solid ground, the ocean will stay with him, will rock with him, and when he stands the world will roll, will dance, be an amazement. And this will make him feel that it isn't impossible, that it isn't completely impossible that he could be happy, that he could come home and live.

He could be happy. He could be loved.

He is loved.

You are loved.

If this is a spell and there is magic and everything that matters can be true, then you can be happy and be loved.

And if I was on solid ground and with you I would give you my hand if you wanted.

I would touch you.

I would touch you.

I would touch you.

I would touch you.

I would touch you.

I would touch you.

I would touch you.

This is the best of me.

But I'd give you my hand if you wanted.

I'd give you everything.

ACKNOWLEDGEMENTS

With many thanks to Derren Brown, Julia Cloughley-Sneddon, Coops, Peter Lamont, Ian Rowland, Ros Steen and Shelby White. Thanks also to the island and people of Sark.